Praise for G

Stories in the Worst Way

"Gary Lutz is a sentence writer from another planet, deploying language with unmatched invention. He is not just an original literary artist, but maybe the only one to so strenuously reject the training wheels limiting American narrative practice. What results are stories nearly too good to read: crushingly sad, odd, and awe-inspiring." —Ben Marcus

"The Lutz narrator sticks its slippery-gendered fingers into the sorest spots on its psyche. *Stories in the Worst Way* is lugubrious mischief, archaeology into inconsolable though jauntily endurable melancholy." —*Village Voice*

"Lutz is the new sad man of contemporary fiction. His first collection turns the official notion of gender inside out, supplying a new kind of creature— call it a Lutz—which is neither man nor woman." —*Interview* magazine

"The book has already become a true cult item, and no wonder: It comes charged with humor, humiliation, odd sexual currents, koanlike thought patterns and an artfully gnarled syntax." —*Time Out New York*

"Lutz is a virtuoso … a language surrealist, with his characters and situations growing out of linguistic caprice, worlds from words." —*The Writer*

I Looked Alive

"What you often hear about Gary Lutz is that he writes astonishing sentences. I think that's true. I also think it undersells the brilliance of what Lutz does. The insanely tight, compressed sentences build into insanely tight, compressed stories that show us what America and contemporary life can feel like, at their darkest core. Gary Lutz is a master—living proof that, even in our cliché-ridden, denial-drenched, hype-driven age, true originality is still an American possiblity." —George Saunders

"Gary Lutz is a revolutionary force in American writing, reinventing prose fiction with sentences that always deliver on their extravagant promises. His new collection is even stronger and funnier than his first, a feat I'd presumed impossible. Lutz's stories reside at the messy, linty, futile core of everything—and he's there, too, at first a tiny figure, waving demurely, but then the nearer we get to truth, the larger Gary Lutz looms, godsome." —Sam Lipsyte

"Lutz has been called an experimental writer—but that's possibly too arid a label for someone whose readers may find themselves taking both prolonged emotional and intellectual journeys... [M]uch of Lutz's writing makes use of the Zen habit of forcing paradoxical statements together, to drive the mind towards profound realisations." —*The Independent* [U.K.]

"[T]wisted aphorisms are strung together in alarming, elliptical monologues of marriage, separation, and loneliness... [S]earing realism... terribly exact... a matter for rejoicing." —*The Telegraph* [U.K.]

"Lutz's sweet music is an English language of vertiginous combinations and recombinations—his linguistic tool belt fitted with Shakespearean inversions and antiquated words. When aiming to verbally fit a triangular peg into a square hole, Lutz succeeds every time." —*Puerto del Sol*

"Gary Lutz is the best writer you've never heard of. To certain stylists, he's a kind of prose god. Lutz ... belongs to a category of sentence geniuses that includes Ben Marcus, Aleksandar Hemon, and David Foster Wallace." —*The Stranger*

Partial List of People to Bleach

"One of the most distinct story collections in years... [Lutz's] droll, abstract world is realism for people who love language but celebrate its mutations." —*Time Out New York*, citing *Partial List of People to Bleach* as one of the ten best books of 2007

"Ominous, creepy, and mind-bendingly alert, Lutz lays out each of his perfectly crafted sentences with the sinister exactitude and obsessive care of Beckett's Molloy shuffling stones between his pockets. These musically torqued, masterful sentences, bedecked with elegant syntax and the glint of a razor-sharp locution, accrue into an equally surprising and angular narrative, creating an explosively original combination—stories as muddy and dark in their exploration of domesticity as they are crystalline and celebratory in their structure and language." —*Rain Taxi*

"Lutz is possibly the premier maker of the great American sentence… He's our own little Beckett." —*Willamette Week*

Divorcer

"Lutz is a master prose stylist… Lutz succeeds where so many other language-obsessed writers fail, because his narratives rise beyond the lexical tricks of which they're composed. Give yourself over to the contorted logic of this book and you come away lugubrious yet exuberant, having lived for a time in a reality at once shattered and inspired… [H]is work gathers a remarkable strength, allowing him to battle convention and win." —*Bookforum*

"… Lutz displays an innate understanding of the grim compromises of modern life but heightens and glorifies these with his dizzying language. He refuses to let the dreary world force him to write a dreary sentence." —*Paris Review Daily*

"Gary Lutz is one of my very favorite prose stylists, and his new story collection *Divorcer* … might be his best ever." —Dennis Cooper

The Complete Gary Lutz

"I have been reading Gary Lutz since his first stories appeared in *The Quarterly* in the mid-'90s, and have never been let down. This incomparable writer presents stories that are consistently inventive, darkly funny, just plain dark, and truly original." —Amy Hempel

"Hurrah! Here's to *heartscald* and *heartwreck* and all the genius of Gary Lutz to be found in *The Complete Gary Lutz*. He electrifies the mundane; he makes wretchedness funny. These original utterances of loveless love and discontent, absence and defeat, work like bolts to the brain." —Christine Schutt

Tyrant Books

Via Piagge Marine 23
Sezze (LT) 04018
Italy

www.NYTyrant.com

ISBN: 978-1-7335359-1-5
Second Printing

These titles were first published individually:

Stories in the Worst Way: Knopf, 1996; 3rd bed, 2002; Calamari Press, 2009

I Looked Alive: Black Square Editions, 2003; Black Square Editions and the Brooklyn Rail, 2010

Partial List of People to Bleach: Future Tense Books: 2007 and 2013

Divorcer: Calamari Press, 2011

Assisted Living: Future Tense Books, 2017

First edition

Book design by Adam Robinson
Cover design by Brent Bates

THE COMPLETE
GARY LUTZ

tyrant
books

To
Anna DeForest

LUTZ WILL ALWAYS ESCAPE
An Introduction by Brian Evenson

About a decade ago, I was in Paris with a gathering of French translators and editors, talking about Gary Lutz's work. Several of them had, at one time or another, tried to translate him, and all of them—some after months of trying—had found this to be impossible. Lutz's work was too deftly sewn into the English language to be picked free of it. Each story is so much about the specific tonal, sonic, and rhythmic relationships within English, and so much about torquing a given historical moment of that language by injecting it with archaisms and oddity, that to reproduce it in French just didn't work. It was, one translator told me, more exacting than poetry, and infinitely more complex. "Technically I *could* translate it," he told me. "I did translate several pages of it. But, then, rereading it, I realized it had, somehow, when I wasn't looking, escaped. Then I retranslated those pages a different way. Still it was gone. I could try again, but no. Lutz will always escape."

These were translators that relished a challenge. They had, between them, translated the likes of Thomas Pynchon, Richard Powers, Mark Z. Danielewski, William H. Gass, and David Foster Wallace. One of them had translated a story of mine that contained a list of more than a hundred varieties of barbed wire, arranged to create certain sonic patterns. "What other American writers are untranslatable?" I asked. They shrugged. "Just him," one of them finally replied.

So, when I say that Lutz is unique, I mean this in a much more serious way than how the term is usually applied to writers.

Gary Lutz is unique. He is perhaps best known for his first book, *Stories in the Worst Way* (1996), which rapidly acquired a cult following. They are stories possessed of a great surface clarity and yet there is a certain evasiveness on the part of their narrators. The stories often conclude suddenly, surprisingly, even gnomically. They are not exactly stories in the usual sense. The plots, when they have them, are extremely attenuated. Characters from one story seem to be echoes or doubles of characters from another story, and doubling proliferates within the stories as well. All the narrators, whether third person or first, whether male or female (and in some stories a great deal of time may go by before one can say with any degree of certainty if they are one or the other), seem to have a penchant for a certain sort of language play, a delicate manipulation of syntax. There's also a love of unexpected word combinations: the "fruitful botch of a girl," for instance, that appears on the first page of the first story, "Sororally" (a title which suggests Lutz's love of the arcane or uncommon word, and his deftness in bringing forgotten words back to life). "What could be worse," begins that story, "than having to be seen resorting to your own life?" Yet, in story after story, throughout Lutz's work, we see narrators who seem to be resisting being ensconced in their life at all, narrators who use language as a defense and as a form of evasion, while at the same time, through language, they fall more thoroughly into the trap of a muted and incomplete existence. These are stories about relationships without relation (sexual or otherwise), with characters possessed of an unrealizable impulse to reach out to touch—and even pass through—another person so as to move into another life. Under such terms, sex becomes a kind of frustration: "The trouble with coming was that I actually did arrive somewhere. I arrived at the place my body had already left. I got there just in time to get a good look at what had happened where things were." (27)

Lutz's early stories are also often mordantly funny. The narrators stumble through situations saying things that are sometimes off, sometimes just odd. Sometimes they seem to address the reader directly: "When I wrote this originally, it was a piece on walking as a disorder of the body: walking as affliction, not function. I am relieved that no one will ever get to see it." (24) Indeed, a great many of these stories might be seen as cleaned-up versions of stories told in a bar by, say, a former professor of literature once he has had enough drinks to be in a confessional mood, but not so many as to be completely indiscreet. He, or sometimes she— or sometimes that distinction isn't important—will tell you their secrets, but they'll tell them murkily. It will be up to you to figure out exactly what is being said, and why.

I speak of *Stories in the Worst Way* for as long as I do because all the gestures found in it are gestures to be found in Lutz's later work as well—though their modulation decidedly changes from book to book. *Stories in the Worst Way* remains strong and original upon rereading. But it also feels like a younger man's book, a book by a person who, despite the manifold struggles of the characters within it, has not yet been thoroughly beaten up by life in the way we increasingly are as we age. The language and gestures are spectacular, even spooky, but there's a certain lightness (in Calvino's sense of the term) buoying them up.

For me, Lutz's second book, *I Looked Alive* (2003), is an even better book. It is grimmer, more confessional, less madcap. It is more deeply suffused with loneliness and longing and loss. Its characters flail to sort out their sexual identity and feel like they might have missed the boat: "for too long a time I lived in the trouble between women and men without taking anywhere nearly enough of it for my own." (142) Characters here seem to fall into relationships without really understanding why, and spouses tend to matchmake for their other halves until their relationships flinder away and are gone. People seem to be wandering dazedly through their own lives—or through someone's life anyway. A strand of hair or a crumpled receipt, disjecta of some kind, is something that a narrator might cling to more than to the person who discarded it. The language is slightly thicker, in the same way that one's body thickens as one gets older, and the syntax a little more gnarled. The stories overall are slightly longer and as a result the reader is steeped more thoroughly in each life. The frequency of Lutz's use of archaisms and unlikely word combinations has accelerated slightly—an acceleration that will continue in his later work.

In other words, in *I Looked Alive* Lutz has fallen even more deeply into the sentence and its dynamics. Whereas his earlier narrators still often acted as if they had an escape route, these narrators seem more aware of their own trappedness. The attenuated plots of the first book are even more attenuated here. Instead each story offers a series of situations with large gaps between, brief moments or encounters strung like beads along the whole length of a desperate, thwarted life.

Lutz followed *I Looked Alive* with three shorter offerings: *Partial List of People to Bleach* (2007, revised 2013), *Divorcer* (2011), and *Assisted Living* (2017). *Partial List* contains both stories written in the years directly before its publication and some of the earliest stories that Lutz published, originally in *The Quarterly* under the pseudonym Lee Stone. Elsewhere I have called it "at once cruelly honest, precisely painful, and beautifully rendered." *Divorcer*, the longest of these three later books, is perhaps the most thematically focused of all of Lutz's books, with its seven stories revolving around both the pain and inevitability of divorce and separation. The title story is one of Lutz's longest stories, and two others are quite long as well; he's beginning to elbow more space out for his characters, to heighten the density of his exploration of their damaged lives. These stories are, like most of Lutz's other stories, oblique, but at the same time there's more interest in mapping a discrete period: the particulars of a breakup and its aftermath. There's a sense of struggle and hopelessness, and also weary recognition: "we were not so much a couple as a twofold loneliness." (367) *Assisted Living* is four stories, fairly concise, and continues in the path of *Divorcer*. Breakup, aftermath, and struggling with a sense of self are prevalent in many of these stories, with faint glimmers of perhaps false hope. "All roads led to the one road that wasn't going where you wanted to go," says one character, summing up her life. But then goes on to qualify: "Except now and then people make a show of themselves, make themselves fathomable in something cap-sleeved, and jam the small talk with wherefores vast and mattery." (430)

The final section of *The Complete Gary Lutz*, "Stories Lost and Late," consists of two long stories and seven very short ones, none of which have been previously collected. "My Bloodbaths," which opens the section, is the longest story Lutz has ever published. It was based on earlier unpublished writings but transformed and repurposed. I place it among his very best work. "Am I Keeping You?," which closes the section, is also long and similarly strong. The shorter stories come from pieces started in the 1990s but finished and reworked only recently, and present an intriguing mix of old and new. The longer stories present a narrator's slow and careful self-evisceration in exquisite detail. They are wonderfully and terribly painful in a way that provides less respite than the shorter pieces, but also greater insight.

The drama of Lutz's work is in the language—in the sentence as a unit in particular. He crafts each part of his sentence carefully enough that there are subdramas in the relationships of the words themselves, in the productive tensions between them. If you are looking for story and plot, you have come to the wrong place. If your idea of character involves epiphany and obvious change, then look elsewhere. But if you are interested in seeing what language can really do when deftly manipulated to give it great flexibility, in seeing how the subtleties of struggling minds might be expressed, and in learning a new way of reading, welcome.

Los Angeles, 2019

CONTENTS

STORIES IN THE WORST WAY   1

Sororally   3
Waking Hours   7
Street Map of the Continent   12
Slops   15
Devotions   20
When You Got Back   24
Positions   26
Their Sizes Run Differently   28
Yours   33
SMTWTFS   34
Being Good in October   38
The Smell of How the World Had Ground Itself onto Somebody Else   39
Susceptibility   46
Rims   47
Esprit de l'Elevator   49
Claims   55
The Bride   57
Education   58
It Collects in Me   63
Certain Riddances   65
The Gist   71
The Pavilion   73
Priority   77
Recessional   79
Mine   87
Steep   89
The Daughter   91
That Which Is Husbander Than Anything Prior   93
People Are Already Full   98
The Preventer of Sorrows   100
Sleeveless   103
I Am Shy a Hole   104
Contractions   105
Onesome   114
For Food   118
Not the Hand but Where the Hand Has Been   121

I LOOKED ALIVE   133

A Woman with No Middle Name   135
Carriers   142
Chaise Lozenge   150
People Shouldn't Have to Be the Ones to Tell You   152
Fingerache   160
Uncle   164
Eminence   166
Spills   171
Her Dear Only Father's Lone Wife's Solitudinized, Peaceless Son   173
In Case of in No Case   188
Men Your Own Age   190
My Final Best Feature   194
The Least Sneaky of Things   199
Meltwater   202
Heights   208
I Crawl Back to People   210
Daught   216
In Kind   219
Dog and Owner   227
All Told   233
The Summer I Could Walk Again   234
Femme   240
The Boy   244
This Is Nice of You   248

PARTIAL LIST OF PEOPLE TO BLEACH   261

Home, School, Office   263
Kansas City, Missoula   265
Years of Age   270
I Was in Kilter with Him, a Little   278
Heartscald   288
Pulls   295
Tic Douloureux   302
You're Welcome   308
Six Stories   314
Loo   318
Partial List of People to Bleach   323

DIVORCER 327

Divorcer 329
The Driving Dress 347
Fathering 351
To Whom Might I Have Concerned? 357
Middleton 378
I Have to Feel Halved 381
Womanesque 396

ASSISTED LIVING 409

Assisted Living 411
You Are Logged In as Marie 414
This Is Not a Bill 423
Nothing Clarion Came of Her, Either 425

STORIES LOST AND LATE 435

My Bloodbaths 437
Grounds 466
The Only City All Blue All Night 467
Pledged 468
Now and Later 471
Cosignor 473
Cousin-in-Law 477
Walking Distance 478
Am I Keeping You? 479

Acknowledgments 499

Stories in the Worst Way

SORORALLY

What could be worse than having to be seen resorting to your own life? In my case, there was a fixed sum of experiences, of people, to or from which I could not yet add or subtract, but which I was skilled at coming to grief over, crucially, in broad daylight. For instance, not too long ago I concerned one of the local women, a fruitful botch of a girl. We worked side by side—did data-entry and look-up, first shift, in an uncarpeted, unair-conditioned recess of the ground floor of a bricky low-rise. I was forever taking her in over the partition of bindered reference directories that bisected our workstation. I would keep a sidelong watch over her as she ordered her daily allowance of cough drops in echelon on a square of paper towel. May the arms of other people be said to have an atmosphere? At the very least, may they be construed as aromatic systems of bone and down? Hers enjoyed, for my sake alone, an intimate publicity above the little dove-gray squares of her keyboard.

And the pastime she had! You are familiar, at least, with those bubble packs that almost everything gets sold in nowadays? She used to peel the clear plastic bubble away from its anchoring cardboard, emancipate what she had bought (yet another handset cord for her phone, maybe, or another pencil sharpener, or one of those tricky tooth-whitening sets), then stow into the bubble whatever she happened to have at hand (blood-gaudied parabolas of dental floss; some saxophone-shaped lengths of black plastic that paired socks had hung from in stores; significant clothespins; muculent tissues), reaffix the bubble to the cardboard base, then post the culled, reliquary results on one of the cork tiles that lined the wall of a corridor, where everybody, including me alone, could not help having to see.

Our days, it turned out, held a lot of the same things. Mornings would arrive piecemeal, filling themselves out little by little, summoning tiny inheritances from the previous day—memorial resources in the form, say, of dust suddenly abundant enough for us to thumb from our screens—until there were valid hours bearing us up and we could at last swoon away from our machines.

My eyes would chance ambitiously onto hers.

The woman possessed an appropriately full, planet-like face. It had things on it I always took for something else—on her chin, for instance, a bluish streaklet that I assumed had to be ink. A bungled complexion, in short, and teeming features.

Inquiry: at what point do people become environments for one another to enter? I was entertaining thoughts along these lines because I had only recently brought to an end a period of clandestine gender on my part, a period of not having allowed my life to register on any part of me that saw the light of day. I had now gone as far as collaborating with my body to raise a pivotal tilde of a mustache.

One night, after work, under the ribbed dome of my umbrella (the one torn panel fixed over the back of my head), I thus led her to a restaurant. We perspired baffledly over our deep soups and did not look each other in the eye at first. I think I gulped around my food without eating very much of it. (I have been told that I swallow air.) I eventually started in on her, tendering the usual explanation—that people banded together into little domestic populations and could be seen getting up, *en bloc*, from tables.

I went on to be understood that I did not expect to ever be cooked for, but that I would probably never stop expecting to smell cooking. I brought my parents into it, too—how I was their descendant, someone who had come down from not too high a height; how I had one foot in the two of them; how in my reflection in the greensick screen of my monitor I could sometimes make out a riling rehash of their faces; how they were no doubt speaking right that very moment at the top of my current voice.

For her part, she told me that as a schoolgirl she had been dismissed late one morning with sticklets of charcoal and clunches of unruled paper, and had been instructed not to come back until she had made rubbings of what it was like where she lived: the fretwork along the upper walls, the nailheads and knots of the floorboards, every unevenness of her household. Always pegging away at some fitting trouble, she said. People were always either coming into money or going through her things.

She paid out her arms toward me so slowly, so concealedly, across the tabletop as she spoke that I did not notice until her fingers had closed around my wrists.

Then her room: an unsociable half-circle of folding chairs. One of those collapsible music stands erect on its tripod—the lyrelike shelf, where the music was supposed to sit, holding out an open telephone directory instead. A sink and a splishing faucet and stacks of hand towels, face towels, bath towels, washcloths. No bed, just some mats we had to uncurl. The lamp made a tinny, frustrated sound when I switched it off. I imagine I must have unbundled her, peeled off her underdressings, dipped my fingers into her, sopped and woggled them around, browsing, *consulting* what she had made of herself inside.

Afterward: sink wash, sponge baths.

Because some days the world holds true at the drop of a hat, don't you find? Things favor themselves: whatever you reach for—a shimmered arm, or parts unknown—is ready, finally, to have itself handled. Other days, you can barely exempt yourself from what you might still be capable of. Instead of sleep, the most you count on getting is some cheesy quiet. It follows, then—should it not?— that in even the thinnest of light there are places at which to come to an accurate parting of the ways. At the most, I may have broken something not too major or prominent of hers.

In due time, though, I had her on the phone.

"Sororally," she was saying. "As a sister."

She walked off the job, or got herself promoted, reassigned, not long after that. I took it in my head to go back to the restaurant just once. I brought along a plump, companionable section of the *Courier-Tribune*—the part with the unremitting regional spot news. Swivel-eyed eaters took me in as I picked my way to the booth. How much harm could I have meant? A woman sat down, unaccompanied, to peer at me from the next booth—a much older woman, a differently futile ensemble of smells and noisings. I remember that during the progress of the meal (I had ordered one of the big, busying specials), I disturbed the pages of my newspaper, spoiling them, melancholizing them with sudden prosperities of eyesight, despecificating the stories until all that was still binding in them was a vague and ungiving sense of people motioning dimly toward me from within their own cumbersome towns.

I left off my reading and brought the paper down a final time, then stared ahead at the woman, with the news, and all I had done to it, still on view in my eyes. I exacted it onto her—*confirmed* it. This was as much as it took to get her up and going, her body irked forward by its clique of meddling organs. For my part, I must have made a decision to see how much of the ink I could soap off my hands.

To get into the men's room, you went through a door and immediately—no more than two feet in—discovered a second door, heavier, unpainted; and before you could get the thing open, you had to make room by reopening, by a good half-foot, the one you had already pushed through.

WAKING HOURS

Three hours after I quit my telemarketing job, I got hired to teach middle-level managers how to bestow awards on undeserving employees. I would run through the presentation on a Monday, say, and then early the next day—when I'd more than likely still be portaging things back from sleep—I would get a call to hurry down and repeat the performance for the same group of people. That would usually lead to a two- or three-week booking at the same outfit and for the same bruised-looking men and women, who eventually got the picture and passed the quizzes, which, admittedly, were hard.

I was in receipt of the mothered-down version of the kid every other Saturday. The bus would make an unscheduled stop in front of the building where I lived, and then out he would come, morseled in an oversized down jacket, all candy-breathed from the ride. I would drive us to a family restaurant where we would slot into seats opposite each other and he would ask me the questions his mother had asked him to ask. I had a quick-acting, pesticidal answer for every one.

When the food arrived—kiddie-menu concentrates for him, an overproportioned hamburger for me—I would tilt the conversation toward him, maybe a little too steeply. I would want to poach on the life inside him, whatever it was. He would splay his hands on the tabletop, arms slat-straight, crutching himself up.

After lunch, in the undemanding dark of a movie theater where he goggled at some stabby, Roman-numuralled sequel, I would plug my ears and loot my own heart.

I lived in an apartment, defined as a state or condition of being apart. My life was cartoned off in three rooms and bath, one of several dozen lives banked above a side street. I convinced myself that there were hours midway through the night when the walls slurred over and became membranes, allowing seepages and exchanges from unit to unit; hours when the tenants, all asleep except me, dispersed themselves into the air and mixed themselves with their neighbors. This at least accounted for dreams that rarely jibed with experiences.

One night, I posted myself at the city's only gay bar that catered to older, self-devastated types. I lapped at a Coke until I got picked out by a drizzly blond—mid-thirties, lightly muscled arms thinning out of his too-short sleeves. He conducted me through a snarl of alleys to his apartment. It was small and airless and hassocky. He was blond everywhere except his crotch, where the wreath of hairs was cola-colored and looked barbered, fussed over. I let him slant himself inside me. My thoughts arrowed from the general to the particular: a kid, an emotionable bad apple, whom I'd sat across from in high-school Honors World Cultures, hounded by his girlishly cursive arms.

I felt something.

I caked some words over what I'd felt.

Days got pocked with facts, names, sights. I was given an office of my own with the understanding that there was no promotion involved, just the freeing up of space. I rewrote my presentations. I lunched at a diner where the paper place mats had been designed to divert bored kids. I always had several pens with me, but they stayed in my pocket. Except once. Once I connected some dots.

Nights were slopwork.

After work, I wasn't above ducking into a large supermarket and picking up five or six items almost at random, then approaching the long row of checkout lanes and skimming the faces of the men working the registers (women were disqualified) until I found one who looked as if he'd had a little too much to live, one who would lavish on my purchases and my implied need for them the most generous interpretation possible. I would choose his aisle. I would get in line. When it was my turn, when he was ringing up my items, we would be close in spirit. I would dizzy him with eye contact. Everything—my life—would be riding on what he would say, on the certainty that he would say something.

The kind of reading I was doing involved pushing the words around on the page, trying to bully them into doing what I wanted them to do. What I wanted them to do was tell me what to say when the phone rang at night and the unfamiliar, expectant, undebauched womanly voice of the misdialing caller asked, "Who is this?"

For the better part of a week, I was ashamed of myself for having refused to participate in a simple little educational exercise the first time I was asked. On a downtown street during my lunch-hour half-hour, a kid had come up to me—a kid with an oily scrub of beard and a clipboard—and said: "I'm supposed to tell ten people what I stand for and then get each to sign this piece of paper. They won't let me back into class until I get ten people."

He had waved the clipboard at me. I'd seen six or seven fake-looking signatures on a piece of steno-book paper.

I kept walking. I'd already known what this kid stood for: animal rights, beer by the keg, all you can eat, perpetual calendars at the back of telephone directories, sadomasochism that had real caring behind it, the right to photocopy whatever you pleased.

"Thanks a lot," he called out as I kept on walking.

On the next block, I was approached by a smithereened-looking woman who told me she stood for unity and excitement. She shoved her clipboard at me. I signed a name.

Some nights the saddest I got was when a street stopped. In a medium-sized city like that, they all did, eventually—guttering out into roads, flanging out into highways, dead-ending, slamming perpendicularly into boulevards and then never picking up their thread again. When a street stopped, I would want out-of-town papers, the advertising supplements of faraway department stores. I would want to know what the people living in those cities were getting that I couldn't get in my city.

． ． ■

I got used to being one of sleep's discards.

I would find myself pushed out, fully clothed, onto my new bedspread, which did not deliver on the promise of *spread*, which did not offer anything in the way of vistas, prospects. Next to me, on the floor, still untrashed, would be the plastic bag the bedspread had come in. It read: "CAUTION: THIS BAG IS NOT A TOY." I kept it there to remind me that everything was in lieu of everything else.

A Saturday, my kid again: my follow-through, my finish line, a livelong shape I'd kinked out of a woman when I could tell their faces apart—when women, womankind, seemed divisible into units, each unit customized with individuating gimmicks and specialties. In this case, the woman, if memory serves, was a well-thumbed, uninhabitable redhead, a health-care provider.

My ex-wife: I could tell that a lot of thought had gone into the things she had taken out on me.

In addition to the wife, I'd had parents. They were the people who had told me, the day I turned seven, that I was old enough to order my own ice-cream cone. They were seated on a bench on the boardwalk overlooking the sand and the beach umbrellas. I was wearing the brace that the doctors had put on the wrong part of me. Pinching a quarter, I wheeled around and squeaked over to the line of concession stands. A voice came out and ordered a cone.

The lady behind the counter said, "No such thing."

I guess I had a look on my face—a disturbance—that made her keep going. "I'm only orangeade, *she's* custard," she said, pointing across the partition—a clumsily nailed plank—to the lady at the next stand. The two ladies shared the same low ceiling.

The afternoon was glassy and overdetailed.

Meaning what? That I grew up on the spot? That years later it would take great effort and willpower to wave away the first available thumby, unsucked dick and wait instead—in line, if need be—for some cunted, varicosed smashup on which to hazard my desolating carnality?

■　■　■

Most nights, I was not so much living my life as roughing out loose, galling paraphrases of the lives being lived in the adjoining apartments and hallways. Someone would make a move (clear his throat, probably, or flush a toilet), and, after a reasonable minute, I would do something that approximated it (scrape a kitchen chair across linoleum, no doubt), something that in the end amounted to the same thing. I developed a vast overdependence on my sources, my fellow tenants, whom I went out of my way to avoid meeting because I hated them for beating me to what my life boiled down to.

STREET MAP OF THE CONTINENT

S ome days his work took him into people's houses. He would enter a room, part the air, odor things differently, then come out with whatever it was. Never a word of thanks from anybody, but he would usually get asked if he needed to use the bathroom—a powder room, more often than not. He would picture the owners listening to the flushes, counting.

He lived with a woman who volunteered at the library and brought a different book home with her every night. She would sit with it open on her lap and work the tip of an uncrooked paper clip into the gutter where the facing pages met, prying things loose: fingernail peelings, eyebrow hairs, pickings and outbursts and face-scrapings. Anything on the plane of the page itself—the immediate, heedless presence of the previous reader in the form of abundances of shed hair, perhaps, or gray powderings of scalp— she swept onto the floor. She evacuated the book, then ran the vacuum cleaner. In the morning, the book went back to the library.

The man had his own chair and watched her like a hawk.

There were a few years of cordial intimacy with the woman, and then her teeth began to lose their way in her gums. They listed and slid. The sticky hair she had always combed into a canopy over her forehead started to droop, and the color went dim. Her eyes seemed to take him in less and less.

One morning she was nowhere the man could see. Most of the clothes she had liked were gone, too.

He called in sick.

He sat in his chair, watching the kitchen from the hour when the table was a breakfast table to the hour when it was a supper table.

He started buying newspapers—anything he could get his hands on, one of each. There were some papers that came out only once a week and printed the menus of the senior-citizen high-rises in town. The man tore out the menus and taped them to the refrigerator door as ideas, suggestions.

The grocery store where he bought the papers was not part of a chain. The floor dipped and sloped. The aisles started out as ample causeways, veered off, then narrowed down to practically nothing. There were vitrines back there. Display cases. Nobody seemed particular about what went into them. The man started bringing things to add.

Her shoes, with the gloating, mouthy look that shoes acquire when no longer occupied.

Her stockings, riveled and unpleasant to touch.

Sheet after sheet of her sinking penmanship.

Numbers, calculations, she had steepened onto graph paper.

One night, he called the home number of the man who lined up the jobs for him.

"Yes," the voice said, over TV noise.

He put the phone down. Her smoking and sewing tackle were on the telephone stand. He put them in a bag to take to the store.

The sleeplessness spread to his arms and his legs. He practiced removing her absence from one place and parking it somewhere else. There was too much furniture in the house, he decided.

The town was one whose name the citizens had never had to spell out on the envelope when paying a bill or sending a card locally. Instead, they could just write *City*. Then came a generation who grew up suspecting there were two different places—one a town, the other a city—with the same sets of streets and addresses. These people were less sure of where they lived and spent too much time deciding whether the shadows that fell across sidewalks and playgrounds were either too big or too little for whatever the shadows were supposed to be shadows of. These were people who dreamed of towers that would never quite stay built even in dreams.

Depending on which authorities the man read, he could be counted as part of either generation.

The only other thing ever known about him was that when it came time to take his car in for the annual inspection, he sat in a little waiting area off to the side of the garage. A mechanic came in and told him that they had gone ahead and put a sticker on the car, but there were oral disclaimers about the brakes, the tires. "I don't know what kind of driving you do," the mechanic said. "Is it mostly around here, or highway?"

"Highway," the man said.

Weeks went by before he thought to stop.

SLOPS

Because I had colitis, I divided much of my between-class time among seventeen carefully chosen faculty restrooms, never following the same itinerary two days in a row, using a pocket notebook to keep track. I had to wear three thicknesses of underwear. By the end of a class day, my innermost briefs would be elaborately rimed, embrowned, impastoed.

Did I ever worry about the smell when I was passing out handouts in class? Because all I did was pass out handouts and read them out loud, then collect them and dismiss the class. None of it would be on the test. There were no tests—just papers. Not essays, themes, reviews, reports, compositions, critiques, research projects—but papers, sheets of paper, stapled together. I'd lightly pencil a grade in the upper-right-hand corner, and that would be it—no comments or appraisals subjoined in authoritative swipes of a felt-tip pen. I made sure no telltale signs—spilled coffee, dog-ears, creases, crumples, crimps, fingerprint grime—would lead students to believe that their papers had ever been read. But I read them hard, expecting sentences to have been spitefully spatchcocked into the running gelatinization of barbarisms and typos to check up on me, to see if I was actually reading. For instance: "Dear 'Professor': You fucking stink. Try wiping yourself once and [*sic*] awhile [*sic*]. Or didn't they teach that were [*sic*] you went to school? Bag it." But I never found any such intertrudings.

I was midway through my shadowed, septic thirties. I had been hired as a generalist. What I taught was vague and interdisciplinary and unchallengeable. Whatever I said, it was bound to be correct up to a point. My credentials were fraudulent. I'd awelessly faked my way through a Midwestern graduate school with a dissertation two hundred and eighty-seven clawing, suffixy pages long, all of it embezzled from leaky monographs. Since then, I'd taught myself to mooch off nobody but myself.

After each class, I lumped my way to whichever men's room my notebook said was next. My life was an ambitious program of self-centrifugalization. I was casting myself out.

Three "once"s:

Once

Once, there was no way for me to get out of having lunch with a colleague. He had the beard, the paunch, the patter. We sat in the faculty dining room, where I had never eaten before and never afterward ate again. He recalled the previous day's special: "chicken cordon sanitaire, potatoes non grata, vegetable mêlée." He said that his profession involved "belaboring the oblivious." He talked about a diffident colleague of ours who, at department meetings, when given the floor, "bent down to wax it." He said that when the annual departmental picture was taken, the camera went "c-l-i-q-u-e." I blinked and swallowed, hoisted smiles, poked at and beveled the block of beef on my plate. When he excused himself to rush off for a one-o'clock class, I sought out the dining-room men's room, one that wasn't on any of my regular campus tours. Unlike the nookish, single-person-occupancy arrangements I frequented (their hollow-board doors securing me from corridoral traffic only by the flimsy expedient of a hook and an eyebolt), this was a vast, modern affair with a line of urinals and three stalls. One of the latter was unoccupied, so, taking a seat, I busied myself with some noodling and valving, the virtually noiseless preliminaries, until, emboldened by the whoosh of a neighbor's flush and satisfied that it would muffle the report of my own bowels, I splattered myself out.

Once

Once, I attended a meeting of the university senate. Why? Because I had an urge to sit in a room with people, adults, salaried specialists. The day before, a sunless Sunday, I'd driven to a mall, where, from the remainder bin of a chain bookstore, I'd plucked a slim paperback by a doctor, a physician, that said the drizzled stools of a patient with colitis should be regarded as tears. So the next morning, I sat among a hundred or so of my colleagues and listened to a soon-to-retire administrator, a dean of some kind, say two things that I have not since been able to displace. One was that during his long career in the classroom he had learned many, many things from his students. I tried to think of one thing, anything, that I had ever learned from mine. Aside from the example of their grooming habits, sleeve-roll-up techniques, the novelties of their wristwear, etc., I couldn't come up with anything. The other thing the administrator said was that we all needed to love our students, that in many cases these kids weren't getting enough, or any, love at home. In the men's room afterward, I thought about my students, the whole faceless, rostered population of them. I did not love them, did not feel a trace of affection for them, but did I hate them? I decided that it wasn't exactly hate.

ONCE

Once, for what must have been well over a month, a dog-eyed girl, a student, a young woman really, at least twenty-three, dimly recognizable from the front-row center of one of my classes, began stopping by for a few minutes during my office hours. She always had at least three questions Magic Markered on pastel-hued index cards, and she asked them in a dampened, worn-away voice. She was an Informational Sciences major. My course was an elective.

One day, after I had answered her questions by hanging, as usual, some suspect, oversyntaxed curtains of explanation in the air between us, she capped her pen and said, "You need a buddy." She wasn't smiling, she wasn't being sarcastic, she wasn't unsteadying me with a stare. Her eyes were a muddy brown. She had an oily cumulus of biscuit-colored hair. She was wearing a windbreaker, a box-pleated skirt, brown socks. There was an untended, blotchy loveliness about her that had my cock smarting.

I balanced the image of her along the rim of my mind in the men's room afterward during an especially boiling, bustling efflux, and it occurred to me: Did people think I was beating off in there? Were people keeping track of the time? Had some busybody logged me in? I had the stink working in my favor, but how long after my exit would it be until somebody actually came in and registered the stink and then put two and two together?

When the girl showed up, uninvited but not unexpected, late one afternoon at the house I rented on a pinched street, I offered her dinner—a microwavable box of chicken. I put her at ease by standing in the kitchen and following the red digital countdown on the face of the microwave. She lotus-positioned herself on the living-room floor, started jerking through the classified section of the paper.

"I'm moving out," she said. Then: "My stepmom, my mother, my boyfriend, school, your class."

"Everything?" I said.

"All of it. Completely. Practically."

I arranged some napkins and forks on the coffee table.

"By the way, that smell," she said. "Now I know."

I watched her eat. I listened to her talk. Then I watched her lead the way to the bedroom.

Undressing myself, lowering myself into bed with someone new, I always reminded myself that whichever women had ever climbed on top of me before had actually just been laddering themselves up onto somebody else. About halfway through, maybe even sooner, they'd be absolutely sure of it. They'd know *who*. What was happening with this girl was this: I was handing her back to her boyfriend on a platter.

After she left, I grabbled around in my desk for my grade book, then slapped on bare feet toward the bathroom. Once seated, I turned to MWF 9:15-10:15, Stevenson Hall 142A, and found her: Ramsey, Val. She'd been doing "A" work. In my course, "A" work meant turning in so many sheets of paper over so many weeks. Thirty sheets, fifteen weeks, I think.

■　　■　　■

There is actually a fourth "once," something I did that didn't involve taking a crampy, squdging shit afterward.

Once, on a table in the faculty lounge in the building where my office was, I found a rain-wrinkled newspaper open to the comics page. There was nobody else around. I took a pencil out of my inside pocket. In the white squares between the black ziggurats of the crossword puzzle, I penciled, in heavy, ham-handed caps untraceable to me: COULD EVERYBODY PLEASE BE A LITTLE LESS SPECIFIC? STARTING RIGHT NOW?

DEVOTIONS

From time to time I show up in myself just long enough for people to know they are not in the room alone. Usually, these are people who expect something from me—a near future, a not-too-distant future. What I tell them is limited to the people I have already had myself married against. Everything I say is to the best of my knowledge and next to nothing. It comes nowhere close.

My first wife, my blood wife, had no background to speak of, no backdrop of relations, customs, scenery. She arrived sharp-spined and already summed up. We ate out all the time and spoke lengthily, vocabularily, about whatever got set before us, especially the meat, with its dragged-out undersong of lifelong life. There was no end to the occasions on which the woman and I got along in public and in private. I remember a smell she had on just her arms, an endearment, something that she had been born with or that had travelled a great distance to land on her. I am almost certain that there was much more to what there was of us—I think we had a house, some coverings at the very least—but the night she gave me what was obviously a severance fuck, nothing needed to be said, nobody needed to be told off. I left right away. The time I looked back, the evidence was slight.

It was the second wife who drank. It was always up to me to cart her back and forth to work. The job titles she had during the time I was married to her could be listed either alphabetically or chronologically; I am not sure what difference, if any, such a list would make. But the addresses—we moved from house to house, although they were never houses per se, just blunt-roofed, boxlike constructions with garages beneath a sequence of airless rooms that I sometimes tried to work some pertinence into—could probably be mapped out to clarify the prevailing direction, which was toward something else.

This was a wife with sunken teeth and runny eyes and a face that darked up when she was finished talking. She had bangs—a blindfold, practically, of black hair. Nights, I watched her watch the babiness go out of her children. I think she was waiting for them to bleed together into a single, soft-boned disappointment. There were three of them, and they all had the same trouble with time—not just with telling it, but with knowing that it had passed, knowing what it separated.

Late one night when the woman had drunk herself snory, I gathered the children into the living room. The four of us sat together on the sofa, a sleepless immediate family. I decided to do justice to the children one by one. The youngest often wet his bed, so I told him: "You sweat a lot, that's all. Who doesn't?" I assured the middle child that he ate constantly not because he had a worm but because his teeth needed activity. And the oldest, whose teacher sent home notes saying that the girl had started speaking up in class about her "stepdog" and her "stepself": I had to let her egg herself on until she got a feel for the busywork of my heart. Everything came out of me in what sounded like a father's voice. I was good at stringing myself along.

The woman eventually brought her disturbances of mind to bear on getting herself under some auspices—some high-up, steep-eaved auspices for a change. There was a man made of money who owned more than one automobile, and she found a way to take charge of the one he liked the least. It was radish-colored and underslung. One night, she took me for a ride in it and explained that the man had put her to work in a vast hall, someplace altitudinous, auditoriumish, where desks were arranged on risers as far as the eye could see. She was careful to keep the man himself out of the description.

I remember looking out the passenger-side window at the mirror and the lopsided traffic it was cupping out for me to take notice of. Decaled in ghost-white letters across the face of the mirror was the claim "OBJECTS IN MIRROR ARE CLOSER THAN THEY APPEAR." This I crowdedly assented to.

Then I did a dumb thing. I moved into an apartment house and grew concerned that the person living in the unit above mine was following me, upstairs, from room to room. For much of the day, my life would be down to just this one concern. I would walk from the living room to the bedroom, or from the kitchen to the bathroom—I had just those four rooms, in that order—and there this person would be, all but squarely overhead, the footfalls clumpy but companionate, solicitous.

Sooner or later it dawned on me that this person had divined how things were laid out in my rooms, had rearranged the furniture and belongings and outsweepings upstairs to correspond to my own—so that if, during a passage from room to room, I abruptly stopped (lowered myself to a region of the floor where a tossed magazine had landed in a rumply heap, for instance, and then lingered over it rehabilitatively, smoothing out its pages, restoring as much as I could manage of its flat, unread, newsstand inviolability), there would be, at that very same spot twelve feet or so above me, a parallel distraction for this person, a consuming project of his or her own.

In other words, there was my life, my offgoings from room to room, and there was the clomping reiteration of it being carried out upstairs. So this is how I got married vis-à-vis my finishing wife: I moved myself and the person upstairs out of our apartments and into a house in another city. This wife was young enough to give birth. The birth was quick and thoughtless.

The child went through life with expressions on its face that were not its own. Bus drivers and crossing guards and food handlers demanded to know whose they were. The best I could do was see everybody's point, then look away. There was always something waiting to be looked at, someone missing out.

As for the child, unresolved questions of attribution drove it far enough out of sight for me to hold down a job. There is almost too much truth in the words when I say that I was holding the job down. The fact is that I was a weight on it, keeping it from getting done. There was a heavy, flattening incorrectness that eventually found its way to the attention of somebody not too high up.

Then came nights when, lying awake beside my final wife, I would spend too much time putting my finger on what was wrong. I was wearing the finger out.

What was wrong was very simple.

Sometimes her life and mine fell on the same day.

WHEN YOU GOT BACK

When I wrote this originally, it was a piece on walking as a disorder of the body: walking as affliction, not function. I am relieved that no one will ever get to see it. The piece was immodest and threatening in tone. I wrote it after reading something somebody else had written, something much better and more mildly put, on an entirely different subject. I wrote it in a single sitting at a card table, an upholstered one with brown vinyl stretched rather slackly over a half-inch or so of foam rubber. That was not the best surface in the world to be writing on—there was nothing solid beneath my sheet of paper as I drove the pencil across it—but I wrote in gusts, furies, of words.

When I finished, I moved in with a woman who had been after me for months. I brought the card table, my clothes, some chairs, all the health and beauty aids I owned. I lived with the woman for a little over a year. It was difficult. She was one of the unhappily happy. We were both in love with the same man. Once a week we took a bus to his building and listened to his records. The man had plenty of pull, so the woman and I would dance together and baby each other in front of him while he resleeved some of the records in his collection, which was immense and off-limits to us. We never did have any turn of events with the man, either marriedly or privately, though I am probably just guessing on the woman's part.

When the woman's parents died—the father first, the mother some months later—I had to tag along to the viewings and the funerals. At a gathering after the second funeral, one of the relations, who was drunk, went around introducing me as the woman's "expected," which almost everybody corrected to mean "intended." Afterward, the woman drove me to the house where her parents had lived. It was a small row house in a run-down neighborhood. She took me to the room that had once been her bedroom. It was right inside the front door. It was the room that in any other household would have been the living room. A couple of days later, she moved into it.

For once, I got a real job. I was selling high-tech surveillance equipment to bosses who were losing sleep over what their employees might be up to. I was living, off and on, in an efficiency apartment with a high-school girl—a senior, I'm pretty sure. I must have been serious about the girl—she had facial features and was already describable to an extent—because I brought some things home from the store for her, things she could easily put to work on her teachers at school.

One night, the girl was sitting at my card table and studying for a test. She wanted to read a couple of chapters and then have me ask her all the review questions at the back. She figured it would take at least two hours to do the reading. I asked her what the subject was. "Some kind of geography," she said. Without even having to be told, I took a walk. I did not even bother looking up at the window of the apartment to see if the girl was in it, with or without my phone pressed against her ear. Part of the truth I had had to keep from her was that when I was in school I had been too dumb to learn the things the teachers were teaching. I had to content myself with learning something else, other things, instead. One of them was how, when taking a walk, you had to calculate what the walk was getting taken away from—what was getting subtracted from what. You had to determine what would be left when you got back.

In the parking lot, I met a man carrying a basketful of laundry. He explained that he had just washed his clothes but there was something unutterably troubling and unfinished about what had happened. His laundry was not done, he said; it was in error. He set the basket down and tugged a pair of washed-looking pants from the tangle and shook them out in my direction.

"Vouch for me," he said.

POSITIONS

T he trouble with coming was that I actually did arrive somewhere. I arrived at the place my body had already left. I got there just in time to get a good look at what had happened where things were. I looked at the person on whom I had been a passenger—in every case, my sister. I looked at this woman, who was a form of transportation, a mode of delivery.

Then what?

I think I stopped looking.

For months it was like that in exactly one room. It was a room in which everything was first on the one hand and then on the other hand, and before long the hands went back into the pockets and were out of view.

Is it coming through that I got myself entailed in her, got conveyed by her body to the room where everything had to be taken out right away but could never be put back in the exact same place because there was nothing reliable to go by?

By rights, certain things were up to me. It was up to me to make sure there was a roof over where her body came apart, where it showed what was inside, where the harsh pink activity of herself kept carrying on. We were on the second of three floors. I was the one hope.

I worked as a substitute teacher, revising a test that everybody, regardless of ability, would flunk. I had the tests printed at my own expense and had a black felt slipcase especially sewn. This is where the money went.

Every so often when I was devising a new test, my sister would notice me from the bed in a way that made me feel myself seen. Usually what she said was: "Your chair is pointed wrong." She would get up and bulk herself against the chair—I would not budge; in fact, I would solidify myself on the cushion with downward, side-to-side thrusts of my rear end—until she managed to angle things differently, influentially. Then I would have to board my sister and get delivered to where things now stood.

One day the school district was through with me. I got a letter with a many-signatured petition attached. My sister was offered a position requiring her to make sandwiches on a large scale in a building where there would be lots of steps for her to climb. On the bed were a bus schedule and an umbrella. She washed her hair in the basin. She sang to herself as she rinsed. She made me a practice sandwich, something thick and colory. She wrapped it in one of my handkerchiefs, then sat down on the bed to watch me unwrap the sandwich and eat.

I could see that the furniture had already been turned, reset, hours ahead or hours behind—whatever it took.

Her mouth did not move with mine.

THEIR SIZES RUN DIFFERENTLY

There were different ways we did not come into our own.

We were warm-armed, hot-handed girls. Our palms burned. We made fists around ice cubes, or squeezed anything else frozen—boxes of vegetables, foiled cuts of meat. When they thawed, we exiled them to the freezer again, reached for whatever had collected a fresh crust of frost.

We knew how to write with a broken pencil-point if there was still a divot of exposed wood stuck to the side. We would fit what was left of the point back into the tip of the long casing, and then, seizing the pencil just above the scalloped border where the splintery wood met the yellow enamel, press down courageously, foolhardily, in the direction opposite the split. That was the only way things could get written out, everything that was spoken into us, the voice drabbing down the line of our bones. "Nature favors the delocalized heart," the voice mostly said.

We had the same oily skin, dripping and dark. We were warned never to let our hands land on our cheeks or our foreheads, told that our blotting fingerpads would make things only worse. By the end of the day, our faces would appear to be entirely behind water. It was just the rain coming back out of us, we were told. By morning, the pillowcases would be moist with our heatdrops.

At a given moment, one of us would always be the first to arrive at the unringing telephone, fetch the receiver from its cradle, then cup the sievelike speaker out for the others to have to hear. We were convinced that the dial tone did not sustain the same pitch from one day to the next—that it sometimes stepped itself up a clement half-tone at the very least, and on occasion lowered itself into a register of pure rebuke.

Our conduct at the mirror was exemplary. We cut ourselves dead as we sponged our faces, groomed our teeth. We dismissed every unsolicited collateral movement in the glass. We kept ourselves secret. We were girls beyond recognition, beneath ourselves.

One day, we were led into a high-ceilinged room and told that everything had already been done for us, that nothing had been spared or held back, that we had been born for no reason other than for hair to have an extra place to grow in the world. A hand pointed to the wide route the hair was already starting to take down our calves. If you cut it, we were told, it will come back. It will haunt.

The curfew was lifted.

I went to where another girl was living and tried to live there too. There was little to be learned, but we arranged ourselves stationarily in the light she had prepared by uptipping only certain slats of the Venetian blinds. I could see down into the side yard, where she was sponsoring a line of gawky flowers. Every night we let sleep reinflict upon us its formulary and useless terrors. Come morning, it was usually argued that we were out of place, and a map was once again pencilly roughed out. I ran my hair over everything the girl drew.

One day, the girl removed a cake from a cardboard carton and explained that she had worked out a method of consumption by which she was not so much eating the cake as allowing the cake to incur a smaller, less rectangular version of itself—much as (or so she said) a body part, if left alone long enough, brings about, takes on, accumulates, the hand or mouth of somebody else, the arriving hand pointfully different in complexion and intent, and the mouth talking (concealedly) about something else entirely, such as how other people's handwriting always looks more legitimate, more artless, than one's own, one's own seeming (in comparison) suspectable, staged, *manufactured*, impeaching the misdirected fingers that still control the pencil, not to mention the arm and its gainless travels.

Am I again covering the subject of her hands and their aptitude for crisis, the left hand more adroit than the right one at communicating itself at long last to the only appropriate knee or saucer or coin? It was a hand endowed with a ruthful sense of what it might next be due on, of what (only moments later) it was to become the final fitting bearer of. I was the opposite—my body irrelevant, just the podium, the dais, from which a face had to speak. My body was where I was instead of everywhere else.

The girl of whom I speak washed herself pertinently in a marble tub. I had acquired a modest capital of gels and oils and salts with which I tinted the water. Some nights I handed her a little tablet of soap. I would follow the course, the career, of the soap as she swiped it across her chest. Other nights there was a pitted mash of fruit that she dwindled onto herself with a strip of cloth. The greasy water tilted when finally she stepped from the tub and I took her place. I became a full citizen of her water.

All too often, though, my life came along and I joined up with it—reconcerned myself with it to the full, enlisted in movement already under way, stood up to myself, made out how my body was lost on me anew. I went to stay with a girl in a building where the girl's mother lived with a woman the mother had known all her life. The girl wrote to me on her instep, and then she planked her leg out toward me so I could peel off the thick sock and read. All it said was: "How will you be mine?" It was presently decided that the girl and I would profit from learning. The night before the start of school, I confided to the girl that what I looked at I looked at only as a favor to what I was not looking at; that the nicest thing I could think to do for a person, the only way I could go out of my way for such a person, the highest compliment I could possibly pay such a person, was to see to it that I did not see the person at all; that sometimes I cheated and applied my eyesight to the person, but so cautiously, so sparingly, that the person was no more than bare shape, dim contour.

I could not take my eyes off the girl as I spoke.

In school, I was placed a grade ahead of the girl. It was explained that the tartaned girls on either side of me, and those in front and behind, were my "neighbors." I kept my eyes on my own paper. The teacher would interrupt our silent reading and tell us to picture something—a different land, or an animal—and when it was an animal, I would see something knobby or protuberant on it that barely belonged and that made its life ungovernable and boonless and sad.

"Who can put it on the board?" the teacher would say.

I was quick with chalk because of how fast it dilapidated in my hand. I would hold the stick of it sidewise between thumb and forefinger, then powder the slate with cloudages that consumed panel after panel of the board. The teacher would follow behindhand, accomplishing arclike swipes with her eraser. The chalk I dropped back into the tray would be worn flat on one side.

I was eventually taken in by a woman whose daughter must have been one of the ones who had drowned. When it came time for as much as possible of my body to disappear behind that of a guitar, I had my choice of the woman's sleek, solid-body electric or the daughter's elderly Hawaiian, an acoustic, which lay in a case lined with wine-colored felt. The Hawaiian, the one I fell for, was tall and full of figure, with *f*-shaped sound holes out front and tiny cracks, crazings, running the length of its voluptuous back. I took the guitar warmly, adultly, into my arms but could not strike off even the simplest of chords. The trouble was my hands: I was no good at crippling the fingers of my left one the way it took to get the strings clenched against the fretboard and to get the chords compiled from the loose, wiry notes.

I fed pieces of underwear—panties, camisoles—into the sound holes to dampen the noiseful predicament I had carried out to the woman's driveway. I operated the strings of the guitar with a Q-tip instead of a pick. I finally contrived an open, cheater's tuning. I clamped out the chords with my thumb curling down over the fretboard. I was thus confined to the major chords, which became heinous, public tollings of my heart.

There were other downthrown girls along the road, with instruments they had never learned the right way to play: a chord organ, a snare drum with a clinky cymbal hanging boltedly and hazardously from above, another guitar—this one electric and overdecorated and plugged into a trebly midget amplifier. These girls heard what was becoming of the chords I platted out with my bone-hard thumb. The noise got onto the girls, overset them. A group of them began to assemble around me on the blacktop. It was a jinkly, bickering music that we frittered and tingled from our instruments and into the last of the summer.

I sang the way I still talk.

Every song was the worst way I could think of to ask for what I did not yet know how not to want.

YOURS

U sually the most I care to say in the morning is: "I have a couple of grown sons." I say it for the neighbors on both sides.

If I have a problem, it is this: there is a store where everything costs a dollar.

These are essentially my outsets and my outcomes.

All I am saying is pick any room and, chances are, there is already enough in it for something situationy to get started. In particular, there is a big difference in the quiet right before the phone finally rings. That is what I listen for the most. The phone itself I just let ring.

One thing else:

There are two types of people in this world.

Just don't ask me where they live.

SMTWTFS

One of the things I mean when I say I could be wrong is that it was my mother, most likely, who told me to shit or get off the pot. This would have been at the dinner table. I was probably withdrawing chips of cereal from the box and eating them one by one with my fingers.

My family: here they come for the last time if I can help it. Mother, father, sister—all of them big-boned, robustly depressed, full of soft spots and unavailing clarities when it came to me.

It was for their privacy that I took a job passing out perfume samples on the main floor at Brach's. It was a woman's fragrance. I splurged it onto my forearms and pressed the sample cards, matchbook-sized with a tiny capsule slotted inside, on men and women alike. I would watch them descend the slope of the escalator. When they stepped within the radius of my arms, the doubts would start: hadn't I already urged a sample on this person or that one? Everybody started looking recognizably unfamiliar. Now and then the supervisor would surprise me from behind and pat some more posture onto my shoulders or float a hand in the gutter of my lower spine.

When the summer was through, I set out for the cinder-block acropolis of the state-university system. My roommate's cousin lived a couple of floors down from us in the dorm and had his own refrigerator. He came from the coal region and called pens "ink pens." By the end of the first week, I had made up my mind to spend money on him. In the gloom of a movie house, I slid my hand onto his and forked our fingers together. At the sink in the restroom afterward, I gave him the conclusive kiss. I kept expecting to get smacked silly. In bed, everything was up to me and happened in the order I wanted it.

We read my roommate's tight, possessive diary every afternoon without ever once finding ourselves anywhere in the wrap-ups. One day, we slipped out of our housing contracts, took an efficiency apartment off campus. We started disinvolving ourselves from our classes more flashily. Once or twice a week we rode a bus to the closest city, a low-rise hub with a couple of perishing business streets. We ate at a department-store coffee shop, strode up and down escalators, tried things on each other in fitting rooms. Sometimes I could get him to piss delicately onto the more expensive clothes. I liked the *shreesh* that abruptly parted hangers made when I returned everything to the racks.

There were nights I could not keep him away from overdue homework—accounting, mostly: ledger sheets, a plug-in calculator with squarish raspberry digits, knife-sharpened pencils. On the floor, with an open textbook of my own ramped up onto my knees, I'd slick flesh-colored polish onto my fingernails and study a chapter—the look, the shape, of it: the sometimes stepwise progression down the page that chocks of white space made wherever paragraphs came to a halt.

One afternoon, in the Old Main concourse, I saw him sitting on one of the long, itchy sofas. There was a girl beside him, a tall leg-crosser with a haphazardry of oranged hair. They had notebooks open on their laps and were contentedly, curricularly, sifting through stacks of index cards. I started going to the city on my own. In a bar, a businessman chuffed commandingly to my side, led me to a table, bought me a big late lunch. He drove me to an office trailer at a construction site, unlocked the door.

It was through this man that I soon fell in with some damselly boys, maidens, a few years older than I. There were too many of us for the one bed, so some of us slept on the floor, on throw rugs, or with the rugs as blankets. We flavored our bathwater with things from the kitchen—fruit syrups, sometimes just soda. The one whose apartment it was, my host, got a summons for jury duty in a special mailer he had to tear open by grasping the thing at both ends and then pulling, the way you do with certain disappointing party explosives. We took turns going over the letter he wrote to get out of going. That day, he looked baffled for his age, indifferently shaved. He had gone after his hair with a blue plastic kiddie scissors, mincing it up in employment-defying ways.

He was the most befucked of us, the first to start filling out. I was the one who finally mailed the letter.

He made us all go to his parents' anniversary party. His older brother was there, under a tarp, with his leg in a cast, and I was expected to write something on it. A pen, a porous-point marker, was volunteered into my hand. I had no problem getting down on the patio floor. The front part of the cast was so oversubscribed, there were regions along the slight curve above the knee that were already palimpsestic. I read from the bottom up. None of the names were ones I could put faces to. There were lots of looping longhand endorsements from women who had old names with fresh spellings: Lynnda is one I remember.

I looked at the line of downcurved toes in their cut-out wiggle room. There was a tuft of black hairs on each of the toe-knuckles. The nails were dull ovals.

"Bashful?" the brother's brother—my protector—said.

I finally signed "smtwtfs," like on the calendar, which is what I usually did when a name got called for on a petition or guest register. The general principle, I guess, was that days were yet to come, big fat days flying in your face.

The one girl I danced with turned out to be the sister. She had swimmy eyes and flat hair and a raisinlike mole on her left cheek. Her arms were long, thin, string-colored. She kept wheeling the conversation around to her parents and brothers. "You picked the wrong one of us to rub off on you," she said.

In her room, upstairs, she had to finish most of my sentences for me. She said it was obvious I had not had my heart bounced around nearly enough. There was a pitcher of colored liquid on her nightstand, and I watched her tilt out cupful after cupful. She drank tediously, dragging it out.

The only one who could give me a lift into town afterward was a friend of the family's I had not been introduced to. He was just barely in the age range, but he had the physique. I agreed with everything he said—that too much happens when people do not get shot and killed, that there were bound to be more at home like me, that things happening over and above did not necessarily ever make it down to the street, and that it was a wonder more people didn't do what he did, which was to recite the dinner order into the drive-through microphone, drive around the building to the pickup window, hand over the exact amount, reach for the bag, then park the car, carry the food into the restaurant, and eat at a booth, where you had secrecy.

"That way, nobody sees you asking for it," he said.

We were stuck behind a truck with a sign on the back that read: "THIS VEHICLE STOPS OFTEN."

"Turn here?" he said, motioning toward the windshield.

My hand was already on his upper arm. It was one more thing in the world my hand could fit around without ever once actually having to hold.

BEING GOOD IN OCTOBER

The wedding was curt and almost entirely without result. At no point during the ceremony did the minister let anybody but himself be the center of attention. The one halfway-decent thing about the reception was that the tables were so narrow, the guests could sit on only one side. They faced the backs of the guests at the next table and kept their voices down.

When the woman got home afterward, she put everything away in drawers and cupboards so that she could not go after any of it in her sleep without waking herself up first and having to know what it was she had on her hands.

THE SMELL OF HOW THE WORLD HAD GROUND ITSELF ONTO SOMEBODY ELSE

From what I gather, I had to have had the sense, sooner or later, to get up and have a look at the outline my body had pressed into the carpet during sleep—the clearing I had made by pushing aside clothes and food wrappers and newspapers and such—and it could not have resembled the shape of any of the familiar postures of convalescence, because I remember thinking there were still some people, two or three people—I kept adding them together differently—who could be counted on, if reached at the right time of the month, to say, "I was just thinking about you," and these were not the people I thought to call.

The phone was one more constant thing on the floor—an old rotary-dial model with a heavyset handset. I must have called the woman and hung on every word of mine, taken in everything I was saying, because I put clothes on and drove to the address I had repeated aloud when it was the first thing spelled out for me to write down.

She was living with a cousin and his blind dogs and porcelain dolls in a rented row house. The cousin could have been out—either at the resort where he worked or at the school he had to go to. I probably asked about everybody else, just to make sure there was conversation, or just to be pulling for somebody, or why would I now swear that the three youngest (girl, girl, girl) were with an aunt and the two oldest (girl, boy) were renting places of their own? What other reason would I have to bring any of them up? Wasn't I the one they claimed had told them things about the human body that could not possibly be true—that it was the grave the heart was buried in, and other misrepresentations of far worse ilk?

A doctor who liked the woman had written out a whole pad's worth of prescriptions, dated at two-month intervals, for a cone-shaped junior tranquilizer, and as a believer in keeping something on my stomach, I am certain I must have taken what was offered and chewed it. And then the woman had to have said, "Come under the covers," because I had only ever gone by what was visible, the parts of things that stuck right out, and what I was seeing was familiar—everything on her that gaped.

The children knew where to find the woman when it seemed reasonable to move back in. It took a couple of days. The house—this was a differently addressed one, with shutters—had three floors. Every room was going to have the same kind of blinds. Everybody who was old enough to work was going to be told how long, in weeks, she had in order to find a job. Names and deadlines were going to get written on a kitchen wall that was going to get painted harvest gold. The woman was making good money and did not have to report to anybody except her boss, who liked her and said, "No need to come in today—just stay by that bonny phone of yours just in case."

At the time of which I write, my middle forties, people were expected to provide their own transportation. The car I owned was not presentable. It did not make an impression. One morning, I drove to a trade-in dealership and stood at the edge of the lot. Within an hour, the salesman had me cleaning out my trunk and my backseat. It had to be done with great haste, he said. A woman was already interested in the car, he said. He wheeled over two large garbage barrels, then dragged out some cardboard boxes to hold whatever I was going to keep. He said he understood what it must be like to live in such a small place and have nowhere to go with your things.

It was the woman and the oldest girl who afterward pretended to be attorneys and made the lawyerly threats over the phone to the salesman, the sales manager, the president of the lot. None of it did any good—once you sign a contract, etc. The new car was a grating brick-red abhorrency in the woman's gravelled driveway. I could look out and see the youngest three peering into the windows of it, pointing at the boxes that were too big for the trunk. The boxes did not yet belong in the house.

The oldest girl kept saying, "I won't bite you." I listened from the other end of the living room when it was her turn to talk legal into the phone. To prolong her threats, she kept up a kind of vowelly crooning between words. It was the first I had ever taken much notice of her. She appeared to be in her twenties and had arranged the freckly lengthiness of her body into a slouch that made her elbows and legs seem pointed privately, inquiringly, toward me. I started siding with her, beholding whatever she beheld—the fishbowl ashtray, the dishful of pastilles and drops, the plum-colored splotch she kept rubbing on her shin.

As thanks, I said I would take the two of them, the woman and the oldest girl, out to dinner, someplace decent and scarcely lit. The girl went upstairs and took a long, decisive shower—I could hear all the water it was taking—and then came down in a slip and knelt in front of the coffee table and looked up into my face as she applied the determining makeup.

At the restaurant, she asked me questions about herself—what I thought she thought, which violences I considered her capable of—and no matter what I said, she would say, "That's a good answer," or "How right you always are."

"But you're so far away," she said, finally.

We were seated at a banquette, the girl in the middle. The woman kept getting up to call her boss.

For maybe two or three nights afterward, I fell asleep on my floor by starting with the woman under my eyes, then adding on the two-inch advantage every new generation supposedly gained over its predecessor, lightening and lengthening the hair, overpowdering the face, inflating the biceps, spattering freckles onto the arms and chest, until I had brought the girl on top of me in her avid, breastless entirety.

As always, I was slow to let on that I knew how far I was being taken advantage of. The girl fell in with some friends of her cousin's, tight-lipped teenagers in floppy shorts that came down to their shins. That was the last I saw of her for years.

One night, I stupidly told the woman how I felt.

"That's all going to change," she said.

• ■ ■

Instead, the woman opted for misery and hardship and unemployment of a high order. These were the years of learning disabilities, loosenesses of mind, downheavals all over. I went through her thick mail. I remember disconnection notices, policy cancellations, bounced-check statements, form letters declaring who was suspended from school and for how long, collection-letter sequences whose initial entry always started with the question "Have you forgotten something?"

What I kept forgetting was that I was nothing to anybody under that roof other than the one who stuck around for it to repeatedly dawn on everybody else—her relations, mostly; the cousin above all—that it takes all kinds. In time, the oldest girl came back. She arrived in a car of her own. Most of her hair was gone. This was the smallest house yet, a cottage. It was still daylight out on the porch. I could see that the girl was looking into the uncurtained window, already figuring herself back onto the furniture.

"You were going to say something," she said in my direction. "You were going to put something to me," she said.

"A proposition," she said.

The woman had to step outside in her graphic housecoat and explain to the girl that there was nowhere for the girl to sleep.

I could describe the circles the other children left the house to move around within. I could describe the walks of life to which they applied themselves. I could describe the beds they slept astray. I would not be the first. There is already a beaten path.

The least I can say is that once in who knows how long you actually get to see where you are living. I can attest to this plentifully. I can speak from experience something awful. Just this once, you have your chance: all the right lights are finally on.

Your first thought is to let somebody else take over the talking.

That summer, the two of us rolled what was left of my pennies—there were still basinsful of them, drawersful that went all the way back to my youth—and I drove the woman to where there was one large body of water, and then on to where there was another, and then on yet again. There were always seagulls, a span of boardwalk, waves, shells to accumulate in our drinking cups. But it was never the sea, she claimed. Show me a sea, she said.

I was a thoroughgoer. There was so much to go back on.

Years must have gone by without my fingering getting any better. The woman kept saying: "A little lower."

Or: "Not even close."

Or: "Do you even know where you are?"

It says something about my wife, which is what the woman had become, that I am saying any of this so voluminously. Because if you are anything like me—*please be*—you have had the sense to keep yourself under investigation long enough to already know what is in store.

For instance, walking in on her when she is transferring everything from one handbag to the other.

Does she say: "Finish your meal"?

Or: "All you do is make work"?

Or: "Occupy yourself"?

In my case, there were only a couple of spots left for me to still fill. One was at work. This was the spot in which I had found out I was not being paid the same as everybody else. I was in the washroom, soaping my hands at the sink, when I heard my name come up in conversation in the stalls behind me. Whomever the voices belonged to had got hold of a printout of how much everybody was making. A distribution. I rinsed my hands and dried them on a paper towel and got out of there in one two three.

Later in life, I brought the matter up with a supervisor. I got called a malcontent, a troublemaker, more hindrance than help. What could she do but put me behind a desk even farther from the public? She took me off light-administrative and put me on time sheets. Work was brought to me in carts.

"Do your dirt on numbers for a change" is all the other one— the one who always gave straight answers—told me to my face.

One other spot I was in—the last—was the one at whose center I kept getting even worse at judging the distances between people. I fouled up every time. If I saw somebody declaring herself with a gesture, I intercepted as much as I could of whatever was on its way to whom it might have actually concerned. I helped myself to anything headed elsewhere. I carried on as if it were mine.

Do I have to draw a picture? The one I keep drawing and shoving in her face is the one of me walking home from work one day when she had the car. I passed a store where a kid was sitting along a landscaped strip that bordered the parking lot. The kid had its arms wrapped around its shins, knees pointing up.

"I cut myself," the kid said to me.

I stopped for a look. I saw a knee with a scab that looked picked-at. A few platelets of scab were loose and afloat in what little blood there was.

The scab was the color of ham. Burnt ham.

I took the clean handkerchief out of my back pocket, squatted next to the kid, patted the handkerchief against the knee. A few circlets of blood appeared on the face of the cloth.

I said something along the lines of: "Just keep that on there for a while."

And here comes what your life will never be the same after which, the same way mine has already never been: my face was bent right over the kid's other knee. The knee was aimed right at me.

I got a whiff of it, all right. I got the hell out of there.

Who hasn't lived life expressly to avoid having to one day inhale something that entire? It was the complete, usurping smell of how the world had ground itself onto somebody else.

Did I hasten home and shut myself in the bathroom and try to bring forth a similar smell—something equally total—from my own knees? Did I wait until my wife had fallen asleep and then expect to drag its like out of hers? Did I slip out of bed and put my clothes back on, let myself out of the house, steer a straight course toward the parking lot at the store, roll up the legs of my pants, grind my kneecaps into the damp earth until the dirt was caked onto the flesh, then roll the pants down again, plunge home, sneak into the bathroom, disrobe, remount the toilet, bury my nose in my knee, and draw in big, hopeful breath-gulps to satisfy myself that the disrupting magnificence on the kid's knee—the alarm—had been nothing more than the neglected pressing smellsomeness of dirt alone; and having discovered, instanter, that it was not a matter of dirt, that the point of origin—of contact—lay elsewhere, did I spend the next couple of weeks before and after supper wending my way around the purlieus of the store, the alleys and backyards and traffic islands, keeping my gait brisk and neighborish, doing my best to preserve the appearance of an unprovoked, unprowling fellow in walking shorts first working up an appetite, then strolling off his meal, but always ultimately, futilely, rubbing the knees against something differently frictional—tree bark or smoothed rock, the blacktop of a driveway or nettles in a vacant lot?

Did I ever once in all of this time bring off anything remotely approximating a get-together with my wife? Did it eventually occur to me to seek out the kid itself? Did I have any luck? Did I have enough sense to burst into my supervisor's office and make a clean breast of it? Did I say: "This is what I've done. This is what I'm doing. This is what I will have done by the time I'm finished"? Because if people should happen to ask, it will be only because they themselves are already sick of being pestered for the answer. The identical let-down looks on their faces are the only way the hostess can tell for sure that the people are all in the same party the one time it occurs to them to venture out to eat as a community.

So go ahead.

Make anything up.

Tell them whatever their little hearts desire.

Tell them I was an only son at the time the world was filling up with women, making everything harder for me to see.

SUSCEPTIBILITY

T his is about two people. It should not have to matter which two. In fact, wherever there are two people, regardless of what everything between them might still be in spite of, this is bound to be the story in full.

One of them wanted to know where he could buy some of those rubber squares you stick under the feet of furniture, either to protect the finish on the floor or to keep the furniture from sliding away, whichever it was.

That one's my father.

The other one's me.

RIMS

From the look of things, there were some openings left in the band, some spaces not yet filled, so I got called out of study hall one afternoon and led into a storage room, where I was told to pick an instrument. I pointed to the first thing I saw that I could play with my mouth shut: a drum. I let them thread sticks through my fingers and strap the snare drum onto me. I let them lead me into the band room and up to the top tier, where the other drummers were already standing. I let them show me which ones to stand between.

I dribbled out a long, mushy roll that was not what I meant. Then I tried a slow, tappy, single-stroke roll that did not come any closer. I did some paradiddles. I splatted out some flams and some rim shots.

The band performed popular songs that were brassed up and flattened out to sound like marches. I kept my mouth closed and my lips still while I played everything wrong by heart. Then I taught myself something better. I brought the sticks down to within a fraction of an inch of the drum's head and just pattered away at the air. I got away with this on football fields, in parades.

There were eight other drummers in the band: five on snares, two on bass, one on cymbals. I received them one by one in the closet where the drums were stored. It never took me very long to get the boys to where I could feel the air go out of them. I got to them first. The girls got what was left. I was doing everybody a favor—slowing the boys down for the girls, making the boys easier for the girls to take. I got between the boys and the girls and clouded up their hearts.

Nights, there was family history for me to go down into, but only so far. I lived with my grandmother above a garage. I made all the meals and changed all the subjects. On garbage night, my grandmother sent me to the curb in one of my mother's things— almost always the brown floral-print dress, the sleeveless one, that she wore in the snapshots. I kept throwing it away, balling it at the bottom of a wastebasket, and it kept getting retrieved and laid out for me to wear. My grandmother watched from a high window as I set the bags down along the curb. I think she found passing references to my mother in the slope of my arms and the blond disorder of my hair. Afterward, in my underwear, I would sleep in the position that put me farthest from everywhere I came from.

One day, the band director finally said, "Why don't you quit the band if you think it's beneath you to play?"

We were in his office, with the door shut. Somebody knocked.

"Hold your horses," the band director shouted at the door.

I looked from his face to the smudgy nameplate on his desk and to the door, which had a poster on it from a musical-instrument supply house. I was looking from thing to thing. You can look at a thing until it gets looked away with once and for all. You can take the thing and just look at it until it gets all looked out. Then you can go on to the next thing and start over. You can keep doing this with whatever gets lined up in front of you to have to see.

This is one way you can go through the whole world.

ESPRIT DE L'ELEVATOR

There were three of them left—sometimes four. Parked not in the lobby but in the gallery above the lobby, though that makes the place—the building, the apartment house—sound classier than it was.

Maybe an overhang is all it was called. An overlook.

Mezzanine?

It was set up like a living room—stuffed chairs, a coffee table, a bookcase with a few magazines. There was a railing so people would not have to spill over into the lobby proper.

These three watched me walking out of and back into the building a varying number of times per day. I was working on bringing the number down to maybe three or four.

I was getting nowhere.

The only progress I was making was remembering to carry something on my way out—a big envelope or a sealed box that looked ready to be taken to the post office. The envelopes and boxes piled up in the back of my car. Some night, I kept telling myself, I was going to stay up late and carry everything back up and start using it all over again.

A part of me said, "Why bother to go get it when it might come to me in my sleep?" I was almost always in the trough of a nap, my arms over the sides, digging around in the carpet.

I kept washing my hands of what the hands kept doing regardless.

Balcony.

Three of the times were for breakfast, lunch, supper.

The rest were for what I was still hungry for.

I carried things up from my car in small plastic bags.

I had different things I did to wear each day thin.

■　■　■

The three were two retired women, or widows, and one fat young security guard, male. The occasional fourth was the oldest retarded person I had ever seen. She had to be pushing sixty. I had never been close enough to make out if the glasses were bifocals. Sometimes when there was no way for me to get around walking past, I nodded hello and she would give me a wide berth. Other times she waved a finger.

I was the only one who trusted the elevator.

Not a security guard for the *building*. He security-guarded someplace else.

One afternoon, I was in the laundry room—I had all three machines going—when he pudged in to throw some trash down the chute. What I was wearing had already been worn.

"Washday?" he said, loud enough for the other two on the balcony to hear.

As always, I had no answers, nothing to put a stop to their wonderings. That night, I began to set down the full account of my tenancy. It became a book of earnest libels. I had three copies copied—one for each. Herewith excerpts:

How often do you get it?
Spend enough time with a person—coincide in the same room, achieve a reasonable congruence—and you will get a feel for, a glimpse of, the party you are sitting in for. It was like this with each of the women. A party sooner or later began to assume a shape in the space between us. I took an interest. I eventually began to court this party more diligently than each of the women could bother to herself. One day this party took me by storm.

Who foots the bills?
I signed up to teach a night class at the high school, an extension course, no credit, for people who had forgotten how to sleep. It took me a weekend to throw the materials together. I baked up a big fat loaf of case histories, pattern practices, whatever else came to mind, then had copies run off. The first night, I wrote on the

chalkboard the reasons people got bilked out of sleep. Afterward, I showed the students a trick, a mnemonic stunt, they could use to remember everything I had just said. They were mostly vast lactic women and self-heckling men in coats buttoned all the way up. All of them stayed after class to show me what they had taught themselves—the feats and magics, the shortcuts and so forth. A man ran me through his eye-sealing exercises, his fingers guiding mine. "I'm not up on myself and what I might still do," he told me. Sometime after dawn we went our separate ways.

What's inside the bags?
Some days my trouble is nothing more than the heavy concentration of both parents in my body. E.g., my father's tendency, at mealtide, to add extra steps to everything he did— cf. my habit of reaching for my tumbler with my left hand and passing it along to the right hand before I take my first sip. In my father's case, the route things took from hand to mouth got longer and longer. Hence for years I have been amassing ingredients for a meal I am no longer in any position to cook.

And your mother?
I am a disgruntled mourner.

Brothers or sisters?
People coming out of the cathedral and crossing the street to their cars expected traffic to part compliantly for them—they held up their hands in hopeful, crossing-guard gestures—and my sister was the only one who kept right on going, not even slowing down. She had some empty boxes in the backseat that I was going to get to use as tables—lampstands, nightstands, washstands, however I saw fit.

Reason for leaving last full-time position?
One morning, the supervisor stuck his head into my doorway and, taking in the undeserved spaciousness of the office, asked whether I thought I could maintain my level of performance

if an additional employee were assigned to the room. Having always been sympathetic toward whoever has hired me when he discovers, by galling degrees, the set of fixations I bring to bear on even the most perfunctory of tasks, I said yes. A second desk was presently steered into the office. A man was brought in to sit at the desk with his back toward me. By the end of the first hour, my every movement had become an exact but involuntary belittlement of his swivelings, his head-tossings and hair-sweeps, the flights of his arms. I felt thrown off my body. The accuracy went out of my work.

Why can't you stay put?
I have always gone to great lengths to keep my life away from the places where I have lived. People driven from themselves are always the ones you see the most of. They make themselves aggressively public. You find them in parks and municipal buildings. They see to it that as much as possible gets rubbed off, ground away, on the chairs and benches in lobbies and waiting rooms, on the tooth-yellow porcelain of courthouse toilets. They make any store or auditorium look fuller than it actually is. They eat at take-out places, the ones with just a couple of tables. "For here or to go?" they get asked, as if there were a choice.

Describe your best marriage to date.
My affiliation with—but never entirely a marriage to—a woman who worked briefly at the high school grew out of a series of conversations a man and I had about his son. The man would talk for hours about the son—how people swore by the haircuts he gave, even though he was not licensed or even certificated as a stylist, had in fact had no formal training, cut only when and where he felt like it, whenever the mood came over him; and as the man talked, the woman—whom I had known only by the rosacea in her cheeks, concolorous with my own—would gain some ground, make headway. I left the man's house one night and cornered her at the library. She had a magazine open in front of her. Her shoes were already off.

I remember that every morning, for the first couple of weeks, we took a kind of roll of everything we owned—called out the names of the appliances, the fixtures, the articles of clothing. Each day, there would be fewer things of hers to include in the tally. Before long, to save time, shirts, blouses, pullovers, sweaters, etc., became simply "tops." (This was her idea.) In like manner, other things became just broad categories of things. We lived in an "area," I was her "associate." She brought me around to her way of passing the time: doing away with the individual filth of minutes—she would move about the room and point superiorly, reprovingly, at scratchy increments of my beard, oily glosses on the slope of her nose—and gutting the hour down to the slow-turning spine of the day. (The clock itself was a square-faced wall unit with a slipping, partisan second hand that was easily derided.) She arrived, in sum, at the age she thought suited her and then halted there.

For the longest while, everything got carried over into the way she filled in for people at work—the vacationers and no-shows, people needed in other buildings. She took their places with conviction. She installed herself behind their partitions. She uncramped her legs in the wells beneath their workstations. She helped herself to the little budgets of condiments, of salt, in their drawers. She drank long, telling draughts from their mugs. The bottoms of her forearms stuck persuasively to the armrests of their chairs.

Then people, employees, were suddenly no longer going anywhere. They no longer missed work or needed to be spelled. They resettled themselves in their chairs, restocked their drawers, reared their stack trays still higher. The day she had to be let go, she went to the administrators and pleaded, then came home to abridge things even further.

What would be visible to a knocker at your door if you opened the door six inches, then a foot, then a foot and a half? That is, from a knocker's perspective, describe bigger and bigger slivers of vestibular floorscape, with an emphasis on what would most likely stand out.

Six inches: a selection of plastic bags, each with its original contents, arranged calendarially against the closet door.

Foot: the last of the exact words.

Foot and a half: men and women both—her and me in general.

CLAIMS

If I go so far as to say that at this point I had a friend, the most it can possibly mean is that once a year, toward the end of it, I had to drive from wherever I was letting myself be lived, wherever I had given consent for my life to keep being done to me, and this friend-person had to drive from his own whereabouts, just so we could meet for lunch in a sandwich shop where, years earlier, while schooling together, we had flirted with each other impatiently, wrongheartedly. By then, things were always his idea. He was the one who kept talking as if there would always be room in the world for whatever he might say. I was merely the one who kept clearing space. The thing I was good at was keeping things sufficiently placeless for whoever's turn came next.

Every year, he told me the same story—he had a double life and was going to have to do something big and final about it pretty soon. He explained that by day he sat at his engineering desk and threw together bridges and such for governments, and that by night he bogged himself down in department-store men's rooms, adult bookstores, highway rest stops. Year after year, I listened to him tell me this.

So I said to this friend-person, "Apart from that, other than the as-per-usuals, what are we harping on?"

He repeated everything already said. There was no other matter for the facts to get wrapped around. In his voice was the enormous gloating noise of somebody standing up for his rights.

I made the mistake of looking at our waitress, who was setting plates down in front of us. It was a mistake because sometimes when you look at someone, especially someone young, you get too good a look. You see the life heaved messily, meagerly, into the person. You get a sense of the slow-travelling trains of thought, the mean streaks and off-chances, everything that has had to be crossed out or memorized so far. The parts out front—the eyes;

the teeth and tongue inside the open, moving mouth—look cheap and detachable, unset, just barely staying put.

What I am saying is that through all this, all through this, I was only loosely in the midst of myself, already lapsing my way into whoever this waitress was, organizing myself within the dark of the body she was sticking up for herself inside.

THE BRIDE

I f this is to be a story instead of what it was initially intended to be—an answer to the question of how you go about finding an outlet for what you are not sure is in there to begin with—then there might as well be two women instead of just one and, for a change, just the one man, who is no longer the one I threw my body away on but just somebody where I work, somebody with little say over what it is I do, which, I gather, is to look lonely from afar.

Which leaves how many more for me to pretend not to see? Because I have actually had people—persons—call me up and plead with me not to think about them. Persons who actually called me up and said: "Promise me."

I am leaving out my brother because of what he said—or what was reported to me that he had said—when there was every chance that I would not be coming to his wedding, which was to be held many hundreds of miles from where I was going to try to be asleep. What he is said to have said was: "If he don't come to mine, I don't go to his." It was probably that alone—the veiled compliment in it—that got me on the bus.

I did not kiss this bride on the church steps. This bride called me "catty" to my face not long afterward, but now that there are children, she tells me her troubles every chance she gets.

Mine—my trouble—is that if you got a good look at my wrists—if they were all you had to see of the world—you would swear you were looking at a twenty-year-old girl and not at a man pushing past forty.

So I understandably keep my sleeves rolled up and try to downplay the rest of me and keep it farther from the masses.

I am waiting to be addressed as Miss? Miss?

It is this alone they must mean when they keep pleading there is no such thing as a stupid question.

EDUCATION

Not long after my youth blew over, I was offered a stipend to help speed along the development of a girl who was being raised in one of the old walled towns in the northern part of the state. I signed the papers and gave away my things. The next morning, I said good-bye to some people I thought might recognize me from the corridors of the building where I had been living. A couple of the older ones unlimbered their arms in a way that I regarded as a wave.

It took me several days to reach the town on foot. The girl's mother and grandmother were waiting for me outside the gates. They were seated on a rock and eating fruit out of basins on their laps.

"She's at home," the mother said. "We were told to keep her away from the school."

"How long does it usually take?" the grandmother said.

Both of them were blunt-nosed and sleep-marked. They kept themselves busy with the fruit. They kept their eyes off me.

"Let me have a look at the girl," I said.

Every afternoon, I walked the girl to the center of town. There were eight streets that led to it, and for each approach to the two blocks of shops and vaguely public-looking buildings, I assigned the town a different name: Townville, Cityton, Burgborough, Townburgh, Boroville, Cityboro, Burghton, and Town City.

With a clear conscience I would stand with the girl in the center of town and point things out—entablatures, drinking fountains, skymarks, misspelled signs in shopwindows, a pair of roofed-over stairwells, resembling subway entrances, that led citizens down to a vast, underlit comfort station. I would ask the girl: "Where are we today? Which town is this? Can you tell?"

She was young, with rude eyes and a block of thick black hair. Her stalky legs were always splodged with bites.

She would narrow her body into the shape, the posture, of answering. "Townton," she would say.

"Not even close," I would have to tell her.

After supper, while the girl played in the yard, the mother and the grandmother would call me into the bedroom they shared.

"What are her chances?" they would say. "How is she to the touch? What should be coming next? Are you going to be doing us all a world of good? What kind of timetable are you on? What should we be looking for? What are the signs?"

The house had two floors, and in no time I had the girl calling them the Land of the Upstairs and the Land of the Downstairs.

"Making them lands—what does that do?" the mother asked me when the girl was outdoors.

The room they gave me had a cot, a table, a washstand with a basin. There was no door. I was pretty certain that there had once been one and that they had it taken down before I came.

Every night, after the girl was in bed, the mother and the grandmother would appear in the doorway.

"How soon?" they would ask.

"Too early to tell," I would say.

In the late afternoons, after our walk into town, I would smatter the names of stars and crops and oceans into the girl. I got facts off my hands and onto hers. She built tiny empires out of the facts and let me see inside them. She was warm to the touch. "You can do this," I said, putting her hands on things. The girl's father, I gathered obituarily, had worn V-neck T-shirts. The girl's heart, I also learned, was set on the slice of florid skin in the mouth of the V. I set her heart elsewhere. I lined things up in the room and pointed at them. I made her put her hands on everything.

The girl had some books of her own, books that her mother and grandmother had not known were in the house. She brought the books to me one at a time, and I told her what was wrong with what they said. They were all about the human body, its depths and its scope. I had to refute every one of the books sentence by sentence. The errors could take days, weeks, to correct. The girl wrote down the corrections, and later, while she napped, I checked over her work, making changes where they were called for, praising her penmanship wherever it deserved praise.

Together, in the yard, without knowing what the right tools would have been, the girl and I built partitions, platforms, folding screens. I remember her turning the earth with the claw of a hammer.

I started blindfolding the girl for the walk into town. When we reached the center, I would take the blindfold off and ask: "Where must we now be?"

The girl was always wrong.

Some nights there were abrupt disorders of where the girl's heart got put. The mother and the grandmother would summon me to the girl's room.

"Do something," they would cry.

I would recite the names of the towns and list the hallmarks, the quiddities, of each town, the area first in square yards and then in square meters, the principal creeks and ditches, the annual rainfall, the population, the manufactures, the number of hospital beds per dozen inhabitants, the elevation, the significant history.

After I finished, I would run over the list again, changing all the facts.

I would watch the girl's mouth.

I would hear a voice getting ready to come.

The mother and the grandmother would not leave the room.

What the mother and the grandmother fed the girl every night, what she ate with us at the table—the cleverly sliced meats, the vivid salads, the cubed potatoes—became the foundation on which, afterward, in my room, with the mother and the grandmother gawking from the doorway, I built swaying towers of candy and pretzel sticks in the girl's stomach. "This is important," I would say. The girl stood still as I patted the food into her mouth. "The towers," I explained, "are the beginnings of a city."

Then my six months were up. My stipend had run out. One day I announced to the mother and the grandmother that I would be leaving the next morning.

"Stay," they said.

"Finish," they said.

They showed me all the leeway they had where their legs went their separate ways. A slucky sound came from their groins, as if a drain were being opened.

I slept off and on with the mother and let the grandmother do what she could to me in the mornings when there was feeling in her hands.

"I remember the day it happened to her mother," the grandmother said to me one morning. "In those days, it was called 'turning ugly.' People would say, 'Did your girl turn ugly yet?' In this case, they sent a messenger from the school. He had a piece of paper. It said, 'Come and get your girl.' She was standing on the steps of the school when I got there. She said, 'The teacher knows.'

"I took her out of that school and had her put in a different one, a smaller one. I sewed her a whole new wardrobe. I told her to make believe she was bashful. She tried her best to become friends with a girl who walked with a limp. She held doors open for the girl and wrote her cheery notes on stationery she bought with her allowance. The girl always wrote back, on plain tablet paper, 'The feeling is ridiculously not mutual.' I would find the notes—dozens of them, all saying the same thing—behind the bookcase in her room. In those days, we didn't know what we know now."

I had the girl in my room. She was sitting on my table, her legs beating open and closed, like wings.

"Tell me something," I said. "Do you have a favorite place?"

"I like them all," she said.

"Each and every?"

"Each but not every."

She flapped her legs.

"Let me see," I said.

She got up and disrobed.

There was nothing to see.

"Which town will you move to?" I asked the girl one night after supper.

"I'll stay here," she said.

Another night, the girl came to my room on her own.

"What else are you?" she said. "Are you anything else?"

Early one morning, I was awakened by the girl's shrieks. I hurried to her room and found the mother and the grandmother already there.

"Let her cry her face loose," the grandmother said. "Let it slide right off her head. Let her learn. She has to learn sooner or later."

The girl wept into her palms.

"She went out for a walk by herself last night, after we were all asleep," the mother said.

"Filthy little thing," the grandmother said.

"She walked all over the place, high and low," the mother said.

"She went the whole way into town."

"Which town?" I said.

The crying got worse.

That afternoon, the girl came to my room to show me that it was there, in place—bristling below the slope of her belly, an isosceles shag of curls.

IT COLLECTS IN ME

Here is a story in the worst way. I have no business being anywhere in it. It comes between me and the life I have coming.

Look: a man who is not me but whose accomplishments are similar (he was the son of some parents, got himself schooled around, circumstanced himself aplenty, placed himself squarely and irreversibly in the employ of somebody who could be counted on to walk all over him, etc.) found a new way to cheat on his wife. This was not the way that everybody else was cheating at the time.

Can I skip over what was popular then without leaving anything to the imagination? Because the imagination has to be left out of this. I would hate for something to have to get created here. That is the last thing I want.

Do me a big favor and take my word that this man I am talking about was a man who paid ridiculous attention to what his wife said and did, what she wore, what she cooked. He took a hectic, grisly interest in everything about her. In bed, he fucked her to the nth degree—never let his mind wander.

What else went on between the man and the woman should go without saying, but it won't. It can't. It keeps showing up in my mouth.

It collects in me.

As it stands, at work one day I struck something up with this man—a little something. I tried to get him at one end of a conversation that had me at the other end. Do you know what the son of a bitch said?

He said, "I'm a married man."

"Personally?" is what I said.

"Go back to work," the man said.

This took place where you're supposed to go if you have an accident, if you get something on you. In fact, it did more than take place. It took up a large area of where we were. It seized it right from around us. We got pushed through each other.

He emerged from me and vice versa, I figure.

I watched him walk off in the direction of where the work was.

This is another way of saying that once, not too long ago, I wrote things down—everything.

A couple of days later, I read with great interest what I had written.

I was a great many far cries from myself.

CERTAIN RIDDANCES

The boss had a long list of reasons for letting me go—most of which, I am ashamed to admit, were generously understated. It's true, for instance, that I hogged the photocopier for hours on end and snapped at whoever politely—deferentially—inquired about how much longer I would be. I was intent on achieving definitively sooty, penumbral effects to ensure that copies looked like copies, and that, of course, took time. Some days I spent entire afternoons reproducing blank sheets of paper, ream after ream, to use instead of the "FROM THE DESK OF—" notepads the boss kept ordering for each of us.

It's also largely true that I had never bothered to learn the names of any of my co-workers. Everybody was either Miss or Sir. I am talking about people with whom I had shared a water fountain and a single restroom for years, people whose office wardrobes I had inventoried in pocket notebooks, people whose sets of genitals had often steamed only inches from my own. Actually, I *had* known their names but could just never stoop to using them. Most days what I felt was this: the minute you put a first name and a last name together, you've got a pair of tusks coming right at you (i.e., Watch out, buddy). But on days when I didn't disapprove of everybody on principle—days when the whole cologned, cuff-shooting ruck of my co-workers didn't repulse me from the moment they disembarked from the sixth-floor elevator and began squidging their way along the carpeted track that led to the office—my thinking stabbed more along these lines: A name belittles that which is named. Give a person a name and he'll sink right into it, right into the hollows and the dips of the letters that spell out the whole insultingly reductive contraption, so that you have to pull him up and dance him out of it, take his attendance, and fuck some life into him if you expect to get any work out of him. Multiply him by twenty-two and you will have some idea of what the office was like, except that a good third of my colleagues were female.

My real problem, of course, was that I could dispatch an entire day's worth of work in just under two hours. It's not that I was smart—far from it. But I was quick. I knew where things should go. I had always liked the phrase "line of work," because to me there actually *was* a line, raying out to the gridded, customered world from my cubicle, with its frosted-plastic partitions that shot up all around me but gave out a few feet shy of the tiled, sprinkler-fixtured ceiling.

With so much extra time on my hands, I had to keep myself busy with undertakings of my own. For instance, there was a young woman, a fine-boned receptionist, who each day veiled her legs with opaque hosiery of a different hue, never anything even remotely flesh-toned. Every morning when I passed her desk, I would glance at her calves to note the shade. I soon began keeping track of the colors in a special file vaulted in the upper-right drawer of my battered dreadnought of a desk. Once, on my lunch hour, I made a special trip to a drugstore near the office to soak up the entire palette of hosiery shades—off-black, coffee, smoke, stone, mushroom, misty gray—because I wanted my record to be precise. Eventually I began to worry that beneath the cloak of the receptionist's hosiery the flesh of her legs was crisply diseased. The worry enlarged and clamored itself into a conviction. Soon it became critical for her to understand the extent of what I had on her. On the first of each month, I began slipping into her mail slot a little unsigned booklet—an almanac, really—with unruled four-by-six index cards for covers. The booklet consisted of as many pages as there had been days in the previous month, and each page recorded the date, the shade of the hosiery she had worn that day, and an entirely speculative notation about the degree of opacity and what it implied about whatever man had been entrenched in her the night before (sample: "June 6, charcoal, glaucomatous—how remarkably hateful of you and your muckworm"). All of this would be jittered out in a near-gothic script with a calligraphy pen bought especially for the purpose in a hobby store on an overbright Sunday afternoon. By and by, I would find each booklet tacked to the bulletin board above the Xerox machine, along with a memo from the boss saying: "This must stop."

There was another woman, a pouncy administrative assistant, with a pair of succinct, pointed breasts—*interrogative* breasts. Even though I smeared past her in the corridor, wordlessly, no more than once or twice a week, I would feel grilled, third-degreed, for hours or even days afterward. At first, whenever the pressure to respond was acute—maybe every other day—I would simply slide an anonymous, index-carded "True" or "False" into her mail slot. But my responses eventually thickened into essays—with longish, interjaculatory asides about my lactose intolerance, my disloyalties, the gist and grain of my extracubicular life—and then into sets of dampish, insinuative memoirs, some of which kept me slumped over my desk for days at a time. These, too, which I photocopied until the words got shadowed and blurry, would wind up pinpricked to the bulletin board, with pealing cautionary memos from the boss.

The last response I sent her—and the only one that didn't end up flapping at me from the corkboard—was a twenty-three-page streak of reminiscence about a belated birthday gift I had received from my grandfather a few days after I turned ten years old. What he had mailed me was a big, gleamless omnibus set of board games. On the lid of the box, the words MY TREASURE CHEST OF GAMES: A DIFFERENT GAME FOR EVERY DAY OF EVERY WEEK OF THE YEAR were spelled out in runny, unweighted block letters. Inside were an arrowed cardboard spinner, a pair of bleary, chalkish dice, an unwaxed deck of playing cards, some plastic markers, a dozen or so flimsy, trifold game boards, each printed on both sides, and an unstapled book of instructions. The whole set struck me as trappy and degrading. I felt as if somebody else's life were being lowered over mine and that it would remain there, bestraddling and overruling, for a whole year. I remember tearing up each of the game boards—they were easy enough to shred—and bedding the pieces of each board on a separate sheet of construction paper and then balling it all up and depositing each scrumpled ball in a different wastebasket. Our house was full of wastebaskets, more than one to a room, because of the people we were intent on becoming. When my grandfather died, about a year later, and I got coaxed into attending the viewing, I noticed a spatter of paint— *hobby* paint, I was convinced—on each lens of his bifocals. Nobody had bothered to scrape it off, or else somebody had made a big point of not scraping it off. On a lamped lectern near the entrance to the chapel was a big book open to a page that everybody at the viewing was supposed to sign with a bead-chained pen. Where my name should have gone, I remember writing: "It goes to show."

The intern I left alone. The intern was just some college kid, a carrel-bound girl with a face full of sharp, unkissed features. She was only twenty, twenty-one tops, and yet there she was, assigned as much square-footage as I occupied after nine soiling, promotionless years. I had banked a digital alarm clock atop a butte of telephone directories on my shelf, and after lunch I would watch 1:12 virus into 1:13, 1:14, 1:15, and I would wish for enough dexterity to fold a paper airplane and then deftly sail it through the space we shared above the partitions, landing it on her desk. But what would I have typed—and left starkly unphotocopied—inside? "Be glad you're not the one who's going to relieve himself on a certain something the next time the boss walks out of the restroom with his suit jacket still hooked on the back of the door"?

The boss was a large man with intricately redefined dentition—a mouthful of wirework and porcelain. His eyes were slow and halting: they arrived at what they were supposed to be looking at only after lots of embarrassed trial and error. The morning he summoned me to his office to recommend that I take the first of a series of renewable leaves of absence, I kept my eyes on the cuneiform scatter of golf tees on his glass-plated desktop. The boss inquired about my "home life" and my "social life," but he talked mostly about his own. He had a teenage son, he explained, who was taking accelerated classes in high school and also a college course in art history on Saturday mornings. He had to chauffeur the kid to the college, because the kid was afraid to drive, and then he had to kill two and a half hours walking around the campus. The textbook for the course had set him back a couple of hundred, he said, and, stealing through its glossy pages one night while the kid was out of the house, he discovered that the kid had styled tank tops and jockstraps onto the male nudes.

"What about you?" the boss said, reaching for a form I was supposed to fill out. "Are you involved with anyone?"

"Everybody," I said.

Because my body was shacky and provisional, I kept it buried beneath flopping, oversized brown corduroy suits. I had exactly six suits—all identical, all purchased from the same discount outlet on the same day, almost ten years earlier. At first, people had predictably, pityingly, said: "He only has the one suit." But eventually their tune changed to: "The guy must have a *hundred* suits!" The once steep wales had been worn down until they were almost level with the wide gutters running between them.

It was in one of those eroded suits that I found some part-time work on the night shift at an office where two dozen or so employees, mostly students and housewives, looked up account numbers on microfiche screens and then penciled the numbers onto mint-green computer sheets. The turnover was high, and I was always the only male. Every time somebody new reported for work, she would see me in my suit and plump toward my desk. I would have to wave her off in the direction of the supervisor, a tasseled toss-up of a woman.

The supervisor began her nightly announcements, a third of the way through the shift, by bleating, "Listen up, girls." I would always sense the eyes of my co-workers on me when, instead of cleaving to my work for a manful, face-saving half-minute or longer before lifting my head and swiveling in the direction of the supervisor, I would swing around secretarially at the instant the word *girls* was expelled from her mouth.

I felt privileged.

•   ■   ■

Unless the landlady counted the number of times water ran in the bathtub, there was no way for her to know that I was no longer living alone. By his own choice, the kid never left the apartment, and we never fought, so what else was there for her to hear? I dressed him in cotton skirts and sleeveless sweaters that I picked out in secondhand stores, using only one criterion: each garment had to be exceptionally confiding. The life of its previous owner needed to have bled vividly into the fibers to compensate for whatever would go unsaid or undreamed of in the new wearer. I had to apply this criterion harshly, because the kid was warm but otherwise unwieldable. I knew enough not to expect much from him in the way of help around the house. But I enjoyed arranging myself into a chair he had just absented for another bath or his hourly shave. He kept the bathroom door locked behind him and took his time.

What was between us eventually got beneath everything.

THE GIST

S he had nothing in common with her body anymore, was how she put it. Her body was going somewhere else.

A place? A direction? I was halfway curious. That winter, there was a lull between my legs that made it easier for things like this to come up. Plus it was bedtime. We were still in our clothes of the day, our work clothes.

I led her out to the car and made sure she got in. Then I got in on the passenger side.

I made her drive with the lights off.

"Show me where," I said.

At first she drove fast and sarcastically. You can get away with that in my state, because it gets so wide at night.

This was the second time I was on this wife, my second marriage to the same wife. Does it figure that neither of us had ever bothered to come up with any nicknames? When we talked, we had to use the same names everybody else had been getting away with using on us.

"I am at the point where," the wife began. For a while, all the talking was about points where. I pictured the points not as the loose, dotty kind but as the arrowy ends of things. This kept me occupied. Then came the parts that started with "As far as my life." Sometimes she remembered to say "is concerned."

"Keep your eyes on the road" was all I said whenever it came time for me to let her know that I was going along with what she was saying, the sticky gist of it. To be doing something, I looked out the side window, where rurality kept taking place in the dark.

When the sun came up, we got out and found jobs.

"Nobody is ever overqualified for this kind of work," the manager said.

He led us into a long room full of card tables. There was a folding chair at each table. The other people would not start showing up for at least another hour, the manager explained.

"In the meantime," he said.

We took turns doing what we were told.

THE PAVILION

I came up with a new angle on how to start a family, an entirely new way of going about the business of it, and went from place to place—parking lots and boardwalks, mainly—to talk up the talking points.

I had pass-outs, outgivings—*literature* was the word people liked. There was a fifteen-minute presentation and a forty-five-minute presentation, and, for some reason, the longer one always went over better. People wanted to stand through such things.

Afterward, men and women alike said, "We'll be rooting for you!" and "Keep us posted!" and "Are you from around here?" A few would hand me money—mostly folded fives. "Put this toward it," they would say.

I did my driving at night and slept mornings in the car. A shower curtain bunched up against the windshield kept out enough of the light. If I couldn't sleep, I shuffled through the little "To Serve You Better ..." evaluation cards I often pressed on people at the end of the longer presentation, expecting phone numbers and addresses to have been squiggled out propositionally, but finding only "Could you maybe go a little more into the nuts and bolts of 'bypassing the problem entirely'?" or "What are you hiding?" Once, a man followed me all the way to my car and said, "You ever even been married?" I told him that I had once had a wife who adored me out of house and home.

Whether I slept or not, by noon I had already washed myself in the basin (I used bottled water and dish detergent) and was back on the road. I drove until I found a promising site. To get a crowd started, I set up my easel and paint set and theatrically slapped out a picture of the pavilion I had in mind. As I saw it, it was a steep-roofed substantiality with cinquefoils, observatories, anything. I threw in lean-tos and tented offshoots, castellar outbuildings with escalators. I had to people the grounds with peoply daubs, though, if I expected passersby to pause and gawp and chum me up. "What is that, exactly?" they would ask. Or: "Would it be an actual place?" Or: "Is it within a day's drive?"

One afternoon, I had everything assembled on an alleylike amusement pier that ledged out over a closed beach. After the crowd was gone, a girl stepped lankly toward me, her hair roughed up, her eyes slimed. She wore a smock of the most besetting blue—a blue I had often seen days acquire difficultly and never let go of without first kicking up a storm. There was a splashy adequateness to the big picture I was getting.

"Highest grade completed?" I asked.

"Some college," she said.

"Why just some?"

"Nobody was telling me anything. Plus all that underlining."

"Boyfriend?"

"No way of knowing."

"Your parents?"

"Still way too married."

"Brothers and sisters?"

"Two sisters."

"Older or younger?"

"One of each."

"What kind of girls?"

"The pep-talky kind. Two-faced behind your back."

"Complete this sentence: Here it must be said that …"

"Here it must be said I just want to get the duration over with."

Later that afternoon, while her smock was being dry-cleaned in town, we worked through the actual mechanics behind the shower-curtained windshield. I had the car parked on a stony crescent of beach. Afterward, I started writing simple booklets for her to read—nothing inspirational or fact-ridden, just whatever came to mind that would advance her from one interim to the next. "Busy books," she called them. "Write me another busy book real quick," she would say.

I had to piece together a diet for her, too. I knew which combinations of which foods on which days would rehang everything that was draped so delicately beneath her skin. In a matter of months, the body under the smock was organized anew, redistributed.

I gradually worked the girl into the presentations, both the short and the long ones, first as an assistant to hand out the handouts and point the pointer at the charts, then as a participant with a speaking part. When she started rounding out and the baby started showing through, I inaugurated a question-and-answer segment and put her entirely in charge.

There was really only one question, though, that the audience could ever think of to ask: "How come the baby seems to be riding so high on you? It seems up awfully high."

The girl's answer would always be: "I'm not sure I understand exactly what it is that's being asked."

Another person would give it a try, but in different words. There were only so many words an audience of any size could come up with. When they ran out, I would have to step in and say, "This is all very new to all of us." I would bring up the pavilion one more time. "Pavilions will take the place of homes as we know them today," I would say. I would go on about if and where the model pavilion would be brought to completion, what kinds of castered dividers would divide it into divisions, the color of the dyed burlap that would be stapled to the dividers as decoration. The girl would chime in with anything statisticky I might have left out—measurements, cost figures, and suchlike—then circulate the evaluation cards and the pencils.

Later, in the car, as I beat the girl's food together in the tureen, I would hear her turning the pages of the booklets in the backseat, biding her space. When I was finished, while she ate, I would try to sleep, curled up, on the roof.

Sometimes the girl cried all night as I drove. I would have to pull over every few hours and get in the backseat and put my arms around her. By this point, she was pronouncedly hump-bosomed. Where her tiny breasts had once reposed, there was the cyclopean, orbiculate business of the coming child instead.

Late one morning, the girl said, "I'm close."

"How soon?" I said.

"Within the hour?"

I drove to the biggest town within reach—it had a Euclid Avenue and a Fifth Avenue and a Market Street and a Wabash Avenue and a Pennsylvania Avenue—and parked at a dumpish shopping center. There was no time to set up the easel. I had the girl doped and laid out upside down on a chaise longue, her head where her feet would have ordinarily gone.

People started gathering. From a box in the trunk, I abstracted a handful of handouts for the fifteen-minute performance.

With a pliers, I gentled the girl's teeth from their sockets.

I dropped the teeth one by one into my shirt pocket.

"Otherwise," I said, "she'll bite the poor thing involuntarily."

Then the tongue.

I had to widen the mouth just a little at the sides.

When the girl started to gag, I reached into her throat and threaded everything out that was coming. The girl went blue in the face. I slapped her first, then the kid, then the girl again.

The two of them—and the crowd—were breathing loudly, busybodily.

I did my best to keep in touch with the kid and its mother afterward and repeated the process with a couple of other like-bodied girls up and down the coast, and in a few years I had become some kind of king, reigning over something noticeable.

PRIORITY

I keep changing my story when in fact it could not be more straightforward or plain. It is a story of none too many people, least of all me. But set me down where there is a bigger turnout and I am one minute picking somebody up, the next minute getting myself picked up—I have no heart for upholding the difference or keeping myself laden with the life of me even this far.

It is too much like work.

To wit, I found something of hers in the bathroom not long afterward—a Band-Aid that had never made its way to the wastebasket and, instead, dropped beneath where the side of the sink cabinet did not quite reach the wall. I was trying a final time to fish up a comb that had fallen down the same crack. The better comb—the clean one—was already packed. I was using a length of undershirt cardboard when the Band-Aid got dredged up. There was a blur of dried blood on the gauze pad. I am just assuming the blood was hers. I am giving her every priority.

Can we at least be in agreement that the things dicks perk out toward vary from one person to the next but are subject in the end to similar spoilage?

Because it is easy to forget that the Band-Aid is still in my wallet, smutted, souvenir-style, but who thinks to look? I never got the comb back, either. I had to use wet fingers to get my hair set aright. I drove across the state toward the house, the close-quartered sorriness, of my parents, talking to myself in an overconcerned announcer's baritone the whole tollway long. It was a voice instigated for letting on that the marriage had never sunk in. Whenever billboards appeared, I read them aloud just as elegiacally.

I stopped just once, at a place called A!D!U!L!T C!A!S!T!L!E. Eight booths, each about the size of a shower stall. The chink of belt buckles and the trinkle of pocket change as the pants came down, mine first; the dismal rumpus itself; then the dirt-colored paper towels—I kept moving myself about within one vast stickiness of long standing.

The same whole world was still waiting to get wiped.

My parents were of course glad to see me, glad I had some time off, glad they would not have to cross the street every morning for the newspaper. I would have the seven quarters heating in my palm before I even entered the store.

My mother was free to fight arthritically with the neighbors about the noise. She sat in the breakfast nook and listened to the people on both sides, warming to the day and the sounds assembling inside it. By noon, things would be organized, bulked, around a central, controlling disturbant—a power tool or stereo or spat. She would shout, make threats over the phone.

I dusted. Carried out more garbage. Tried to replace the doorbell. Afternoons, I did the marketing. The name of the checkout girl would get printed in pale-violet ink at the bottom of the receipt. The receipts accumulated in my pocket. I would reach into it for my keys and feel the girls feel the sudden extra weight on themselves. People could tell when they were being dwelled upon.

Nights, I put myself through conversation. There was a sister for the three of us to discuss. She had had two children so far, the boy and the girl. The boy kept everything to himself and did not want to be seen eating. The girl claimed she never ate.

"Bragging or complaining?" is all my father said.

I have no real way of knowing how many nights it took until a man my age let himself into the house and ventured steadily from room to room. He entered my parents' bed, saw how much space remained between the rims of their bodies, then fidgeted himself into it. In no time, he had a finger of one hand deep inside my mother, had my father's undertrousers pushed all the way down to the knees, had a finger of the other hand as far as it would go up that crack.

The idea must have been for it to become somebody else's turn to bring somebody else into a world.

RECESSIONAL

F or the sake of argument, know everything about me.

I was a flask-shaped man in a velour shirt sitting at long lunchroom tables in business schools, cosmetology schools, junior colleges, community colleges. My business was buying used textbooks and crating them off to a distributor. Kids would come up and lunge their thick, thuddingly unread books at me. I would lip the names of the authors and the titles—Gurson's *Invitation to Secretarial Science* or Fritchman's *Accounting Principles Today*, third edition—and flirt through my blue loose-leaf price guide while the kids gloomed above me. Then I'd reach into the tackle box I kept my cash in, slam some dollar bills and quarters onto the tabletop, watch the hands grubble for the money.

I no longer even looked up at the knocking incoherences of the kids' faces, which were mostly acned rinds, fuzzed-over globes. Instead, I concentrated on their arms. In short-sleeve weather, especially, their arms were the most vocal parts, each one clarioning a need that had nothing to do with what the face might be asking for.

I never had to say a word, either. The kids never questioned how much I paid. They would just pivot around, happily disembarrassed, lunch-moneyed.

I'd been floating this version of myself for nine months in a three-state territory, paying off bills and piling lots of cash aside. I was on the road every other week. Each morning, in a motor-court cabin or motel room, the woman expertly folding everything in sight—starting with the special sheets and pillowcases I always brought along so I wouldn't have to fall asleep atop the heavily dreamed-on bedclothes provided by the motels, with their unbleachable residues of heart-scalded travellers—was never the woman I lived with. In each case, she was an unaired, hamsterish woman with a mouthful of loose fillings and certain thrilling agitations of speech. She had a flicky way with a pair of pants, my ice-cream pants, which she saved for last.

She had her grateful housekeeping-staff counterpart at every motor lodge on the map.

The man I was in each of those rooms with that woman or her equivalent was down to three hundred and twenty-five pounds in the mornings.

With her, my undecidable life was in remission.

I was losing my hearing. The words trending toward me in conversations often arrived pumiced, their meanings smoothed off, rinsed away. If I wanted, I could squint my ears toward the words and make out the gist, funnel them down to the threats and insults, the "You fat fuck!"s. But could I be blamed for preferring everything foamed over to a thwoooosh?

Still, I kept the appointment that the woman I lived with had made for me with an audiologist, a no-obligation consultation. The audiologist was a pulpy blond. She bracketed a set of earphones over my skull, and I compliantly uncurled a finger and raised it each time I got a purchase on one of the fugitive tones she let loose in my head. Afterward, she graphed the cordilleras of my nerve deafness on a blue-gridded memo pad. She swiveled on her chair to get closer to me and, syllabizing exaggeratedly now, explained the test results. Then she corked a sample "hearing instrument" into my ear. I instantly reacquired the honk and slam of the world, only tinny and trebled, a clacking souvenir-soundtrack version.

Then I noticed what the audiologist was doing with her face—louvering it open and shut, open and shut. I'm not talking about blinking or a tic. There was nothing metronomic or involuntary about it. She was slatting her face closed and opening it for me again, shuttering out what she wanted me to know about her, keeping things safely unsyllabled but unmisconstruable.

It wasn't just this one woman, either. Lately, people had been flagging me with napkins at lunch counters, inclining menus toward me meaningfully. Morsing me with the rataplan of fingertips. Wigwagging their arms at me in clammy rush-hour crowds. Browing and swallowing vividly, declaratively, for my benefit. Worse, they expected me to get what all the sirening and signage added up to.

Everybody was a sexual emergency.

Once, in a department store, after witnessing some seizured semaphoring near a rack of summer shirts, I tagged after a man up an escalator and into a vaultlike restroom. We stationed ourselves in adjacent stalls. He cupped his palms against the metal wall and megaphoned, "Do you miss someone?"

I unlatched my door. He brisked his way in, a recklessness of chiaroscuroed forearms and a dank, rebusing face. He unhaunted me for five minutes tops. Then I junked him from my thoughts.

So what I said to the jalousie-faced audiologist was, "Let me sleep on this." I unstoppered my ear and set the demonstration model on her desk.

I watched her pull her face shut with a tantrummy tug.

Then I went home to the woman I lived with.

Gloria had three daughters by her ex-husband. She had provisoed from the start that a second marriage was out of the question, exactly what I had wanted to hear. The girls were espaliered on their mother—tamped down, battening on her. When I wasn't on the road, I ghosted parenthetically through their days. But I made an effort to figure those kids out. I did. I delved into them, parsing and plundering swatches of their fissured nervous systems. They had been through a lot, I reminded myself. I imagined that they had started out as tidy, exact quotients of their mother and their father (an amply brainsick, runaway refrigerationist named Sandy) and the things the two parents had said at the table—the household slang they had evolved for borborygmic high jinks and the like. Then Gloria and Sandy had begun farming out a large share of their hatreds, fractioning it among the three girls to see how much they could take and what they would work it into. And then the beatings, ambulanced trips to the hospital, hushful visiting hours by Gloria's intensive-care bedside, the daily hand-holding ceremonial walk to the hospital gift shop for candy. After the divorce, watching all the newcomers single-file in and out of

Gloria's bedroom, the girls had resignedly rounded themselves off to the nearest full-time adult: their mother. They never mentioned their father. I am certain that during my absences my name never came up. Each of the girls despised me in a different, unexploded way.

Late one afternoon, returning from a weeklong book-buying trip and squattering into the living room, I found the three of them, batched and mumpish, on the carpet. The second-oldest was beached three feet from the dust-filmed TV screen, folded in on herself, thighs pressed against chest, crossed arms propped on the shelf of her knees, her thumb plugged into her mouth. All of this took place beneath a huge, tentlike T-shirt, one of mine, tie-dyed into Day-Glo swirls without my permission, the neckhole pushed up all the way to her nose, armless sleeves hanging limp.

The other two girls were idling on either side of her, still slung in the underwear they had slept in. I waded midway into the room, then halted, cantilevering my paunch above their heads.

"Hi, girls," I gargled.

No response.

Lineamentally, though, they were good kids—sparrowlike, blue-veined, each with an aureole of gingerish hair. My own face looked as if it had been sketched out as a shenaniganal exercise and then immediately, apologetically, scumbled over and shaded into something you could at least linger on without thinking, "Is he simple?"

I gave the contents of the TV screen, *my* TV screen, a distracted appraisal, then lobbed toward the stairs.

I knuckled on the bedroom door before entering.

I found Gloria in bed with a magazine and a cigarette, her hair still spongy from a shower.

"The girls came across that female-supremacy literature you ordered from that club," she said, dictioning each word as a favor to me but not looking up from the page she was on.

"Then shouldn't they be doing handstands?" I said. My voice was fat-clogged and remote. I couldn't even be sure my words had gotten all the way out.

Gloria shot me a stay-thither look and returned to her magazine. Unstuffing wads of bills from my pockets and slapping them onto the dresser, I watched her read, watched her eyes dartle across columns of type. She was a speed-reader, steeplechasing through more books and magazines and newspapers in a month than I managed in a year, and yet I was the one with the diplomas, the certificates, the letters of recommendation.

She had a strapping, hoydenish body. She maintained a sunlamped handsomeness. But she was hygienically delinquent. I wondered what my predecessors had made of the ashtrayish, perspiry nimbus she almost always hazed around herself.

I'd emptied my pockets. I flattened and stacked and justified the wads, trued them up for her approval. Then my eyes chanced upward at the mirror. I looked strewn.

"Did you eat? Are you hungry?" she said.

"I didn't stop anywhere," I said. The words fogged out of me.

"Bluh-blub-bluh-blub-bluh-blub-blub. Talk right. Jesus."

"I said no." I was forming the syllables slowly and effortfully this time. "I haven't eaten anything."

"The only reason I ask is that the girls are going to their aunt's. Somebody's coming over I'll need to be alone with."

"Who?"

"Who? Whoever. Go eat."

"No…I mean, just for the record."

"The record? All right: you know that checkout girl at Foodtowne, the one you're always carrying on about right and left? With the biceps? I've been fucking her all week as a goodwill gesture to you. It's an act of largesse. There's no recreation involved, hardly. She asks about you all the time. Okay? Now go somewhere and eat."

My hands fisted as far down as they could go in my pants pockets. I stood there, a shadow-slopping, chronically howevering man in a room that sloped slightly toward an uncurtained window. An erection began to dumbly press itself out.

"Obey," she said.

"Look," I said.

But I wasn't pointing at anyone or anything. There wasn't anything for anyone to see.

To my credit, I knew which days were over. Days, for instance, when I could stump into any diner, canvass the menu, and, commanding the vocabulary of entrées, side dishes, and beverages, feel confident that the waitress scrabbling out my order on a guest check would understand everything that the Swiss steak, whipped potatoes, buttered noodles, chowchow, and orange juice stood for from my standpoint. Days when, minutes after the plates and dishes and tumblers had been arrayed in front of me, the waitress would reappear to ask, "Everything okay here?" and her words would pour out in a clear broth, and my "Yes, ma'am" would be weighted and epigrammatic, foreshortening the entire history of my lives in and out of women. After dessert, I would leave the diner satisfied that I had placed a rendition of myself in the waitress's memory for safekeeping: not the whumping, flagship version— crowding forty, flabbed over—that restroom mirrors kept serving, but a charitable likeness of the uncramped life I was conducting beneath the threshold of myself.

For months now, however, what I had been trying to get out and put across in public—not just in diners and coffee shops— had kept sinking deeper inside myself, blotted up in suety layers, dendrochronological rings that archived my departure from the world of speaking and listening. I was sealing myself in. When words did manage to spurtle forth, they wrenched off and garbled themselves surrenderingly in the air, finished with me.

My last time at a diner, a week or so earlier, I'd ordered Salisbury steak, parsleyed potatoes, and applesauce, but what the waitress set before me was a pair of crab patties, French fries, and coleslaw. When I fluttered out a yodelish, hyperventilated complaint, she bustled through her memo pad, unperforated a green-shaded page, and shoved it at me. On it were my booth number (17) and, in a dribble of misspellings and abbreviations, the order for the crab patties, fries, and slaw. "You don't see anybody else raising a stink, mister," she said.

．　．　．

But I was hungry. Leaving Gloria to her appointment with her Foodtowne girl, or whomever, I pursed my way downstairs and out to my van. My bags were still tossed over the heavy cartons of books in the back. I climbed in, turned the key, inched out of the hedgy suburb. I ramped onto the loop of parkways and bypasses that cinched in the city. I bucketed along beneath the speed limit, let myself be overtaken by homing secretaries and paralegals and telemarketers, all sleek in their toyish cars. I finally exited onto a service road and fell in with a vast taillit recessional notching past diners, family restaurants, cocktail lounges, fast-food dispensaries. I kept going until the garden apartments gave way to the warehouses and turreted row houses that husked around the battered downtown business district.

A couple of years earlier, when I'd miscooked myself into the guise of an employment counselor and reported each morning to a frontless, ribbon-windowed building off Center Square, I'd wambled away long lunch hours downtown. But I hadn't been back since.

I parked the van at a meter that still had seventy-five minutes left on it and started huffing the two blocks to McDonald's. Except for a few gibbering solitaires halted at crosswalks, I was alone on the overlit street.

Inside McDonald's, I humped down a long aisle of plastic booths in which offcasts from rooming houses roosted alone or in liverish confederacies, most fingering the barely sipped cups of coffee that entitled them to stay.

I fetched up, short-breathed, at the counter.

I watched a bulgy, sweat-sluiced man point to the wrapped hamburgers heaped behind the counter, then slowly, fatly, heft his index finger. I watched the countergirl ring up the sale and then turned to watch the man carry the hamburger, trayless, along with a couple of ketchup packets and a shock of fist-rumpled napkins, to a lone, tenuous table wedged near the side-street entrance. I watched him hunch into his seat and then whisk off the wrapping of the sandwich, jerk the beef patty from between the twin cushions of the bun, deposit it on a bed of napkins, and, with another napkin, strenuously wipe the ketchup, onions, mustard, and pickle from the underside of the bun's crown. I watched him turn next to the patty, first mopping up its sickly slather of condiments, then swaddling the meat between thicknesses of napkin and drubbing the grease out of it with his overfleshed fists. I watched him swab the pickle, shred it, then rain the fragments onto the patty. I watched him slit open a ketchup packet and gingerly squish out curlicues onto the meat. I watched him caliper the patty between the thumb and forefinger of each hand and lower it onto the heel of the bun. I watched him give the finicked, reconstructed sandwich a blunt-fingered tap.

I watched him venture a troubled lunette of a first bite, then hulk up from his seat, hamburger in hand, and take a few slow, expeditionary steps across the several feet of littered floor that separated his fastness from a trash receptacle. By this point, I guess everybody else was watching him, too—even a cassocked old man, tenanting a booth close by, who until now had been gutturalizing contentedly, eyes shut, over the wreckage of a caramel sundae. Everybody had decided that this damp, widespread man with a hamburger was history in the making.

I watched him, only a step away from the trash receptacle, abruptly change his mind about jilting the sandwich. His thoughts friezed across his doughy face, every one of them an open secret. They were so clear, and they followed in such a tidy succession, that I could have written them down for later. Instead, I watched him prize himself back into his seat, guttle the rest of the hamburger in four or five bites, rear up again, then pant and swivet his way out to the street, leaving a snowdrift of napkins to be cleared away.

I watched him thump the two blocks to where his van was parked. That was when I got the feeling I was horning in.

That was when I was sure I had outstayed my welcome.

I watched him hoist himself into the van and drive off.

MINE

Do what I do: come from a family, have parents, have done things, shitty things, over and over and over. There was the one day I got too friendly with my friend. The next summer, I welcomed men into the house while my mother and father were at work. I did this to the exclusion of everything else I was cut out for at twenty-two. The men passed through me one way or the other and came out narrowly mine.

That was the one summer my heart had clout.

In the early evening, I would sit on the patio while my father stooped among his flowers. I could never sit for more than half an hour without having to get up to walk to the bathroom at least once. I don't know what I was expecting to come out, but I never once looked. I would put the lid down before I flushed.

Later, in the dining room, where the table would already be set, my father would say his piece. It always amounted to the same thing: if there was a problem, I should let Dr. Zettlemoyer know.

After dinner, I would go straight to bed. I crossed each night by linking one minute securely to the next, building a bridge that swung through the dark. I did my real sleeping in the morning sun, and around noon the first of the men would knock. The fact that they spaced themselves out assured me that they all knew one another and got along and were reasonable. Whoever was first was never a matter of surprise, but I think they would have liked the sequence to hold meaning.

My father never came home sick in the afternoon to find me on my knees in the living room with my mouth full of somebody's grave, helpless perpendicularity. I never got to see my father eye to eye like that, the only way I wanted to.

My father: what stood out about him was that his life got put past him.

It was my mother who taught me the one worthwhile thing: when they ask if you like what you see in the mirror, pretend that what they mean is what's behind you—the shower curtain, the tile, the wallpaper, whatever's there.

STEEP

The gray bowl that my husband ate his cereal out of, the bowl he had brought to the marriage from someplace else, a bowl from which I had never eaten, did not break or chip or go back to where it came from. It simply stopped coming to the table. Up until then, events had been uneventful: I washed and dried the bowl, then returned it to the cupboard. The exertion involved was minimal—in truth, I welcomed it—but I screamed bloody murder every time.

I think I already know what comes next: a stipulative definition of marriage as an accidental adjacency of flesh in which small, unbegrudged exchanges of affection are fitfully possible provided that ... and then you get so many pages of *provided that*s. The pages are wrinkled-looking, as if somebody had read them in the bathtub and then set them out on the floor to dry. The definition is the foundation of a vast, steep, plunging counterargument against which I am defenseless unless I spill two beans that I have been saving in my blood because what other privacy do I have? These two beans have been prowling in my blood for too long. The first bean is so simple, so obvious, that I have to work extra hard to keep putting it back into words, just to keep it in words: the woman he was seeing stopped letting herself be seen.

The second bean I have to condense. I woke up and he was biting my finger in his sleep. Not sucking—biting. An irksome switch, his being the container, instead of being gouged into *me*, slopping around inside when I was dead to the world or pretending to be. I was inside *him*. I was the one getting chewed up.

What I did was swack him on the head twice, three times. He eventually woke up. I told him what he had done.

He said, "Is that right?"

Because I was a woman he knew to speak to.

Ever since, the fundamental unit of discourse, the basic building block of speech, has been my mouth asking: "What's scarier than two people in a room with their nightstands and the things they keep on their nightstands?"

I make it sound as if I know an answer.

THE DAUGHTER

T he man was afraid of heights, of looking up. This was well known around the house. It was a household fact.

It was well known that when the man went outside he wore a cap with a long bill that awninged off unreliable tracts of sky.

The daughter knew all this.

One day, the man walked into the kitchen, which was shooting up several stories and becoming elaborately, sculpturally, tiered and balconied. He kept his half-closed eyes trained low—on the countertops, the slats of the chairs. He found some semblance of his wife at the table.

"We need to look for another house," he told her.

The silence was more vertical than ones he was used to.

"Do you hear me?" the man said.

"You can hardly notice it," his wife said.

The man put on his cap and walked to the daughter's school to talk to her teachers. He watched their faces when he gave them her name.

"She never comes" is all the teachers would say. They each showed him a columned page of a roll book on which she had been check-marked absent every day of the term.

"Describe the girl for us," one of the teachers said.

The man talked at reckless length about the daughter. The teachers complained that the more he talked about her, the less they could picture a girl or even the outline of what a girl might look like. They said that what he was talking about seemed more like a place, the capital of someplace, than a person.

"I'm not apologizing," the man told them.

When he got home, he left his cap on and panted up flight after flight of stairs to the daughter's room.

She was in bed, asleep. He looked down at her face, into her ears. He looked up her nostrils. In the left one he saw a stalactite of dried mucus. He left it alone. He sniffed at her underarms. He sniffed the entire length of one leg. He smelled her mouth. He gave it a spitful, plunging kiss.

A city was steeply taking shape around the daughter. The voluminosity of it made the man want to give up. He felt he had to see. He threw his head back and, clinching his tongue between his teeth to keep from swallowing it in fright, watched skyscrapers stunting overhead, crooking and curling, blousing out.

THAT WHICH IS HUSBANDER
THAN ANYTHING PRIOR

I stopped mistaking what the husband was doing for merely a new way of coming and going. I started regarding it as what it more likely was: a series of faultful, pestering steps taken farther untoward me. I had to adjust my own footing accordingly.

In bed, I kept my nose stuck in a book that listed pairs of words people often confused. It was something the husband had brought into the house early on, in a violent bout of furnishing. For instance: *intimidation* versus *intimation*. Only, I did not necessarily see where the versus came in.

I lived in a town that had sourceless light falling over it at all hours. At the front of the phone book, right after the dead-blue street map, came the claim that the town was within a so-many-mile radius of an immense fraction of the country's population. But every time I set foot on the streets, they withheld their longitude from me. They reneged on distance.

It was a town of meantime everlasting where, for homework, sheets of paper got numbered from one to fifty. The homework was unacceptable unless submitted in folders the teachers could drop off and pick up in the old metal milk box on my porch. The only time I had to meet the teachers was when they were new and thus understandably doubtful until I brought them into the bedroom, where they could see for themselves the picnic table with its jars of shining stick-pens, the banks of papers and folders, the bulletin boards shingled with teachers' handwriting samples and grade-inflation charts. Afterward, I would walk the teachers to the door, watch them tuck themselves into their cars.

In the folders, I would always find that some of the pages had been balled up and then sorryishly, second-thoughtfully, smoothed out. Others would be torn and flapped, pleated or petaled. Occasionally I came upon papers that had been soaked and crinkled and fancifully dyed or shaded until there was something cabbagy about the results. The greater number of sheets, though, arrived with coatings, toppings—not just spilled coffee and soda, smeared chocolate or pizza, but rampancies, offscourings, of the body. Often, opening a folder, I would be greeted by the concentrated smell of underparts preserved with uncanny loose-leaf fidelity. Whatever the students could get out of themselves, they put on paper for whoever collected. "Hand something in," I could hear the teachers saying.

Before the husband who kept leaving left for good, he accused me of two things: hirsutism and "self-dependence." It is true that I had hair scribbled fine-pointedly over my arms and the backs of my hands and a few other places. It is also true that I liked to keep the marriage almost entirely to myself. There was more to get out of it that way.

I started keeping the hair sleeved out of sight but went to doctors about the rest of the body, because it was not tiding me over. It did not suffice. There was the general practitioner who wanted to overcome his disinclination to heal just long enough to help me retain what I slept, because by morning all of it got away from me. And the neurologist: she was the only one I could think of to go to about the commotion in my face, the twitch that made my cheek blink separately from my eye. But it was the dentist I visited the most. He filled my cavities, the same ones, again and again, each time with something different: artful arrays of streaming silk threadlets, cleverly tinctured plasters and slurries, crystals whose enchasement could take hours. By the time I left his office, my tongue was already working the fillings loose, and everything would get swallowed later in my unbottoming sleep. In the morning, I would stare in the mirror at my rows of teeth—the slanting, headstony front ones, especially—until I found the holes. I would drive to the dentist and let him put his hands back in my mouth. I would go home afterward and put my own hands in places that did not have as clear an opening.

It was soon after that—after the marriage and the appointments—that I started the invitations. In one folder, I found a sheet on which was typed, red-ribbonly, "Every floor your on, is somebody elses ceiling, step lightly, please, show some feeling." This was biology, the science of life—a lab report for the junior college. I looked at the name: Lu Clovis. I looked down at my hand, which, at the foot of the page, was already writing: "I'm not the teacher." Beneath that, I gave my suppertime whereabouts, the name of the restaurant, for the week ahead. I pictured what they called the "nontraditional student": a housewife on the brink. But she showed up young, maybe twenty-three, and incompletely clean. She let a collapsible umbrella spill onto the table before she sat down. Her hair was brown and streamy. She had a forward body building up toward something already. She wanted to know where my youth had gone, how long at current address, what I had to go by, which people I held my life against, reasons for leaving whatever I might have left. But when I started to give her a factish rundown of some sort, keeping my palms up, hair-enshadowed sides down, her eyes went right out. I shut up and ate my sandwich until they came back on. They were brown, dry, blinking fast.

"I read that people who work at home put on suits just like people who commute," she said. The gutter above her lips—the downspout that there's a name for; it was in the book of pairs: *philtrum* versus *philtre*—started getting trickly with sweat.

"In my case, no," I said.

"I'm pissed," she said. Then: "Not about that. I'm here for something else, simultaneously or something. This is my fault—all right? I'm entitled? This is forgotten? This doesn't have to go down in memory? Excuse."

One thing led to another when there was no reason for the advance. Days were something I had to put myself into regardless. There was no getting around where they were going.

In another of the folders, I found an over-epigraphed Child Psych term paper with the research broad and abundant at one end and, at the other, following a blank page, this: "I TAKE MY DAY ONE LIFE AT A TIME, I LIVE MY LIFE ONE TIME A DAY, ALONG THESE LINES MY BODY WILL ONE DAY WANT MY LIFE ON IT." Below that was an exorbitant red signature that flamed out only after repeated bursts of paraphs and descending curlicues. The name was Tracy Frick. I did the "I am not the teacher" business again.

Because at home my bed was outdoors and amphitheatrical and, by this point, open to the public. Or because the husband, when there had been one in place, had run his finger up my leg as if untracing everything along the way, putting anything else in place of what was already there.

Look: here was folder upon folder full of words issuing from one aghast organism after another. The folders were in my house, in the room where my bed should have been. Which is why the bed was where it was and why I wrote what I wrote to a girl named Tracy, who showed up.

Only, Tracy was a boy—not even that, actually: just a display of height and posture. An unparentlike adult had followed him at a plausible distance, a woman with a squeezed, prevailed-upon face who boothed herself close by and now and then disappeared, a fresh cigarette skewed into her mouth, in the direction of the restroom.

I watched Tracy make a ketchuped muddle of his sandwich. His cheeks were stippled with acne—tender pimples that made me think of baby corn. We ate in swallowy silence.

Then he spoke.

"Is it possible to get away with talking about certain people as if they were far more distant, far more farther off, than they actually are?" he said. But this was already a speech—his eyes were nowhere near mine. "I ask this because I have been looking for a basis on which to talk about exactly one person. I have been imagining this basis as something plinthlike. The plinth would have to be high enough so that people walking past could not be sure who was doing the talking."

I looked over at the woman in her booth. Her hands were doing as much as they could with a paper napkin, trying to get it to the point where it was anything else but.

I entered into partial, tentative cahoots with her.

■　　■　　■

From here on in, I am speaking as someone with a sleeping disability—someone whose sleep, when it comes, is disabling to herself and others.

The last folder I ever graded was full of what looked like conjugations—page after page of permutational wordliness that struck me as overpostponed progress toward a second, fuller language. I red-penned the usual invitatory sentences at the end.

The man who days later sat down opposite me in the restaurant explained that he had a houseful of daughters who no longer wanted to be seen with him. He was many years my senior and loomed against himself in a way that was hard on the eyes. There was his body, which for some reason did not get the picture, and then there were its retractions, which, he said, had names and rooms and crawl spaces and undivided attentions of their own, and which poor-mouthed him, day in and day out, in notes magneted to the refrigerator.

The man had his bearings and was polite. I got him to go over his marriages, which had all been wide of the mark and not to his liking—spotty, topical impromptus set against a larger and larger landlessness. Between bites of his food ("The meal of the day," he called it), he tried to bring me around to where he claimed to be, which was the place from which you could see that between where the skin separating one body from another stops and where the air begins there is a place where nothing much should have to take place.

I said either "Ever?" or "How so?"

I was not keeping track.

It later turned out that I did not marry this man off the top of my head—there was no marriageable surface left on him that I could see—but when he got up to leave, most of me likely followed suit.

PEOPLE ARE ALREADY FULL

I was down to just two, the two of them, the two I had left.

It will be both convenience and courtesy—and I am hardly the one to overlook, as well, the pronominal luxury I will enjoy—if I make them, just this once, a woman and a man; but in actual, inadvertent life, you are sure to understand, they both were men—men of similar setbacks and altitude.

The man: I had to drive practically a week to reach him. My car niggled away at geography. The days were wide.

When I got there, the town was up against a bay. The slim streets were neither gridded nor ranked.

Later, on his terrace, he did not want me to call them photographs, and I did not want to call them merely pictures before I had a look at them for myself.

"Snapshots," one of us must have said, because by then the first of the albums was already being reckoned onto my lap. On each page, a listless, imperfect suction barely held the prints in place behind the clear plastic sheets. Toward the end, there were just glaring stacks in envelopes.

The depictions were last straws, old hat.

When it is two men—I still insist, I'll keep insisting—the one body disputes the other. What you see is one of them playing itself down, throwing off most of its weight, averting itself.

The pictures! A lot can happen if you stay awake, is all I ever got out of the things people kept shoving in my face and expected me to make instant snotty comments about.

But I elaborated myself into his arms: he was still a way for me to get a better grip on my body.

As for the woman? She lived in a city. Not the great scarped one you're right away imagining, but one that interferes with its inmates a lot less flatteringly. I wanted to know what she was doing up so early.

She explained that the moon operates on you for only so long, and then it stops and you're your own.

"Are you dry?" I said. "I am."

There was a cabinet on legs—not an ice box. The woman reached in and deducted some drinks, warm juice in cups.

I had to follow her to the sofa out of rude habit.

Until somebody tells me different, I am saying only that people are already full. The most you can do is lay yourself out on top.

THE PREVENTER OF SORROWS

At some point I played up to myself long enough to be living in a room that was scarcely part of the house it was tacked onto. Mornings, the open space between the bottom of the door and the carpet admitted a scalene wedge of light from more substantial regions of the house. Things besides light could have got in. It was my fault for not having insisted on a door that locked.

My troubles in the room were in fact few. I was living cajoledly as a woman. I worked in an office and was on concise, finite terms with the men I mixed with. I gave certain of the men permission to hunt and peck.

My thoughts at the time are said to have concerned proximity. Transportation was abundant. There was always a bus coming.

The properties of rooms are sometimes said to differ from house to house. I once rented a room in a row house on a through street. The room, it was insisted, was a convenience by which some extra, unruly space had been rectangled off to enclose someone for whom carnalities had become moot. By this point my lovers no longer recognized me on the paths along the river. They passed me with packages under their bare arms. I never managed much rest. The cubed air of my room hardened into a medium resistant to the through-passage of sleep. I could pat the air where it hung above my head.

How secure should you ever feel about anything that might go up on a wall?

For a time, I found that whenever I was on a street, I looked at people until I saw one who looked the way I expected the person to look who could put a room in my favor, bring it around to me.

I am speaking horribly again of where I was young.

It was a room in which the reception of articles, effects, was incomplete. I had been keeping to myself for months when a girl appeared to help me straighten things up. She did not think highly of herself. I hated to see her have to touch anything. I had to stop her fingers each time they were about to reach whatever should have been belonging only to me.

I convinced the girl that what I needed most was that she keep me company while I did the actual cleaning. This arrangement continued, awkwardly, for weeks. I was more and more beholden to the girl. One night I noticed a change. It was not a matter of light, of the turning of seasons. The girl had a new history on her—a different clutch on things. She had been admitted to the room: I could see her life coming down on her all at once. My possessions were now massily hers.

The woman was a stickler for partnership. She was smitten with better things to do. I followed her across an areaway and through an anteroom and into the room where the husband was already fixed up. The woman's face was narrow and red again. I could smell the deodorant on all three of us. The woman achieved her smile. That being so, I wiped my feet.

"I'm just starting out," I reminded her.

She touched my arm, as if to say: "That would be lying."

In return, I felt pushed.

I heard the door close behind me like before.

In time, the husband and I had everything packed into boxes and had the boxes piled high against the wall, leaving the center of the room clear. The husband stretched himself out on the floor. There the similarities should have had to end.

Something goes terribly wrong with a room when it has held only one life for a long time. I had been over this and over this with people who claimed otherwise. There was a room of mine that was looked at and taken the wrong way. I opened this room to a man who was bringing up girls his wife had already had. The girls became raucous, cocky explorers of my bed. I tried to level with them.

■　　■　　■

I was the new girl, the trainee. They had me behind the register. My room was across the street. The manager was driving at something.

"Drop all idea of this being a cake job," I saw him saying. "Don't think that the things people line up on the belt spell something out. There is no 'whole other life.'"

I remember an attic room to which I brought sackfuls of used clothing from thrift stores, rescue missions. The clothes were complicated by the lives of the people who had worn themselves onto them. In each case, something of the wearer had worked itself into the fabric and defeated the detergents and bleaches. It was often the least celestial thing.

I did not draw the line at underapparel. I did not limit myself to what had been worn by men. There was a boxful of maternity dresses and another of maillots. There were children's sunsuits, snowsuits.

I never found opportunity to wear most of the clothes but arranged ways for them to impinge upon me outnumberingly. I slept beneath enormous odorant piles. The clothes pressed their way into the upper reaches of my sleep.

Dressed, I could feel myself spoken for.

There were men throughout the city to whom infants of a certain age had to be brought at least once a week. It was said that there were never enough of these men at any one time. Once, I ran into one of them on his way to his room. There was a woman at his side who did all the talking. I forget whether I was expected to do anything spectacular on her behalf.

The world was one place, and then, overnight, it became someplace else. This was brought about without a significant redistribution of landmasses or weather, without any change in the vocabulary people had to fall back on when asking for admittance.

I taught myself to live in water.

SLEEVELESS

I 've had things in my eye, sometimes too many at one time. Except this once.

It was during a standstill in some otherwise eventful unemployment on both sides. My wife was asking for permission. She was sleeveless. The car was already in her name.

"Let me at least have a look at him," is all I said.

He was waiting in a booth at a coffee shop. My wife slid in beside him. I don't ordinarily drink coffee, but he ordered it for all three of us. I was going to count the number of sips I took.

"This isn't my day," he said. He told us what had happened on his way over—near misses, thumbnail bios of the principals, etc.

We sat in the misorderly, picayune midst of my wife.

I let him butter me up. I tapped my foot on his. Just a tap.

Because I know myself from somewhere, surely.

I've been within an inch of my life.

There are no big doings in my heart that I know of.

I AM SHY A HOLE

I hate it when it gets all languaged around like this. I don't want it to be "If I had a dog" or "If I don't have a dog." What concerns me is how to get it past the point where I can decide whether I want to do anything next.

In other words, this is always going to be about my mine, not yours.

Last night he told me we could narrow it down to a boy-girl thing, and I let him disrobe me. I had to think about the knees of the girl I sat across from last year in school.

This much is figured out: the thing about being a girl is that stuff gets stuck inside you—but with a boy, stuff goes away and never comes back. A boy keeps losing himself. A boy just keeps watching himself run out. How much should this explain?

That *boy* is open wide at one end so things can make their way out? (Say it and you will never hear it stop until you make believe there is something else your voice could be for.)

Girl is shut tight: say it and it's already done away with.

None of this is in my face.

I am always saying *boy*, no matter what people think you hear.

CONTRACTIONS

When I was an old-enough kid, I prepared an exhibit of things I wasn't supposed to know—things my parents had done before they got married to each other. It was almost like a science fair: posterboard displays, Styrofoam props. I had been secretly working on the project for months, excavating most of the facts I needed out of spavined shoe boxes at the back of my parents' closet, and early one Saturday night when my parents and sister went shopping, I set everything up in the basement, mostly on the Ping-Pong table but overflowing onto the washing machine and dryer. The centerpiece was a four-paneled entry titled "My Mom Was Married Before, and I Have a Stepbrother I Have Never Met." Among the evidence arranged beneath cellophane was a mildewy set of Gregg shorthand manuals, each opened to a flyleaf on which my mother's spiderish, inwrought handwriting spelled out her first name and a rude-sounding, unfamiliar surname and then a month, a day, and a year before I had been alive. I had also put lots of work into the diptychs "*Another* Stepbrother of Sorts: Daddy's Secret By-blow" (I provided a dictionaryish sidebar, as well as photocopies of the legal papers detailing the terms of the settlement) and "The World of My Sister" (featuring a time line ticking off the five and a half months between my parents' St. Patrick's Day potluck wedding and my sister's birth). Breaking up the Magic Markered text were Xeroxed family snapshots I had shaded with coloring pencils and then captioned destructively.

I spent the night out with the kid who considered himself my boyfriend—a gripless unethnic type who always had an unlit cigarette slanted apostrophically into his mouth. At the kitchen table the next morning, I found my mother looking unslept, tear-swollen. My father was administering to his bare forearms the same slow sequence of slaps, brushes, fingertaps, and hair-tugs that years earlier I had decided added up to his stab at a formula for making himself disappear. My sister, however, was the one who was missing.

The upshot was that I eventually turned twenty-eight and found myself married. I fumed and soured and stenched in bed beside a husband who himself was a cloud of exhausts and leakages. Sleep became a contest: by morning, whose smell would prevail in the room?

My husband's piss drippled out day and night, slavering through his underwear, blurring the crotch of every pair with a corona of orangey yellow. He had an enlarged prostate, and he kept a plastic ice-cream tub beside the nightstand. Every five minutes or so until he fell asleep, I would hear him, sodden and unfaucetable, bowing and curbing himself along the edge of the mattress, the tub in one hand, the other jigging his penis against the inner rim until a driblet or two finally plipped surrenderingly against the plastic. Sometimes, after he had resettled himself in his zone of the bed, I would reach across and pat his slobbering penis. My hand would come away clammy, vinegared.

I had always been struck by how other people spoke so casually and unembarrassedly about their beds, as if a bed were merely an unshaming final destination on the day's itinerary. When I first lived alone, I thought of my own bed as a softer, more expansive version of a toilet, a fixture on which things got discharged or unrecoupable selves got squeezed out, then flushed away in cleansing eddies of the sheets. Later, when I began making myself available to others, every body that trespassed on my bed left behind a new, unfillable furrow in my mattress. Some were more like clefts, gougings. In college, I had had a roommate whose bed I one day stared at too long. The roommate had gone home for the weekend without having made her bed. I stared at the swirls and crests of the waved sheets and the bedspread. I felt their tidal coaxings. I was determined not to get up from my own mattress, where I was lying with one hand wound around one of the cold metal legs, and dive onto hers. I could hear the siss of showers in the lavatory down the hallway. I had probably already missed lunch. I contented myself with the explanation that what was playing across my roommate's bed was simply the afterswell of a certain kind of sleep, a slopping, heavy-going sleep that had excluded me *unslightingly*. My roommate had left a sweatshirt lying on the floor, and that was what I ended up wearing all day. It was the day I went up to a boy I had never talked to before and asked where he came from.

I had to buy things—little things—several times a day: tweezers, permanent markers, newspapers. With every purchase, I should have stood in a fixed, unambiguatable relation to the person behind the cash register, but the transaction almost always got complicated by the accompanying thermal exchanges, the glancing flesh of palms and fingertips as payment was tendered, change dealt out. Some days when I counted on these seductions, all I would get was a clerk who slammed the coins onto the counter or trayed them atop bills he then let parachute onto my outstretched palm.

I would rock an empty shopping cart back and forth in the aisles of stationery departments, notebooks and thick packages of filler paper cliffed on either side of me. Sometimes I would reach for a coilbound themebook and riffle the pages, unsticking them, vaguely sickened by the washed-out pink and blue of the margins and ruled lines. I would picture the prongy, unparallel outlines onto which teachers were going to drape unmemorizable facts.

Mostly what I wanted to find was a special piece of chalk like the one my third-grade teacher had always used to mark our positions on the linoleum floor of the stage. It was a sausage-shaped cylinder of soft chalk swaddled in flocky wool. Back then, I had wanted my words to stream out as smoothly and as scrapelessly as the lines and circles and X's that flowed from that overscaled piece of chalk. Instead, everything I said or wrote seemed to scratch something else out of the world. On tablet paper and on blackboards, my letters were bony and tined. I begged classmates to recopy my homework for me so that each answer would come out curved, clawless, quieted down.

I'd had a friend once. For years, our goosefleshy lives had abutted in classrooms, on playgrounds, at library tables. Even when we outgrew the stage when we could jungle-gym across each other's legs and trunk and arms, I kept piling my life beside hers. Once, an overclouded July afternoon when we were both thirteen, we were lying in a weedy field behind a shopping center. I managed to land my head on her belly and listen to the guggle and burble inside her. My ear was pressed against the bare skin between the hem of her T-shirt and the waistband of her shorts. She let out a laugh. It was a flat-voiced laugh, but it made my life seem suddenly solvable, performable. I started thinking about unpillowing my head and letting my hands balustrade up her long arms until our faces were close together, and that was when she jerked away. The fleshy suction of my ear against her skin, the vacuum between us, broke. She hunched up, propped her chin on her knees, began tugging blades of crab grass out of the earth. I hunched up, too, and looked at her. Her shins were hatched and shaded with darkish hairs that I liked because my blond ones were uninsistent, practically invisible. "What are you looking at?" she said. "Nothing," I said. But the next time I saw her legs bare, a couple of weeks later, they were razored, girled-up.

Late every night, my husband watched a black-and-white 1950s variety show on a nostalgia channel. Eyes shut, shoaling in some puddly near-sleep, I would listen to the splashes of applause and the effortful laughter of the live audience. Inevitably, a member of the audience, usually a man, would let out a sudden, petitioning laugh, a laugh out of sync with the lilt of the jokes. I found that I had to assign the man a face and mete him out a life as unfinishable as my own before I could shark off into sleep.

Once, returning home from work, I found my husband kneeling raptly before a wicker hamper from which my dirty laundry had overspilled. He was bobbing for my socks, incisoring into them one at a time, then craning around, depositing them onto the carpet, tandeming them off. There were already at least half a dozen heel-soiled pairs, each a different shade of off-white, laid out intently. His hands, meanwhile, were making slow, winging dips in the air around his cock, now and then grazing it as the angle of its levitation shifted.

I backed my way unnoticed out of the room. In the kitchen, I settled myself squeaklessly onto an upholstered chair. I thought about the sad, outcropped, lavatorial world of men. I had once met a man, a limericky professor, whose secret, unairable life's work was a definitive atlas of women's body-hair distributions: an oversized, plywood-covered volume, full of thick, eraser-pinked pages, that he kept clamped shut under a terraced heap of accordion files in the trunk of his car.

Men wanted my toes in their mouths or my torso roped against a chair or my mouth lipsticked and wordless or my brain ligatured to whatever unknottable neural twist that in their own brains winched their rawing, blunted dicks into place. It was always just one thing they wanted, or could handle, at a time. I had myself convinced that I had so many lives recessed inside me that I could afford to portion my body out part by part and not miss anything, that everything would grow back.

But I had a hard time finding anything even marginally fetishizable about a man's life. I would grub through my husband's nightstand and bureau-drawer dross—the siltage of receipts, business cards, watch straps, and crease-blurred newspaper clippings that shadowed him securely into the apartment. I would poke my finger through the front slit of a pair of his jockey shorts before I tossed his wash into the machine. I would stand in the bathroom and stare at the pepperish encrustation of his whisker-hairs in the unscoured sink.

Eventually he stopped haranguing me with sex altogether.

The only way in and out of the building where I lived with my husband was through a dim lobby furnished with a sofa, a card table, and some folding chairs. Coming and going, I had to walk past a pair of plaid-dustered old women who early each morning organized themselves onto the sofa and kept watch. Each had a cathedral of yellowish-gray hair whose bobby-pinned buttresses and pinnacles the other would frettily oversee. Gangling through the lobby, surveilled, I would occasionally let an unlipped, falsetto "hi" butterfly out of my throat and into the nets that the women's squeeching hearing aids unreeled into the dead air. But the women never even nodded. It was real work to operate my body past them, my life beating down on me with every step. It was even harder when I was dragging women in and out, one at a time, never the same one twice, during roiling, elongated lunch hours. Because by this point I had to have women, their knee-shine and susceptibilities, even though every one of them left me staled, depopulated.

Every year for six weeks in gym—a whole grading period—we had had what the teacher called "apparatus": monkey bars, parallel bars, the pommel horse, the high bar, the stationary rings. The teacher was a loudly married snoop with blunt legs duckpinning out of the same sort of salmon-colored trunks we were all required to wear. She knew I couldn't do a forward roll, which was the prerequisite to all other stunts, so she confined me to a special mat. Twice a week, and for forty minutes at a time, I was expected to kneel on that gashy, eraser-soft mat, tuck my head between my legs, and wait for a somersaultic force to exert itself on me and overturn the cinder-blocked gym and loop me forward into the same world everybody else was living in. But I remained untumbled, earthbound. Through the triangled space between my thighs, I would watch the spoked bodies of my classmates as they spiraled down the matted trackway that led to the apparatus, blazing their legs at one another. Then I would watch them skin the cat or stick-arm their way along the parallel bars.

On my mat, singled out, looked after, I bowed obediently into my groin and developed an overacquaintance with the inletted, divulgent body I presided over.

■   ■   ■

I started spending lots of time in my car—a rust-mottled, incognito beige Chevette. It was suddenly the room I felt most at home in, and it had enough of a sick-bay look to it to be thief-proof. The passenger-side leg well was table-solid with a pile of sallowing unread newspapers, and the crumb-strewn passenger seat made a companionable, multipurpose side-surface. I kept some extra cups and a box of plastic forks, knives, and spoons hutched on the dashboard. The radio gave out nothing but static, but it was the deep, bearable variety, not the kind of organized insect-kingdom roar that always brought on headaches.

After work and on weekends, I drove, rivering through the city and the suburbs. For a while I ate nothing but tiny meteorites of fried chicken that came casketed in clumsily slotted and tabbed cardboard. The arm that angled out of the drive-through window to hand me my box was almost always the same one: fuzzy, overbraceleted. It was an arm I wanted to have something to do with. Instead, the window would shut. Back on the service road, I would molar down the crumplets of chicken and let the grease terror through my system.

The women I was seeing were becoming less disappearable, and some started having names. There was Karen, a pharmacist with straw-blond hair and an asterism of nipply pimples that, during the days or hours I spent away from her, seemed to belt across her face zodiacally, never coming to a rest on one cheek or the other. The one with the chopped hair and paper cuts was Marcia: she drove a UPS truck. Dianne worked at an electrolysis studio. The waiting room would always be full of sleeveless young men hovering behind fashion magazines, and she would lead me upstairs to her uncurtained efficiency apartment, where she talked about her incumbent boyfriend and about the two other men who were after her and about how she was getting drummed out of her life. Gretchen was the one who kept saying she lacked the courage of her contradictions. She was afraid of losing her job at the community college because she didn't flatter the students enough. Each of these women was an exclamation of salty, spoiling flesh.

■　　■　　■

I came home every night. I would hurry through the underlamped lobby, ride the elevator to the third floor, find my husband on the living-room sofa. By this stage of the marriage, he had precipitated himself so exhaustively into the apartment that the air was urinous and unparting. Every room was snary with his life. His sleep trellised over towel racks and chair arms and shoe trees. It filamented from the handles of coffee mugs and the pocket clasps of mechanical pencils. Sometimes I would wake him and point to the bedroom. As he slippered past me, I would see his life training behind him, floor-fouled and unlanguaged, littery bits of myself magpied and particled into it. I still slept in the same brinkless bed with him. I would want to get up and shut off the candescence of the white shirt he had hangered to the closet door for work the next day, its collar pennanting in the breeze of the electric fan he ran as a noise filter.

My life had started to pill. I was fuzzing out little balls of myself that people would come up and twist off and flick into the already overpacked air.

At stoplights, I began to slope my neck sidewise so I could glint into whichever car was laned beside my own. The bloodshot, circumstantial desolation of the windowed faces—the splather of fingers against a cheek—was how I wanted things: wrung out.

I started wearing shopgirlish shirtwaists so that when I drove to the malls after work, I could be certain that if I lingered long enough at a display, restacking saucepans or arranging a strew of shoe boxes into a neat row, one old woman or another would eventually ask, "Miss, where would I find…," sealing off her question by salivaing the name of some unfamiliar-sounding kitchen utensil or sewing-box instrument. Her gaspy mouth would be a burrow of caries and glazed tongue. I would do my best to crease my face into blank lines and busy my hands menially with the merchandise before me. "You don't work here?" the woman, unanswered, would continue. I would wait until I no longer felt her stare singeing my cheek, then watch her flutter off toward a real salesclerk.

People in malls had it coming to them—even the girls wristing one another along from store to store or willowing about in a subjunctive sulk. The girls all had their lives marqueed brightly on their faces. My eyes would dart straight to their skirted legs, the flesh that glowed above the cuffs of their socks. Their skin was a threat.

A few blocks from the memorial park where my mother was staying put was a convenience store where I one day decided that the man behind the counter knew what he was doing. He kept an old metal dustpan on the counter. If you wanted to buy something, he pointed noncommittally to the dustpan, and sooner or later you figured out that he expected you to put your money on it, which you then did. He would grasp the dustpan by the handle and set it atop the cash register. He would ring up the sale, drawer the bill you gave him, plink your change onto the grooved ramp of the dustpan, and shovel the change toward the very edge of the counter, toward you.

This made sense.

It was a Saturday afternoon, early. What I bought was a stapler, a cheap blue plastic one, for my car.

ONESOME

To get even with myself on behalf of my wife, to see just how far I had been putting her out, I began to ingurgitate my own seed. I had to go through with everything twice the first night, because it came out initially as thin as drool and could not have possibly counted as punishment. The next time—I had let an hour or so elapse—some beads of it clung to a finger, and a big, mucousy nebula spread itself into the bowl of my palm. By the time I got everything past my lips, much of it had already cooled, but I revolved the globules around in my mouth slowly, deservedly, several times before allowing myself a swallow. There turned out to be nothing clotty or gagging about it—why, then, her gripes, her grudges?—just a bitter stickiness that stuck with me.

I repeated everything in the morning before work and again before bed. I began to hear—or imagine—a glueyness, a tightness, in things I now said. It made me think twice about opening my mouth.

Is it news to anybody that my wife had already given up on me hand and foot? She wanted her own room, and she got it, the small one downstairs we had never settled on any lasting purpose for. I went along, knowing how little it takes for a room to become the opposite of room.

Let me ask myself something else: should a father and his daughter have to fear each other tit for tat? Did I not make sure the door to her room was open when I made polite bedtime conversation with her? There was a prolixity of purple-blue veins legible beneath her skin, and on her face I could see my own features garbled, corrected, redressed. Childhood had cumulated in her and was getting ready to sour into something far worse. She had her own secret life and a circlet of friends who all had nearly the same name—Loren, Lorene, Lorena, I could never get all of them straight. She was a decent kid—picked up after herself, got high marks in the hardest subjects. I had no bone to pick with her except that she kept breathing down my collar and then expected me to provide the food, the clothing, the shelter she needed to rule me out for good.

Marriage is what—the most pointless distance between two points? Or the foulest? Which?

My earlier marriages had all had a ring of adultery to them, because they were concise but inexact. For a long time afterward, I still looked in on the women in the supermarkets where they shopped, but we kept out of each other's eyes. I eventually saw every one of them vehemently pregnant—they deployed their bodies to brilliant effect for the men who came after me—and I was always on the verge of sending well-wishing cards with notes attached. But I kept my mind on getting in good with myself and watering down what I wanted from people.

Now I had another wife, and a daughter, to both of whom I was the last person on earth. I have already said everything about the daughter. But the wife, my last one: she was the one I married because how else this late was I going to get an idea of how many things a person did during the course of a day and then make sure I was doing the same number of things—only different ones, to keep me from looking too dependent? I could be civil to this wife once I knew her plans for the day, once I had an inkling of how much work was cut out for me.

Whatever my wife did, I would come up with something collateral, an equivalent. I would keep pace with her—chore for chore, personal occasion for personal occasion. Except that everything she did fell inside the marriage and everything I did fell anywhere but. I was no good at holding it in.

Example: two nights a week, my wife volunteered with a program that reached out to anyone for whom speech had become a hardship. These included the people who said *they* instead of *he or she* to jack up the population in their private lives. The county college offered a course the same two nights. It did not apply to the source of my livelihood, which shall remain nameless, but I signed up for it and bought the book. A girl sat next to me for weeks before finally markering "How are you fixed for people?" on a page of her thick semestral notebook. She tore out the page, folded it, fillipped it toward me.

I wrote back what—that I am people-proof, a onesome?

A story can go on only so long before it stops being a joke.

It was a three-hour class with a fifteen-minute intermission that the prof kept postponing until later and later because nobody but a handful of studious illiterates hung around for what followed. One night, at the start of break, the girl pointed out the window at a car that was a black oblong on the parking lot.

In the car, she said, "Guess what I made for supper—it stank up my hair."

I sampled a shiny hank of it in my fingers but could not place the smell. She drove me to somebody's house. We stationed ourselves at opposite ends of the living-room floor. When we both saw that that was all there was going to be to it—that just because there is a place for something doesn't automatically mean it belongs there—she drove me back to the lot where my car was.

I told everything to my wife.

Who wouldn't have?

She tracked down the girl by first name alone—called the registrar's office in one of her voices—and barely made trouble.

I called the girl just once after that.

"I know we had a falling-out," I told her.

I went to grocery stores, expecting to find her buying further things to cook.

My teeth started sticking to everything I took bites from.

One morning, I could not get out of the house. I tried all of the doors and a couple of the windows. It was as if they were pasted shut. I turned on the radio, expecting nothing but static or long lists of school closings, but there was music, music with words rising from it familiarly.

I had to call in sick.

I looked at my wife, my daughter. One or the other said something about being hungry for something substantial.

I watched my wife reach into a cabinet for a frying pan. I watched my daughter open the refrigerator door. I duly unloosened myself from my chair. I started off in the direction of the silverware drawer.

I went on with their life.

FOR FOOD

He was a head taller than I, but he had arrived, midlife, at a way of scheming himself downward as he walked, of wreaking onto his considerable body a succession of indentations, curtailments, so that whatever memory of him the townspeople might, if pressed, recuperate later in the light of their houses would be that of an incompletely statured, sideswept man of unfixable purpose. He was not my father (my father had remained unheard of); but because I never addressed him by name (I instead tutoyered him left and right), observers understandably conformed the two of us to their familiar, cleanly notion of father and son.

He would tolerate no footwear under his roof. It was an issue, a policy, of hygiene. He held to a conviction about the unmanageable filthiness of shoes—that once you suffered contact with the bottom of one, you sank to the level of everything the shoe had ever been brought down upon. The piss slopped onto lavatory floors and then tracked everywhere by dint of the retentive sole of a publicly worn slipper was his standard, weary example. And then the house would have the entire clientele of the lavatory circulating throughout it: the house would be thrown wide open again.

The man designed promising clothes.

I adolesced diplomatically by his side. I put in long days in the wide, thorough rooms. My heart *performed*. I fetched whatever the man pointed to. He had a rapid, nominating hand.

I was his head of hair. He would lay claim to the tacky mass of it—redisperse it, superintend it differently, complicate it with ribbons and barrettes, adjust the lights in it, provoke it to fresh successes. I would allow him to have his full say where I was just nerveless, slippery lengths.

In turn, he sought control of the cooking. He plotted our meals with a dismal rigor, mobilizing faded cuts of ham, even paler partings, sectionings, of fruit, jeopardizations of it, along the narrow extent of countertop. (An article of food should present itself as something else, he demanded, arranging lesioned vegetables on a tray for the headboard. "To cool the backs of the knees," he said. Or: "For where your feet will one day have to go.") The days I locked myself in my room, I could count on a raggedness of beef, in sheets, to be slid into thick wallets of bread and then be remitted, relinquished, on the mat outside the door I knelt behind.

For I had already flung myself into the books that were expected to cause me the most trouble: our sickliest histories. I loitered in them: I stooped on the sentences, bestrode the tensed, buckling words, squatted there until the spread of events became mine alone.

The man knew, too. "What will you use for money?" was how he couched his knowledge.

Our life continued in this train for months. With my ear against the door, I could make out, when I wanted to, the fussing snitter of a scissors or the motory commotions of the sewing machine or, less often, the cantillation, intimate and menial, of the man's telephone voice. (There was a backer he was required to call.) I noticed that a woman from time to time passed by my window: we began to exchange waves. Nothing serious or signific at first— but, before long, a greeterly incontinence took hold of the two of us: our arms shivered away from our sides: even our wristfalls became communicational, *summative*. The first time I climbed all the way out, she guided me to where she said she slept: an ulterior milieu of lotions, spot cash, pedestaled cake savers ajar with the surrounding town. My hands lent themselves to her pink, winking undernesses. (She had the prevailing anatomy.) We made plans to meet again halfway between us. She named some eligible district.

A less penalized course of retrospection, however, would find me having already found that there was a living to be made by furnishing grounds for others in the town to regard me consanguineously: to knock on a door and be shown to a seat and then, by polite, solacing intervals, be drawn out as the furthermost yet of kin. I thus fingered their ashtrays, left informing redolences on their sofas and chairs. I wore a welcome hole in their lives. For once, mothers would have been in the right to talk in secret twos and threes. But how wrong could they have been to keep counting their children on the sly every hour on the hour? When at last the time came to eat, we confronted a speckiness in shallow bowls. Afterward, I would be alternately detested and regaled—the butt of every confidence. I remember setting enough nights aside to compose a hat: a serviceably curtaining and commemorative number that was later to be accorded that ill-intentioned popularity.

The strings one neglectedly—neglectingly—pulls!

For it was on the strength of this hat alone, the boxed mock-up of it, that I advanced to another man: this one importunate, futureless, adept. We mostly had to travel.

His house and his "finds" (I am free to quote merely from the will) in time demised to me. I had to be driven out for a look at the place. What I could make out had a loose, unmastered aspect in the supplementary light I had been reminded to bring along.

After the auction: prompt, forgivable descents into marriage.

Delora: she must have lived her life in advance of the actual events, because her stomach would accept nothing further. (But she had advantages of height, of moisture.)

Grete: mornings, after shaking out our sheets, she claimed to see "blue minerals" all over the floor. (These she is said to still be sweeping.)

Liann: a whiled-away, vanishing girl. (She had come up through the ranks of her sisters.)

I hope I was impossible.

I hope I told all of them the same thing—that under no circumstances should the body ever have to depict *itself*.

More in keeping, then, with the nature of this anniversary confession are my chances, much later in life, of having had a boy looking in on me after work. (The work was the boy's alone.)

Then the boy fell sick.

The doctor squeezed his, the doctor's, face shut while he, the doctor, spoke terribly of English.

Both of them gave me their money so it would not have to go for food.

NOT THE HAND BUT WHERE
THE HAND HAS BEEN

P eople will hold you to your secrets.

So put your finger, for the time being, on a man whose daughter is already grown.

By grown, I mean she no longer lives where I can.

By daughter, I mean she gives off, suffers from, comes down with.

Sometimes I still go where she stays. The bus is more like a waiting room than a corridor, but I am hardly one to sit.

Have I as much as said that, once, an afternoon, I had to ask to use her bathroom, and something turned up, naturally, in the cabinet under the sink? It took me at most a minute or two to get it figured out: it was the fluted plastic rod whose office it is to steady the roll of tissue lengthwise in the toilet-paper holder. But at the time, for the moment, I had it taken for something else. Because it was all by itself down there—set apart, put out. All *treasured*-looking, and privileged. Women, because of how much better they are, or how much better they have it, get to own things—instruments—that men should almost never have to find reason to touch. Even at my age (I have reached my thinning forties), it is a misfortune to be reminded of even where they get stored. But this, for once, was something simpler to put right.

The sound of small things being rearranged has always been, for me, among the hardest to abide. But I remember taking hold of the roll of tissue, working the rod through the cardboard tube, slotting everything into the assembly glued to the pink tile.

"Dad," I heard her say, not even tapping at the door, or at least clittering her fingernails against it, but just barely *patting* the thing. (I swear I could see it move a little in its frame.)

Spare me the spectacle of people fending for themselves.

■   ■   ■

From early on, it had been a marriage that held no real sway. (Littlenesses, piled high, do not suddenly amount to anything immense.) None of it would even deserve reminiscence if the outfit my wife was working for, a realty, hadn't relocated to a newer building, one that had been rushed up, I'm now guessing, to throw people together. (Sliding glass partitions, everything modular and portable, impermanent.) My wife liked her men noticeably put upon, conspicuously ruined. (He was a title searcher upstairs, I later learned.) For a time, I worked out a compensatory adultery of my own: the source was a woman of immediate physical utility and careful demeanor, a phlebotomist. What we felt for each other lacked any basis in either one of us—it was a hard-nosed tribute, I'm supposing, to people before and yet to come—but we catered to some unrealizable ideal of infidelity and kept up the cattish decencies it called for. Quickly: I was going with her, and then the two of us were going, "together" (her word), with a third, and then there were just the two of them, coupled, professing surprise and self-reproach.

Then I did what I'm still answering for.

Even so, I ask a lot of what I can't see.

If it's a question of looking into a face you haven't run across before and inquiring of yourself just how far it's a corruption of, a judgment on, some other face you are not yet sick of, and then, in the time left (let's insist the two of you are on a bus), doing it some swift, scathing kindnesses—if it's a question, that is, of bestowing upon it an undeserved deprecatory merit—my answer is that my regard for such faces has become almost entirely subtractive, that I do my best to fatigue and deplete their features until the faces go blank and I can thus institute her onto (*found* her looks upon, call her to order on) everybody I see: I put her squarely in my way every place I get.

I mention this because there's a store I can make it to on foot, a drug and grocery combined, where I look at people who are almost never her.

I tack from aisle to aisle, an accumulator. I carry one of the red plastic shopping baskets.

Things between me and the checkout girls could hardly be more tacit. The first of them is reducible to deep hair, a lofty forehead. The second is a bolt of college material fading fast. She twiddles each item she rings up, editorializing with a wry cigarette cough. Everything—grapes, bleach, disposable razors—earns a familiar tussive dismissal. The third is actually a boy (spared so far!), but surely, slenderly, alert that his current body (the lint-white scraps he gets for arms, above all) counts for nothing.

Today I get the third girl, the near miss. I watch the thickspread man in front of me set up his homey skyline of cartons and cans on the black span of belt. The things I live on—the chocolate chips, the noodles—sag behind the sleek planes of their packaging. They don't hold up.

It's then I see her enter the store, choose a cart: my eyes and my mouth still secure on her face, though she can barely bring herself to wear the things—the lips bitten shut, each green eye sunk, minimized, behind its thick, remedial pane.

We do what we always do: we see each other out.

A voice-activated tape recorder keeps me abreast of most of what gets said in my sleep. I keep the thing on the headboard and listen each morning to the playback. What I hear is beyond the range of speech, but I usually have no trouble making out distinct trains of feeling, burdens, better ways of never knowing what it was that hit me. The most useful method of assorting the sounds, I have discovered, is according to the people they were leveled against— the people who get me to pipe up without my knowledge. The supermarket cashier, for starters, the one temporarily a girl: she has me coming out with an opportune murmuration, very throaty and unlike me. The one with the disapproving cough provokes a hectoring, refutative bark. The tone I take with the wife I had to have is, I think, by and large a steady, reasoning tone. And then there is the one to whom I speak as if through what exactly—a gag? a surgical mask? a hanging of handkerchiefs? It comes out struggled and inspissated. I admire the thickening consistency of it. I can tell it's big talk.

• ■ ■

I hear myself out like that, unpersuaded, for the better part of the spring. Then I decide to move into a different, nearby city, a less handy one. Within a week, I am complaining to the building manager about noise from the apartment below mine. The offending tenant is described to me as "a woman away on vacation." The manager grudgingly sympathizes with me for however long it takes the two of us to get to the bottom of the same stairs. From my new address, the commute by bus is fifty-five minutes instead of the accustomed, preoccupied twelve. My career, in fact, breaks up. ("Uncollegiality," "insufficient service to the community," a "fat backlog of name-withheld-by-request grievance letters, for photocopied samples of which please see attached," etc.) A week of busy sleep, and I become an indexer, a freelance. I manufacture indexes for university-press books. I discover I am partial to narrow lanes of type, ragged rights, the appearance given of a settled intelligence. It's private, satisfying work. (A mimeographed pamphlet, a hornbook provided by an editor, describes the ideal indexer as "a person prepared to content herself, minutely and anonymously, with water under the bridge.") I work independently, get paid by the book. The trick is to push your way into the society, or coterie, of facts that the author has pushed his way into first, and then it's a matter of making up your mind to cooperate with what you read. Next, decide on your headings, your *See also*s, and (when appropriate) your subheadings and sub-subheads. As for the rest of the job, who can't handle page numbers? Who can't run the alphabet? (The pamphlet devotes a stocky paragraph to the matter of how easily, given a rogue shove, the "entire works" of a book can be tilted away from the author, or "be made to tick differently," and cautions against the temptation, understandable though rarely understood, for the indexer to take one or more "keynotes," "unheard concerns," of her own life, then fudge them into the run-in, alphabetized biographical arraignment that follows any entry whose headword is a person's name. Other warnings, monitions, mostly concern the treatment of numbers.)

I set my own hours and operate out of my bed. For my off-duty periods (though the pamphlet insists that "an indexer is never not working"), I find it helpful to arrange things around the apartment as prompts, cues. In the bathroom I hang a picture of a woman enjoying a shower (I am otherwise prone to baths that go on too long), in the kitchenette an instructional clipping about a man who saved himself from choking. Early one morning, I am tipped backward in the dentist's chair for a cleaning. The hygienist is new to me: tall, unquiet, not too removed from herself. From a laminated ID card pinned to her waist I learn her name in full. She presents me with a suave handout about gum sicknesses and a packet of hooklike floss threaders for my bridge. Afterward, up they go on the wall above my bed.

Weeks pass: a book every two days or three. (The pamphlet reassures me that it is not unbecoming for an indexer to perform with such dispatch.) I start skipping the recommended three-by-five cards, the shoe boxes, the colored pencils. I do the alphabetizing on plain loose-leaf, then press the results into the dirty pica of my manual typewriter. (The hollows of the *o*'s come out shaded.)

The stream of my bathroom-sink faucet, I notice, gets thinner and thinner. I come to rely on the faucet of the tub for the water I splash into my eyes. I take down the picture of the showering woman and substitute a newspaper cutting about the problem of getting to sleep and the problem of knowing what needs to be done once you get there.

The second time I eat with the dental hygienist, a new fact (according to her, the simple reason you forget the things that come to you in the middle of the night—the things you think up and regard as yours to carry along into the day ahead—is that the next regime of sleep comes and demands them back) mixes itself in with older ones (her brother's freezer isn't freezing anything, just keeping things soft and damp; she sat on her aunt's deathbed, just a corner of it) and begins to lose some of its narrow value. People have children, she is already saying, to export themselves into the future, which on the face of it I know to be false.

"How many have you got?" she says.

I develop a small following among the local editors, referrals are made, I get asked to do this book and that one. For instance, a man gets around to jerking out a little history of labor unions. The call comes. Within the hour, I have picked up the galleys, begun my dingy involvement. To the hygienist, at my side in bed, I let slip the remark that one instant your life is a complete, if hard-to-see, accumulation of people and all the wrong ideas about them, and then you're already halfway through the next, garnering moment. (The limited light from the lamplet puddling on her bare leg. The unprevented oppression of her hand on my arm as I write down a page number. My tender reminder that there are ways to keep to oneself that do not entail reaching one's full length in bed.)

She is so pleased with herself for having told off the receptionist at work that she repeats the speech in its belated entirety, working wonders with a rich, accusative *you*. My preferred way of being addressed: directly, but as a substitute.

More weeks. (Mornings that get going as if by cranes, hydraulics; then movement with confidence through the long, paraded hours.) Returning one evening from a walk, I find a paper towel balled up (messagefully?) outside my door. I carry it inside, unwad it, run my eyes over its receptive cellular surface, discover no lip-smears, discolorings, notations, desquamations, gouts of mucus, modest holdings of crumbs or dirt. No communication of even the dustiest, most negligible sort. So I desert the towel on an end table. The moon at my window is glib and complete. The hygienist no longer answers her phone. I go back to baths. I find a way— transparent plastic report covers that slide over the pages, grease pencils, etc.—to bring my work along with me into the tub. My naps, when I start taking them again, are adversarial and to the point. (I come out of them cleared.) A not unforeseen sloppiness, a retaliatory inattention, eventually finds its entrance into my work. I get a call from the editor of the labor-union book. "Can you take criticism?" she says. ("As I believe I told you..." is how I have come to initiate all responses.) On the bus down, I watch a man busy himself with a snug, compatible rubber band. On the bus back, I open the folder, squint through the boscage of green question marks that shoot up at me from every page, and read what I remember having submitted:

INDEX

Daughter: approaches to the body of, 00; as baby of the family, 00; on "being fallen asleep upon," 00; on "being low on people and places," 00; on being the "slower of the two of heart," 00; on being told to "put something on those feet," 00; on being wanted on the phone, 00; on believing in "giving people their dwindling due," 00; birthplace of, 00; bonbonnière, hiding place for, 00; books, being hard on, interfering noisily with what the words said, reinforcing the punctuation with stabs of a stick-pen, "dimpling the thick, accommodating page," 00; buying more of her "rosy" soda, 00; "census" of "people not yet become," 00; childhood ploy of occulting objects in nostrils and ear canals, 00; clumsy employments of, 00; on "complications in which there are no parties involved at either end and the middle is wide open to sights and sounds," 00; consequential redness under left eye of (burned off by doctor who had to remind her to sit still), 00; cornered, 00; corrective hairstyle of, 00; "cutting others in on her injuries," 00; daybed of ("only this one with throws instead of sheets, the toilet muttering until morn"), 00; decision to be "a connective, not one of the things connected," 00; on the "detergency" of naps, 00; disagreement over whether there should be limits on how much can be spelled out on people, 00; discovery that one's pulse can be felt down around the ankle ("How many hearts does that give me now?"), 00; on disqualifying oneself from one's actions, 00; disrupture of mail delivery of, 00; on "doing things to her voice to make her sound uprooted," 00; on "doing whatever does away with dirt," 00; "dumbing" employments of, 00; dust ruffle (gift), 00; earlier trouble of, 00; "effusive" cigarette of, 00; entitlement to "bodies of knowledge accumulated during sleep," 00; on "the ethics of being asleep versus the ethics of having slept," 00; excerpta concerning the advantages the mouth has over the "other crannies," 00; excuse for recumbency ("Just resting my heart"), 00; on "facts having yet to do their job," 00; "fair enough," repeated by, 00; "faraway powder room" of, 00; fastenings of, 00; feeling of being walked rather than of walking, 00; first swing taken at parents of, 00; footage of foam rubber on which she sometimes drowsed, 00; on forgetting whether it was an alderman or a magistrate who served the papers ("It looked like legerdemain"), 00; forms of greeting, 00; game made of sitting in chair still keeping the heat of, 00; as "gazingstock," 00; glassy, almost transpicuous incisor of (unsuccessful attempt to inspect untrimmed arclet of fingernail through), 00; on going "behoovedly to work in hideaway pants," 00; "grabbiness" of, 00; handbag, inventory of contents of, 00; handholds, footsteps, stays, 00; on having the air blow right over her, 00; on having been followed night after night to the locality's movie house, and sitting in the same fusty dark through sentimental documentaries about "fatal but honest mistakes," 00; and the "heart's chores," 00; heavy lifting and, 00; "hellhole recreations" of, 00; heyday of, 00; high-school career of ("girling herself around the boys retiring behind their guitars"), 00; on how "it's not you yourself who turns nineteen, twenty, twenty-five— you *get* turned. *Dialed* forward and

therefrom," 00; on how the strip of cellophane tape captured dust and hair on the way to the page waiting to be mended (volutions of the fingerprint grimily visible in the face of the tape), 00; "husky" pillow of, 00; "huttish" characteristics of bedroom of, 00; "I have always had the best reason in the world to be afraid of my own shadow: it's of me," 00; idea for a book printed on paper specially treated and weighted so that when the book was removed from the display and browsed through, the book always fell open to the same page, 00; on the "importance" of furniture ("It elevates you"), 00; on "the incidental, auxiliary violence one might do to what has already been done," 00; "inconsolably okay," 00; insistence that "all the words available to me have already gone through too many mouths—all come out meaning the same thing," 00; "insomniac eminence" of, 00; intercrural entertainments with, 00; intervening decades of, 00; judged to be visitable, 00; kindergarten experiences of (having been told to bring in something from home to exhaust a couple of minutes in show-and-tell; having brought in the only toy she had ever cared for—a toy drive-in theater [tiny cars, a tiny projector that beamed film-stripped cartoons onto a tiny screen]; not speaking up when a boy in the class claimed the toy was his or when the teacher naturally took his part; how, that quickly, there was every way for her to go about not rising in the world), 00; kitchen of, lit by pilot light, 00; on later being told by a telephone voice to stretch her right arm out as far as it would go; then being asked, "Are you up against anything?"; then replying, "The back of the sofa"; then being told, "Slap it so I can hear it's really there," 00; laxity, 00; on "learning to live without yourself," 00; legs gone out from under, 00; libraries, behavior in, referring to spines of books as "snouts," 00; life briefly coming to a head on, 00; "lifelikelessness" and, 00; local-calling patterns of, 00; locomotor misalignment, autodisjointure, skeletomuscular discontinuity, maladhesion, "shifting," etc., 00; long, hangy hair of, 00; malice in the way she got everything into her head, 00; on "meekening" her soda with tap water, 00; memberships in circles, 00; "mending talk" to (the "perspectival protection it probably should have brought"), 00; "mixed, disintegrating good looks" of, 00; moles, pair of, on left inner thigh, referred to as "umlaut," 00; as "monoxide blond," 00; moonless fingernails of, 00; "moseying dicks" and, 00;

mottoes of, 00; necessary music of, 00; on needing to be warned again that "people won't keep," 00; nervature of, as imagined by, 00; nicknames desired by, 00; "night-eyed, grimed, sofa-ridden," 00; nightstand drawer, inventory of contents of, 00; nosebleed hankie kept under pillow "just in case," 00; nosewings of, 00; on "not taking form on anybody," 00; "not the hand but where the hand has been," 00; on "nothing new pooling in her heart," 00; observation that "Sundayish light is seeking me out already midweek," 00; observed eating, 00; others as ringers for, 00; papeterie of, 00; parents of, constructive potshots taken at, 00; "the part of the light I am no longer part of," 00; "a parting of the ways," 00; as passerby, 00; peach fuzz of, 00; pillowcase of, darkened by wet hair, 00; on "pointless turnabouts between turning points," 00; poster of human anatomy mistaken for map, 00; procedure for dividing room into quarters, 00; proposed elevated footway for, 00; puberulent surfaces of, 00; on "pushing, being pushed, almost twenty-seven," 00; ragweed season and, 00; "rained-on" smell of inner bend of elbow of, 00; readerly behavior of (tendency to drift to the horizon of the page), 00; records of acne of, found (atlaslike notebook, a double page for each day, on the verso an oval representing the left hemisphere of her face, circles representing pimples; recto showing right hemisphere; legend at bottom explaining system of shading and crosshatching devised to indicate stages in growth cycle of each pustule ["emerging," "peaking," "receding"], everything done in faint pencilry; "like page after page of star charts"), 00; on the "reigning" voice of, growing more professive by the mouthful when the subjects must have gotten touchier, 00; remark that "the opposite of saying something still involves making way too much noise," 00; on "representing the side of humanity that fostered a fern on every stick of furniture," 00; on the "responsibility of taking on an appearance," 00; "roof falling in on," 00; room of (tenpenny nail protruding from wall at eye level of, resultless attempts to extract the nail, the window envelope thus impaled upon it as a warning), 00; "rug pulled out from under," 00; on "running down a day in the solid clarity of the town, holding only the most lulling of things against each other," 00; on running into people met during former educations, 00; "rushed and rubbishing" months of, 00; "scenic cosmeticism" of face of, 00; on the "scrattle" of a neighbor's snow shovel on the sidewalk out front, 00; seat cushion of, 00; "self-eclipsing" manner of entering a room, 00; self-spectatorship and, 00; sheltering car of, 00; "shingled heartwreck" of a house of, 00; shower-curtain pattern, 00; shown to have typing ability, 00; sightlines of, from bed and desk chair, 00; on sinking one's heart into, 00; in slacks, 00; as sneak, 00; soilures of, 00; "speaking against the language," 00; spoken ill of, 00; "spurning bed" of, 00; as stacker, boxer, bagger, shelver, 00; status of neck of, 00; storm-felled tree branches compared, playfully, to antlers, 00; stretch of wall between hamper and dresser of, 00; on styling more and more feeling into her morning farewells, 00; subclothes of, 00; on sudden kisses in the car ("smushy and considerate, but only at first"), 00; at table, 00; taking the sun, 00; telephone as a "calamity of black plastic," 00; telephone, misdescription of the "strainer" of the "talk cup," 00; telephone personality of, 00; temptation to concede that "the world sorts itself out into people stuck to their stories and people walking scantedly up the stairs to put out," 00; tendency to be hard on acquaintances the second time they are run across on any given day, 00; as tireless obliterator of the hours before bed, 00; toiletries preferred by, 00; trouble with throwing things out (there not being a sense of anyone on the receiving end to acknowledge the arrival of any particular piece of trash, the desire for the process of disposal to be a "requited act," for things not so much to disappear as to be "put in the way of" somebody else, the necessity for such a person to know what was someone else's at some point, reassurance of something's having changed hands, etc.), 00; in the tub, 00; "underhouse," tablet sketchings of, 00; "unmixed" with others, 00; on "the unseen world as an apology for the seen," 00; venation of (face and neck), 00; verification that "it starts when you discover that you can keep yourself at arm's length: you practice conducting your life at farther and farther reaches from the body—except you do not want to be allowed any longer to get away with calling it a body (which would be an arrogance) and insist instead on being required to regard it at most as a *steadiment*: the station, that is, which the heart, the mouth, the eyes, etc., can be said (variously) to occupy, to be the 'guest' of, or to trespass upon," 00; visitor book discovered, 00; voice of, said to "desert" the mouth, 00; on the "wayside tendency to let things just pale," 00; "The well-made bed is always fuller of discoveries than the blowzy one," 00; "Whatever you eat, just make sure you look it over real good before you eat it," 00; where found, 00; window coverings sought by, 00

I get myself roped into further jobs: product assembler, loss preventer, Clerk Typist II. The way the other passengers on the bus keep bringing up what they had for lunch in thrifty, time-killing esophageal aftersurges, I discover, by accident, that I can fetch the tastes, the flavors, of things I once ate at her side, things we swallowed together when she was still in school. I become a specialist in summoning the tang of cheap, bygone candy. I bring the taste back, release it from what has long been claiming it, then waft it out of my mouth and into the already spoiled air. I accomplish this extramolecularly and with a contempt for whatever minimal physiology it requires. People—for some reason men, especially—sense what I am up to, take a liking to what they are inhaling, reseat themselves by hopeful, discreet stages. Before the bus reaches their stops, some of the men ask me to spit onto little scrips of newspaper, which are then folded and secluded into sports-jacket pockets, for later. One afternoon, a man who has taken the seat next to mine starts thinking aloud about how long he has set store by a waxen variety of hollow chocolate, with a stalish pallor, or bloom, all over it—and I remember a marked-down, end-of-season bunny I bought her one year, and I bring the far-off, hushaby savor of the chocolate up into the trough of my mouth and fit my lips punctually, resuscitatively, onto his.

.

I Looked Alive

A WOMAN WITH NO MIDDLE NAME

I had not come through in either of the kids. They took their mother's bunching of features, and were breeze-shaken things, and did not cut too far into life.

They were out in the yard, often as not, standing childheartedly and hasteless near something barely coming up beyond the fence.

But had I at least put myself across in my wife? I had twenty years on her. They were packed down so hard on the two of us, those decades, that it was all but murder to get even so much as an arm moving concernedly away.

I should be saying what her draws were instead of what they drew me toward.

One day, in other words, I chose the toll road on my way home from work and pulled over at a rest stop. I began mixing with the men in the toilets there, tapping them for their hourly saps.

Stalls they were called, and how fitting, because they were structurally apt for delay, detainment, holding over. I started dashing off a private life for myself inside.

One afternoon I go in one and there's a hair kinkled up from the rim of the bowl, stuck. It's an upshooting thing that I pluck and take into freakful consideration.

I travel a little of its crinkled, coiling span.

Somebody tries the door, is not persistent enough.

From the next stall comes the beginning of a plea.

I go visit.

This one is keen-haired, wide-kneed. Wants me to piss justly but off-aimedly between his parted legs where he sits.

I'm not lacking a knack for anything this chummy with a scrawny, lopsided cock.

Then there's talk.

Him: Some days the whole world lags and withholds.

Me: Everything makes a point of taking itself down a peg.

Him: Other days, you see straight up through the hours to where things might still have a chance of getting started.

Once he's gone, I sit a little, wiped. Through the open rectangle beneath the door, I take note of the blind, dodgy society of passing shoes and trouser cuffs. Now and then there is a giveaway, interested pause.

The next one in has cleansed himself first at the sinks.

When I start on him, the hair on his arms is still wet, streaked flatly, linily, across the skin. By the time we part, it has gained back its upreach, its fluff.

My wife comes clarifiedly to mind:

My love for her has surely got to be *convex*.

I mean, there might as well be a dome I keep seeing put over it.

It's underneath, booming unharmed.

My wife: the way, in bed, undressed, she bent the lower leg back against the upper one gave you, where they met in a line, the thin, shy, wibbling mouth of it. A dolphin it was, or a porpoise— whichever. She was good at getting forms and shapes to come out on her like that.

But I do not want to make her out to be anything other than a wife who mostly hoarded herself and now and again insisted on knowing something of the world's trickier wordings.

E.g.: *I got up on the wrong side of the bed.*

The bed, I tried explaining, is more widespread than either of us can ever have reason to hope to know. The whole mattressy vastness of it gets zoned and rezoned and terrained anew while you doze. Step off of it come morning and don't expect to be certain of what all you're deserting.

I pointed at sheets impressed topographically by our pokes, our tossings:

Empire after empire we had turned our backs upon.

The attendant? There was sometimes more than one. I worked up a gaunt understanding with each. I explained my indisposition as a collapsion, an intestinovesical circumstance, that obliged me to make a prolonged, daily stop about halfway home. I was sorry to make their lives harder, even offered to fill out the cleanup-schedule checklist posted by the hand-dryers if they ever felt like blowing off their hourly rounds. How I marvelled at those charts, the narrow rectangles taking the day so completely to pieces.

Today a kid I figure for someone newly torn off—still fresh, I guess, from having the news finally broken to him. He's nervous but clean-breathing in a T-shirt relieved of sleeves. Just blond frizzle under his arms, rimmed by deodorantal chalk. I tell him that whoever she was, he'll be burying her beneath whichever one he'll have under him next.

What comes to hand is on the order of tears, only clingier, better condensed.

I place the taste: chlorine.

I go home and fish for compliments.

What's sauce for the goose is sauce for the gander.

We will both see need, I tell her, of sneaked flavorings and creams—worthful droplings pestered from whatever is hardest put on some other body.

That night a leg of hers shoots up in her sleep and keeps itself aloft, playing, I gather, at departure.

One evening I put in some time as the father and treat the kids to budget golf. We take to the welcome, vivid obstacles, the flimsy windmill, the slopping low waters of the moat. You don't get to pick your ball out of the final hole. It goes clanking down a pipe. This the kids decide is distress.

I find I favor the confectionary complexion of the boy. (The girl's trifling, offsprung body has already gone to the trouble of widening its pores.)

I ask after their friends. The girl names a quick, organized three. The boy doesn't come up with any. A look of annoyance looks tossed onto his face.

The migratory blemish on his arm has reached the gateway to the fingers. (But the fingernails are bright, baubled.)

The cigarette his sister finally shows me has gone much too long unlighted. (The tobacco has come unpacked. The thing sags in her lank grasp.)

Afterward, I drive them past the rest stop. I backtrack, then leave them with shallow, gaudy sodas while I drop in for my functions.

A few minutes and there's one close to me in age, a fearer first, then a negotiant, then an eye-closer certain of something coming to him. His slim face is a theater of twinges and tics, the strict hairs looking splintered into the chin. He takes some getting used to, and then my feelings for him thin.

A house is not a home.

It's just an unflattering brick-and-shingle apparatus for seeing to it that people get bulked into belittling intimacy on the unlofty proppage of furniture.

Still, something big should have happened every time I dried myself with her towel. Smitches of her dead, departed skin should have held fast to my back, my arms.

I should have felt enlarged, defended.

These men—I knew what was inquirable about most of them, and I fetched it out: modicumal indoor data about the upbringing of their dogs, setbacks and obscurities in their livelihoods, milestones in their ungreatening associations with whoever might still have had the upper hand at home.

Then some of them wanted to have something on *me.* There were three memories I circulated, all slenderly accurate.

The first, and least excludable:

My parents hit the ceiling when they found out I had not been seeing a thing on the blackboard. (All along I had been reasoning that the teacher kept going to the board and turning his back on us just as a courtesy.)

Thus the rush-job eyeglasses: I got them strutted over my ears, and watched every face break out into unbeneficial linearities, crevices, pockings. A snug indefinitude fled the world. I saw what was written up front in chalk: the tilting, calculatory digits, the names of stars and states. That was thorough enough sorrow for me for weeks.

A few times, though, I just sit in my car outside the place. A down-rolled window attracts eventual, diplomatic conversation. I invite the man in. He's deep-faced and deserving in his daintihood and modest designs. My hand joins his in his coat pocket, and then come tender knee-knocks, and in no time we are describing fundamentally the same faceful of spiteless, tolerative wife put to hazard at home. They're alike, these wives, down to the marriage marks along the stoutened back of the leg, the unshunning eyes. We're of one mind on it: eyes look better on a woman.

Then a late afternoon. From the neighboring stall, an at-long-last, loud-whispered "Nor I *you*."

He leaves, is succeeded.

The new one clears his throat.

Then: "Fewer words were never spoken."

Then: "What are you thinking?"

I give my kids a thought: had I bled them white enough to start them out all right?

As for marriage, husbandhood, wife-having: I liked variety and novelty in how I was still not quite up to the task. I no longer pried into her body, but that night I made sure I took a felt-tip marker to her knee and darkened it with just abbreviations, things we both could see.

A.M., F.M. "Against me, for me," I said.

WWII. "Wuv wou too."

H_2O. "Hate to overstay."

The second memory I get passed around in the latrines?

The twenty years I was her senior, the years just before I flopped down on her—they had not lent themselves too steadily to duration.

The calendar kept troubling the seasons with three-day weekends. Enough of their minutes would get pressed together into one hour, then another, and at long last one day got itself driven through the next.

I seemed to be the one person always seen going out for the mail.

I was a notifyee.

Then I fell on vaguer days.

Then one night it's finally her telling *me.*

No news is good news, I say.

"How wouldn't it have hurt?" she says.

I killed two birds with one stone, I say.

"Don't flatter yourself," she says. "They would've crashed into each other anyway."

The way to a man's heart is through his stomach.

"Only if you come up through the ass."

But I count on every one of them to be at least privately, illiberally, beautiful. I count on even the most foul-browed and unfingerable to admit me to at least one beautiful place.

This one has blocky teeth, a beety face.

Hair frustrated forward into a dirty-blond surge.

A juvenility to the unmuscled upper arm.

I get almost all of him out into the open before I find it: hard by the ankle bone, the charm of a scar, a volant, darksome swash looking unsettled enough, I decide, to be ready to make the crossing from his body to maybe finally mine.

And the third memory?

It was only of what sleep had been like back when dreams still briefed me for the day ahead, instead of just shaking up what little the finished one had thrown my way.

■   ■   ■

"But shouldn't we be painting the town red?" my wife is the one to be saying one night. "Don't we look like people who would be so much better off painting the whole town red?"

We're already in bed, though, and through.

Then she pulls the monthly thing out from between her legs by the string that might as well be a fuse.

Daubs a little of the warm stickiness onto the back of my arm. Sparingly, but fidgetless in her thrift with it.

"Get your clothes on," she says, and throws on a robe.

In the car, her passenger, I am of course the one to keep holding it, and I am the one who folds.

CARRIERS

Were I to keep talking about barely the one thing, which is that for too long a time I lived in the trouble between women and men without taking anywhere nearly enough of it for my own, I would humor myself at least as far as discovering, all over again, beyond example, that the thing to do with a man, the fittest way yet for a woman left like me to get a man put to rights, was to set him three, maybe four paces in advance of me on the sidewalk and let him block out what would otherwise have been my view of even more of the town—the sun-porched, shingle-thin enormity of where I was still hard up in the hours. How else to get it explained that I one day fell behind a slow-gaited man whose back was presented to me as a helpful column—a wall, practically— of broad-shouldered, long-skirted topcoat? For I walked as far as this man went, trick-stepping in back of him, letting the bulk of him give momentary concealment to a birdbath here, a mailbox there, or, farther off, samples of regional humanity, the women and measlier men, whom we could depend on to cross to the far side of the street at first sight of our staggered, our loose-coupled progress. By week's end, I had put myself permanently to the rear of this man, enrolled myself matrimonially in the confined violence by which he was taking the place out of visibility, one piece at a time, for my sake alone. He had failing, aimless hair of a muddled gray already, and a well-founded nose skewed just a trifle to the right, and an inclement complexion, and he brought a modest outlay of emotion to a house I had already filled mostly with shelving—miles of it, I would have then imagined, that ran like elevated tracks from room to faraway room. I remember a year or so of sharp smells and shared expenses and half-swallowed avowals, and then we were sudden, slapdash parents of an eyesore son. Low birth weight, premature, got up in cottons—not a girl at all. "He flatters you," the nurse said to my husband's face. "He favors *you,*" the doctor whispered shrewdly at mine. And: "I'm not just saying that." We spent a couple of months on this infant, fetching affection from its mouth, from the graspless, uncatching fingers, but it gave us up, it gave out on us, it did not stick with us for long. The director of the funeral wanted to have a word with me in a side room, not the office they usually used. He was a short, honed-looking man, condensed in his speech, and there was sordid hard candy in the footed dish he kept pointing to. He said that people, left to themselves, revolved in a very slow, a very limited circle of feeling, and, oh, how he wished that to have been clumsily loved could just this once be counted a life in itself. Then came a spoiling silence, and a silence following that, and finally he said, "I should get you to the things." I let my face color for him just a little, the way I now and then did for people in positions.

Words were a little looser now in the things I hardly said. You will want to know whether we worked, my husband and I, and the answer is an unemphasizing yes: we both had jobs, we both kept books, but in different places, for different concerns.

There was a desk I went to, a back-office destination of concentrated gray, and as a person who looked kindly on all openings, I would admit my legs into the kneehole, then fall out of my feelings long enough to nurse the numbers I worked with, getting them to hold up or, with a pencil with extra-hard lead, trapping them just beneath the surface of the ledgered page. Whenever I looked away from them, I became less and less certain of the term, the longevity, of any "hello" I might have earlier fixed upon any of my co-workers—of how long the greeting would stay in force, how long until it had to be renewed, or updated, or varied—and I sent my gaze out onto a woman, a new one, at a wayside desk, and onto her sleeve, a short, side-slit one of rayon, and the way the flesh of the arm seemed to come washing down out of it, toward me. There was a defective hour toward the end of the workday when, elbow propped on desktop, I would let any little thing, whichever had worked its way up into my sight, come between my cheek and the flat of my hand. I would thus arrive home bearing the perishable impress of the twinned, concentric circles of a cellophane-tape refill, maybe, or just the trombone-slide tricksomeness of a jumbo paper clip.

Any other husband would have said, "Let me have a look at you."

Instead, I would have to shout, "What's stopping you then?"

But I had to remind myself that my husband came from a desk of his own, a desk that constituted itself, it's true, out of unoverlapping planes, plywood sectionings, splinty and unvarnished panels, that came ramping out at him and were held up, kept aloft, by the top rails of certain cast-off folding chairs of unrivalling heights. It was on this unhelpful surface that he fitted the numberings he was good at into preset stopgap calculations. There was a hole in the left pocket of his blazer (my fault again), and much of whatever was entered into it would get sent down into a second, more deepgoing pocket, whose lower limit was some overburdened stitchwork of lining that gave out just above the blazer's woolly inner hem. In this further pocket were pencils, a rainy-day dozen of them, that tunked against one another in sheltered and futile abundance.

So we worked, yes, and kept up the sneaky peace between us. But now and again life falls due on certain parts of persons, the most tampered-with parts, the ones best centered on us—or is this something we take a vote on now, too?

Because what came next I can get to come out civilly only in numbers:

1

He found a longer, a more dissenting way to lure himself homeward at night and started smelling, I was sure, of other men: their lonesome deodorants, their waning aftershaves.

2

He acquired the same narrow stripe of mustache I had been noticing on certain of the lesser local men. (The little hairs seemed needled into the upper lip.) He began taking fresh pains with his wardrobe. Everything he now wore smelled rainily of the iron.

3

At dinner one night, a tiny slip of a bracelet, thin as thread, stole down from under the cuff of his buttoned sleeve and sent a glimmer out over his plate.

4

"No going below the heart" was the line he started using to clear my arms and keep me on my toes.

5

His things came out of the medicine cabinet and vanished, one after another, into a toiletries bag he now favored on a makeshift shelf set high above the toilet. I went after it just the one time. The zipper made a fretty, testy, *protesting* sound, a little-sister version of the full-toothed aggrievance I kept hearing from the never-ending zippers of the garment bags, half-closetfuls of them, holding his clothes in shaming separation from mine.

6

Another night: a dinner of unplanned sandwiches away from the table, and a shift, a repositioning, of his leg brought the hem of his trousers a half-inch or so above the upper reaches of his sock. In the clearance I caught the sheeny meshwork of nylon.

7

Another night—one is never through enough with one's meal— he called me "sisterfamilias," then placed a disaffiliating hand over mine.

■ ■ ■

Look: is it only the question, all over again, of how to keep yourself innovative emotionally when men have easier, dicky stuff all their own?

Because this took place back when soda still came in grave, shapely bottles—the slender ones, violently unsteady once you withdrew one from the carton and stood it up at last on the table. In this case, it was a towerlike and topplesome sixteen-ouncer that brought a fresh unrest not to the kitchen table (how could I eat?), but to an outlying one, a step table, a side table, the one I strewed with my collectings, my pertainings, my daily securities of tissue and receipts. I remember worrying my hand around the bottle and bringing the thing close enough to my face to see how chipped the glass might be around the lip. But it was the carton itself, the carrier the soda had come in, the host, with its eight flimsily flapped and tabbed cardboard compartments, that gave me ambition.

I ran out to one of those office-supply places and brought back a cheap little printing outfit, the kind that sets you to tweezering tiny rubber letters the color of brick into gutterlike slots grooved into a little wooden holder that soon enough finds itself, meanly, at the ends of your fingers. I pried open the stinking stamp pad, then stressed my message ("There are two of us to one of you") and the petty digits of our phone number onto the little dibbled squares of scratch paper that had come with the kit. Then I put myself into the car again and, making a tour of the supermarkets, shoved the paper squares into the compartments of the soda cartons, one to a carton, the outermost cartons on whatever shelf was at eye level of the adult, useless, stand-alone male.

Then of course days, the minutes pounding around in every one of them: you wait, you wait, the phone rings finally one night, and at the other end there is a voice at first untoned and already in decline, then clearing itself afresh, the words barely filling out what has to make itself get said, and then my own contribution—the crisp specifics of time, of address, and of what to watch out for on the way. Because there are people who cannot wait to be met by the airs of anyone else's house—the private, longtime vapors of the human catastrophe differently contained.

Or there's at least one such person.

Except he called back and said we should meet him instead outside a bakeshop we were to recognize, he promised, by the unsoiled upstretch of its blond brick in a close-by town that was otherwise all smudged, charmless horizontals. We thought we were early, and then a man came out, taller than either one of us, but knuckled-under-looking, all silent treatment, and he brought to his face an expression—in answer, I supposed, to one of my own— that put him nicely along, I decided, in lives he had yet to lay eyes on. Wastes of hair, curls the color of iodine, showed between the collar blades of his shirt, and I watched my husband get himself taken with the man, or take his part at least a little. There was a tiny paper bag in the man's hand, and without having to dip his fingers into it, and by means, instead, of clever manipulations of the bag from without and beneath, he worked a cookie up into the throat of it and pinched off the rest of the contents. It was a crumblish sugar cookie I reached for and took one bite of before passing it along, festively, to my husband. The man had still yet to speak a word, but my husband and I must have felt spoken to completely, for we let the man guide us across the street to the car he kept pointing to, and we let ourselves be put into finicky automotivation with him, my husband of course up in the front.

The voice that finally broke away from the man was hard on words but got it put far enough out into speech that he was strapped for companionship, and the reason was always for a number of reasons, naturally, but the one he was offering us was that he was one half, the more spacious half, of a marriage to a woman who wasn't just anybody but who was hardly a shop-lifter, either, though she had an overactive feel for merchandise— juvenile cosmetics, mostly—and knew how easily the motions of their molecules could be made to shut down until the lipsticks, the compacts and applicators, suffered a persuasive, deserving absenteeism from the pegboard wall of the store, then declared themselves with renewed materiality in the pockets of her coat. "Life isn't apportioned equally into people" was the line he said she made good use of on the store detectives, and were we ourselves willing to go along with him that far?

"Or it can go the other way around for a change, can't it?" the man said. "You two can be the ones asking *me* how it's any fairer to keep saying it's the woman who puts out when in fact she's the one taking it all in? It's the man who ends up *minus*? He's the one you see leaking all over the place?"

This voice of the man's sounded messy, squirky, from disuse, and in the rearview mirror I enjoyed a pretty decent view of the mouth it was coming from: I could see past the settlement of crowns up front to the slummy molars, packed high with fillings, and now and then get a glimpse of the gumline, a corpuscular dirty red. I was probably making saliva lap against my own gums in response.

But the man raised himself up on the subject of his grown children, a couple of "undressed, knucklekneed housebounds," and how they landed their legs on each other, and how, the way some unfortunates could throw their voices, these two had now started throwing their sight, taking in one person, toiling away at his face, while appearing all the while to be giving full, bratty regard to somebody else entirely. The man rushed us past where he had put them up in a place of their own: some scarcely windowed blockwork the hard height of two stories. But he was already remarking how you kept seeing more and more drivers advancing through traffic with the left arm stretched to full length out the side window. This was not to be taken for the stage business of lazing an arm around in the breeze or testing the sky for drops; this was high-minded dirty work—putting one tensed section of the body as far out of touch with the rest of it as you could manage in passing.

"But you two," he said, "you kids aren't up too far on any high horse yet? You're still new to the problem? You can see your way to where I am practically half the time?"

He brought the car to a stop in a garage whose door was already wide open, and we followed him through a breezeway to a kitchen, then up some stairs and past a diversity of doors, all shut, and into the room with the comprehensive bed.

Then there was big talk, all the man's, about how some people spotted easily and others could not even be bothered to wash their hands.

In the powder room off to the side, I had to make up my mind between how mushy the cake of soap seemed underneath and how smooth and solid it still looked on top. Then it was either a lank hanging of towel trapped halfway through a hoop on the wall or just tissues I could tear from a tight boxful on a shelf. I had always been rough on whatever I shuddered to think, had always lived a little in advance of my feelings, had always exempted myself from much of whatever I might have found reason to have to touch, so what else needed doing other than keeping myself reminded that to think a thing through meant only hollowing it out, letting it cave in, seeing it to a successful collapse?

By the time I reached the bed, the man had already tugged most of the dayshine out of the blinds. There was the worsening sound of persons parting themselves, sorry-leggedly, from underclothes, then my husband going for what was posted on the man at midbody, taking it into his confidence, and I going unfavoredly for the leftover mouth, which was luridly elaborative while I was still on my way but then went vague altogether once I got there.

Because this was just once more only me at my least: getting one person drawn through another, cutting myself dead in the two of them.

CHAISE LOZENGE

M onths accumulated. I was nowhere nearer female.
The look I had been shooting for? You've seen it on girls
who are studious about unpivotal things, on older young women
looking cornered already, pushing forward in unelegiac life.

Then the tresses came off. Bracelets no longer plinked on my
wrist. No more nail polish, not even the clear. A moderate overhaul
of the vocabulary—purging of qualifiers and the airier adjectives.

By this point, I was living entirely in effigy. The city made a
yellow amoeboid splash on the road map of the state. Sleep was
choppy, unproductive. My car was getting keyed. Lots of hastened
engravery on the side panels, the trunk.

I chippered up my mumping tenor with telephone-solicitor
effects, taught myself to space out my swallows, breezed through
screening interviews for temp positions as telefundraiser, tele-
activist, appointment-setter. I would get hired, pile my self and
scripts and fizzes into a cubicle, crook my long legs into a sleep-
defeating stance, then get called down after the first monitored
exchange.

I had soon made all the lateral moves allowable in my
lonesome lines of employ. "Suppose we gave you some bad news,"
a supervisor ventured one afternoon. "You're sure there would be
someone for you to really tell it to?"

Once it was only a Tuesday, but I felt already deep in the week,
through with so much that still was new, untried. In my father's
house I had a room to myself but did not reign in it. My father was
always at home. Beyond that, he was no nonpareil.

You can buy just one fork, I found out.

Or you can take the other view: that *cunt* had to be the
contraction of something, and somebody just forgot to pop the
apostrophes in.

I.e., *c'u'n't = could not.*

Because I couldn't.

"Meaning now you can?" one of them—the women—was first to ask. People talked about the airs this one gave herself, and I sometimes did do her the favor of picturing an essenced mist adrift above her head, some ozone she alone had. I should have been able to bat it away, get it to settle over somebody else, let it drizzle down onto this or that walkaway replacement, who would enrich me or finish me off.

The next one went about in low-hanging sweaters and was a cherisher, true, but there was always something probationary in her regard for whatever she cherished. There was a fine-lined signature of hair on the backs of her hands.

Then my father's heart got backed up. Things weren't getting into it, or out of it afterward—there was one stoppage or another. I should know the words.

When he died, I handled everything with the local paper. I sat at the kitchen table with the dummy résumé I had only weeks earlier freed from a library book. I beefed up his education, work history, community service. The obit ran the next day with just one misprint: "chaise lozenge."

After the burial, a buffet at my mother's. My sister was there with her peer—not the one she married but the woman one. They insisted I come stay with them. I became known as the perfect guest because of how good I got at sponging mouth-marks off the glasses.

PEOPLE SHOULDN'T HAVE TO
BE THE ONES TO TELL YOU

He had a couple of grown daughters, disappointers, with regretted curiosities and the heavy venture of having once looked alive. One night it was only the older who came by. It was photos she brought: somebody she claimed was more recent. He started approvingly through the sequence. A man with capped-over hair and a face drowned out by sunlight was seen from unintimate range in decorated settings out-of-doors. The coat he wore was always a dark-blue thing of medium hang. But in one shot you could make out the ragged line of a zipper, and in another a column of buttons, and in still another the buttons were no longer the knobby kind but toggles, and in yet another they were not even buttons, just snaps. Sometimes the coat had grown a drawstring. The pockets varied by slant and flapwork. The father advanced through the stack again. His eye this time was caught in doubt by the collar. A contrastive leather in this shot, common corduroy in that one, undiversified cloth in a third. And he was expected to make believe they were all of the same man? He swallowed clumsily, jumbled through the photographs once more.

"But you'll still have time for your sister?" he said.

Her teeth were off-colored and fitted almost mosaicwise into the entire halted smile.

A few nights later, the younger. A night class was making her interview a relation for a memory from way back and then another from only last week. He was not the best person to be in recall, but he thought assistively of a late afternoon he had sat at a table outside a gymnasium and torn tickets off a wheel one at a time instead of in twos and threes for the couples and threesomes. He had watched them file arm-in-arm into the creped-up place with a revived, stupid sense of how things ought to be done. A banquet? A dance? He never stayed around for things.

He saw his words descend into the whirling ungaieties of her longhand.

"And one from just last week?"

Easier.

At the Laundromat, he had chosen the dryer with a spent fabric-softener sheet teased behind inside it. He brought the sheet home afterward to wonder whether it was more a mysticization of a tissue than a denigration of one. It was sparser in its weave yet harder to tear apart, ready in his hand when unthrobbing things of his life could stand to be swabbed clean.

(He watched his daughter wait a considerate, twingeing minute before she set down the tumbler from which she had been sipping her faucet water.)

"Your sister's the one with the head for memory," he said. "You ever even once think to ask her?"

Most nights, the man's hair released its oils into the antimacassar at the back of his chair. The deepening oval of grease could one day be worth his daughters' touch.

He got the two of them fixed in his mind again.

The older went in for dolled-up solitude but was better at batting around the good in people. Her loves were always either six feet under or ten feet tall because of somebody else.

The younger was a rich inch more favored in height, but slower of statement. Men, women, were maybe not her type. But she was otherwise an infatuate of whatever you set before her—even the deep-nutted cledges of chocolate she picked apart for bits of skin.

They had tilted into each other early, then eased off, shied aside.

Then they were wifely toward him for a night, poising curtains at his streetward windows, hurrying the wrinkles out from his other good pants, running to the bathroom between turns at his dirt.

The older holding the dustpan again, the younger the brush—a stooped, ruining twosome losing balance in his favor.

They were on the sofa afterward, each with a can of surging soda.

"Third wheel," he said, and went into his bedroom to sit. Were there only two ways to think? One was that the day did not come to you whole. It was whiffled. Things were blowing out of it already. Or else a day was actually two half-days, each half-day divided into dozenths, each dozenth corrugated plentifully into its minutes. There was time.

He sat, stumped.

When he looked in on them again, they had already started going by their middle names—hard-pressed, standpat single syllables. Barb and Dot.

The next couple of nights he kept late hours, pulling his ex-wife piecemeal out of some surviving unmindedness. The first night it was only the lay of her shoulders.

On the next: the girlhood browniness still upheld in her hair—a jewelried uprisal of it.

The souse of the cologne she had stuck by.

Budgets of color in her eyelids.

The night it was the downtrail of veins strung in her arms, he had had enough of her for him to reach at least futilely for the phone.

It was the younger's number he dialed.

It was a different, lower voice he brought the words up inside of. She had never been one to put the phone down on a pausing stranger.

"People shouldn't have to be the ones to tell you," he said.

One night, he went over their childhoods again. Had he done nearly enough?

Their mother had taught them that you can ask anybody anything, but it can't always be "Do I know you?"

That you had arms to bar yourself from people.

That you had to watch what you touched after you had already gone ahead and touched some other thing first.

That the most pestering thing on a man was the thing that kept playing tricks with how long it actually was.

For his part, he had got it across that a mirror could not be counted on to give its all. Should they ever need to know what they looked like, they were to keep their eyes off each other and come right to him. He would tell them what was there. In telling it, he put flight and force into the hair, nursed purpose into the lips, worked a birthmark into the shape of a slipper.

Each had a room to roam however she saw fit in either fickleness or frailty.

Rotten spots on the flesh of a banana were just "ingrown cinnamon."

The deep well of the vacuum cleaner accepted any puny jewelry they shed during naps.

The house met with cracks, lashings.

They walked themselves to his chair one day as separates, apprentices at the onrolling household loneliness. The older wanted to know whether it was less a help than a hindrance that things could not drop into your lap if you were sitting up straight to the table. The younger just wanted ways to stunt her growth that would not mean spending more money.

When they were older, and unreproduced, he figured they expected him to start taking after them at least a little. So he now and then let his eyes slave away at the backs of his fingers in the manner of the younger. He raised the older's keynote tone of gargly sorrow up as far into his voice as it deserved when it came time again to talk about his car, any occult change in how the thing took a curve.

Some nights he saw his ex-wife's face put to fuming good use on each of theirs. His failings? A waviness around all he felt bad about, a slovenry mid-mouth. Before the layoffs: timid, uncivic behaviors that went uncomprehended. (Tidy electrical fires, backups downstairs, wastepaper calculations off by one dimmed digit.)

From where they had him sitting, to see a thing through meant only to insist on the transparency within it, to regard it as done and gone.

But adultery? It was either the practice, the craft, of going about as an adult, or there had been just that once. Poles above the woman's toilet had shot all the way up to the ceiling, hoisting shelves of pebble-grained plastic. The arc of his piss was at least a suggestion of a path that thoughts could later take. He went back to the bed and found her sitting almost straight up in her sleep. Her leg was drawn forward: a trough had formed between the line of the shinbone and some flab gathered to the side. It needed something running waterily down its course. All he had left in him now was spittle.

At home afterward: unkindred totes and carryalls arranged in wait beside the door. He poked into the closest one to see whose clothing it might be. His fingers came up with the evenglow plush and opponency of something segregatedly hers. A robe, or something in the robe family.

One night he paid a visit to the building where the two of them lived on different floors. First the older: buttons the size of quarters sewn at chafing intervals into the back panels of what she showed him to as a seat. He had to sit much farther forward than ordinarily. He gave her money to take the younger one out for a restaurant supper. "How will I know what she likes?" she said. Then two flights up to the younger, but she was on the phone. A doorway chinning bar hangered with work smocks blocked him from the bedroom. The bathroom door was open. Passages of masking tape stuck to the plastic apparatus of her hygiene had been left uncaptioned. Everything smacked of what was better kept to herself. When she got away from the phone, he gave her money to pick something nice out for her sister. "But what?" she said. "You've known her all your life," he said. "But other than that?" she said.

No sooner did he have the two of them turning up in each other's feelings again than his own days gave way underneath.

The library switched to the honor system. You had to sign the books out yourself and come down hard when you botched their return shelving. (He gawked mostly at histories, portly books full of people putting themselves out.) He recovered a gorge of hair from the bathroom drain and set it on the soap dish to prosper or at least keep up. There were two telephone directories for the hallway table now—the official, phone-company one and the rival, heavier on front matter, bus schedules, seating charts. You had to know where to turn. He began breaking into a day from odd slants, dozing through the lower afternoon, then stepping out onto the platform of hours already packed beneath him. It should have put him on a higher footing. He started collecting sleeveless blouses— "shells" they were called. Was there anything less devouring that a woman could pull politely over herself? The arms swept through the holes and came right out again, unsquandered. He tucked the shells between the mattress pad and the mattress and barged above them in his sleep.

The younger stopped by with an all-occasion assortment of greeting cards from the dollar store. She fanned them out on the floor so that only the greetings would show.

"Which ones can't I send?" she said.

"What aren't you to her?" he said.

"I'm not 'Across the Miles.'"

"Mail that when you're at the other end of town, running errands."

Then the movie house in his neighborhood reduced the ticket price to a dollar. It was a frugal way to do himself out of a couple of hours. He followed the bad-mouthing on-screen or just sat politely until it was time to tip the rail of the side door.

He became a heavier dresser, a coverer.

The older called to say that while the younger was away, she had sneaked inside to screw new brass pulls into the drawer-fronts of her bureau.

"It'll all dawn on her," she said.

Before the week wore out, the two of them came by together one night, alike in the sherbety tint to their lips, the violescent quickening to the eyelids. Identical rawhide laces around their necks, an identical paraphernalium (something from a tooth?) suspended from each. Hair toiled up into practically a bale, with elastics. High-rising shoes similar in squelch and hectic stringage. They were both full of an unelevated understanding of something they had noticed on TV—a substitution in the schedule. He had noticed it too. It hadn't improved him.

They were holding hands.

Each finger an independent tremble.

He had to tell them: "This is not a good time."

How much better to get the door shut against them now!

His nights were divided three ways. This was the hour for the return envelopes that came with the bills. The utilities no longer bothered printing the rubrics "NAME," "STREET," "CITY, STATE, ZIP" before the lines in the upper-left corner. The lines were yours to fill out as you wished.

Tonight: electric.

_____

_____

_____

He wrote:

Who sees?

Who sees?

Who sees?

The night his car had to be dropped off for repairs, the older one offered to give him a ride home. He faced a windshield-wiper blade braced to its arm by garbage-bag ties. Come a certain age, she was saying, you start thinking differently of the people closest to hand. You dig up what you already know, but you turn it over more gently before bringing it all the way out. It might be no more than that she catches a cold at every change of the seasons. But why had it taken you this long to think the world of it?

He started listening to just the vowelly lining in what she said. He skipped the casing consonants that made each word news. It was carolly to him, a croon.

The daughters had wanted their ceremony held in the lunchroom where they worked. Other than him, it was only women who showed—a table's worth of overfragrant, older co-workers. The officiating one, the day supervisor, first wanted to run down her list of what she was in no position to do. It was a long, hounding list of the "including but not limited to" type. (This was not "espousage"; it was not "conjuncture"; it was "not in anywise matrimoniously unitudinal.") Then she turned to the daughters and read aloud from her folder to steepening effect that no matter where you might stand on whether things should come with time, it was only natural for you to want to close up whatever little space is left between you and whoever has been the most in your way or out of the question all this long while, and let a line finally be drawn right through the two of you on its quick-gone way to someplace else entirely. Nobody was twisting your arm for you to finish what you should have been screaming your lungs out for in public since practically day one.

The kiss was swift but depthening.

Then the reception. He was a marvel for once, waving himself loose from the greetings and salutes every time he realized anew that they were intended for the person beside him, or behind.

FINGERACHE

Have you ever known me to be anything other than a woman shitty years of age but still standing by as much as I had lived of it, listening to her air the last of her intelligence on the family dirt, letting her butter me up for once the way she should have always? Because the day after the funeral it was her husband coming down to my level and wanting me to tell him whether he was saying it right—that since I knew where the things were kept and was up on the kids' chance triumphs at the chalkboard and their sizes in whatnot, wasn't I the one to have a go in what was left unstained of her clothes? (There was a cap-sleeved dress I could try on in the bathroom already.) But give him credit, I guess, for being the kind of man who kept his body set back a little from how he would have otherwise come across. It took effort to pick out just how off-base the hair was or to get an influential view of the minnowy mustache or, lower yet, a violet vein close to gaining the surface of his upper arm. I must have turned to him anew, this time with a more mature, closing eye.

Look: it's hardly as if I hadn't already put myself through marriages all my own—marriages small, it's true, of their kind. Which is to say it's a shit list I could be giving you now, a fecal census of bodies that were little more than backdrops for sickling emotions, though it was the emotions I remembered afterward, not the shapes of the men or anything else physically exclusive to them. I will bring up only the one I keep throwing in my face: he was a man of knowledge, granted, but before long he had slaughtered most of what he knew, or he had been losing acquaintance with it all along, or else the whole of it had swung suddenly away from him something awful—whatever the case, he had to go back and look everything up again by hand. We polished our differences in a house he bought from his parents for a dollar. I stayed only long enough to be accused of hiding out in a "personality."

So yes: I'm all for assuming novel difficulty in even moodier rearrangements of one on one. This latest husband made okay money, at least, but it was money with pieces, whole corners of it, gone. The house was mostly beaverboard and ungroomed carpet and concerted backdate appliances. I looked pushily at the walls and took his mind off things in the high heat of those first few weeks. There was innuendo even in how he rinsed out a glass, then set it, mouth downward, on the drainboard. I followed him into a bed that was on casters, brought to it some haphazard adult behaviors of my own. A low-lying smell was as much as he got out of me at first. Nights were fringed with the few things he said— "Far be it from me," "Not a day goes by."

One by one the children sought me out with pissy sorrows. The oldest said it would help if she knew who it was she was growing up for, and I said in that case, then, a way would have to be cleared for such a person. For a few days she started picking up after herself and was a little more wide-going in her affections. (A run of goodwill sometimes ran through her partway.) The middle child usually let a silence mature around her but now and again complained of shooting pains, of fingeraches and daintier misfunctions. These I told her to take as signs that her body had an interest in her and was making definite plans. (She prided herself on bringing back whatever might have rolled far beneath the furniture—her arms, her hands, were that meager already.) The youngest, a boy, was a little loose and unfortified in what he knew. He called the floor "the ground" and did not so much walk as trifle his legs forward: there were negligences, even criticisms of the filled world, in his lawless progress toward the table where supper could no longer wait.

One day, after lunch, I convened a fatherless full-house family assembly on pillows fronting the headboard of the master bed. There was copper trinketry, hobbied, untinkling, abroad on all three of the children—wristwirings, neck-hangings, anklets. None of what followed was to go beyond the room. I told them that should they ever be called upon to give the names of the parts of anything or another, it was always safe to go first with "base" and "projecture." I made it plain that I was a done-with portion of woman in the main but had once slapped along for years with arms the color of oysters. I explained that people made destinations of one another but no longer knew whom to live with; that people did not change but the spaces between them were forever going to have to. I said that as soon as they felt ready I would show them how to take any emotion and put a nice, bright costume over it. I said that you were always wrong about how it all goes wrong, because there were fewer people to put in place of the ones you had already gone aground in, and there was a shortage of places left to go on the people coming up next, but with the extra lips set out on her, a woman was never not saying something somewhere, and most of what got said was only that once you get to where your body feels hoaxed over you, you start to skip mirrors completely and just nerve your way direct to whoever else is got up as a woman or a man, and you get a good look from your eyepits at whoever it is until you're rewarded with the fate of finding your own features tugged and quirked just a little differingly onto the other's face— you're that far at large in people, a dead ringer for everyone else.

"She's saying there's no need to tell people apart?" the middle one said.

A night or two later, the man brought to our room something unsturdy and uncustomary in his face. He produced from his pants pocket a smart little packet that I at first took for the colorsome wrappage of a prophylactic, but no, when he undid the thing, I could see it was just a moist towelette. He squared it out to full size, patted it first against his cheeks, gave a fast shine to his forehead, the incline of his nose, the neck, then ran it up one forearm and down the other; and then, seeing my hand opened receptacularly, he balled the wilted thing and tossed it beyond me.

"What could be that bad?" was as conclusive a lie as I could provide.

They took me back, though, at a place where I had worked once before. There were only so many reasons for a person to be in the line of work I was in, and I had thrown myself open to all of them at one time or another. I am not denying that I found bloodshot relief in sitting at the desk again and having my lower half neatly concealed from the remainder, but my arms were forever front and center. I suffered an insinking overintimacy with the things. I would look down at the desk pad and find the arms already there: there was no way around them. I started going out of my way to convince myself that the arms were no more than delegates of a commanding intelligence and not the intelligence itself. But there they were again, ahead of me on the papers; I was trailing behind. For a while I went in for longer, broader sleeves. Then I started taking things out on the arms themselves. Bought a watch with a wide strap that did away with an inch and a half of the left one. Arranged a formation of bandages to the left of the strap. Excited a patch of the right forearm with an ink eraser until I had provoked a brush burn of sorts. Slickened that with a discoloring preparation. Teased the little hairs off both arms until the skin went red. I made as many examples of them as I could slowly manage. When you're doing yourself out of a life, I guess, the arms are always the last to go.

UNCLE

S he was a milk-warm girl in bad odor with herself, glad to have at last come down in the world. So she undoubled herself from the boyfriends, the girlfriends, to better herself under my roof. Mornings, she would struggle to the kitchen faucet and put a finger to the underside of the spout. There was usually enough water still hanging from it for the finger to come away with a big, rudimentary drop. This she would use to loosen the crumbles of sleep from the corners of her eyes. Breakfast was just soda she stirred bubbleless with a paper straw.

I was the one stuck making the bed. I would interrupt myself only long enough to raise a fingertip of her silverous lipstick from the tube, then with rushed reverse turnings send it down again.

Afternoons, the sky volunteered its birds and its sun-showers. We would be out on the patio again, each with a rubble of white chocolate in a ruffled paper baking cup. The one skymark was a radio tower, laddery and ablink.

Anything, she kept demanding, is the seat of a passion.

I would have to remind her, counteringly, that you don't pick the person who fronts your life—you *get* picked, you watch the picker's ankles vanish into the scrunched socks afterward (his whole body going blank behind the blue-black of the uniform), and the picker goes off in the starkest of transportations: you keep an ear cocked ever after for the return of his van and its paraphernalian clatter in the gravelled driveway.

You might consider chumming away at somebody your own age, she would say. Or who's hailing now from whom?

I would answer that we come by our austere perversions and then do our best to get out from under ourselves.

She wore her T-shirts in wearied, vanishing colors and would hold my hand retardedly in public. A short-streeted city was a habitual drive away. We would arrive just in time for the waning daytime plenty along the one horizontal avenue. We would walk around the people. The local public! They all had the look of having been made too much of already—each citizen a subsided mystery with hard feelings and staying power.

Afterward, restored to the house, close-piled on veers of the sectional sofa, we would haze each other into a shared, mutual nap. Her lips allotted little to mine, but there were always fresh runs of emotion inside.

We could wait until later to watch whatever got passed into the cars of the boys and then out through whichever of the girls the boys would prefer not to leave deluded.

Her own heart never once cracked down.

EMINENCE

T here was a time I would not hear of women, and a time I looked to them as my betters, and months when my heart went out to anyone done up as a person, but it was usually men I suited: men who liked to keep their words a little stepped back from their meanings and mostly wanted to know whether I was still in school or was hard on shoes. I would awaken to the poundings of one or another of them taking his elbowing ease in the shower stall. The bedside table would of course hold quarters, and a lone dime, out-of-date and valued-looking, and no doubt a patched-up, gadabout ten-dollar bill—I guess the test was simply how much I would be just the sort of boy to take. So I would let pocket change of my own drop to the floor in what I counted on amounting to an answering reproof, then top it with a spruce twenty. I would usually think better, though, and pick everything up, his and mine together, and disappear into my clothes and be gone before he was dry. Still, I suspect that I went unrepresented in much of what I ever did, if I get my drift even now.

There was a father, for instance, who wanted me to help save his daughter from him, or else he wanted to be saved from *her*— at some point I gave up keeping track of the ones I had been a party to seeing spared. There was a drumble of TV noise from the apartment below; that much is still with me. And he ticked off the points of nervy resemblance: upraised veinage, standout nose, teeth looking stabbed into the gums, arms unfavorable for even the joke sports. A broth of sweat came off him, and I hate it when they talk right into your mouth, but he kept it up until he convinced himself there was nothing set out between my legs other than whichever mishmash he figured on being a lot like hers. (At the time of which I write, circa my youth, there still were glories to be brought out in people behind their backs.) Weeks later I was introduced to the girl at some function I showed for. She was clean-lined, nothing new or unearthly—a desponding thing in a shirtdress, looking care-given and sided with beyond her years. The father was at the steam table, turning over the local foods. He had a tousled smile. "It's like you never left," he said.

I had been staying with four or five others on the top floor of a three-story sublet. Freaks of drapery to keep us from the morning sun, double-strength cosmetics and pills of the moment in handbags nailed shoulder-high to the wall—it hardly helped that this was in one of those little cities that had been thrown down at the approaches to a much bigger one once enough people were pinched for time or too moody for a commute. The town had already run afoul of its original intent, and there was a misgiven majesty to the newer, upstrewn architecture that left people flimsier in their citizenship, less likely to put their foot down. So we walked ourselves into recognizability in and around the plazas, the pocket parks, the foremost shrubberied square. You could run your feelings over one person and get them to come out on somebody else a little distance off. There was no need to even come face to face to be stuck in a failing familiarity forever.

People eventually answered any purpose or were no skin off my nose.

There was Joeie: clean-tasting but a trace too saline. Colored easily, needed his full eight hours every night, believed in taking each of his meals in public. His loves were drugstore luxuries and the fitting instant you knew for sure that something was finally finding its way down the wrong pipe. But sometimes the rope I woke up with around my ankles and wrists was only laundry line, and the knots were not even all that serious.

And Tarn: he was either off doing somebody a wonder or having something further burned away from his complexion— you looked for the underlying advisory in his motions and let the whole of it loll in your understanding for a while. Nights I found the key to his car, there was a minor toll bridge I could have just as soon avoided, but I liked surrendering the warmed quarters to the collection attendant in the booth, his arm a sudden, perfected thing of the open air.

It was the night Tarn was first threatening to move out that an ex of his came across with a car trunk's worth of guitars. These were junk guitars, folksinger styles, with the strings raised penalizingly high above the fretboard. He wasn't satisfied until one was strapped onto me and he had his hand spread over mine to depress my fingers and get a few clunked chords going steadily. When he started to sing, the better part of the lyrics reminded you that with a stepmother and a stepsister, the prefixes alone, if you bothered to do even any of the thinking, made it all but expected of you to walk all over these women and, if you were still up to it, climb them stairwise to a height from which their originals might at least look easier to buy for, easier to mistake for two good eggs. It's not that I mind it when a pack of lies with real effort behind it gets pitched way over my head to somebody reliably cruel at a remove. But the song was going on and on, with too much chorus between verses. He later offered to make it up to us by driving everybody to a party in the city. There was a kid there with an isolative refreshment, something he alone had been given to eat. His fingers kept bringing it up from a plastic sandwich bag opaque with condensation. I was among the least encouraged to get an arm lilting leanly toward him. One or another of us stayed in touch with him for months afterward in notes that amounted to mostly "More soon."

I do not want to make it seem as if this is all we ever did. There was a neighbor lady's dog we agreed to feed when employments led her away. He was one of those full-natured, kerchiefed dogs that liked being bossed around. Days it fell to me to fill the dish, I did not so much call his name as thin it out to the scanty inner vowels, but the dog would still put in a complete, hustled appearance. I would watch him eat, take advantage of his company, draw myself out about things, any part of life I no longer was any part of, just to get listened to without bias or retention. There were also some weak-willed plants to be doused if I thought of it, and dresses that were all too tight on me and seemed to smell of more than just one person.

As for women overall, though, I went along with what Lorn had said about how they were set deeper within themselves and moved about reproductively in a world spaciously different from ours but sharing the same sorry places to meet up for a bite. And there was nothing to be held against any of them, either singly or in the dissatisfied aggregate, even if you now and then had somebody's sister coming forward with rundown makeup and a mugginess to her arms to tell you that the only reason you were a waiter instead of a grill man was so you could stand above people in seated couples and make a living looking down your nose. (There were only so many things you could say in return that would come across as both the truth and a dig. I had worked up enough of them to put into conservant, fallback rotation, but lately I just pointed to my groin and explained that if we give them names, it's because they spring from us, we bring them up, we're forever wiping their snotty little mouths.)

So what's left? The only other question still worth entertaining should not have to keep being only "Who else?"

Which I take to mean that the answer can't be parents, or even brothers and sisters, because we all were done with practically the exact same ones. Mother would signal the end of the conversation by saying she could feel inside her skull the precise contours of the space a headache would require, though she did not yet have the actual headache. Father had grown a beard that was more like a black cloud loitering in front of his face. (The beard was purposely mostly air.) The sister or brother was younger and had to have it drilled again and again into the head that it was one house if you came into it from the back and a different one altogether if you came in from the front: the people were the same, they were nice to you to your face, but nobody was being fooled: no one was living here everlastingly.

So that leaves whom else? Kittrick? Reese? Malin?

Or is this the one time the question becomes only "What other bones do you have in your body?" or "Where are you going to go with all those clothes?"

Because the answer could then be nothing more personal than that at the rebounding municipal college I was a figure of considerable scholastic mystique because I looked over my notes before the quiz and tried not to seem cross when the chairs had to be pushed back into a circle. The late-afternoon section of the summer course in speech was mostly boys, because it was mostly boys—repeaters, sweet-naturedly tardy, rug-burned in their undershirts—who had trouble sticking to their points and making it even as far as the middle minute of the three-minute impromptus. But when my turn came, I was slower-hearted in walking them all through how I saw it: that I was not the good listener everyone kept insisting I was, but I liked hearing people out the way I expected balloons to be quick about losing their air—I wanted the breathy, informative smell on their mouths right afterward; that the busy signal doesn't always have to sound like bleedbleedbleedbleedbleed; and that I could kick myself every time it did not come out to even so much as a syllogism no matter how often I got it stacked up onto the three needful tiers:

Major premise: You go with whatever is most available on people.

Minor premise: On men it is an eminence that luckily never lasts.

Conclusion: Except there was a farmers' market open only a couple of nights a week, and I could pick out the one to follow from a produce stand and into the men's room. There was just the one stall, and the latch was broken; it was up to me to lean against the door to keep up the privacy. Then the unzipping, and we were standing a polite foot apart, my arms retired now behind my back, his eyes already more wishless than mine. We let the things shy off from ourselves, boggle out the way they always did, twitch and dodge and stickle a little, until they were kissing unassisted. It was out of our hands, or none of our doing, and I could afterward witness the differences from me amassing in him almost instantly.

SPILLS

The youngest of the girls had proposed herself out of the least promising of bodies and had ever after let her life take its line from the coercive slants and downturns of her sisters. She could go through their wastebaskets and find, hived away in envelope after envelope, discarded wafers of soap that were tongue-shaped from gloried use. These she could press against her oiling forehead until they stuck.

It was a town in which a night sky showed through the streets and trouble was often missing from things. To be fair, the only boys were sulkless local pollutables. Whichever one of them picked up the phone when she called would right away reach for anything close by to eat—suddenly unforgotten breakings from a pretzel, if need be, or jellied candies of abrupt magnitude. She would listen to the boys' encompassing swallows and take further swift steps against herself.

She became a forthputting girl of mixed intent.

Beyond the sweep of low-peaking buildings lived a boy about her age who had been held back one too many grades. With a slip of her heart, the girl would tug at the sails of the shirt that had been tucked too constrainingly into the boy's waistband. "Blouse it," she would say, and her hands went to work. She folded a cuff onto each of the red socklets the boy had been made to wear with the loose, flared shorts. His saliva was easy enough to elicit, and in it she could at least enjoy a loneliness to her taste, briny and warm, conclusional. She would pass the boy's stubbed, unfirm fingers inside her as far as they could be made to go.

Breadthless days piled everyone closer to the fall. The girl turned old enough to work, but the employee entrance was sticky and hard to get through with her handbag and magazine and snack. Her boss was a downtaken, suitorly man married full well. She returned home every evening to the expectable little pool of lucid soup that had been set out for her at the table.

She would let things faze her one at a time.

She would settle alertly for things.

The fingery disposition of bananas in a basket.

The way the high-set window cropped the crown of a tree.

The cuticular bloodiness to her hands; vague shinings in the nails.

Some nights she would come home to find a money order from her father, or another of the letters full of smart-mouthed affections, bruising tributes. He wrote of "rural torments," of "tumbles taken out of court," but would be "returning anon to resume certain backhanded familiarities under the mackerel skies of our town."

One afternoon her boss was fresh from a haircut. Slashes of gloomful hair still stuck to his forehead, were visible down his neck. He was all revolt and filthied principle. He had a bone to pick with everything she did—e.g., the ruthless, valedictory business she apparently resorted to with her hands after she shut the lowermost drawer of her desk.

The rest of this just parallels anything else entirely.

Viz., she trailed him to his car and became the woman I should have been instead—quick to disappear from as much as she understood of one person, quicker to get going in whatever might be likelier of the next.

HER DEAR ONLY FATHER'S LONE WIFE'S SOLITUDINIZED, PEACELESS SON

I f, then again, I had been put on earth to hurry up and come between any noise the world might think it finally needs and whoever is fittest to produce it, who better to have been still living at home when it came time at last for hers? The day, I mean, when your best friend throws you over for an emissary from the opposing sex, and for a glorifiable afternoon your bellyaching strikes just the right note of retrenched intimacy and spite, but spite that is holding out some hope.

For we were brother and younger sister, cobelligerents on the centerpiece of a pushed-apart sectional sofa, and I told her, naturally, that when it had happened to me, the "friend" was a boy with a disadvantaging face, big and round, much of it still to be filled in, and before the day was out, I had gone sick for the first venereal do-gooder to come my way. He was a seller of house paint. He brushed the fingers of one hand down my arm, escorted me to a car, and, before I parted from him later, wanted to go over it with me one more time—the difference between *hiding power* and *coverage,* the former being the capacity of a paint to disguise that which is to be painted over, the latter merely the area at last thus treated, expressed in square inchage or however else it could still be stomached.

So I told my sister that I did not want the two of us to be wasting her day away, or holding her back from people, but she said no, there was no real rush just yet; and if, in putting her up for depiction here, I insist on having a few stippled liberties taken with the complexion, and the teeth kept completely under wraps, and the hair dinged and torn up afresh, and the sleeves drawn all the way down and buttoned beyond the wrists, the tack I am taking, please understand, is to preserve her this side of recognizability on the one hand and just shy of the very picture of forgottenness on the other. But what wooing good would it do me to keep her in anything other than the skirt that was just plain curtaining? Because sunlight had caught the line of her shinbone suchwise that the skin above it was aglow, and you don't let light like that just run off from a person, though you don't go crying it up too publicly, either. You might, at most, assure her that an hour spent in your company right now would hold its own against any hour she was likely to pass with anyone who had not come to such good-sport maturity under a common roof; and no sooner had my sister signalled shruggy agreement than she uprighted herself, set the lower leg swinging from the fulcrum of her knee, and the shining line that had got its start on her shin spirited itself out across the room to the telephone stand and let itself sink into the oaktag portfolio, the accordion-pleated clutch, that I toted about instead of a wallet.

So I got up from the sofa to claim the thing, and on the way back, having unsnapped the elastic band, then fishing around inside, bringing up a catch of fives and tens, I asked whether she had troubled to notice that people, loneful ones, had taken to writing in the margins of their currency—beseechments and pleas, mostly, to pass along—and since I am not a person who ordinarily requires a reply, I said only, "What ever shall we be writing on our very own?" I lowered myself beside her again and ventured a ten-dollar bill face-up and longwise onto the downy wealths of her leg, then inched a stick-pen between fingers of hers already spread acceptantly. There's an unpuncturing penmanship held in reserve, of course, for just such moments when there's pertinent skin—snug-pored, flushingly tender—underneath; and it was with just such leniency of longhand that she wrote, in the upper margin of the bill: "Hindsight is always 50/50!!!" I brought out a narrow-barrelled ballpoint for myself and, starting in the right margin, then working my way down and around, wrote: "I am grateful even for people whose beauty is just a sideline to how they really look." But her writing hand had already set out catchingly for the left margin before mine was entirely withdrawn.

Again: is it that one thing leads to another, or that the other has been tugging the first one forward all along? Because the instant your sister is whispering into your mouth, words lose all consonantal bounds.

They're down to just vocalic mist.

Ah-aw was as much as I could make out of it.

Back off?

Dad saw?

Paths cross.

Then years.

I saw my parents to their graves. (They went neck and neck in a November remembered mostly for the rectitude of its weather.) I moved to a close-by city with a dip in its population. (People were either accumulating attentions intended for others or picking over available holes.) There were days, though, when the dick was deputative of a clear thinker and got itself responsibly aloft: I thus married easily enough. I will shoot ahead of the peculiars of her rearing and emotionality, and report only that the woman and I prospered ammonially in close quarters, the washing machine was almost never not going, neither of us was ever got the better of in the heart-to-hearts, but I put myself out of her misery early on.

I threw in with a man about my age who made a game of losing a finger in the hairy slough at the foundation of my spine. (I could count on a separate, alkaline smell to him come morning.) Then a woman who said I looked like someone who would be good with tools. (She had lineature already around the mouth and was unrepaired overall. But I liked taking orders for a while and co-signed for the pleasant car she said her thoughtsick son required.) Next the son himself, minus the mother and motionable only in the ebb and flow of semesters. (Nights, he sat up late in a shower wrap and turned the heavyweight workbook pages. The hand I now and again admitted between his legs came out unclaimed and little different.)

So agreed: that allegiances, alliances, turned on a dime, and it was a dime that stuck to whoever's bare back was turned to me at the time, then worked itself loose and dropped to the floor so I could stoop for it and put it later toward the newspaper, the thinning local of good comfort, which ran the discount-chain ads in which I had been following the downsloping progress of an unmistakable pair of long-natured arms from sale to sale, through one set of abbreviated sleeves and then out of another, no matter that the face above got cropped and that the ink, meted out in unevenness, had blotched everything before I ever got my spattering chance.

I lived like this, yes, and took to calling everyone "Miss" for the nice emphasis it put on my failure to have made any of them even palely mine. My seniority at the office began developing tiny pockets of fallibility, creases too easily taken for weals. I lacked the criterional patina of my peers, or so it got sworn in a file somewhere. I alone was never invited to join in on even the wider-blown windfalls. A "failure to thrive," in short—unless it was some higher-up's mortuary newborn I kept overhearing them describe. The afternoon I was told to empty my desk, I dropped eventually to my knees to get the carpet smoothed underneath. I teased the tufts into a uniform, satisfying, outbound drift.

But was it only "years" I said above? For it must have been decades I meant: a couple of them—solid and volumed and columnar, though demolishable the moment someone thought to say, "If you don't mind my asking," because the oncoming question was either "How goes your sister?" or "Your dentist die?" The former I could turn my back upon in time to remind myself that the error of my ways was actually an assorting of errors, though there was only the one way, which, once I came into a sense of it as nothing more than a *route,* did not even seem to pass through any of the places where actual dirt could have been done.

But on the matter of the teeth: I concede that there were breaks, crannies, in the bulwark of cracked enamel I held my tongue behind. (Who has time to be minding bony minutiae?) I figured one or two of them must have snapped off in the thicker and gristlier of the things I ate. (Meals were taken counterside, in stand-up haste and minimized light.) Others might have backed out while I slept, then got carried away, and drowned, in deepsome overnight salivas.

So if that is all this needs to be—a behindhand recountal of a man who may have let a thing or two slide—then it might as well come to a head one day not too many months after I had settled in with somebody new (a great one he was at first for paddling the air between us with hand mirrors, fanning me with gilt-framed glimpses of everything amiss between my lips), and I got myself dressed and went out for a comparisonal look at the run of teeth in other open mouths—the layouts and lineups, their bias and skew, how snugly everything was packed into the lavish salmon of the gums.

It was early afternoon: the people about were mostly older people. I came to a dental studio with a sign welcoming emergency walk-ins. Was admitted, told to lie back and relax in the chair. It was not a dentist but an assistant; I tasted beauty soap on the instruments. She had barely begun inspection before whispering, "Oh, you didn't want to hurt anybody—is that what it was? Because these are well above the fray: ground to a fault and altogether fine. A few may have dropped below the gumline, but not for long. In short, I find much to admire. I wouldn't change a thing."

I said, "Now the dentist has a look?" She did not treat it as a question that had an answer. I went out to the receptionist's station. "They're not talking to each other," the receptionist said. I paid; was handed a receipt and then, afterthoughtfully, a much-thumbed leaflet called *You Can Hardly Even Notice*. It was printed in one of those frail, sticklike typefaces that make everything look a little religious and overpersonal. I read it on my way out.

Courtesy permits a synopsis?

A man who claims to have lost his teeth to love is walking down the sidewalk when he notices an approaching figure still several blocks off. Not a moment to lose. He stoops for some flower-bed pebbles, orders them archwise into the gutter of his lower gums, vows for now to go without swallows. Reaches next for a piece of blown-about cardboard, beneficially off-white; tears off a strip twice the length of a finger; makes thirteen tiny, halfway tears at roughly quarter-inch intervals along the lower edge; tucks the strip only far enough under the canopy of his upper lip for a curved and dividered line to achieve jaunty visibility just beneath. The approacher by now is less than one block away. It's a woman, obviously. Saliva puddles in his mouth. He smiles sloshily as she walks past, arms aswing. But how much does she see? For the tract ends on the burdenful note that, unbeknown to the man, the woman's long sleeves are stuffed entirely with kneesocks and wadded homework papers, except for mouthwash-bottle caps poking out where the elbows would ordinarily, jointedly, go; that the fingers of the glove sewn to the wrist of each sleeve are filled weightily with dampened sand; that the sandbox from which the sand was spooned belonged once to the woman's daughter, who, as a child, and still later, was a clinger, a clutcher, a tugger at the sleeve, a hand-puller, a wrist-wrencher, an arm-twister—a hanger-on, in short, who grew up to become the only person ever eligible to behold the amputatory triumph of her love.

Below the last sentence, though, the receptionist or someone else had written, reconsideringly: "There's a man in a shanty behind the old shopping center who's been doing some interesting things overnight in ceramic."

I went out there while I still had the verve to hear news I could take hard.

The door was open just a sliver. There was a worktable inside, and a washstand, and a man and a much younger woman sitting on patio chairs in front of a kiln. The man got up and moved toward me, reached into his mouth to lift out the lower crescent of his dentures, rinsed it at the washstand, then placed it in my one hand and a laminated snapshot in the other. It was a print taking in a little business district in a sunny aerial sweep; some of the buildings had been circled helpfully in red. I looked back and forth between the photograph and the shammed teeth long enough until I could let on with a nod that, yes, I had begun to make everything out—the mansard-roofed hotel memorialized, underexplicably, in the lower-left molars, and the across-town hospital in the lower right, and a limited line of commercial buildings in the lank rhomboids of the incisors, and the water tower in a plasterlike bicuspid pitched so steeply, I had to hope its upper-arch counterpart had been hollowed out to allow the man the boon, at least, of shutting his mouth without too much harm.

I set the things on the worktable, expressed admiration, then added that I thought I could probably get by with just a partial. Here the woman let out a quick little cry of affinity, and as she got up and came closer, I watched her uncatch some chainlets that were belted about zodiacally in the vault of her open mouth, fastened here and there to kernelly canines and some stumps toward the rear. She lined out four or five of the things, gleamingly, in the bowl of the man's palm: fanglements I would have anywhere else taken for overintricated fishing lures, maybe, or the contraptious miniature hardware you resorted to when nobody else's hands were steady enough to hang a picture treasured too long in secret— except there was a charm or token or two dazzled along the length of each.

The man assured me that I could go with tooth-colored ones if I wished ("You can't eat with them in, of course"), but either way I would be pleased to discover in my speech a fresh, enlivening meander. He told her to put them back in and favor us with talk. I watched the fingers hooking, reinstalling, and then, if I heard her right, she was saying, in a voice that sounded bitten away at from within: "This isn't kissing. It's just the way he goes about getting a better feel for how everything is spaced out inside." And in fact the man's tongue was already lukewarm and adart in my mouth.

Afterward, I told them there was somebody at home I would have to talk it over with first.

I am calling him my familiar here, but in sorry truth he had begun unversing himself in me almost from the outset. It was an intimacy, after all, founded on little but joint dislikes and congruent cross-purposes. Not that I was his opposite—I was more like his reverse, going back on things he was just now coming into. But his face! He had a face that had you taking sides again every time. You were expected to either fall all over yourself the moment you caught sight of the hair he had hanging in a pair of black, glossy sheets, or else woo yourself half-blind with the weak green havoc of his eyes.

He was not yet a full-fledged tailor, mind you, but freelanced in alterations to trousers that gave the wearer more play in the seat and the crotch. Men in shirttails and underpants stood stock-still for him in a room with a separate, backstairs entrance. I went up there sometimes when he was out spreading word of mouth even wider. There were pants pegged to the walls in hangered fraternities, and a couple of full-length mirrors slanted to afford a plunging perspective, because what sort of man did not need to see himself relieved of his face and that much the deeper in things? My own body got its start an inch or so north of a belt orbiting loosely, unupholdingly, in the loops, and ran itself down to the dust-hoarding creases in the vamps of my shoes. That's how I remember myself at my best, anyway—cropped at last to the lower, better half.

I hope I am speaking for more than myself, then, if I insist that when two men pool their solitudes, there is none of the ruthless, finite symmetry still said to obtain between any woman soever and a man, but only an obstructive redundancy intent on doubling itself out indefinitely. I offer as lonesome, sidewise example the fact that after we chose the house, we could never settle on a fixed purpose for any one room. You worked your way down the hall and opened any door to yet another independent setting in which to eat or lie down or hide. These are not criticisms or judgments but simply flat-out truths I have tapered just enough for them to come eventually to the point that when he brought people around at night, clients and prospects, men of a mind to leave shallow, souring impresses of themselves on somebody else's sofa for an hour, it would make little difference in which room I was keeping to myself upstairs. There would be spells of laughter, then a lone voice sending itself up through the floorboards, then sudden, unanimous inquiries about the house and whoever else might be acquaintable within. Sooner or later I would hear myself come up for description as "an old family friend getting back on his feet."

That night, I heard one of them take the stairs, treat himself to a tour, then loiter at the doorway of the room in which I had unwound myself for a nap on a much-trod gangway of a carpet runner. He came in, lowered himself to a sociable crouch, and explained, unencouraged, that when you worked for an outfit that was mostly cheatery anyway and was down now to just the two phones, you got confused about which one was ringing, though it was usually hers, so if you had already, mistakefully, reached for yours, you had to fall quick to mock-dialing, and you understandably wanted nothing more to do with the woman other than starting to dress a little like her, which meant only absorbing her ruling colors and throwing them back at her a day later in the downcourse of a scarf or the baggy vastness of a shirtfront, not out of snot-nosed deference, because it would be lost on her, but in the interest of whatever continuity that backbiting best provided as you made passage from the delicately errorful hours before lunch to the fouler hours of digestion thereafter.

By now I had been made curious enough by the man's voice, which sounded as if something were cutting into it, or costing him some crispness, that I lifted my head a little and turned his way. The teeth in the upper half of his smile looked unstationary. Not as a unit, though—these were teeth that seemed individually, isolatedly, motional and asway. I tried to push my eyes along to anything else, entertaining myself first with the campaign of gray in his stubble, then with the wire-spun consequentials of his eyeglass frames, and to be saying something I said that what's worse is when the firm is pairing off every stick of polished deadwood with a new hire behind just one door, and it's a door she covers right away with kindly cartoons and screwball newspaper cuttings, and before long you are so worried about passersby walking away in a smiling conviction of some united, craven good humor in force behind the door that you tape to it a little note saying "All postings by—" and then see that her name gets a large-lettered outspelling in marriage-hyphened, horse's-ass entirety.

But who doesn't know when it's only his mouth being talked to, and whatever is most equivocal by way of teeth inside?

Because he reached between his lips, jerked the thing out, draped it stickily and braceletwise across my wrist. It was just a few slicings of board-game dice that had been filed down further, then trained along the length of some black elastic with a tiny, molar-encircling clasp at either end. He hitched the ends of it together with a pitiless pinch, then started toward the stairs. But I did not let him spoil it, the moment most to my liking: when the house had gone quiet except for the drawn-out smack-smick of the suckage that people expected we lived for but in fact was just the way every other one of us, down at last on bended knee, knew best to tender his pledge of farewell.

If nothing else, then, I caught a bus late the next morning to the outlying locality where I had been set upon by the faultful, godsend sister in the first place. I stepped off at the public library. At the reference desk I inquired after any picture of the town that might have been taken from on high. The woman hurried off in a sidesway, returned with a sesquicentennial panorama in a back number of the auto-club monthly. It was just hobbywork, irresolute in its focus, but I could stare down into the sprawllessness of the neighborhoods and make out the upward pleadings of individual roofs. I must have had a look on my face, because the woman was saying, "If it's that important." She had the scissor blades already parted.

On the bus back, my pen was wobbly, and I doubt I was circling the exact houses. (The photo, as I have said, fell short of splendor.) And I was confining myself to just fourteen—enough alone for the lowers. I would have the remaining ones out a.s.a.p., then let the ceramist behind the shopping center trick something up for me in terra-cotta, scale a little of the town down into my bite, make it bear annihilatively on any further talk of time going faster when you're giving yourself away.

I numbered the circles as chronologically as I could.

The annotations were typed up later and are laid out for you hereinbelow, precisely as I dumped them all on him, because I am a believer in treating everyone equal, or at most as one and the same:

1. 63 EAST JUNIPER STREET

Since the living-room carpet was deep-tangled and untamed, she would fetch any fallen pencil by sliding a sheet of letter-writing paper, corner first, beneath it, then pick the pencil up off the *paper*—a civilizing enough thing to have been in her nature to learn from me while our parents still could sleep.

2. 87 EAST JUNIPER STREET

I taught her, of course, that although it was easy enough to get the sound cleansed from most of whatever she did (e.g., destining her pee, as she had already discovered, not into the water proper but onto a cloudpack of tissue allowed first to mount purposively in the bowl), things would be better for all concerned if, instead, she timed any little personal noise of hers to coincide with a larger, outer sound (postponing a cough, say, until the instant a cupboard door was clumsily shut, or bringing her whispers in unison with the rustle of pages being turned across the room in Father's evening paper). In next to no time I thus was hearing her, bodily, behind every household stirring and thud.

3. 292 NORTH MAIN STREET

Just the grade school from which she brought home papers of hers the teachers had not cared for. (Sheets dressed with disobeying, hideaway penmanship that lapped over itself from line to line. Or others on which you could make out words, but the words had all been chained together with hyphens, and the hyphens were darkful things, thick as equal signs.) I acted the patron, paying her in pennies she could take to the man who sold cough drops by the piece. Better for her to prefer anything coming cherrily to nothing on the tongue instead of whatever a teacher might still be working up to such expert verticals on the board.

4. 1031 WEST GROSVENOR STREET

We were always moving, but hardly moving far—a couple of blocks up the same sharp street, or only one street over, or three or four bountiful doors down. I wish I could say it was just the neighbors and their noises, or the animals the neighbors began favoring, or a bay window too beholden to its view. But it was more often a weakness, indiscernible earlier, in the scheming out of the rooms themselves, how perplexively one led off onto the next, so that you had to put yourself through this room, then that one, to reach a place to which you thought you were bearing an emotion still distinct and unopposed, though once you got there, it was scarcely any longer even yours alone to feel.

5. 211 NORTH EIGHTH STREET

I told her that between any two people in a family there was a big block of feeling for them to do with as they wished.

I spoke her mind.

I lowered her sights.

6. 835 NORTH EIGHTH STREET

The night I let it drop that the body is mostly a body of water, she tried to boot me out of her room but was prevented, I sensed, by a leg already fallen asleep.

7. 17 SOUTH FRONT STREET

We came by contrary motions to the same place—a paradise of vacant shade beside the moving van. I re-introduced myself, this time, as her dear only father's lone wife's solitudinized, peaceless son.

Shirtless in her dun-colory jumper.

The umbral hollows of her underarms.

A dry run for everything certain to follow.

8. 71 WEST RAILROAD STREET (REAR ALLEY)

I told her I was an only child but had consented to being repeated here and there in the sketchiness of her chin, in the forehead that was all uphill, in her fragrance without undersweat.

She was just a later arrayal of what had figured foremost on me.

I had a right to require all of it back.

9. 74 WEST WATER STREET

We were side by side in the laundry room the night the light bulb finally burned out. There was the petite spectacularity of the filamentary ping, and then I let her be the first to do something, and then I did something in character with it, only much wider-about, in the interest of knowing better trouble.

10. 333 SOUTH EIGHTH STREET, APARTMENT 2-C

Days had the same onsweep, and off-bearings, and hours with me lost in earshot.

My mother telling my sister, "Because you have friends and he still doesn't."

My sister telling my father, "He says the rooms have us divided up all wrong."

11. 1414 EAST LOCUST STREET

When she went off for her bath, I donned her watch for any indrawing warmth still current in the strap, got as much of the clutch of her jewelry on me as I could manage, given that I was broader all around, and harder on things I wore out. (Only the tops of her dotty pajamas could fit me without stitches starting to split.)

12. 19 NORTH GRAVEL HILL ROAD

Or when you are the wrong way around in how you now feel, you can say: Here's the person herself, and here's the person scraped together on top. Then the way is cleaner to things.

13. 393 EAST LOCUST STREET

My assurances, again, that whatever she felt hanging over her head would appear to others as no more than skyward extenders of her hairdress—raylets, wingings.

14. 2187 BUENA VISTA DRIVE

I eventually let a boy in her grade play himself slimly into my hands. He had a deep, lax mouth stocked with teeth enough like hers in the cuspidal setbacks above and in the lusterless huddle below, and arms that in their blunt, bluff panels could have passed for the ones she tossed overboard in her naps, and eyes nicely competitive with hers in their downcast hazel exactions, and hair—unrationed on her head, kept almost portionless on his—of a resemblant, fellowly nutmeg-brown. We coaxed his parents into letting him exchange his room upstairs for some moist space in the basement. I steeped myself in his gamier hours before the first of them returned from work. There was the thutter of a dehumidifier to draw off any sound I got made on him. They should count for all the world as something of a heyday, then: the fingerworn weeks until he said, "I want to thank you for bringing me to the brink of girls."

IN CASE OF IN NO CASE

M y younger brother was having trouble with his dreams.
The trouble was that some of them had been obviously,
insultingly, intended for somebody else. They arrived in his sleep
after having been turned away by other people. He would recount
the story lines for me. We would have no luck finding any of his
belongings anywhere inside. We would look and keep looking.

This was the brother who "tonsured" his arms and legs. "The
well-groomed man," he insisted, "is never not shaving." It was up to
me to hold the lighter whenever he did the bust-ups of his acne with
the pin of a name badge he had to wear for work. His answering-
machine presentation was a greetingless, trilled avouchment of his
being out, gone, anywhere else. I would sometimes call just to take
it in, all that tonal flaunt of progress, forgettery.

I saw some valiance in how he raked us over the coals.

Neither of us was allowed to bring men into the house.

My mother was fluent in all the current forms that violence
took between mothers and their middle sons. Every day she
re-befriended me. I would go crazy over whatever she heated up
on the stove. She had her own way of deconcocting what had been
cooked originally. We were big on off-flavors.

She would tiptoe to the room where my father endeavored
heavily over his symptoms. It had once been the utility room. She
would make sure the door was kept locked.

"In case of in no case," she would say.

I fell away from myself every now and then. I would slide right
off whatever I was being held up as. I would come home and once
again be the butt of my mother's love. I raised myself to a higher
level of endearment to her. She decided that everybody needed an
epithet, a prank appellative for the frolics ahead. Humor broke out
of her in bulk. I was "lonelily unalone."

My father? His gumption went into penciled reckonings of his pension. He went otherwise unexpressed. From him I got my likeliness to tally and retire.

My bigger brother knew none of this.

Other than that, everything I say comes straight from him.

He was the one who understood the need for furniture.

"It sets you above," he said.

MEN YOUR OWN AGE

There was some thrifty rigmarole I used to manage with the ring finger of a T.A. I knew at school, when it was my sister he claimed he was after.

This was a ring finger whose ring was tricked out with a bigger allotment of surface novelty than you usually got with even a college ring. The thing had inlays, bossings, oversets. It was as availing an obstruction as I ever allowed that far up inside.

The college? The college was a state college with little but brick in its nature. We came out of it in the guise of people thriveless in pairs.

Him and my sister.

Me and a boy I later could make no lasting light of.

That said, forget them.

I was twenty-three already, in poor order among the other clerks and mistakers in our state's junior city. We got jerked forward into the economy regardless. A man at the office had flowers routed to my desk. In the copier room later, he joked me around to a deplenishing kiss. But the one I moved in with breathed more cleanly into my face. He was set on swifter sorrow, spoiling for it. So I let myself get handed along to high-schoolers, busboys with transportation, escapeways.

Then twenty-five, and thickened out, but you could still see a little of me around the eyes, the fitting mouth. I was off and on with an illustrator. He had the bottom half of a house and soon all the blazonry of that new disease.

He perspired and shrank.

It had to be closed-casket.

Then an immediate cleanout of his fair-haired porn before his parents and sister had their dullard turn at the shirts, the charms.

I moved into a cheesily carpentered apartment house and within days was timing my baths to the unpeaceful baths a neighbor on the other side of the wall was giving her toddler son. He would slap brattily at the water, and I would follow suit—accepting the threats, hogging scolds through the sweating tile. I otherwise kept my own counsel and did not answer the door, the intercom, the phone.

Resolved, then pooh-poohed:
That the body is far too big a place.
Or that it's actually just the same two frivolled, sex-sickened places every time I get there.

I was going for total strangers, men methodically unfamiliar, unrememberable, in clammy concisions of limb after limb. I patrolled my body for purplements, lesions; found only the ordinaria of dim good health. And I bought a radio, one that pulled in stations from farther away. I listened to call-in programs for the gist of the distant gripe. One night it was incivility, and prices. I huddled together some examples of my own—six-fifty for five tablets that hardly smartened the bathwater; twenty-three for some jarred froth that returned little of my old gloss. I picked up the phone, dialed the long distance, was soon talking perfect, morbid sense to the screener.
"You called earlier tonight," she said.

A trick I learned: alternate your late lunches between one restaurant and another—but just those regular two. Keep it up long enough for the counterpeople at each place to hurry to smug, merciful certitude that you're in there every single day.
You've doubled the mark you leave on the town.
You're coupled.

I was what—thirty-one?
Let this sound better: I was cozying up to whatever was nothing to people. A loose string on the sleeve of someone's workweek

sweater? I would pick it off unnoticed and give it place, keepsaken privilege, *perpetuance,* behind a window in my wallet.

That's how I hauled people off. I divided them from their lives one fiber at a time.

Then the men your own age start passing fussily into ugliness. You can point to exact places where death is already imbibing them.

Women, even the older ones, no longer seem that big a step down.

I took the ribbing and pursued myself into a few.

The first and second were swanking drunks of splendid wasted education and an abiding antagony of eye. The third did not feel up to any actual idle friction.

People are picky about any tribute they will take.

Or wait:

To make things easier on people, try looking at them from on high. Straight down. Then they're mainly hair and swollen waist, but mostly just the headway of their pointing shoes.

Which is to say: I married at forty-two.

The first letup in the reception and I was upstairs again, picking over the pews—programs left behind, mostly. Notes had been exchanged on a thumb-marked blank back page:

"Think he even knows who women are?"

"Low blows today at least reach a certain altitude."

Quick question: my wife?

She was slow-legged and bound to me only loosely in household hindsight already. I kept bumping into her in rooms lit only by night-lights. There was a circle of friends she said she would not give up—a thick-packed circle that went round and around in its fumings under our roof.

One day the circumference lost its give.

Thing just snapped.

Wound itself around one of the women, the least hurried to alarm.

Then my wife trying to part her from it, and the two of them fallen into each other's arms. Not "Here we finally are," but "Look, you know me better."

I learned to stir a finger in them both.

MY FINAL BEST FEATURE

I was going to lay off those years for a change, but here were people in what might as well have been asking attitudes, and from the whole of what I might have told them, I said only that in me they had yet another girl who had gone as far as she could get in life without somebody else's body to back her up, but I for one had at least come early into the sense, thank goodness, to keep a book open in front of me at all times, a heavyweight paperback I was not so much reading as working a different, less stable shape onto, putting leisurely violences into the turning of pages so that when I was through with a book it was a lopsided thing, something far atilt that could be pointed to, publicly, as an example of someone's having stuck something out, and then one morning I fed myself far enough into the population until I came to a like-sized, schoolworn girl doing just such pointing, a girl a little unpretty but with a heart dangerously in use behind the buttony blouse, and the way the two of us instantly took to each other gave us a leg up on marriage—we each set out hours for the other to fill with just shy breathing, pinned hopes to the ribbonry we hung wherever there were bulks of hair further discoverable upon us, feigned a unisonal swoon whenever a forearm of either one of us was by chance drawn forward finally against the unsleeved upper arm to produce, at the shadow-lined seam, a mouth, surely, an unbiting mouth, which, were it to break into a murmur, would let everything between us be a lesson to us—for most of what any two people of that age together might do (we were each, you see, a drowned-out, undominant twenty-three), most of what they manage in the way of advancing the loveliness in each other, was in sorry, well-known fact addressed to, aimed at, an unseen and unknown but counted-on third party (it was the only progress we could see a point to), and the girl and I were now looking to each other for a glimpse of who that person might turn out to be; and for me, soon enough, it was a man I was sitting only a handbreadth away from on a bus, a thick-mouthed man in need of an underling right away, who led me from the bus and down an off-cutting street and into a dark-ceilinged building, where he showed me to the plasticized outercoat I was to wear while doing the rudimental cabinet chemistry itself; and that should have been the extent of things, but the man brought me home to say hello to the sister he lived with, a woman bearing victorious versions of the man's off-sloping chin, his wide-set nostrils, his gristly ears, and the two of them, brother and blinking sister both, were pounding away from their forties under one roof with only a shared kitchen between them, the sister a little more under the weather, hoarse, watery of eye; and in no time the sister and I were impartible, and even though there was a voice she used solely on her brother (a sharp, finite voice that put things straight up into the falsifying affirmative whenever he asked whether she was all settled in for the night), and a different voice altogether for persons who brought things to the door (this one bracing, salutatious), she had a further voice reserved uniquely for me, a duplexity of voice, complex in address, which might have sounded, up top, to be saying only "He pushes you too hard" or "I should see to supper," but which, if you went straight to what was lowermost in it, was saying, "Catch my cold, get yourself knocked up by the snot of it, feel it fill you roundly out, carry it around inside of you, bring the thing to term, blow out a mucousy umbilical string, be sure to have saved every sluttery tissue, because I am going to come to you in demand"; and it was not long afterward that she packed the brother off to a faraway bachelorship so the two of us could pass some agreeable, willinghearted months as a close-set couple, keeping each other looking looked-after, building the world up with our home truths and sore points, ready-handed, for instance, in our agreement that a man was just a frame from which a single useworthy but renounceable thing was suspended; she let out the prediction that we would be turning up eternally in each other's endearances in new, unprompted, uncurbable ways; and then one night, after some errands had removed her from the house for a run of days, she began wondering aloud whether our intimateness, agreeable as it might still seem, was in fact just a fluke accord of matching dank genitalia, whether the worst of life in fact gets its start when you are attaching feelings not to other persons but to feelings those persons have already put out of themselves, whether I had not yet come into the discovery that if one truly knew what one was doing with one's eyes, people did not actually look like what they looked like, men of course above all. The invitation to the wedding shower was forwarded to what was now my forwarding address.

The last place I stopped was out in the sticks, at the weld of some piddly tributary highway and another Old Airport Road. I found a couple of low buildings—a news agent's, a sistering sandwich shed. In the sandwich shed a blackboard listed drink flavors; chairs were paired badly around the few tables there were. I did not discourage a slump-breasted woman from piecing some beef together in a sandwich for me, and when she made mention of a basin of wash-water in case I wanted to rinse my hands, I wandered over to it, let my fingers while away some of the graying suds. That was when I noticed a kind of jumble shop—a few shelves and racks, really— toward the back of the place, with grab bags, lunch-sized paper bags stapled thoroughly shut at the throat and labelled, in orchid crayon, "Boy—backward," "Boy—receding," "Boy—scotched," "Girl—earliest teenhood," "Girl—done without," and so on. They were going for a dollar apiece; I bought just two: "Girl— personal life" and "Girl—beauty problems." The things within went through the fingers of one hand while the fingers of the other brought the bite-marked sandwich toward my mouth, then took it away from me again.

I went next to the news dealer's. On the floor, just inside the doorway, some tablet-paper leafletry, pamphletary curiosities, one-of-a-kind newssheets, had been weighted down with rocks. *The Stairstep Complainer* one was called, and there was *The Bedstead Unfortunate*, and *The Housetop Crier*, and *The Storm-Cellar Early Riser*; there were *The Porch-Lamp News Minder*, *The Hat-Rack Disastrist*, *The Doorstop Detractor*, *The Haulageway Daily Flare*. The window where you were supposed to pay was just a glassless rectangle cutting through the wall and into the kitchen of the sandwich shed, and when I asked how much for the papers, it was the woman from before who said, "Whatever you think is fair." I laid a five-dollar bill on her palm, then noticed a girl—I will call her a girl—standing suddenly by my side. "You bought all my papers," she said in a voice straining its way upward again from the big, killing, pubertal drop. There was just jacketing over her bare legs—it was one of those men's lightweight things (she had plunged her hips through the neck of it, worked the zipper up as far as it could be made to go, sashed the unfilled sleeves around her waist). An overlarge, gray-gone T-shirt, a man's as well, was draped stolewise over the shoulders. The line of her arm could be followed in either direction—all the way past the wrist, wreathed with shreddy, brick-colored rubber bands, to the finespun fingers, if you needed a preference, or back to the well-boned, shivery shoulder. As for the heights of her: the hair up top was short and stickied until it was barbed-looking, prickled up, and there was a skimming of fainter hair already on the upper lip, the chin. The eyes: the eyes were faithworthy eyes already getting a jump on how things would stand between us after the difficult, intermediate minutes. And the Adam's apple—it seemed to push itself out even farther after each certain and unnervous swallow. Someone, then, who in no small part had unlikened herself blow by blow from spoilsport parents—"fuckards" was the word that would emerge for them— to become a one-girl show of hands for me alone.

For inside of a quarter-hour she had walked me to the house and up to a room whose walls were covered with crayoned skyline— big, upstricken rectangles for the buildings, little dark squares for the undisclosive windows—and over to the confining bed, where she said, "No, wait, this won't have been where it was." She escorted me past a sewing room, a utility room, a storage room, and into what I took for the parents' bedroom, onto the lofty bed of it. I must have been thinking that anything and everything fingerable on her body was keyed, pardonably, to something still unowned on mine, because before long I set my hand down on a curve of her leg, just shy of where the kneecap horizoned off. In answer, she sent an arm out flatwise onto my lap. There was a downthrow of emotion in the room, and before I even took hold of what was least obscurable on a girl of that sort, the thing had already gone withoutwards, grown away from her as far as it could go. Like most of what I had known of the world, there was a perfect, low-road way for it to take inside me. How small of me, yes, or how like me, but the way an only child becomes only an adult, the deep red I was turning became, sight unseen, my final best feature.

THE LEAST SNEAKY OF THINGS

There were strides being made in human error, and it was middle-school arithmetic five columns wide he had been hired to teach with a couple of stumpy, yellow, mortal chalks, though that was not the half of it. He had been told not to fraternize with the staff, but the women among them would look him over and put a little something forward of themselves—an arm taken up with an enhancive, practiced fidgetry, perhaps— and then give him the full, accumulated thinking behind it. Only one of them will come into much value here. This was a woman with a rutted forehead, and bare forearms gone velummy from the crossings and recrossings, and glasses that did not give you her eyes at anything like their true size. She rucked her face up at him in the entranceway one morning and said, "Have a high opinion of anything?"

The day came, in short order, when he presented her with a splinty segment of a homemade ruler he had fashioned inchily from guitarwood. (He showed her a tonic discomfort to be had by slipping the thing onto the insole of her flat, murky shoe just before the foot itself returned.)

Then a cinder-gray eraser one had to operate wheelwise. (This she appointed, pendant-style, to the already intricated chains engirdling her neck, all the better to outcompass the strawberry mark hard by the collarbone.)

And one of those all-in-one drawing aids, a thing that was at bottom a protractor, which is to say only that there was a protractor set centrally into the clear plastic sheet of it, but the whole works was pranked up with off-curving flourishes and cut-out circles the diameter of practically any fattening finger. (To take hold of the thing almost anywhere, as she was quick to do, was to become a carnivaller for at least the clinched, worldly instant.)

At best, in other words, the man got himself shooed into marriage, married in fact into disease, but it wasn't disease that took her off, it was some sick-abed she fell in with, and what mattered most remainingly was a cushion she prepared for him not long before she left: it was a squarish cushion, big enough to fall asleep atop if you balled yourself up just right, and she had covered the thing anew with blithely striped fabric of a coarse, heavyweight, farewell sort. For weeks afterward, this cushion was the man's lone seat. Then one night a seam came open. A tiny unparting of the threads at first, and then a liplike tear that took on howling length and width as weeks went loudly out. What showed through wasn't the siftings, the stuffings, he would have expected, but an earlier coverature, a dated floral patterning—plushier, staled—that was trouble to touch because of how thoroughly it mongered up the previous, unhelpful life of hers: the off years, the fair shares of misdevotion, the hard water and dirtier looks, the last straws and accelerating changes of heart. It was all there, confidential and contagioned in what he took for rotting cotton.

Only two things further need saying to clamp down even worse.

The first is simply that there was a pencil he set out, in secret, early-bird provocation, for the other teachers to reach for, then put down again, unstolen, on the deep-pocked countertop of the full-house faculty lounge. It was a worktable pencil he had sharpened to a fetching, irresistible half of its original span, and he had gone and scribblingly reduced the point of it to a long-suffering, well-rounded bluntness, and he had then left it to catch and collect as much as it could of his fellows, because in no time even the least sneaky of things will have already been handled awfully, will have drawn onto themselves a commonwealth of squandered touch: anything eventually sports the lonelihood of people who could no longer keep their hands to themselves. Why then own up to having any further unsanitary use for the people themselves when you already owned so much of what had gone ruiningly through their hands?

The other, final matter is that in the classroom thereafter he no longer had the heart to insist that his pupils "carry" any leftover digits from the rightmost column of workbook numerals to the summit of the previous one. He instead had the pupils laying the surplus numbers aside ("These loose, glutting, ridiculable tidbits of ongoing arithmeticizing" they were now to be called): the pupils were to set them out on the bed of a separate piece of paper, the backmost sheet of the dwindling, unlined tablet, and then he would lead the pupils in tearing the sheets cleanly free, would recite the grave, tribulationary instructions on just how every numberful sheet was to be folded into a weak-bodied box, and then each was to be walked single-file up to the desk so that the teacher might give it the completive tuck and fold. His touch was the touch of a precisioner—and the boxes were stacked flimsily tall on his desk as a wall against parents who were overlappingly dissatisfied, who showed up in jolty patrols of two or three to pull their sons, their troublable daughters, from his classes. But looks alone would have told you that the children had been put, at most, only a little further forward on the vanguard of everything going by the board.

MELTWATER

Here was a man, he claimed, who had caught his life early and already was bottoming on the parts of the world available to him, and I remember saying, "It won't happen again," and then the two of us broke away from the line of urinals in careful, patient unison. I followed him to the building where he lived—a free-standing single room, a garage-sized office, as things would have it. He explained that the most to be expected of anyone in his circumstance (the world was hard put to keep itself looking full) was to have both a girlfriend and a boyfriend, in hopes that the two would cancel each other out and leave him at the center of an enlarged, more compassing loneliness. I had nothing further to do with him other than getting the people's names and looking them up.

Of the boyfriend I have little to pass along, except that he turned out to be my equal in the overintelligibility of his face— teeth the color of margarine, I'm afraid; eyes that rivalled the lights; a rampant, unlimited nose. There was a garland of dark hair growing around his neck and shoulders (he was shirtless the little while I knew him), and there was much talk—rumorous murmur, really—all that week in the apartment below his: a pair of voices, male and discussive, that got pitched even lower as they were channeled up through the floorboards and the deep carpeting on which the man and I lay after all our trouble. Sometimes I could make out a third voice downstairs, that of a contestant female, just a visitor, no doubt, and a laugher. I never got to meet her and to this day still suspect that she had a smoky hood of unshampooed hair and the sleep-buckled arms of a quitter. But this boyfriend: had I sought merely another reminder that everything always gets stuck being slightly more than just itself, that objects flourish in the thick of their own innuendoes, and that the trick, therefore, is not to look directly at any one thing but instead to concentrate hard on the haze environing it, until whatever it is, the form emerging thereunder, wobbles a little further within its outline and becomes separable, easily chased out? For I came away with nothing more than one of his combs, a largely ornamental one, the crown of his toilet, and another new reason to keep from touching all the old things.

The girlfriend, on the other hand, was in some sort of accelerated rehab. I slipped in on family day and sat by her side on a lawn that sloped toward the expressway. She was undodging and level-chested in her baggy sundress, and she necklaced her arms around my shoulders to confide that she had a private room and that these were merely the sick days and personal days she had long had coming to her, taken now in one salutary lump. Afterward, assisted out of each other's clothes, we displayed ourselves at full length in the coarsening fluorescence of her room (I remember a port-wine stain enriching the goosefleshy preserve beneath her left breast). By day's end, she had already bargained for an early release (she had some vague, undefiable kind of pull), and I came to stay at her house. The next morning, she was back at her office, and I began humbling each day down into heart-drowning dozes of roughly equal length. After every one of them, I would turn myself around, unespoused, on the uppermost bedclothes (alone, I drew back none of the covers, seldom resorted to a pillow) and throw in my lot with what I was already in the middle of.

For the woman had a son, a collegian in his late teens, who was mostly at work or in class, and who went around the house in exactingly parted hair: the parting was a coercionary line, an unfailing divider, that I came to reverence as a segment of a much longer line that I formed a niggly segment of myself: a line that travelled by inchmeal through unpined-for bodies and spreadless, low-pitched towns and now and again hit an improving stride and was manifestable, broken up anew, in the vivid transection of a boy's head of hair or in the outgoing, eminent prolongation making a fresh, last-minute mess of my crotch. The line, as I thus set about reconstituting it, directed me, soon enough, to the boy's room; and it was in the course of making a first search of that room (prospecting in the high-posted dresser, the desk with its deep drawers, the heavy-lidded hamper, as soon as the boy and his mother were both at last out of the house) that I turned up his pornography, the little there was of it, in a night table that opened, cupboardlike, from the front. It was a slender magazine, a one-shot, a "special" dedicated to I forget precisely which partialism, and I dallied in the drab thing until I reached the page most singularized by the boy's touch—a recto, ten pages or so from the rear, marked off with a batch of proprietary thumbprints and depicting an ignorable girl, foul-eyed and recumbent in pajamal diaphaneities, one hand raised unshieldingly above the triangular murk showing through at her center.

It was the backdrop of the photograph, though, that brought me up short: a remote, all but vanishing blue—one of those decrescent, lesser blues, with nothing the least spirituous or skyey in the cast of it, yet crisal, crisic, just the same: a blue that did not so much give out on the world as give up on it (but without tossings, without vehemences!) and that sent me, almost at once, and without a sweater or a shave, to the paint store closest by. The salesman spread out a fan of color charts, then fed them one by one into my hands. I charged through the charts with disappointment until, on a thick, palette-shaped card of enamels ("finishers," the salesman called them), I came up against something close to a match: meltwater it was called, and it had to be whipped up specially in a countertop mixer that gave off a temperate, alto hum. I came away with a sploshing gallon can aswing from each hand, and a stirring paddle and a paintbrush in my back pocket; but that first night (an early-autumn night sloppy with rain and coiling traffic), I merely committed a dauby specimen of the paint to my fingernails and arrived, unventilated and ready to catch him out, this "commuter," at the dinner table. The boy, however, was unfazed and unrecognizing as I sent before him with my upcast fingertips the bowls of stew, the gleaming salads. I remember a notable excurvature of muscle, not unbecoming, beneath the snug drapery of the boy's short sleeve each time he accepted a dish.

The next morning, with the run of the house once more, I regained the boy's room and, this time, with my paint at the ready, let myself into one of his spiraled notebooks ("SOC SCI," he had written in prissed, lessonly caps on the cover) and at deserving length skimmed my laden brush down the margin of the page where he had left off. (The notes had been recorded in soft-penciled, back-slanting abbreviations that seemed on the brink of retreating from the page.) The boy came home from work, vanished into his room, and, I gathered sorrily, went untormented about his assignments.

A couple of mornings later, with all the windows in the boy's room thrown open to a low-going, unmetropolitan sky, I gave a slapping introductory coat to the baseboards. That evening, I arranged a quick dinner for all three of us (the boy unperplexing the salad I had stocked with bouillon cubes, tindersticks of pasta, enfoiled chocolate exotica; the woman recompressing her slipshod sandwich), and afterward parked myself in the living room, nose lowered alertly into a thickset volume of the scarlet household encyclopedia. But, once more, whether through simple imperception or the killjoy composure of a born flirt, the boy gave no sign—merely kept up the tit-tat of his lap typewriter as he harbored words for his "comp." The woman was at her phone for the night, and as on all such occasions, I took up the incontinent crusade against my body, trying to clear my face by going after the late-day hair appreciating on the chin, the cheeks, abstracting the hairs one by one with a slant-tipped tweezer, enough of them to cumulate into broken lines down my shirtfront and onto a double page of the encyclopedia spread now across my thighs. There was a bulblet at the root-end of every hair; and certain of these, when subjected to an experimental pressure of the thumb, could be made to excrete a dark, private ink that left a tiny smouch on the page. (I had so little else to show.)

The next afternoon (I had slept well into its steep-rising shadows, because, come night, almost everything was costing me my sleep: the almost coppery taste of the dry heat as it reached my open mouth, the woman's least turnings on her span of the bed as my life kept pivoting filthily off her own: I was always on pain of waking to the snottery monotone of her snores or other earthly maneuvers of hers—and yet with what whispery concern I would test the nip-and-tuck vowels of her name: Sael!)—the next afternoon, I applied harrying fluences of blue paint to a zone of stucco above the boy's bed until I was satisfied that my jittering brushwork had yielded a sightworthy, window-sized rectangle.

This, apparently, was as much as it was going to take, for after dinner the boy interrupted my reading, escorted me to his room, assumed a vibrant position on the brim of his bed, and conducted me by suggestive, irregular swallows into his hardship. It started with the car that gave him no peace (it was slow to get going, he said, then squirted of its own accord into traffic that always took its time to part), and the shortcomings of commuter life (the "dormitorium," to hear him describe it, was not the bricky, box-shaped residence hall of the sort I could still call up from remembered youth but, instead, a far-reaching yet indefinite complicacy of stone and shaded glass whose central escalators, I gathered, would afford the "nonresident" an aggrieving vista of students dead to the world in humid pairs and threesomes on the marbled slabs of groined galleries that were ranged about the base of a foggy rotunda), and his boss (a franchiser given to intimate insanitations, scratch-paper threats), and, finally, "girlettes," "feminatrices," as the boy termed them, and their inconvenient, pinksome anatomies. I explained to the boy that in my day we had counted ourselves lucky if, once a month, rummaging through the family ragbag, we turned up one of our fathers' forsworn T-shirts and hacked off the sleeves and the neckhole and then pulled the remains down, sacklike, over our hips until the hem got as far as our knees—and that, in sum, midway down a body, man's or woman's alike, the trouble is always original and always suits. Here I fixed a hand on the boy's upper leg and spoke, at last, of bachelorisms, slipslops of the heart, and, most of all, how to hold it, the troubler, aloof from yourself, how to regard it at most as a guest of the body and not a permanence on it, because the truth is that the thing did not originate from within you but in fact grew onto you from afar—you merely *hosted* it. I thus came into a rash knowledge of the boy's differentiae—distant, backside moles he could have only guessed at, the tensed setting of every rung of his ribs.

On the floor, a skyline of furniture curving above us, I set him forward in his larger life just a little.

(Days thus passed under the woman's nose.)

An hour or so before the woman returned from work late each afternoon, the boy and I would now share a confidential foremeal of chocolate bric-a-brac and a thinning, sepia-toned liquid that trafficked from a high bottle to a tumbler I had taught the boy to keep upright in the blowsy yarn of the carpet. His hands were newly productive, formatting dinner napkins into bonnets, depressing cookie batter into shatterable hearts. There were other gustoes of mine the boy would not soon escape. And I told him to forget words from here on in—that once you got even one of them out, a whole cortege of others would be bringing up its stinking rear.

Early one night, the woman came suddenly from behind my chair and said, "You better would've not've." I craned my neck to meet her halfway. There was an alien, liquorous tilt to her features.

You only get way too many chances, I must have put in, because I remain of the enormous opinion.

But I "walked."

I came, in due course, to the food court of a mall (for the world was yet to be taken by mouth) and worked myself toward the Chinese bay: behind the counter was an overblooming, low-hatted girl, a blond (youth is vast!). I ordered by number and presently accepted a routine, rimmed density of chicken and vegetables. At my table afterward, devoting myself to the meal, narrowing my gaze to the limits of my plate, I discovered amid stray splinters of fried rice a rich, characterical hair: it was more than an inch and a half in uncurled longitude and of darksome human gloss. I had not had a look at the food-prep station or the cook (they had scrims nowadays, dividers), but I pictured somebody down on everyone else's luck.

For this hair—there was a body surely recoverable from it: putty in my hands and no great shakes.

HEIGHTS

She had always kept up an interest in the avocations of the familiar. One could return to a room, after all, and find that paper, ordinary paper, had since been folded until it was bladed and held danger. Or one could pass into a kitchen (for one had been away, sullyingly, again) and descry, on the stove, mere finger-breadths from the oniony ebullition in a saucepan, a tablespoon already beginning a career as food itself. If she fitted the bowl of the spoon into her mouth, there would be the discovery that the stainless steel had a filling and satisfying taste all its own.

She married, in other words, a fellow who had decided that women alone could ever be man enough for him now. He would entertain the pressure of her hand on his cheek and have his blood tapped and inspected once a month. One night, the man wanted to have people over, people more like himself. She sat in the bedroom and listened to the men's voices, thick and inept, playing with what had already been said, making good on her misgivings.

Or so I gathered as much from the deteriorating alphabets of her doodles, and from the faces with which she kept resoiling paper for me to have to regard—shapes of accumulating unease one minute and slaphappiness the next, each finally evicted from the page with jerked expunctions of her eraser. For this woman was no gabber like the ones they usually put next to me now that they had us working two to a table. The regular pencil looked heavyset, out of scale, between her hurrying fingers.

She was a worthy opponent of herself. Gray fillings discriminable in the thin teeth during a rare, airy yawn. A depleted comeliness to her face. Not one word out of her, ever. But one day a switch of her hair fell finally across my sleeve. I forget who followed whom out onto the landing.

We sat in her car because the passenger seat of mine had been stuffing itself all along with steadfast pilings, elevations, of newspapers, circulars, discarded cardboard. Her voice was melodial but economic. She explained that her mother had always claimed that hours weren't bait, something laid out to trap with, but to her mind, time was still waiting to get itself told. Thus her hand came to rest so livingly on my own.

We became another arm-swinging pair waging walks on the town, fooling with heights.

I CRAWL BACK TO PEOPLE

LEATRICE

There was a kind of woman you could spend weeks with, months even, and never get it settled to your satisfaction whether she was on the mend or not yet finished being destroyed. This one was no different, only younger than I by a couple or so years, though on a second or third life already. We were together one spring, briefly, tickledly, and then it came to her—in a dream, in a diary entry; I forget—that I would not be having her very much longer. Then I lost her altogether. I remember the tears she provided in a waiting area at the airport before she left, and how she insisted on being the one to make the trip to a snack bar for some napkins to blot the tears, and how it looked like little more than perspiration she was wiping away when she got back. Then she fell in line to board, and I went out to seek my car. I lay across the seat until I heard a plane take off and could satisfy myself that it might have been hers. I drove back to the city. In a couple of days I was already picking her out by the piece here and there on other people, because people came to hand on other people or drifted up out of one another availably. There was always some scrap of her arising usefully in passing on somebody or other.

What I mean is that people shaded into each other pretty easily, and all I had to do was find her somewhere there in the gradients.

I found tender burlesques of her hair on one girl, and exactly the scoop of her underarms on another, and approximations of her forearms on an uncavorting kid of seventeen. I could get him to feed me the seizing feel of her sometimes.

In fact, it was this kid, a high-schooler, that I mostly got her dwindled down to by the end of that first summer.

The attic he lived in was underbeloved by the rest of his family, so we could generally count on privacy. If a parent stuck a head in the room, I fell back on instant dramatics of mid-level math, pad-and-pencil finesse left over from taunted years at the commonwealth college.

The kid showed me his middle-school yearbook, his tapes, some bitter, unvisionary pornography.

He had a big dictionary that contained mostly disappointments—*bottle tit*, for one. It was just some dim, skinny bird nesting in the holes of trees overseas.

"Are troops the individual guys or bunches of guys all huddled together?" he seemed to wonder. He had balmed lips and novel, weary whiskerage that looked crafted on.

So I took to frocking this and that onto the kid—got him gowned in a bedsheet, skirted with a bath towel. Brought him a sleeveless thing for him to slink deep within. Got his starter razor buzzing above the ankles, taking out the blond dither along each shin.

I milked his arms for further thrill of her farewell.

CAULEN

He already had a way, when passing alone through an entrance, of keeping the door held open a little behind him, in hopes of a follower.

He was the type not ruinable ordinarily.

But I knew what to buy him—blood-colored underwear, man-tailored shirts from women's stores.

Knew how he could be stood to outpourings of infallible citric alcohols.

Knew I could get him to where I guess he expected only better things to push up through what he already thought of me.

So at last he was professing it—an excruciated fellowship I would have some share of.

■　　■　　■

Together, housed, we banged each other up with contestable affections.

He had grated good looks.

He cooked savvily on a berserk four-burner.

A few hairs of his came loose during the bustling solitude of a shower. They stuck to a block of soap already claiming several of mine.

We were that much together even in toiletry.

There were exactly two bars in our catchwater town upstate. I forget why I started sending him off alone.

One was a warehouse revived for dancing. The other bar had only stools, in my clumsy opinion.

He came home with something against wallets—something about how the way to get one thing to belong to another should not have to require putting them side by side in a leather packet and then sitting on them until, if you wanted just one, you had to practically peel it apart from the other. It bothered him that it took a rear end at rest to make sure that things would stick together.

Things came and went on his face, his back, in pustular debuts, crusting retreats.

Some days his hair stole over him differently.

It riffed out more racily under his arms.

In his defense? You could work only so long at a furniture outlet before minding it that every sofa and chair was plushly, or hard-armedly, dramatizing its lack of a suitable sitter.

Every stick of furniture was a history of spurning asses.

You get better and better at dialing down the light to the point where passersby decide the place is probably closed.

He later sold phones and had glum dominion over a teenager with repatterned teeth and a rubber band bangled swankly over his wrist.

For a couple of weeks, I commanded repeat condolences from our pallid little crowd.

KELL

The idea was to marry lightly, not go overboard or be private about things, just let affections string out however they might. I expected to see streamers of feeling coloring up the air between us.

Each of us said: "I'm not going anywhere."

She was none too grubby for having dug herself out from other people. I could smell the same dud soap on her always.

I was sometimes by her side while she shopped. Her "Thank you very much" to the change-tendering cash-wrap girls always had in it an acknowledgment of applause.

We lived without onslaught. The days did not clobber us or break new ground. She did some kind of surefire statisticizing during the day. Collected informations, forced them through a formula until they came out pestled, floury.

She would sweat off her makeup over dinner.

Ruffled nostrils, wear and tear in the eyes, pressuring escalations of a competitive pink in the complexion—her body wasn't pioneering anything, it wasn't hectic in its decrepitude: she wasn't shading off ahead of schedule. Her vaginal efficiency was unchanged.

But more and more ornaments got hung from her. There was fierce hoopla in all those boostering units of chainwork and chatelaine.

She began vanishing into jumpsuits, quilted coveralls.

I would say something, and she would chop or wrinkle it into something else, but she was never far from wrong—neither of us could have ever been saying much more than "I won't keep you."

I understood, but then there was a shimmy to my understanding, and I no longer exactly could follow.

FAISAL

There were holes in what I felt for people, and it was through these holes that I slid finally toward this fourth.

I bummed a touch from her in the subway. I let the touch aggrandize itself unquietly.

I moved to her steep-streeted city downstate.

She decided I was a deserver.

She was a woman of punctual life-tides, ate right, had suffered at all the right hands. She had a drafty manner and jewelry that tailed off asymmetrically from her ears in a show of what looked like sugar. She had been grossing all of this great, capering beauty for something like twenty-six years. We did the giveaway pharmaceuticals of the season. We went out with her friends, busy-headed kids her own age, to crack up over menu English. I loved her sundrily and all at once.

There was, to start, the givenness of her bare arms, and legs you could pick out of a dress and follow all the way down to the pewtery hue of the toenails.

Childhood, teenhood, were still refrigerating inside her. I could make out the timid din of who she had already been, a hum of harms hardly done.

The question put to me by skeptics was: "What is she doing with you?" I was swift to answer: stapling personal papers together, breathing providently in her broad-hearted sleep, bearing junk mail straight from the mailbox to the trash cans in front of her building.

"No," they would say. "What does she see in you?"

I told them I was doubling for somebody. It's hard not to be standing in for people jokingly slow to show. Go-betweens impart important impromptu breadth to any population, keep cities backed up and abrim.

They would say: "How can this be good?"

I said it's called middle age because everything is just circling around you now. You're at the discouraged center. Why should it all of a sudden be any ruder to reach?

She had never been to a drive-in movie, so I withdrew an address from the phone book, drove us to some gravelly outer county. There was one shack where you bought the tickets, another where you bought unsatisfactory snacks. The screen was a folly of peeling panels. "I'm not your pillow," she taught me early in the first picture. During intermission, I directed my twinkling, postponed piss into a metal trough. Through the wall I listened to her relaxed, sassing abundance in the bowl. No flush, no siss of faucets afterward. In stinting rain on the way back to town, she complained that my windshield wipers were too loud.

The doubters said, "It's over, isn't it?," or gave us maybe another week.

The way she left things when she was done with them—narrow ranks of cutlery, a high-raised figurinal telephone, dish after dish of jotted chocolates—the weight seemed thrown around in them differently, they looked plummety or fickle in their molecularity, they harbored her touch with too much rumpus.

It got harder to get her arm through mine.

One afternoon she mentioned a brother somewhere else who lived on one floor and was host to a lonesome federation of straight-backed chairs, pull-up chairs, TV chairs. It was time for her to see him again and be ready for what he was facing. I gave her a lift to the airport. In the car, she lowered a balled fist onto my lap and explained that we were set up much too differently in our bodies; that there were no lasting or reliable handholds on each other; that I would turn up something nicely remindful of her dry-boned elbows or collisive knees on somebody nearer my own age; that the xoxoxoxoxoxoxos given as sign-offs in the few, close-written letters she had sent me were actually tallies, each x standing of course for a mistake I had made, every o just my final score.

I have probably got her features collated all wrong in memory anyway.

I have no doubt given freehand failings to the line of the mouth, leaving the lips figgled, defaulting.

Jollied a lone, focal mole along to the slope of the nose.

Undarkened the down at the bounds of the cheek.

Brought the eyes to unfinal idle crisis.

The world has since figured her into its fixed emotional fare.

I count on others to cough valiantly, or turn on aquarium pumps, run the loudest of fans, when I think to bring her up.

DAUGHT

No sooner had my husband and I fixed up a place of our own than a book arrived on the well-meaning subject of landlordry. I was in no mind to read it, but I interested myself in the graces and attractions of its manufacture: it was a loose-jointed but otherwise well-kept old thing, and if I thumbed ahead to the midmost pages, a little nether passageway opened welcomingly between the arched edges of the signatures and the inner strip of the spine, and I could either admit a finger into this hollow and then shut the book to feel some barely favorable pressure, or I could bring it up to my eye scopewise and enjoy a narrowing, exclusive view of the ashtray serving as a caddy for my thermometer, perhaps, or of the chromatic strata of pills in a see-through canisterette—I was not much troubled that things could now and then look so suddenly, relievedly, independent. Still, the stacked pages, however stale, must have exhaled at least enough of their purpose to influence my choice of what next to allow into my hand, because it was a plump marker and not the thermometer just this once, and it must have been big and wishful of me to think that by printing "ROOMS" (largely, coarsely) on the back of the envelope the book had turned up in, and then by tilting my little sign against the bow window, I was putting out only some benevolent, overdue description—an explanation, I mean, and not an ill-vowelled cry of availability.

As for the passing woman first to knock: if her cheeks were pock-pitten and mealy, there was a complexional rosiness in the upper reaches of her arms, which were wisely left unsleeved; and if her breasts fell inobligingly short, there was a way I could get her to sit with her knees just wide enough apart for them to see duty as a second, hardier bosom when my head needed its place for rest; and if her mouth struggled to hold in the dim, shifting masonry of the teeth when she kept letting out that she lacked "destiny, remedy, delight," there was a more opportune mouth forming at the jointure of the thigh and the calf when the leg was at last drawn in, and this one could be kissed without risk of return; and if there was anything else that did not instantly suit, there was sure to be something cater-cornered to it or not too distant that would do in a pinch and no doubt prove even warmer and more aromal in the end.

Then I must have remembered that all along I had probably just needed someone to walk in with me when I finally went around to see the teacher. Classes had let out by the time the two of us, the roomer and I, reached the high-vaulted desk up front. There was a line of transparent party tumblers near the edge of it, in one of them a razor downside up in scummage, in another a toothbrush abob in a streaky solution I trusted was recycled mouth-rinse—by then her fingers and mine had to have been braided together even tighter, I can at least now hope.

A towel was draped around his neck, and he was guiding a cake of soap dryly across his forehead. He took us in with his full nostrility. His shirt was off, so it was all to the good that he was heavy enough for the vaccination mark on his arm to have swollen out to practically a sunburst, glazy-looking and something to keep my eyes away from his. He did not think to ask about my lady friend, but he wanted me to know that although the boy had nothing against the "material" per se, he would lay aside the lessons and pass most of his days in the lavatory; that on the walls and door of the stall he favored, the boy had rendered creditable side views of bunk beds, four-posters, foldaways, cots; that the custodian, who was getting ready for a move and needed to dispose of things anyway, had donated to the stall a plant stand and a floor lamp and a parcel of foam-white carpet, which in its day must have surely kept guests on tiptoe in even their most allegiantly cleansed stocking feet; that visitors were admitted only one by one, and after they emerged (this one's pullover now inside out or smelling of smoke, that one's arm sinking beneath its new load of roped jewelry), they pleaded for time—

But I cut him off, either on the principle that they're no good until you've got them to where they rule the roost, and then they're worse, or else on its opposite, which could still keep me bullied into believing that somebody should always at the least be the one being wooed.

"For your information," I said, "it's my daughter, anyway, that I'm gunning for."

He had started poking his sunny arm into a sleeve.

"I would ask, then, whether you even have any idea of what a daughter is," he said.

It was of course only one thing for her to chime in with "A person, pushedly female, who daughts," and altogether another to be first to define "daught" the way I should minutely let it stand.

IN KIND

To hear me talk, I had come out of college at the time the profs were just starting to get begrudging again about grades, and after graduation I found myself in a town with just groupings of confusable buildings and some fields to be treated as parks.

I had no friends, just timid emergency contacts.

I married the second woman to come along.

The first had been clear-hearted, and hair-colored, and the few times she spoke, it sounded as if water were running over her words. Something was coursing through her speech that was other than what she was saying, even when all she was saying was: Tell me your news.

My wife—in third grade, she had called her teacher at home one night to ask what he was up to. (He said he was right that very moment being dragged toward the door.) She was a hard-boned girl afraid her heart would halt between beats. She went around with her hand covering it, until somebody finally said, "Must you always be pledging allegiance?"

Anything she related came only from this same short strip of girlhood. So one assumes, naturally, that there were other years long ago set fire to, or put unsafely away into other, worldlier people. More likely, though, it was only that life had covered up her life.

We lived, my wife and I, in a morbid swither, and were inaccurate in our passions, and now and again frightened ourselves into feeling on the verge of something that could lead to change or at least a better examining of who we already were.

I was halfwise through my loose-fitting forties, chumpy and rump-faced.

My tendencies boiled down to the tendency to have trouble seeing what was right in front of me, then to follow anyone else's eyes to maybe just a larger situation of noodles stymied in a dish.

I had a heart cleaned out and in need of new keep.

I liked telling people that their secrets were safe with me, but I was in fact a deadliness to them, each and severally.

I wrote stapled manuals of policy and dampened encouragement for outfits that sold "financial products." I mostly just copied, substituting "should" for "shall," then substituting "might have at some point in the past" for "definitely should have." I insisted on "she or he," then cut out the "he" altogether. All the bosses, managers, executives, decision-makers, vessels of discretion in my clamping paragraphs were female in body, female in parts.

As for my parents? They had let life drop away from them.

And I had a brother, younger. We were not close, but something must have been jumping around in his feelings for me and sometimes hit against his heart in a scrubbing way.

Rather, there was the city you called home, and there was a companion city, a comparison town, some miles downlake, and you went back and forth between the two, working in one and living in paining well-being in the other, or elating your family by marrying in one and buying rousing flowers for some other in the second, until a third place went up in the neutral form of tents and tarps, thank goodness. This was where I came to associate my life with my body in ways that there was definite bloodied overlap.

Or they judge you by what you make a run for, and I made a run for a kid not even out of the district. He had thorough hair, with a blonded backstream to it, and earaches, nose aches, and no sensation at all on one side of his tongue, and his family spoke to him only through block parents or glory holes.

So which was the bad sign—that I had no influence over him, or that I came to him so often with militant doses of alleviatives I crushed with tablespoons myself?

Women were ring fingers, toenails a pickled purple, powdered belittled features, panics laid bare on stationery, then sharpened in forthtelling agony over the phone.

My wife taught eleventh-hour math to twelfth-graders. It was just glorified arithmetic—the friction of recipe fractions, check-cashing-service subtraction. The students were imaginative nincompoops quick to sign petitions.

I would awaken unquietly upcity, shower with some figure of fun, whoever it was. Often a colleague's son, a kid unbeaten at the comedy of his lengthening life and possessed of jabbing stops in his voice. It was a voice that dumped glassy vocabulary over anything left of his good nature.

The muck wouldn't get into my days until later.

I was otherwise talked about in an interested and summarizing way.

There were uncles I saw mostly as pallbearers and peacemakers. There were lug-along, unlofty aunts. The grandmother on my father's side was eye-sick, dry-throated; an upheavalist in the mornings, a regretter come night. Afternoons, she took her tragedies with tweezers and reasoning.

It was my grandfather on the other side who brought the caustics to the bloodline.

My office had a window, but it gave out on the corridor, not on the renewable contrarieties of the world outside, and I covered the glass with bare cardboard, though not quite completely: there was a narrow band at the bottom through which anyone up for the bother could see clear through to where I was, often as not, leading a throwaway razor, without balm of water or foam, across a freshly despised portion of forearm, or simplifying an underarm snarl with pinking shears.

These were things I did on the job, yes, as if the job were a base, a foundation, on which I threw myself around inside myself.

Home, I was budged but unadvancing. For whole weeks what came to me in dreams went right back again into the stream of sleep, unminded.

She talked aloud in her dozes, this wife, though much of what got said sounded only like toasts or alerts.

The parts she had come from were mostly farms, with here and there the hardened variety of a village.

And that neighbor I drank with during the stinks of summer: he was barely half my age, but his life was leveled against him in ways that made his past look ledged with trick precipices.

I could never get the chronology right—construction first, or carpentry, then the pinching year or two as a package handler, the engagement (torched) to somebody unfavorable in baby fat, then the mono, the money damages, the meatlessness and drinking, the death of a friend with whom the friendship had been veiled and failing?

I would have him over when my wife was out for sitdowns with sisters or another ireful, untiring walk before bed.

I liked the differing trueness of him when he made his mouth unwelcome to mine, and the resting eyes he had, and always that raincoat, always those annulling motions he made with the hands.

I had to get along with what I could gather of myself, and what I could gather was mostly this—that I had to answer every question with a question, and it had to be: What else might you have missed?

Two children, yes. There must have been nights when there was patience on offer in my heart, nights I sat beside them when they were still in school and could be ruled or at least feared without too much fright.

These were a sturdying girl of vague obediences, a boy hidden in his hardihood.

Their names, their first names, formed a blatty, honorary off-rhyme, I want to say.

But they must have felt buttoned into each other, those two of ours.

The excusatory note the girl had forged to her teacher: in forky penmanship, it said she had been "homesick," not "home sick."

And the boy: the climbings and depressions in his backhand posterboard alphabet were, the teacher wanted to warn, without apparent parallel.

He later shirked his gender or got himself ousted from it, and had a curt, spiking life, little of it limpid.

The girl grew up to browse herself hourly for allurements. I am getting ahead of myself if I say that a ruin shouldn't ordinarily start out as one.

The departing manager was having me throw together a memoir for her, a dignification, really, of any dent she might have made in things behind thicker partitions upstairs. She was a woman of unhurrying readiness, and anecdotes already deserting her, and scarcely enough names to go with faces, faces I let putresce and appall in pagelong sketches in the chapter on hirelings, associates, lunchmates easily fathomed. There was, for each, a paragraph of fallacious acclaim, a word on domestic conditions, and a single, fair criticism.

Myself I wrote off as a town wonder now toned down—low-spoken, overmuch of body, slow to show his undersides.

People did not expect to stay on in my affections, but I never really finished with anyone, never really saw them off from places they had filled.

I brought my work home, meaning I was still on the job, meaning I was athwart some notion of it.

An afternoon might feel original and culminating, or else the hours had hardly a touch of time in them.

My neighbor needed someone in front of him to express his difference from, and I was content to face his features whenever they afforded me the wide weekday arrays of his woe.

There were the beginnings of a rip in her visage, and cakier gloomings of makeup on her eyelids, but still an ingredience of sympathy in our evenings overall.

A lot of well-wishing went on just before we went to sleep, plenty of warmest regards and the like, though in remembered and confided dreams we were hurtful, encumbering, believable.

I can't take it upon myself to say there weren't others, familiars for a day or two, thankless in kind. And a girl once, too, though she had seen herself formed into a woman who absorbed men only by accident, and with women was even less guiding.

And a word about the house where I lived liably with this wife and these flimsily boned loved ones and whatever was kept drumming around inside them: it had several and a half baths, and was sectored into vestibules, entryways, and other prefatory thresholds. You had to take a breather from this person before reaching that one. In like manner, the big, fat lies added up.

Months, and whatever else there might have been to catch or cadge; jury duty and cautions in the mail; a few more neighbors, every one of them a presentable disgrace with a body barely squarable with mine; an undegenerate but consequential blotch on the upper leg; niceties it was in my nature to deny; replies that more and more often had to begin, "If what you say is true…"

It is true that I had bought, some years back, at the one thrift store in town where men's and women's T-shirts were racked emboldeningly together, an armful of the women's things, the plainest ones, varying from the men's only in the girth and in the length of the sleeves, and under my dress shirts and sports jackets these held me closely for a decent while. I held up dearly in them, yes. I wore them to pieces.

And then one whose bearings I shortly preferred to mine: he had done cruelly in school (maps were rolled down like window shades over anything he had sneakingly chalked onto the blackboard, the mystifying anatomies and such), and in college he had to chase any accurate inconsequentiae out of the handouts because the quizzes were quick and graded on machines that had to be wheeled in. He wanted me to declare him looted of youth.

It was the truth, or there at least was truth arranged around in it somewhere, or it had been true enough of somebody else, anyone approximate who had wanted to be a girl and grew up to content himself with the offsloughs of a wife ruddily losing her looks.

Case in point: whenever a large dog died, a crate even larger was left behind to fill. My friend—for I had a friend at the time I am considering, someone lonesome even in his chosen loneliness—knew somebody in just that sort of bind. The dog had been a huffy lug named after a seasoning or a garnish. It had died of bloat and a heart hard to make out. My friend had the crate brought over, and we looked at the thing for a while until he thought to say, "You'll fit."

This friend locked me in certainly. There were a couple of stainless-steel bowls to be hung—one for food, the other for water—and he promised to keep both of them topped off. There was a long, shallow pan for him to slide underneath.

I must have let out a whimper, because he said, "You're not a dog. You're in a dog's crate."

So for a few days I felt cramped, no argument there, and my skin was waffled from the wired sides and floor, but I have only one remaining complaint. My friend one morning brought me a magazine, a jubilating weekly, and I opened it and laid it on my floor, but there was no way for me to read the thing. My eyes were too close to the pages. So I spread the magazine up against the side of the crate. That way, though, I was just blocking the light. I told myself to remember to tell my friend to leave the lamp on the next time he came to refresh the bowls. But I never did. The magazine was eventually in the way, and I accidentally dirtied it, and my friend brought around someone who brought in bedding from his car—oversheets and undersheets, foam-rubber stuffings, an unfrilled duvet. The two of them went to waste on each other in stages upstairs.

Inside of a month, I had already been living alone in a new apartment, adjusting to the parquetry and pilot lights, waiting for this to be the one time I thought better of myself and my marriage, when I began to hear, at unpredictable hours (once as late as weekday midnight), a couple of men on good terms of some stubborn sort in the apartment under mine. But whether what I was divining in these voices was the residential ease and ridicule of companions or the trucelike give-and-take of repairmen on call, I could not finally get it settled.

In sum: whether the night befell the day or vice versa, the hours of either were soon full-laden with little else than these two vocal but unintelligible presences downstairs.

So I brought over my wife. She pressed an ear humoringly to the floorboards, harked, then pronounced the two of them father and grown son working puzzles in the paper, hand-minded folks finding holiday hours on the comics page.

My wife once more: that little rizzle of hair on the upper spread of her foot, for one thing, and bullying breasts muted by a bra the color of those bandages you were expected to stretch resourcefully around a sprain.

She would take her dinner to the telephone table—a treacly salad, a clod or two of chocolate—and wipe the hair out of her eyes when it came time to play it down again that something was considered forgiven, if only in a newsy sort of way.

DOG AND OWNER

Not too long after having insisted, when the day finally arrived, on being seated, by myself, at an arm's-length remove from tables now pushed together in makeshift, banquet-style annexation, and then (once the guests, the few of them there were, relations of hers, with a few drinks in them apiece, had at last taken their leave), having made short work of fussing myself free from whatever might have been "put sacred" between the two of us (because the girl and I had never been close: at most, I had seen to setting up, by her side and in my stead, in eulogy to some vague, perishing beauty of hers, an ornate and embellishable absence into which, from farther and farther off, I had been good about throwing even more endearments, encouragings, and so forth)—not too long afterward, in short, I remember having stopped one afternoon for an overpostponed lunch, something quick and unconsidered, in a bystreet coffee shop whose narrow band of windows, once I had got myself established at last in a booth, cropped the second, and terminal, stories of the buildings across the street in a way that gave a persuasive, even elegant, suggestion of a grand upsweep just out of view, as if the little I could make out were in fact foundationary of something vast and overtowering, an abrupt city impending over the low-strung town I was despised in. This last, of course, was exactly the sort of conviction I was getting much better at keeping propped up, sawhorse style, above the lurid floor of my forties; and thus, after the meal, chancing the streets again and resorting, almost at once, to the town's one catchy avenue, the line of buildings looking understandably stooped and unfinished to me now, I would halt every half-minute or thereabouts to tilt my head back in regard of, say, a storefront that shouldered a couple of floors of sooty apartments, and then, taking the full, unruly measure of what I saw, let my eyes step everything up to what, until now, had been merely implied heights. In no time, I was entertaining, banking

on, similarly enlarging abstractions about people, persons—
namely, that they no doubt had to be just getting started right
there where their bodies stopped short, and that there were bound
to be further, more considerable attractions just above eyeshot;
and it was then that I noticed it, a figure hunching its way with
unsteady gait toward me along the sidewalk, as if there were at least
one extra foot to be worked into the problem of walking, and when
this form drew close, I could make out an outnumbered-looking
man of about my age, arms blundering outward, one hand busying
itself with the ticky clickwork of a ballpoint, and a face devoted
to an assailant nose and metrical eye-blinks—the eyes, it seemed,
forever figuring their owner in and then out again of difficult,
riskful head counts. There was such an aboveboard loveliness in
the joinery of all parts of him, in the way his body seemed to verge
away from itself and into the space upkept between the two of us,
that I decided, at once, to make an experience of him, to call him
up out of himself then and there, though it might well have been
little more than tricks, hoaxes, of reposturing that I was capable
of bringing off, and it is entirely likely that I had already dropped
to my knees, and it could have been either one of us, in fact, who
let out, "Not here, not here," for he was by now stretching an arm
toward a car across the street, a four-door dejecture done over in
a low-down, militarized olive-gray, and we went to the thing, and
got in, and he took off in the direction of some watercourse or
another, because it was a town dulled by water, streamy silences
of it, fits and starts of a bigger, dishevelled river downstate; and
letting him be keeper of the quiet, I threw my mouth open to the
knowledges, the crammed expertise, I fell back on in just such
sudden but slow-going crosstown companionships, remarking, to
start, that there was a way to cough without even having to part
the lips—the most it required was setting off a dampened clicking
just behind the Adam's apple; and that at the baccalaureate
shithouse that was still keeping me on, "with reservations," from
month to month, I had helped myself to the discovery that if you
were true to the same pair of trousers for four or five days running
(here I pointed, by way of example, to the set of flagging flannels

in which I had been carrying myself about), your faithfulness would make of the change collecting in the pockets (and here I gave some demonstrational tinklings) a weighty, wallet-rivalling wealth; and that it was not so much that the dog and its owner come to look like each other as that they both by degrees take on a trim, unbidden resemblance to a third party, a truant, dancing an unseen attendance on the two of them as it plunges its way forth to take at last the delayed, necessary spills.

The man's watch, I now noticed, as he ventured some even more finical turnings of the steering wheel, had not been strapped onto him so that the dial, the outcase, would face below the arm in the routine, oblivion-securing fashion of the deskbound, but instead was posited at the outermost bend of the wrist, just beyond where the half-globelet of bone stuck out, and thus fronted away from him entirely, so that no carpal motion, or any greater chance mission of the arm itself, would ever risk bringing the dial into his view. For this, you see, was the weekend we gained an hour, and people, persons, were understandably slower, more bashful, in prying their way into further others, or running themselves on a bias through whoever else there was, or keeling forward into a chosen one, once and (let them hope) done.

But this man, perish the thought, was nobody of mine, though my fingers steal, stole, forever downward everywhere regardless.

They could make a day of it on anyone.

I remember coming to, much later, in a room, an uprooted-looking bedroom, where a woman was operating an opaque projector, one of those big-bulbed, plastic gimmicks, half toy, that gave off the private and chastening smell of clothes being ironed and that was throwing any chosen small objects onto the one undecorated wall at many times their meek, certain size. (This was a shovy, fast-swallowing woman with an unheated air of seniority about her and thick, lengthsome hair parted so severely, so opponentially, that it fell onto me in twinned antagonisms.) I know I sat up, at once, on the brink of the bed as her pinked fingers ushered things in and out of the display area of the projector (she had the thing propped up, you see, on her lap), and I remember her making a show of the discernibles, incommodities, released from the pockets of my pants: my keys, the mostly invalid few of them I had strung along the lower bend of a paper clip, the snaggled serrations of each now looking gouged out, geologic; the butt of a pencil I had once held dear; a little breaking, an abruption, of kitchen-floor linoleum I had taken to carrying about because there were gabbing faces and sheer, intentional geography discoverable within it once you got the knack of how such things demanded to be seen.

The man, of course, was still lying only several, witting inches away from me, compact and delicate in his sleep, packed into it, practically, and there was such a kindly deportment to him, and such a thrift in the inturning of his limbs, that I kept my voice down when the only thing for me to tell the woman, the one thing left to get rubbed in, was that I could remember having sought my father's counsel only once: I had needed some help with getting around the endearment called for in the salutation of a postcard I was destining for a friend, or for a stand-in for the friend I was impatient to have come forward, because this was the summer between the grade when I last looked to people for what they had already seen of everybody else, and the grade when I started seeing that the people I looked at were blocking my view of even fuller numbers of people behind them, that people up close were in fact coming between me and the rest of the world, that the most I might make out of the people on the other side would be the perimetrical fraction of midriff that now and then showed through when the person behind was a hair broader than the person out front, or (just once) a pair of arms spiring above a head in what might have been mere exercise but which in my eyes acquired the status of purposeful beckoning; and the criticism thus set down now with greatest, red-inked frequency on the backs of report cards was that my voice no longer travelled direct to the teacher's face, but went around the face, or to the side of it, and that my answers not only were louder than what the acoustics of the classroom called for, but seemed addressed to someone in back of the teacher, someone on the other side of the wall behind her, or somebody several rooms down. And thus the postcard—the front of the picture postcard I was subjecting at last to reminiscence, the one I had been intent on seeing off: the thing threw in your face, naturally, the name of the beach town, the resort, spelled rollickily in hollowed block letters, every one of which gave out, windowlike, on a different span of the same boardwalk, the plankway on which I had to keep to my latecomer's place between my father's sogging trunks and my mother's tagalong dress when, at mealtime, my parents halted in front of one concession after another to have a look at whoever had been at the meat, and what had been made of it, how unproportioned or lonesome the sandwiches looked once they had at last been let down onto the paper plates, and my father or the other always saying, "We can do better," or "The day is still young"; and on the matter, at last, of the salutation for my postcard, what my father therefore recommended was *Buddy Walt*, but when my ballpoint got going between my fingers, what I was writing was *Friend Walter* instead, and then I of course crossed out *Walter*— more than crossed it out; overspread it with stickied opulences of the violet ink—and then got rid of *Friend*, put it out of my sight, cancelled it with even more busied stickiness, and, after many an airborne hesitation of the writing hand, I simply wrote *You!*— *Y*O*U!*; i.e., Why, oh, you!—and left the address panel blank, spotless, unmolested, on the strength of the unforeseen conviction that like-natured postmen would certainly recognize virtues in the high points of my penmanship and keep the card in noticeable motion along the upper currents of the mailstream until the thing got itself claimed, finally, by anyone eyewatery and room-ridden enough to have expected delayed, devout word from somebody anyplace else.

For, you see (I told the woman), the actual writing of what I wrote on the postcard was brought to happen in a tent-trailer, a sulfur-yellow, boxlike concernment that had been hired only for the week, vacation week, and that was hitched to the car and had to be folded out at both ends to get the up-spreading canvas portioned into taut walls and a roof, and to produce the cantilevered ledges on which we piled the bedding and went through the hours of degraded nighttime that we had come to expect in place of sleep, my parents at one end, gone weak in their horse sense, and I at the other, still picky about my feelings, all boned up on myself, contesting my life—for the little I had set down in the message panel of the postcard could have been only the first of many reminders to stop siccing my heart on the locals and just get my loneliness finally right.

ALL TOLD

The day my sister died, I was the first to make a parting from the packs of shadow in the tall room. She did not exactly look hemmed in by death.

I still remember her telephone number. Something happens to a phone number when it is held too readily in recall. The movement of those digits through memory gains the unheaviness, the fated headway, of haiku. You feel foreordained in even your faintest of furies.

I mean, there was something physical about the way I kept ringing her up—a finger maybe in the ribs.

My parents later attracted a calamity of their own. Crossed the center line in their cozy sedan. (I was the one who had put them up to "seeing some lights.") I thus had an inherited house all to myself. But if I came around to learning that places can have consequences, too, I hardly mean only the easy contagions of furniture, or any room's inevitable, irreversible digestion of its contents. What I wish to insist is that anything you look at can have a way of holding itself against everything else. I thus became a specialist in the fevered and exactive marriage of a week to ten days. The women all had shrewd, fortunate hair.

But I can bring most of them back—my family, at least.

I will forever be cueing them up in gesture, throes, locution.

My father: I can read a book as uncleanly as he could. I leave a luxuriant organicity to behold on most pages. Hardenings, cakings, fingertrails.

And my mother: I line my upper teeth behind the lowers until my jaw shoots forward a little and I am no longer speaking up for others.

But my sister! I cannot carry out her life with anything I am currently putting over on people.

Even in dirty weather, my hands are tied.

THE SUMMER I COULD WALK AGAIN

They are never in the house at the same time. My cousin's skin isn't packed on right. It bunches up at the knees. When she talks, she hoops a bracelet back and forth along her arm from the wrist all the way to the elbow—that's how thin.

She's low on people and places, you can tell.

She knows better than to call me the man of the house.

She says a new day is too big a thing right away. You have to nap it down until you fit inside.

She's allowed in my bed. Her snores come in long lines that tip way up at the end. What I hear is questions—somebody asking me the same thing over and over, something simple.

My answer is no.

I place my leg over hers, then hers over mine. Her limp hand goes anywhere I decide. I uncurl her fingers and put them over where I am all wrong. I'm allowed in her purse. The mirror inside her compact holds exactly my face.

"Did you sleep?" she says afterward.

There are two of them next door, brothers, a year or so apart. Their names would just ruin everything. I loop electrical wire around my wrist, pale my neck and arms with talcum. I let them practice on me one at a time.

First it counted only if I could get them to keep their eyes open. Then it counted either way.

Today it's the younger.

My hand on his arm, the promised rise of bicep.

We sit on our hands and our feet. Different parts of us go to sleep at different times. Nothing gets put away.

There is a list, my cousin says, of everything my mother knows is not right. I cannot get her to show it to me or even tell me what room it might be in.

"It is all written down about you," she says.

"Your mother works where?" my cousin says.

"For the state."

"Only time anybody ever tells me that is when they work in a liquor store."

Leaving, she says, "Is everything off that gets taken off?"

She looks me over for signs.

"You don't know the first thing about it," my cousin says.

I tell her about the brothers.

"Besides those," she says.

She takes my fingers in hers and puts the two of us into where she is nothing but mush and pulp.

"You're one hole short," she says.

They come out of the water, new hair staining their shins. To get them into the house, I tell them I can give birth.

They follow me up the stairs and into the bathroom. I am good at pulling down my pants. I sit on the toilet and squeeze and squeeze until I get something finally sizable to come out.

It's the only reason I eat—to get off the seat and point down into the bowl at what should be the beginnings of arms or a heart.

The best way to clean a carpet in the long run, she says, is to pick everything out of it by hand. I'm on my knees, going from room to room, filling my pail with fuzzballs, bits of paper, pebbles, shells of beetles. Every room has something different for her to flop on.

"One summer, I was like that with girls," she says. "Every ponytailed little brat up and down the block thought she had me spoken for."

She comes from a family big enough, she says, for everyone in it to have always been looking the other way. According to her, this is what makes her an only child.

■　　■　　■

"It's not a mouth," she says. "I already have a mouth."

I am folding the big towels.

It is long after dark when I knock on the screen door.

The younger one comes toward me through the kitchen, his eyes and mouth shadowed off, his face just a blacked circle.

I know him by height.

"We're not allowed out, and you're not allowed in," he says.

I look down at my clean feet.

Is it one mistake after another, or is it the same one divvied up to make it last from one day to the next?

The door to my mother's room is always shut but never locked. Her life is private but not secret. I have to remember which way the hooks of her clothes hangers point before I take anything off them. My body has no smell of its own yet. Nothing remains of me on whatever I put myself against.

Nothing settles on me, either.

That's the thing.

Nothing ever comes to any kind of rest.

I am standing along the road when a car comes close, slows.

"Are you selling something?" a voice says.

There is a man and a woman in the car, a couple.

"Don't anybody sell anything anymore along this road?" the man says. "This looks like the road."

"She's not looking at us," the woman says.

"It don't look like it," the man says.

"Maybe she's not selling something right this very minute but has plans for the future," the man says. "That could be it. How about we drive around some more and come back in maybe half an hour and then see if she's gotten a head for business?"

I run back to the porch, where my cousin has the carrots ready for me to peel.

"Who was that?" she says.

"Somebody looking for Dad."

I get into their room just once. I ask which dresser drawers I am allowed to open.

It's not a dresser, they tell me. It's a chest of drawers.

They are ready for bed.

My cousin no longer gives out information, because of things I do with it.

She tells me about where she came from originally. At one time it was the seat of something, she says. The world wore itself onto the people who lived there and onto the legs of the pants and the sleeves of the shirts and the raincoats that the people put themselves through to get out of its way. When they undressed at night, the clothes fell onto the floor along the track the world had taken.

Otherwise, she says, nobody slept.

The doctor tells my mother to stay off her feet for a week.

"You have the air blowing right over you," she says.

I get up and turn things off.

My reading matter is the warnings on the backs of cleaning products. I have the bottles lined up on the bathroom floor. The stickers come right out and say Do Not.

My mother is downstairs making the sandwiches the way she was taught. My cousin's are just stacks of sliced bread, nothing in between unless she's in a mood.

I come down in my underwear.

"Is it doing you any good?" my mother says. "Does she go over things with you? Is anything coming across? Does it pay me to keep her? Is she ever on time? What does she do around here all day? Do you listen to a thing she says?"

I have been told that when people say they see my father in me, I am to do one of two things.

The first is just to tell them that it must be only because he's trying to get their attention because he wants something again. Otherwise he wouldn't be showing himself in me of all people.

The other is for when people have already stayed too long. I'm supposed to say, "Where? Point him out. Show me where, so I can pull him out all the way. Maybe I can shit him out. Think that would work? Let's go see."

I have done both, but sometimes I just picture my body glassed over and my father motioning from within, bobbing up now and then between my bones, no big trouble.

My mother is back at work.

"I took some things of mine to a dry cleaner once, as a treat," my cousin says. "The man behind the counter looked everything over and said, 'Who wore these?'"

I'm in the grass when they come up from behind. One grabs me by the ankles, the other under the arms. I like them this quiet. They carry me across the field—the sky is bowled above me—and drop me into the stream.

The water is cold but not deep.

They run off, leaving me staring up.

Then I'm on the warm macadam. One has my shirt and shorts and is riding his bike in a circle, whipping them dry.

I am in his.

Everything sticks.

"You're the instigator," the other says.

Who can sleep? There was a penlight flashlight on a beaded chain my grandmother bought me once. I had to keep clicking it on and off and on again to make sure the thing still worked. It finally no longer did. It was a relief to go on to something else.

In like manner, I count on losing the use of my eyes because of what I do with them—closing and opening them too many times, expecting fresh letdowns in the way things look from one instant to the next.

■　　■　　■

I'm upstairs in the bathroom, hearing everything.

"Are you the mother?" It's a woman's voice.

"I'm who the mother pays," my cousin's voice says.

"What about the boy—he's here?"

"Can't say. I might've dozed off."

"He was obviously here earlier. I understand he had some company."

"He's in and out."

"Tell him the mother of the boys next door wants him to know he's made two very nice boys very sick to their hearts."

"Count on it."

I'm on the bowl with my legs tighter together, not ready to see what else might have happened since I last had a look down, when I first saw toes on a foot, a definite mouth.

FEMME

I used to visit a younger man in the big, voluminal city, the one that maddened itself out between twin rivers. He would call and say, "Just get here." I would drive half a day to a town within two hours of the place, then park, and ride a bus the rest of the way. There would be the rummaged abundance of his hair, the blooded trouble of his eyes, hands runted becomingly—but he always just wanted me to go out with him with his friends, a characterful alumni brigade. Once, one of them had found the "perfect winter bar," and it was in fact winter, forced-air heat had dried up all their faces, and my younger man returned from the barkeep with some timely femme sparkle for me to spurn through a straw, unobscured spirits for himself. Our table was two tables brought together unlevelly. His friends were lounging quietly in whichever private, humble injuries could have then been current.

But my love for him must have been flush with the line of his arm as often as he got it propped up to make his point: that things should be kept figmentary on people, between people—

So I suppose, yes, we were serious about each other, only graver than two men usually are about failings they are fleeing.

Later, in his apartment, a walk-up, I watched him beat himself back from me again.

Before him, I had had a wife: a wife, true, who kept a glaze over everything. I would have to scratch my way through it if I hoped to find anything unhypothetical. (She exhausted her hair with denigratory tints, and there was a stirless dark to her eyes. Contact was chancy, ungladdening.) It was a period, understand, of rationed, grating embraces, and then one day she came out with a baby, sprang it on me in a bassinet upstairs. I know I must have eventually confused the thing with mock holidays, and lonely toilet drills, and homemade cereals that just sank in the milk, and I know I must have stood the kid up in front of uncles and ball-rolling aunts, and then this wife vanished with it into her vague-faced, waiting family. These were people who uprooted themselves tooth and nail, hurried their furniture over highways into ditchy, isolating towns. They were letter writers, but they mostly just wrote, "We know about you."

I have since turned many a corner in what I know of myself.

I can take apart a marriage, and sense when a possessiveness might be difficult to undo.

One morning I found a pill outside a neighbor's door. It was reason enough to have stooped some more. This was a vagrant, gray prescriptional with narrow characters sunken dingily into the face. I went back to my place and gave the thing a concerned chew, then put my system on alert for any improving diddling within. I waited half an hour, an hour, an hour and a half.

I was living in an apartment complex. There is no use in hearing the term "apartment complex" unless it is taken immediately to mean a syndrome, a fiesta of symptoms.

On the other side of my bathroom, someone was living a life that called for lots of water. I would almost always hear it streaming remedially into the tub, the sink.

People, co-workers, naturally inquired about whether I had a girlfriend, and if I mentioned somebody "now gone from this world," I did so in the expectancy that by "this world" they would understand me to have meant not the entire subcelestial estate or national agitation, but just my unlargening residential snatch of it and the few places I might have once taken someone—the second-hand-clothing stores and bested restaurants of the unample town.

This town—you had to get your hands on a different, specialized map just to find it.

It was a hollowed-out dot of round-shouldered population. Roughnecks ran the college.

My younger man: he had moved around a lot on people. A lot of casework, social work, had gone into him. He lived on purified tap water and spangled baked goods. His face rarely carried an expression to term, but there was expression in his elbow, a mien to be made out in either of the underarms.

Some nights it was all I could do to keep from adding my lips to the mouth of a bottle he had once put his mouth around when pausing for effect in some gracing self-criticism.

His face? He called it a rat face.

His ass? He said there was a word in his grandmother's tongue for the way the flab seemed to be coming up from it in little bubbles. It was a pimpling or a pilling my dabbling eye had never minded.

There was a bar of soap he had used a couple of times, a woman's soap, with womanly incurvature. I had held on to it. I would draw it unwetted along my cheek, the distance of my arm. I would try to bring a little back, however much of him might still be sticking to the thing, because I understood the molecules of soap to be especially grasping and retentive, and the skin of a man to be not all that loyal to the body.

When you live in apartments, understand, you go over the communal walls daily, fingering for sightways, cracks, exposures, scopes.

You resort further and further to the TV, just to hear voices coming physically out of pictured people and not through ceilings, cupboardry, the floor.

I was no model rider of the bus, either. I saw arms, swaying legs, that might have belonged on anyone. Everybody was the same body, no matter the twists of personship, the agonied differences of fit and build.

Then I must have been caused to fall for a woman, a regular on the jumbly, crosstown run, because one day one part of her would be arisen, pivotal, summonsy, awag—a chancing hand, perhaps, or gleamed, unsecretful ankle. By the next day, the center of her would have shifted. A couple of public weeks like this, and finally she said, "So what do you think? Could you use a friend?"

I moved my things in. This woman turned out to have a daughter, a struggler, who was late to take after her. The girl's body was now in brutal pursuit of the mother's. The girl seized the mother's most liable features, and brought them—panging, pushful—to semblant possession on herself.

The mother's face gave ground. I watched it unpile itself.

Her voice was a gurge.

I would tread tenorlessly on floorboards on my way to the stairs.

Our life thereafter was just another huddledom of sorts, the three of us jumpy, barely belittleable, usually of a piece.

THE BOY

T he boy was raised in a city that had the look and feel of a state capital but in fact was not even a county seat. The buildings—big, brutish granite piles—gave everybody the wrong idea. Travellers would see the castellated skyline from the highway, sheer off at the exit, park their cars, then climb steep steps to what they hoped, despite the absence of signs, of plaques, would prove to be a mint, a museum, a monument. Once inside, they would find themselves in cramped, fusty living quarters. Somebody—an old woman in a housecoat or a bed jacket—would look up from a sofa and say, "Let a person sleep." The boy, on the other hand, did not have the look and feel of anything big or promising. You couldn't look up his name in books. Even as a child, he had always remained many removes from himself. Wherever he stood—near the swing set on a playground, say—he was never inarguably there, but his absence was always firsthand. His absence, in fact, was so commanding, so convincing, that people around him were often confused about just exactly where they too now stood. Obviously, his parents must have caught on very early to the unexampled form of ventriloquism the boy had evolved, a ventriloquism that entailed displacing not just his voice but his entire flute-thin body, and they made the necessary adjustments—sudden half-steps or about-faces—in their own strides. That's why people thought they walked funny, that's why people thought they looked funny together as a family.

One day, well gone in childhood, the boy sat at the kitchen table and watched the father solder together two wires on the boy's tape recorder.

The tape recorder was of the old, reel-to-reel type.

The father was not especially good with his hands. In fact, the soldering iron—the risk that its use introduced into his life—was a terror. More important, the father was unforgiving. He was so unforgiving that he gave in, time after time, doing everything for the boy out of a big, banging spite. With every splenetic dab of the soldering iron, the father thought he was defecting from a deductive scheme that always runs: Father, Mother, Son.

The boy was convinced that by destroying his playthings he was accomplishing something similar.

Walking home from the high school he attended at the other end of the city, the boy would often linger in a park near the very tallest of the buildings. Crestfallen tourists would on occasion approach him. Once, a long-throated, heavily talcumed woman asked, "Have you a pen on your person?" The boy slued around slowly and exaggeratedly, as if to see whether there was a third party involved, an attendant bearing supplies. There was only his own angled, outbound body and, at a respectable distance, her own, the globulet of a tear glissading down her cheek. The woman moved on. There were plenty of men in the park whose pockets were full of pens and whatever else there might be a call for.

One day early in his eleventh-grade year, the boy was summoned from his social-studies class to the office of the guidance counselor. The guidance counselor was a short-winded block of a man with corned teeth and an overexerted vocabulary. He explained that to the best of his knowledge it would be in the best interest of both the boy and the school if, for the remainder of his tuition, he were enrolled as a girl. He explained that the parents had already been informed and that the papers had already been drawn up and dispatched for them to sign. That night, the boy's mother took the boy shopping for the pair of Mary Janes, the jumper, enough white blouses for a week. The boy became very popular at school, excelled at all his subjects to the extent that was then expected of girls, and enjoyed many boyfriends and admirers, all of whom he did his very best to delight. At the commencement ceremony, the guidance counselor delivered a long speech about the boy and his progress. The speech was full of words like "miracle" and "rapture" and "angel." During the peroration, the guidance counselor publicly proposed to the boy. They were married a week afterward in an elaborate but rushed ceremony, during which the minister looked content in the knowledge that this smell would cover up that smell and so forth down the line, domino-style. Two weeks later, the guidance counselor died loudly and tumultuously in his sleep. The boy slipped out of his negligee and slumped across the dark city to the house of his parents.

With his diploma and a cajoling, loopily handwritten letter of application, the boy was offered employment three hundred and forty-two miles to the right of his bed if he was facing the wall that held the window, a position he favored. He engaged a room, sight unseen, over the telephone.

A week before the boy was to depart, his mother decided he would need a rug. She drove him to a carpet store to have a look at remnants.

The boy watched the salesman slide a licorice cough drop into his mouth from the box in the pocket of his shirt.

"You certainly know your way around in here," the salesman said eventually to the boy.

The boy turned away and paged through some carpet samples bound together in a thick, shaggy book.

"I was saying, ma'am, that your son here has sure been spending a lot of time in this store," the salesman said.

"We'll want something for the floor," the mother said.

"Okay," the salesman said. "What are we talking about?"

"It's just one big room," the mother said.

"How big of a room?" the salesman said.

The mother looked at her son. "How big a room?"

The boy did not answer.

"It's one state over," the mother said.

There is an explanation for patricide that works in every case. In every case, there is a soda machine close at hand.

The boy was always thirsty. The boy was always hurrying across the street to the machine, buying one can at a time, carrying it back to his room to drink at the table. The father was in town only for a visit. The greasy whorls of the father's thumbprints had already blurred the cover of the hobby magazine the boy had bought for the father to leaf through. Also on the table was an iron that the boy worried was prowing in a different direction every time he returned from the machine.

"You drink way too much soda," the father said, finally.

"I'm thirsty," the boy said.

"Then drink water."

"I hate water."

"Soda don't even quench your thirst. Look at the money you're throwing away."

"If it doesn't quench my thirst, then tell me what it does do."

"It makes the inside of your mouth and throat nice and cold for a couple seconds. That's it. Water would do just as good."

The boy and the father sat and wordlessly pushed their points.

The knife presented itself to the boy as if in shimmery italics. The boy could not remember ever having bought the thing. It was a heftless, nervous-atomed, self-disowning simulacrum of what a knife was supposed to look like in such a low-built town.

As on so many occasions, this was the boy's first time, but everything rang a bell—a cracked, mootish, spanging bell. Each clank of it brought him a clangorous bit closer to the understood *you*.

THIS IS NICE OF YOU

I was a man dropping already well through my forties, filthy with myself, when, taking a turn at the toilets one afternoon, I met two brothers—they said they were brothers—who swore they had a sister, a schoolteacher, an officer of instruction at the county college, a whirlwind midlife turmoil of everything already put to ruin, who had gone off from a new marriage in an old car, an upkept and ennobling sedan, but had returned now to the apartment and was living there alone with the little runoff there was from the marriage—some outcurved appliances, apparently, and low-posted furniture promoting its own mystery but becoming figurable in certain concentrations of TV light—and, above all, a telephone (on a pedestal, they insisted), the handpiece of which she gripped in lieu of exercise, or in fury, and I thus let out my little, reliable cry that I was in fact a student of the telephone, that it was a debasing apparatus in the main, with its meager economy of bells and tones, and the intimacy of the mouthpiece that sent your breath, tiny aftervapors of it, back toward your lips, so that regardless of the party accepting the outgoing products of your voice, you were, at most, in a further, rivalling exchange with yourself alone, and this is what must have brought the two of them around, the men who proclaimed brotherhood with the woman, because they offered me her phone number, put it at my disposal on a piece of paper one of them had already committed it to, a snipping from a menu, and the looks the men were now giving me had deletions in them, already, of my exact, beanpole shape and size. So off I went to a pay phone, the nearest canopied one I could find. The woman answered after the second ring and said she needed a lift right that very minute into the little, unlevel city close by.

She was idling in the doorway of the building when I pulled up in front, and I helped her into the car, then got back in myself. I had always had a way of not having to look at people that nonetheless brought them to me in full, and so I still am certain of the susceptive and impressible complexion, the shimmer on the mouth, a lipstick of low brilliance, a difficulty around the eyes, the hair short and rayed out exclamationally, skin bagged up over the elbow bone, conflict even in how her arms stayed at her sides— in sum, a spinal loveliness for me, an off-blond quantity with shadowed, thumbworn hollows that put me out of as much as I might have ever known of women before.

I set the two of us into the narrow traffic, and I remember telling her, by way of explaining the little burden which I had shifted, by now, from the shelf of the dashboard and onto my lap, that when you lived as I then did, a daily newspaper came to count for a lot, although instead of the thick-supplemented local paper, I bought a trimmer one from a backlying town—not, of course, for any affluences of native data it carried, but as an article of houseware: a rough immaculacy in four lank sections, a set of fresh, hygienic surfaces to come between the table, say, and whatever I had going for me on the table, if the table was where I was going forward—because what else so cheap comes so clean and far-spreading?

The woman told me that her own trouble with paper was that through a modest hole, no larger than a quarter, that had been drilled a foot or so above the floor (the standard height, she had reasoned, of legitimate electrical outlets), and by means of which her faculty office had at last gained communication with the roomier but unoccupied office next door, she more and more often shot a single sheet of paper, plain copier paper she had rolled just barely into a tube, so that after landing on the floor of the neighboring office, the paper would preserve little if any of the curl, and there would be nothing written or typed on it, of course, and it was always a blank sheet that had been ageing on her desk for some time and had already been moved around, or advanced, from station to station on the desktop, coming into further creaselets and crimps and other infirmities—paper, in short, still too bare and unfraught to be thrown responsibly and forgettably away, and yet too seasoned and beset with irritations of the surface (a molelike blemish, say, or what looked like a tiny hair, an eyelash, sunk into it, or frecklings, or notational pressings of a fingernail), too *wrought,* in sum, for the paper to be appointed to any secure curricular purpose. Her office, she claimed, was in fact full of such paper, much-handled and singularized sheets of it by the loose, functionless hundred.

I had to get it across to the woman that I myself no longer had an office, or any other place to divide me reliably from everybody else, and that for much of the daylight I thus appeared to be among people because I kept putting myself where people came together into even closer-fitting assortments, the viewing areas and showrooms and rotundas and such: I took in the lean-to look of the women, the tongues coming and going in what the men kept thinking of to say—whole families of low knees for me to bark my shins against during the crowded and involving way out. At home afterward, in the one room where my life was packed down, I would keep my nose stuck in the safehold of the phone book, where the names of people suffered reduction to mere episodes of the alphabet and underwent humbling declensions down every column (Lail, Lain, Laine, Lainerd), and the names of streets, of the towns and townships, got docked in crude, heedless abbreviations (the vowels almost always the first to get poked out), and I would run my eyes over the telephone numbers themselves, each sequence of digits another fallible run of the infinite. I thus corrected my feelings for people and assembled myself emotionally into whatever else I had at hand—the obligating arms of the clothes hangers, usually, or the keen-angled understructure, the guardian legginess, of the ironing board.

The woman said that in her case, though, it was more a matter of making slow circuits of the classroom where she had to put across the Emporial Sciences, retail theory and methods, to heat-giving and suggestive young women, some of them world cruelties already. There was the cooing of empty stomachs in the hour just before lunch, and the braying and fizzle of loaded stomachs in the low hours of the afternoon. She would recite her notes in a voice barely loyal to any one octave, a tiny alluvium of slaver hardening at the corners of her mouth on the days she gave the glassy lozenges a slow, warming suck, and she would take lowering notice of how whatever she said succumbed at once to freak spellings and razzing paraphrase in the big, dividered notebooks; and because in midafternoon light the world looked as thorough, as filled in, as it was ever going to get, a better way to set about ruining her eyes was to review how hair had established itself on the arms of the young women, because almost every arm had brought across itself a welcome and diversifying shadow. On one girl it would be a fine, driftless haze afloat above the white of the arm, never seeming to touch down on the skin itself. (An atmosphere, at most, of Brazil-nut brown.) On another, it was as if copper wire, the narrowmost lengthlets of it, had been stuck into the fleshy batter of the thick, freckled forearms. On a third: a field of it—wheat-colored, thin-spun. On a fourth: a differencing, darkish updrift that shaded off as it approached the inner bend of the elbow, then re-emerged at the base of the upper arm as whiskery fringe. On others it was a brassy or rust-colored frizz, or it was as coarse as corn silk, or it looked fussed on, as if the arm had been slowly stroked with charcoal.

But here the woman broke off, or I may well have made an interruption of my own—I think I must have asked whether she was hungry, and she said if I was, and so on one of the lesser streets I parked the car and led her down into a belowstairs eating house I still remembered. Sandwiches were presently lowered in front of us. I watched her remove the festooned toothpick from hers and then play her fingers over the toasted planes before she took a fond, first bite.

"This is nice of you," she said.

I must have looked at her in the way I then had of getting people to speak so they would not seem to be dwelling any longer on my features, because if on the well-set face the mouth and eyes are said to seem frozen in elegant orbit about the tip of the nose, then mine was a face that beholders, regarders, could not help trying to round off with greater success, to goad the particulars of it back into the arcs they had wandered away from—the mouth, for instance, having been pursed and pinched suchwise that it

seemed resident more on one side of the face than the other—
and there were other signs of original strife to be busied with
(slapdash eyebrows unbunched, it appeared, from reserves of hair
elsewhere on my person; a showing of adult acne, a shrivelly little
relevance of it, confined to the declivity of my nose); and so to
be polite, the woman thus sank her gaze into her sandwich, and
told me, in a voice lowered accordingly, that, one late-childhood
summer, she had devoted herself to collecting postage stamps: it
was a tongue-involving sideline to early-arriving puberty, and she
liked having to lick the pale, gummed hinges instead of the sticky
backs of the stamps themselves before entering everything into the
hosting album; and once, during some foul weather between her
and a brother (the older, thrown-over one, who had already made
a habit of fooling the underside of his arm across the top of hers
and calling her "pussified"), she reached for the shoe box in which
she had let duplicate stamps accumulate—Spanish ones, mostly,
of a fading orange—and sent the box slooshing through the lower
air so that the stamps showered onto the brother's bare legs with a
full, delicate harm.

The woman was now touching up the surface of her iced tea
with tiny activities, initiatives, of the longspun spoon. I myself
was good at getting my touch onto things, although in a way that
seemed to mix up the motive atoms inside them, but I was satisfied
that for the moment my sandwich, the unbitten-at half of it, was
still displayable and stable and local to my plate.

The woman went on to say that, as a child, she had been
bundled off, many an afternoon, to the slope-ceilinged quarters of
a bachelor uncle, who, when speaking of anybody not immediately
present, could not bring himself to use the person's name but
instead would say "an acquaintance of mine in..." and then
mention the name of some lapsed homeland, or little-loved rural
orchestra, or backset building about to come down; and it was
never a riddle, this device of his (not once could the girl have been
expected to identify any of the subjects), and no matter how often
and aloud he insisted that particularizing persons any further—
bringing even a first name down upon any one of them—would

have been indecent, he claimed, much like doing things to people while they slept, the girl accepted all of the uncle's prim and extravagant evasion for what he surely must have intended it to be: a neat, protective trick to space the world out a little further in her favor, to scatter the population so that wherever her hand might at last come down, it would have to be on herself alone.

And here I could sense that the woman wanted from my mouth an account of as much as I myself might have ever managed of attachment, so I told her I had once owned a house (a rising, really, of much-fingered, handwrought architecture that amounted to a little family of rooms above garages: a boxlike building with a rattly thorax of downspouts and drainpipes and an unfolded but full-toned fire escape), and I had had for a time a boarder, a student, a high-colored, loose-packed representative of declining girlhood, hung with necklaces and barrettes, a girl of precise but shifting leanings and inclinations; and the afternoon she had come around to ask after the room, I stood in the entranceway, handshaken and asweat, and from what would later be my memory of the girl, I made off with, first, how every pore of her nose seemed to be sheltering within itself a tiny dark seedlet, a grain of something immediately, enormously valuable. And an almost lipless mouth (just a slit, practically), the teeth inside looking wet, watered—it was my life's chore, at that instant, to keep from sending the back of my thumb blotterlike across the line of them (I was later to learn she drank everything cold and through the narrowest of straws). And her hair: it was tea-colored hair she had, long and reachful, an unstopped downcome of it. Tall for a girl, but she managed to stay out of much of her height and put herself across as somebody backward, or behind.

I must have told the girl, as best I could, that I of course had a wife, a full-faced, imperishable partner, though for the moment she was gone otherwhere in the marriage, and here the woman, my present companion, my tablemate, whose feet were now parked, in parallel, on the grade of my upper leg, interrupted to say that her husband, too, had been such a liar, and what could I bring up by way of reply other than that a lie is a truth struck through with other, further truth, or that a lie is the present multiplied by the past, or that a lie is an outcry of borrowed hope? The woman gave me an allowed look of disgust, her eyes lowered but still popular with me, and on I went with what had now become the girl of my story.

For there had been a great, gainful carpet in the room I put the girl into, a matty expanse of coarse, grabby piles, an engrossing affair that took things into itself and held them tight, misered them, and I of course insisted that the girl not bother herself with its upkeep, that I enjoyed weekly access to a prestigious, upstanding vacuum cleaner; but no sooner was the girl out of the house each morning than I would withdraw from my room, where time was unportionable, and loose myself into the ticktock impertinence of the girl's room and get down on my knees, and, going after the carpet first with my fingers, then with a forceps, and finally by unspooling lengths of clear package-sealing tape and pressing them against the tufts in neat rectangles to catch what I might have missed, I brought vast tracts of the carpet to depletion, recovering not simply the girlinesses, the girleries, one would expect (buttons, straight pins, downed jewelry), but flirtier personalia in the form, say, of a stray confetto brought into the world when a page had been wrung without caution from a spiral-bound notebook, or some pleated paper shells of the chocolates she required, or one of the bargain antihistamines she took to get her naps going, or a trash-bag tie ragged enough to show the kinked line of the wire within (this I would get wound around my finger), or a cough drop enwrapped like a bonbon (I would undo the wings of the wrapper and have to decide whether to suck the drop all down or begin chewing it midway)—I became the following, the public, that these things, these off-fallings, had come to have; but mostly there was hair, afloat above the uppermost pushings of the fabric of the carpet an almost continuous haziness of loose hairs of all lengths and sources, and I would have to set them out on a fresh sheet of paper and assort them according to the regions of the body they had taken their departure from, and in no time I had nestlike filiations of broken filaments and smaller involvements of the hairs that made me think of hooks, of barbs, of treble clefs, and each pile required a separate envelope, to be filed in a separate shoe box for every sector of the body until, I hoped, the boxes themselves would no longer be enough and I would have raised something semblable, brought up something equal in volume to the comprehensive girl herself.

And her wastebasket! For every bit of rubbish, every dreariment she tossed into the thing, I would, in secret, deposit a reciprocal discard of my own, matching a spotted, confessory tissue of hers with a lurid throwaway after my own heart—the cardboard substructions of a fresh parcel of underwear, maybe, or tearings from pantyhose I now and again pressed against a span of my forearm to work onto it the complications of female shading I otherwise made do, choosily, without.

I thus built the two of us up together in her trash!

One afternoon—it was another of those unsampled days when the world humors us each a little differently to keep us nicely on our last legs—I discovered in the wastebasket an inch-deep textbook of hers, a paperback with a celery-colored cover that had come partly unglued, and this dilapidation I paired off, naturally, with a name-your-baby guide to whose pages, during my recurrent turnings of them, in bed or at table, I had contributed dried produces of my person, a chemical splendor entirely mine. This coupling sent a sudden spigoty thrill from me that forced an unbuckling and an unzipping and a cleanup with a handkerchief I then ventured responsively into the wastebasket as well.

It was in the bathroom afterward that I found a suds-clouded puddle on the unlevel floor of the tub, a little undrained remainder, rimmed with offscum, of the girl's prolonged early-morning soak, and this was as much as I needed to get on my hands; I pressed them flat against the wet porcelain, then flapped them around in the air, and that was when I noticed it—in the amphitheater of the toilet bowl, an orange-yellow tint, or value, to the waters.

When the girl arrived home that evening, I told her, of course, that I had discovered fresh, unforeseen trouble within the tank of the toilet (a misalignment of the trip lever, a waywardness of the float ball, a misarticulation of the lift wires, kinks and defects, really, throughout the entire system) and that, in fine, it was a contraption now operable only by means of advanced and strenuous equilibrial manipulations that it would be unseemly, inhospitable, of me to presume to burden her with—so that from here on out, following any leak or evacuation she need merely lower the lid and then, before quitting the room, ring the handbell that had been placed on the sink; I would see to everything else.

But the bell never rang, not even once, and from my window the next morning I watched the girl carry from the house a little plastic bag distended balloonishly, much like those bags you will remember having seen in the hands of children bearing homeward their solitary, carnival-prize goldfish. In fact, I never ran across the likes of the girl again. The man who came to collect her things— not the father, apparently, but an advocate, an upholder—I found to be dull-eared and lax in his speech, and the better part of his face seemed to have already begun making tiny, rotational departures from whatever it was that the eyes, themselves impressively mobile, were just that moment having to take in. (Was there a lamp in the house that was not that night slopping its wattage over everything?) I guess I was waiting for the man to take a laggard, last-minute interest in me, and by now I was pushing everything out into the paired first-person—it was, I said, "*Our* night shot," and I began including the two of us in whatever it might be doing out, the expected sprinkles and such—but he was no friendship buff, and he paid no heed to my telling him that the only dress of hers I had ever scrunged myself into even part of the way had been the simplest of them all, a large-buttoned wonder of depthless blue, and then only on the principle that one naturally fits whatever one has into whatever somebody else had first, or how else would the world keep getting any fuller with people? The man just went about the removal of the girl's things without having to be reminded too noticeably, I guess, of how every dick hangs by a thread.

My listener, though, had by this time brought about some becoming slowings of her arm—it was an arm inclinable to languorous diagonals and magicianly swoops through the air above the tabletop—but it no longer was involving itself with her plate, so I suggested we shove off, I made payment for the food, and on our way to the car, and then in the car as I took to following her pointings, the directional tilts of her head, she said that you naturally kept putting more and more of yourself into another person, at first wondering how much she can take, how much of you is accumulable and how much she can hold, and you're letting things out, disbursing yourself, and you've soon got things set up in her, and room is being made for even more of you, and if you bring this off with enough people, even two or three, what you've got is at first a comfort, because you can pass yourself along and move a little more widely through the world and leave it to these others to man your grievances, your disappointments; and what brought this to mind, the woman said, was a term of financial hardship she had contrived for herself a few years back, an unpaid leave of absence from scrupling letter grades onto quiz papers (propped-up As, and upended Bs made to look, rather, like fannies; all As and Bs, no Cs or anything lower, the difference between an A and a B having less to do with the accuracy of whatever facts might have been impounded in the space the woman had provided for an answer than with anything recallable about the way the enrollee had conformed her body to the confining perpendiculars of her chair and the navel-level writing surface that projected from it, or the way there might one day have been an unignorable blush on the instep of a once-moseying foot, disburdened of its shoe, that had got itself trapped in the grillwork of that cagelike involvement, intended for books, that was welded to, or otherwise schemed into, the underworks of the chair)—this had been a duration, in short, of controlled difficulty, when the misexpenditure of even a twenty-dollar bill had set her thrilling, gloating, over everything she would miss out on, and one afternoon she had made an engagement for a haircut, just a trim, and very early in the session the haircutter, a woman poorly defined in the face but otherwise full of conspicuities of emotion, set down the prevailing scissors and pressed the flat of a lukewarm hand against the woman's cheek, held it there for a good minute or longer, while the other hand eventually found its way into a drawer, a shallow treasury of slender specialty scissors, one pair of which the cutter withdrew and began routing deductively through the woman's hair, the other hand staying put on the cheek, longer and longer, and the woman went home and for weeks afterward the bathtub was now a more likely destination than any of the upright furniture, and it got easier to fill the tub with further clarifying volumes than to clear space on the difficult heights of the sofa, and she was hardly claiming to have become a cleaner person in result—she in fact would often discover, voyaging about her body, a browned, fractionary detail of a larger crepe of toilet tissue that must have got itself stuck in some assy crevice and was impossible to get plucked out of the revolving suds—she was saying only that she spent more and more of her time thus immersed, ill off in water, and the haircutter had surely had a hand in it, the woman was doing some of the cutter's life now, coming into some of its wrong, because you sometimes have to look to somebody else's life to get the dimensions set back even part of the way around your own, and it should not have to be any less your own life when it comes from somebody else, and you could surely fudge a society out of any one available person and get this person doubling for the many, so that in the little run of things perpetuable from one person to the next, every loose moment stood to become a complete, active ultimacy.

But by now this was a new day, with only an hour or so off it already, and the place the woman had made me bring us to, the man's place, with a promise that the man was elsewhere—this was on a little offshoot of a street, a stewy efficiency apartment the color had long ago gone out of; and when, once in bed, still clothed, I found among the sheets and blankets a spoiling pair of the man's underpants, one of the leg openings of which was puckered into an avid, sloppy mouth, I held myself accountable for redisposing the fabric until I got a befitting featurelessness back onto it; but all the while, I am sure I had to make myself go over again in my mind that if the body is the porter of as many organs of affection as there might one day turn out to be, then the idea was to let the thing carry you to where you would otherwise never have any reason to arrive, because I listened for the unmelodious downslide of the woman's zipper, and then the woman made me put myself out of my own clothes, the attritional corduroys and overshirt, and got herself up at last onto the topic not of the man whose apartment this was (because his story was scarcely the story of how the boy who decides he is half a girl no sooner starts to worry about where the other half might be than he gets careless with where he rests his eyes, or what he gives even the feeblest of fingerholds to, and anything, even a crumbly triangle of pie offered on a saucer instead of on a pie plate proper, comes in easy, ready, wronging answer), but of her husband, and how, no more than a couple of months into the marriage, he had begun snugging away in his undershorts a little source of chance, reliable frictions to nudge him onward through the workday—anything company-keeping that could be counted on not to slide out of the elasticky leg holes: a half-dollar packet of chocolate tittles, maybe, that was barely noticeable in the baggy surround of the wide-cut trousers so popular at the time.

For by now the woman had at last brought what is usually called the other mouth to within only inches of my lips, but it is not a mouth, obviously, although I let myself go along with the goodwill behind the comparison, the way I will remain loyal to anything deliberately and faithfully misunderstood, and I fussed my tongue against the vital trifles hung inside of her, as much of the curtailed finery as I could find, and gave the whole insimplicity of it a slow-circling, examinational lick, until I was taking a sudden tepid downwash on the tongue.

It was a familiar, latrine indribble that must have tasted, no doubt, like trouble just starting out.

Partial List of
People to Bleach

HOME, SCHOOL, OFFICE

I remember buying something once—I can't remember what—
in the stationery aisle of an all-night drugstore, something I did
not need. All I remember is what the card accompanying it said:
"101 Uses for Home, School, Office." I remember thinking there
was a home, a school, an office in my life, so why not? Make the
purchase, look alive. This was how long ago?

HOME

The home in this case was actually two homes. First, my apartment,
which was just mounds of filthied clothes, newspapers, index
cards, depilatories, razors, and paper plates forming a ragged little
semicircle around wherever I happened to be sitting on the floor
when I was home. (I owned no furniture; I was afraid of heights.)
And then her place, a house she rented, a place she vacuumed and
dusted, where I slept with her, where she made the bed. She had
a name, a job, a kid, a parrot, a couple of ex-husbands, relatives,
neighbors she concerned. When she wasn't drunk, I was her project.

SCHOOL

I taught at a school, a college—a community college, to be fair.
The students hated me, and most who got stuck in my courses
eventually dropped. I would step into a classroom on the first
day of the term, and a good third of the kids, furious that I was
going to be the teacher, would get up and walk out. On those who
remained, I got my revenge by ladling out all A's—even an A for
the kid who slept through my entire last semester, because I was
jealous of his frictionless, rubber-limbed sleep. I would often want
to stop talking—there was never any discussion; I filled the room
with words for seventy-five-minute sessions, displacing the air
with sequences of salival syllables arranged to give one the feeling,

afterward, of having heard something like a lecture, something that could survive on a margin-doodled notebook page as a plausible outline of a plausible topic—so that I would not wake the kid up, even though it was obvious he could sleep through disquiets of any kind. (My own sleep was and continues to be a tiresome business—battering, sloppy, unproductive.) Shall I admit that more than once I wanted to share that kid's sleep—i.e., to be fucked and fucked and fucked by him until I bled?

OFFICE

I shared what had once been a large supply closet with a history teacher, a woman who smelled like the exhaust fumes of a bus and who cancelled her classes at least once a week. One morning, as I was repositioning books and papers on my desk, an elaborately coiled pubic hair—it called to mind a notebook spiral—slid out of a folder labeled "TO BE FILED" that I had been trying to find a new place for, and landed on the carpet. This was carpet the color of pavement. My officemate was nowhere to be found, and the office door was shut, and locked, so I got down on my knees and sought out the hair. I thought the thing would be a cinch to find, but it wasn't. I just couldn't put my finger on anything. I borrowed a piece of cellophane tape from my officemate's desk (I had never asked for any supplies, but my officemate had a metal tape dispenser—a big thing, a console, really—and a stapler and a hole-puncher and a telephone) and thought that if I dragged the strip of tape, with the adhesive side down, along every square inch of the carpet, the hair would eventually cling to the tape. But after about five minutes, I gave up—not because the phone rang (it was my officemate's phone, obviously, and it never rang) or because there was a knock at the door (I had signed up for five office hours a week, but nobody ever came by except for students asking after my officemate or dropping off get-well-soon balloons), but because I did not know up to what point, to what extent, I was supposed to keep going along with my life.

KANSAS CITY, MISSOULA

I moved in with my sister and her girlfriend after my little marriage had started to wear itself to the bone again.

I was twenty-seven, mostly unknown to myself, known best by my sister, who said, "You won't have to do anything just yet."

But I had always made sad work of persons. Even now, in these later, unarranged times, everything is just modicums of what it once was.

My sister and her girlfriend were, both of them, paralegals. They were renting a house at the confusing end of town. This was out beyond where people still felt any need to mix.

The girlfriend was the tallest of us three. She had lots of that mobile jewelry all over her. Her body seemed to crowd around her life in ways that kept her from being too social with me.

But Sister was the sackier one. Blurts of blue still in her hair.

My first full day was a workday for them. They had me using the edges of one of those disposable-razor caps to scrape away the crud from the insides of their tub. They would be wanting a bath, a long, lemon-laden, embubbled soak, they had said, after they came home and before they took on the night's carnal charges.

They would be arriving antsily together in that nonnative sedan of theirs.

I had to shove a brood of good soaps aside.

The tub's guck came off in a powderish gray. This took hours, but what was time to someone with nothing to wait for but take-out pad thai, hoi polloi, potpie, whatever they were calling it?

The house was actually more of a cottage, with bookcases built bluntly into the walls. The books I could not exactly read (I had disorders), but I could land a hand onto a page, spread my fingers, then make out whichever words that showed in between, though these were mostly just ingredients of words:

firt   *leen*   *bini*
aze   *oli*

They kept their bedroom door shut at night.

Mornings, I went through their drawers—but things were much too plush and tingly for me in there, all that underwear inalienably theirs, plus some shapely drugs, mostly robin's-egg-blue and dazing.

I took another of the tabs. It was quick to get me feeling renewedly mortalized and minute.

I couldn't log on to either of their boxy old laptops. No diaries or journals or such for me to see whatever each might have finally dared rue about the other. Those two more likely lacked even a line of wiseacre poetry to their name.

I could have written a poem for or against them right then and there, and tried to, something merrimental and penciled, but it got to be all about my own catchy life and what all had gotten caught in it—the set bedtimes and slant-tip tweezers, any old TV screen with the power off, the less-than-a-year-left stuff that dragged on and on, the chances begged for, the overnight bags that were actually technically for the next day, if you woke up and the world was still looking coy.

I needed to find something better to know like the back of my hand.

The last time I had gone looking, I'd found that woman with the tiny floes of green in her eyes. This was a woman like nothing else floral at all. She had had concussions, and blackouts, and years later was still blinky when she turned up looking ousted from everything peaceable in the species. So, yes, I loved her calamitously and however little. But she was a braggart, a cheat, and a back-stabber. I'll keep her mostly out of this reminiscent business, though. I'm under orders to tend to just about any other hill of beans.

Regardless, I'll venture that marriage spreads itself filmily and spherically around two people until you're doing your damnedest to poke your way back out.

Truth be told, I felt less joined than merely jointed to her in little fiscal fashions.

She'd say, "Are we ever even talking about the same thing?"

She hoped to be a guitarist. It would have had to be one of those half-size guitars. The songs were going to be bouncy and sagacious about having a cunt with more mystique than most. For a minute there, in the stairwell, her singing voice got something trapped in it, a real shiver that brought you revealments from afar.

Making her way up the steps was a girl who must have heard. The girl looked to be about that age when instead of places to go there were only worlds to come.

They just shook hands at first, exchanged names hard-headedly, then sniveled until the two of them were kissing.

I didn't hear from my wife for a while.

I'm not telling you anything I won't have already one day come to have known about myself, at least the parts about life's not being right for everyone, and how I've no reason to know why; but for a couple of semesters, I'd pushed myself over at the community college, the one they had set up in the older hangars. My fingers kept driving themselves into the books until every binding gave up the ghost. One of the profs, some even-minded soul, took me aside, said, "All work and no play." I said, "I'll play when I'm dead." But it was a stretch, and then I took up with that man who day in and day out looked loveproof and bloated.

What—all that water and blood in him wasn't enough to drown his sorrows either?

His story was that I was using him just to brush up against myself. But I must have looked redundant even off on my own.

Men, you must know, are behind everything, meaning only laggard, backward, passé.

But I keep coming back to my wife as if she weren't the one coming back to me black-and-blue.

This was all in that make-do conurbation between the state's two hardening and unfavored cities nobody even snooped around in anymore.

We didn't really tell anybody about the marriage. Whom could we have told?

Her sister was dead, and her parents weren't the type you would ever once think to describe, and as for friends, there were none left aside from me, though she might have sent notes, potshot postcards, to lorn pharmacists she had leaned on, or mentors long spurned, or pushover crisis-hot-line troubleshooters, or any other sobber who might have once bashfully asked her to piss on him as a finale to something long since finished anyway.

As for my acquaintances, I knew a man who kept daintily to himself in an enlarged house with six sinks and a tub from which the water, he claimed, would never completely run away. It had the plumbers stumped. He was hit with bills you wouldn't believe. I called him every now and then to go over the eventualities.

"It's all been pushed back," he would say, then hang up, then not answer when I kept redialing, thinking: By which he had meant what—it's been moved forward or further behind?

I had a dictionary, but it was the kind that hedged on everything.

"Bound, adj.," or so it said, meant just the opposite of "bound, vb."

So I tried to keep my wife to the fore and laid off sex.

We lived in the perfect timing of our passions for other people.

Some people, I now see, are idea people. The idea might be only: Eschew bloodbaths.

My mother had never done much besides lose her heart to the dial tone. It must have seemed a threnody of a kind. That was in the times of landlines only. I believe she lived mostly in silhouette.

It was my father who had taught me it would be disloyal to buy another town's newspaper, even the one from the town just down the road, where the people liked it when the hours finally got themselves all balled up into a day that could just roll itself right off from them.

So my sister's girlfriend, to let something be known: I did in fact try her out in their bed. It's no bombshell, though, if the other party is mutinous in even the twiddliest way against your own sis. She buttoned her lip. Everything went without brunt. Next morn, she said, "You're a man still here. You're a breach of the peace."

But I've never been very immediate in things. I've skipped out on myself every time.

My wife had married me in a huff. There had been somebody else, somebody before me and later to come back—a man of clean riches. Any affection from me went straight through her.

I'll say one thing for her, though:

She looked for all the world.

YEARS OF AGE

M y sisters had turned out to be women who wore their hair speculatively, lavishing it forward into swells, or loading it again with clips, barrettes. The younger worked for a store that still had a notions department, a dry-goods department, a toilet with a coin slot on the door. Her affections raced in undaring ovals around co-workers.

The other lived on her own in a safehold of foldaways and one-player card games with crueler and crueler rules. She had a couple of dogs that she wanted to see something of the world.

I was the middle child, never the central one, and a son. I had gone through life unfetched.

We were resemblers bent on coarsening the resemblance.

I had been a suggestible kid, senseless in all I foresaw. I'd had the kind of parents who taught you to tell time, then taught you that time would tell. High school I had liked—the hourly hallway travel, the breezy hygiene of the girls—and in college most of the profs shook your hand on your happy way out of the amphitheatre.

A diploma was at length made out to me. I was free to apply for openings. I liked the festive attention allowed me at interviews—the questions put to me pointedly but unpersonally. My first job involved scourging printouts with proofreaders' marks in a metropolis of sorts mocked up for regional commerce beside a thin, palling river. I prinked about the offices in baleful well-being, maybe awaiting ovations.

Or was I already taking the long view—that the world we lived in stood in the way of another world, one where you need not keep going back into things with your eyes wide open?

I took to taking things calmly and degenerately.

I moved to the forefront of the city, shared an apartment divided four scarcely distinct ways, now and then brought home discouraged hitchhikers or delicately shaven teenagers—wrathful, facetless kids easily regaled with things neither strange nor true. I thus got roughed up in my roommates' regard, found "FOR SALE" signs taped everywhere on my car. Then the first, brute months of a new year. I spaced things out in my luggage and hauled it all to the outskirts. I became one of those secretive types who want you to know everything about them except what should most catch the eye.

People, in truth, had got the *wrong* wrong ideas about me— that I responded well to cosmetics; that I had already come to know most of the disrobers in our town of halfway houses and rehab socials; that my teeth had been sewn tight into my gums with thick black thread.

In awful point of fact, I rewrote my rent checks until the dollar-amount and the signatural hurrah were just so, and I called my parents almost any Sunday. I would force myself to talk for exactly twelve minutes, the better to counter criticisms that I could never be kept on the line for more than ten.

I would have to answer the same question every time: "Why are you always so out of breath like that?"

Shall I say that I eventually shamed myself away from men, though they had all still been just boys, actually—boys too much alike in the rough patter of their pulse? They were happily acrid in shorts almost too long to be shorts.

It's not every day I let any of them come cohering back. But there was one whom I will call by some other name, *Floke,* and who called me both timid and vicious—tender in only an investigative way.

Or, rather, there were men I offered the luxury of witnessed private conduct, and women who set out bridge mix or pretzel twists, women with colorless good looks, women who picked fights with their bodies.

I always walked away a differently unchosen person.

■　　■　　■

The one at whose side I worked that summer was deep-set in family heartaches, and facially inhumane, but she sometimes came out from behind all the etiquette.

Eleven was the only clock word she liked. She would insist it sounded lilting and relenting to her.

For me, though, the hour itself—the work-shift one, I mean, and not its trimmer twin in late evening—did not slope toward anything better. I never budged for lunch, and I liked to do myself in a little. I would postpone a piss until I had to brave rapids, practically. (There was a vessel I kept beneath my desk.)

This was the property-management division. We were sectored off from the rest of headquarters by little more than particleboard. The job required the luxurious useless indoor fortitude it has always been my fortune to enjoy.

Then some unsought weeks with a silkened fright of a girl with mutiny in her stomach, unfellowly elbows, lively fatalities in her thinking. She had a ring of relations around her—impressionable cousinry, commanding aunts with bracelets by the silverous slew—and we moved in with her parents, early retirees, who swanked away at the prospect of the two of us unpairing before the year got thinned of its holidays. Her father would stand outside our room, knock ungallantly on the door, shout, "We hear you in there." Then the mother would say, "We most certainly do not." It was her reproofs that counted.

Men of my kind kept cramming themselves into marriages, violated hindquarters and all. I mugged for a minister late one morning myself.

This was hazing July, and the days just burned away.

My wife came from a family with vaulted closets, kitchens with doors that locked. Every dress the woman wore had to have vents, slits, pinholes. She drank excitative mixed drinks of her own fixing, was swayable in her credos, drove home the sobering groceries.

Her hair had something almost auroral about it, plenty of sparkle in its upper reaches. But she wasn't eating.

When the day came that she wanted something frothed and resolving to daub onto her face, I walked her to the makeup counter at H--- Brothers. A saleslady came over. We made it sound as if we were picking out a gift.

Was the skin about which we were barely making a peep a dry skin, or an oily one, or was it splotched, or papery, or combination? What was the one thing the woman—if the intended recipient was, indeed, a woman—wanted most to change?

"Should we be telling people?"

I might as well have kept going through life repeating: Consider the source!

There was, a while afterward, just one other taker, somebody else at city hall, a man who leaned on me during the last-ditch derisions of election year. (A stuffy, unbowing couch in his office, a provisioning little fridge, curtains and blinds both.) He expected to compound some things he still felt for his wife with his unriotous feelings for me, then come up with a new, totaling emotion that he could offer to the woman he wanted to clean his life out with. She was a recent hire in the prothonotary's office, level-voiced and unshifting. Mistily, immediate one minute, undivinable the next.

As for the man, there was little he still did in his role as my resister. I started bringing things home from the library—magazines mostly, the pages brightly outdated. Touching whatever someone else had touched first was going to be fellowship enough for me.

This was punctual, unbrilliant winter. My car got harder to start. The thing just scoffed, razzed. The library stayed open later and later. The one I liked behind the circulation desk had lips dulled plumly, some final drifts of girlhood at peril in her voice. A becoming boniness to the fingers, and that hardening and seaming of the face achieved, I was certain, from having too soon seen the pleadings in things.

I must have been hoping for someone deep-eyed and hampered and unfancied like that, someone with consolingly different dislikes—pretty-witted antipathies I would not want to trump.

This library had a back-corner department of cassettes thick-cased into sets, series. I signed some out, drew myself into a few. I did not own a player, but I would poke the cap of a pen through one of the hubs in a cassette, jostle the tape forward a little that way. Such were my heaves, my advances, in the hours before I would pass myself back into the unmonopolizing sleep of my nerveless, earliest thirties.

Hard to imagine anyone's ever having had cause enough to wonder what in my life might have once been worth a count—dying adorations, maybe, or playsome enamorations going way back to nursery school, or any hands most recently mislaid on me, then on bedposts, then on banisters on the bullying way back down the stairs.

My sisters were just sturdier, vulval versions of myself. We kept in touch by tardy and typoed e-mail. Greeting cards arrived on time to clear things up again about Mom. ("Hi there guys. Sorry for the form note.")

When I asked how things were going, the answers came out more like pledges than anecdotes.

The older of them rode the bus over one night and knocked, tunicked and flip-flopping, a bismuth-pink on her lips. She had gotten herself a flu shot some days before, and would I have a go at the Band-Aid? She whisked up her sleeve. Her bare upper arm was pale and asquish.

I saw her home afterward to her troves.

My younger sister threw herself into her work, battled away at largely moony evenings. For a time, our feelings ran in parallel toward the same woman. A yearning for her firmed in us both.

This woman put wrong names to our faces, and there were oddened tilts and tonings to her voice as often as we approached. Her wardrobe was a rowdydow of oranges, beckoning reds.

Eyes an acorn color.

Hair she kept ruckussed upward.

A finger sometimes presuming upon a front tooth—to test the sureness of its set, its hold?

These were weeks of endangering heat. My sister and I were of like violences of mind about this unrelished, unensnared piner throwing herself aside. We plotted a past for her: meadow hockey in college, weddings called off, devotions forever obsolescing. We left a brood of brazen tulips on her doorstep. Pictured her kicky and ambitious sleep, an exercise of caution in her days, her vague but chaoticized dailiness. We started eating where she ate— ordered the same boffo salads, with just scribbles of onion, parings of radish fillipped in just right.

Still, we made no grabs, no gains, until my sister wondered, Maybe *we* were the couple?

What at first doesn't sit right might eventually be made to stand at least to reason.

Then came crackdowns at work—freezes on travel, on "favors" for office affairs. I liked how things got worded on the stop orders, and I liked how a day harshened around ten o'clock and again about three; I liked personal bombshells—the miscarriages and surprisingly affordable addictions.

But I mostly liked feeling pinned down, sized up, taken for.

The new guy they paired me off with was just some kid, formerly rural, with a headful of unmastered mathematics and specialty jests.

He figured in my toilet ruminations, true, but only as someone spooked, not spooking.

The library girl had the disease in its early, bashful stage. "Watch and wait," she said the doctors had said. But it did not come out of its shell the little while I knew her.

I would help her off with her coat, and she would put everything she had into a practiced shakiness that could not be ignored. The money we threw around was mostly money torn most of the way down the middle.

She had a diary she decorated alertly but wrote in only here and there—tidings, updates, mostly flashily inaccurate. I know because I, too, tended to peek at life and generally save my breath.

Then a boxier month holding more than I knew what to do with. My mother died idly and lopsidedly in her sleep, and within days had begun her cindered foray into the infinite. My father threw himself truantly into grieving, claimed he could hear his mind clearing up too soon. My older sister had started courting some galled dab of a man. He kept his back to the rest of us while we whiled away the days of bereavement pay.

This was supposed to be broad-skyed autumn, don't forget.

Slants were falling all across my life, too. A sore, a lasting blemish of some sort, had asserted a fresh residency on my chin.

Then my older sister had a change of heart, married her man's grappling brother instead. The ceremony was swift, inventive, isolating.

A year or two of slower considerings, and then another year broke out its days. I was newly forty, and veinier, but now and then still had a crack at people.

I squibbed myself this way and that into a few more women, fled the coming fruitions.

Then Elek.

I had known him for only the hour, but he left that scathing of citrus on my lips.

In years to come, I shared a house—some plywooden, hideaway housing, really—with a much younger woman who had a daughter, a keeper, from a man who had left. This woman and I helped each other off with high-collared sweaters that verged nearly to our shins, ate take-out pizzas that had been rechristened to sound like sensible dishes. We fought like equals. When the daughter grew up a little further and started overdoing it (she had a finessed, triumphal bloom on her), the two of them got mistaken for sisters almost anywhere they went. They took to explaining that they were just good friends with hopes of someday being something more.

I WAS IN KILTER WITH HIM, A LITTLE

I once had a husband, an unsoaring, incompact man of forty, but I often felt carried away from the marriage. I was no childbearer, and he was largely a passerby, minutely berserk in his bearing. We had just moved to one of the little cities that had been set out at intervals—they formed a kind of loose oblong, I imagined—in the upper tier of our state.

He had an unconsoling side, this husband, and a mean streak, and a pain that gadded about in his mouth, his jaw, and there was a bumble of blond hair all over him, and he couldn't count on sleep, on dreams, to get a done day butchered improvingly.

He drove a mutt of a car and was the lone typewriter mechanic left in the territory, a servicer of devastated platens, a releaser of stuck keys.

I would let him go broadly and unseen into his day.

These cities each had a few grueling boulevards that urged themselves outbound. Buses passed from one city to the next and were kept conspicuously to their schedules, and I soon took to the buses, was taken with them: I would feel polite and brittle in my seat as a city was approached, neatened itself into streets and squares, then petered out again into bare topography. It never made much difference in which city I got off. I always had some business somewhere of a vaguely gracious, vaguely metropolitan sort, if only a matter of inquiring at a bank about exchanging some uncomely ones for a five. Sometimes I resorted to department stores, touched handbags, clutches (I have always preferred the undoing of any clasp); and I liked to favor a ladies' room with my solitude. I knew how to make an end of an afternoon, until the day lost pace and went choppy with a fineness I could refine the finality of.

It was mostly younger women on the buses—women barely clear of girlhood, dressed for functioning public loneliness in tarplike weighted cottons.

I one day sat down beside one.

My fingers were soon in the pan of her palm.

This city was a recent thing built in pious, cutback mimicry of someplace else. The streets were named after other streets.

I had been hired, probationally, as a substitute teacher, which meant I was not hated by any one student for any length of time, but I made enemies aplenty in the short haul.

I would write my name on the board, and then I would usually have one girl, a roupy-voiced thing, who would say, "Wait, I know you," and I would say, "I don't think so," and she would say, "Not from here."

Back in the practicums I had been taught to ask, "Who belongs to this paper?" Because you do run across cases where the possessory currents seem to be running more forcibly from the paper to the kid than the other way around. You're taught to feel something for anybody caught in that kind of pull, though I never once felt it.

I had, I hope, a dry, precise smile, a good-bye smile.

My husband: he had sized his life to deprive it of most of the right things.

I had been meaning to get something in here of our incensed domestic civility, and the queered quiet of our nights, and the preenings of the weather all the following summer, a summer that never cut either of us in on its havoc and seethe, but the mind's eye is the least reliable of the sightholes, and I might have been looking all along through only one of those.

It was availed away, our marriage.

We got tardier about every fresh start.

If I am talking them up again, these women brimming hectically now on buses, it can't be only to keep throwing pinched perspectives over their low points, every rut in their loveliness.

It's just that I tend to get all devotionate when I sense sore spots and unaired ires in any shrewd mess densening suddenly in my ken.

A Tuesday, for undiscouraged instance: a vexable, vapory girl.

My one hand mulling its way into a pocket of her coat.

(To join hers there at last.)

My other hand fluffing up the leg of her pants.

(The hair on her shin a chestnut-brown emphasis.)

I helped myself to their charity.

Ruthfully open arms, blind sides, always a general alcoholature to their breath—it was true a few of them might have been cautioning me all along to look out for myself, but I took that to mean what? That I was the fittest object of my own suspicions?

Women of muddled impulse, lonely beyond their means—I let my drowsy heart drowse around.

Then it was decided it was time to fix on just one of them. I was on a bus homeward from work. She was steadfast of face, and it was a situated face, or my idea of one, but her dress curtained her off so completely that the breasts were cryptic, the legs undefined.

Ideally, the way we sat, the way our forearms were set out in a line, her bracelet should have slid with ease from her wrist to mine. But the rumps of our hands were too thick to permit a crossing.

Then her apartment, a barracksy large, lone room: tenants on either side of us, and above, beneath, making overheard but unintelligible dead-set headway.

She had sweepy arms, a squall of dark hair, eyes a slubby brown. She spoke through prim, petite teeth of favors she was owed.

There was relief in how quick we could find the hardness in each other.

Then weeks, scrapes of inquisitive affection, kisses kept quiet and dry, unluminary movements not undear to me, a clean breast made here or there, every passing thought treated to a going explanation (people combine *unneatly*), an inaccurate accusation, a principal I had to have it out with.

They weren't hours, these classes; they weren't even forty-five minutes—they were "periods," which sounded to me as if they were each at once a little era and the end you had to see decisively put to it.

I would be summoned from school to school, grade to grade, and I would advance through a class, a subject, a unit, by picking on yet another nobody undergoing youth, and I would peer into her worried homeliness, let a trait or feature advocate itself for half an hour's discrediting endearment.

Eyes, maybe; eyes of a sticky green that looked fuddled with the world and its ongoing insistence that things, people, remain detailed and unalike.

Or an unblunt arm unsleeved in late autumn and within esteeming reach, though I had come to believe miserably in seeing arms not as the pathway to a person but as the route the body took to get as far afield of itself as it could.

Evidence pointed directly to other evidence, never directly to me. What influence did I have? I spoke from notes.

When you are no good at what you do, it does you no good to triumph at whatever you might come home to, either. My husband was in fact my second one. I should be making a case for the first, for the avenues of feeling I must have taken with him, though he mostly just roved from room to room between charley horses, was studious in his insults, twidged a slowpoke finger into where I still trickled against my will.

Let me remember him, at least, for being the one to teach me that there was only one polite way left to say "yes," and that was "I'm afraid so."

I am admittedly leaving out a kid I left eventually with an aunt, my one uncornering aunt, but I imagine I did later write a letter to be given to the kid when the kid finally aged overnight.

I wrote it in emotional accelerations of my pen on hotel stationery on an evening when the fitness of the word *evening* struck me for once, for isn't it the business of that first reach of the night to even out any remaining serrations of the day?

I was a woman heaping all alone into her thirties.

Things allowed me mostly lowered me.

My young woman, then: she was technically out of the nest, but there was a parent she reported to, and I must have known there were other goads.

In the nightlight, I could see where she had been C-sectioned. A weak grief usually strutted her up. She sometimes thumbed an hour aside with habits, practices; brought an abruptly feared finger down on the pricket of a candleholder, maybe, to gloat over dribbleting blood. But the nail of the finger had been cheered an opera pink, or a mallow purple, and there was nothing uncourtly in her intonations.

I was thus kept milling in her feelings still.

For a living, she banged about tables in a downstairs restaurant scaled back now to only breakfast and a rushed late lunch. She would settle her stomach with formally forked portions of what had unsettled it in the first place.

But how best to be usefully afraid for her? I could never get a sense of where others might be perched in her affections.

Her name—I dare not draw it out here—was a huddle of scrunty consonants and a solitary vowel, short. I should have done a better job of learning how to say the thing without its getting sogged somehow.

A family? That was where you got crooked out of childhood.

I had been sixteen when I grew into my mother's size—an already tight and terrible ten. Our wardrobes overlapped for a while, then no longer got sorted at all. We would pick a day's dark attire out of the dryer, and had to go from there.

Or you could go back even further, to when you are barely untucked from childhood and finally get the full run of your body, and feel secure in all its workings, then learn that everything on it will now have to be put to dirtier purpose.

But my brother? I was in kilter with him, a little.

I turned on him, then turned back

There was already wide plight to my tapering life.

One night, though, I had to use her bathroom. It was mostly men's things in there—shaving utilities, drab soaps, an uncapped deodorant stick with a military stink to it.

When I came out, the phone rang.

"Let it sleep," she said.

(The handset had, after all, a "cradle.")

Then later, someone slapping away at the door.

The slaps were all accumulating at one altitude at first, but then travelled unmightily down the door panel to the knob.

Then sudden, fretful turnings of the knob.

We listened, hands united, until the commotion at the door was a gone-by sound, followed by the gone-by sounds of feet in the hallway, then of a car entered, roused, driven expressively away.

Prescription oblivials gave her an assist with her moods, veered her toward a slow-spoken sociability sometimes, sometimes made her meaner.

We would sit down dearly to a dinner of whiskery import vegetables, close-cropped meat gone meek in the sauce, everything on side plates, everything a lurid obscurer of itself.

But why lie when the truth is that the truth jumps out at you anyway?

Before me, so she claimed, it had been a narrow-faced shopmaiden with a muggy bosom and a catastrophal slant to her mind.

To hear her tell it, there were girl friends (two words), there were girlfriends (one word), there were friend girls, and there were women. Women were never your friend.

■ ■ ■

Baby talk like that must have put the lacquer back onto my life for a while.

I stood up quite handsomely now to my husband's entire, perspirant heights.

One morning I thumbed out most of the teeth from a comb of his, stuck them upright in rough tufts of our carpet—whatever it then took to get a barefoot person hurt revolutionarily.

But the days arched over us and kept us typical to our era. It was an era of untidying succors, follied overhauls.

Her manager gave her more hours.

Her feelings came down to me now in just dwindlements of the original.

She started showing up in the snap judgments of a glass-blowing uncle, and was an aunt herself to two nieces already girthed and contrarious.

We had them over, those two, to her place, our table. They had been lured through youth with holiday slugs of liquor, had put themselves through phases but always stopped short of complete metamorphosis.

The younger was the more bridelike. Skewy eyes, a dump of dulled hair. A sparge of moles on the neck, the shoulder.

The older's shoe kept knocking against my own.

She picked a hole in her biscuit, didn't seem to have any tides dragging at her.

They each later took me aside to tell me what they had had the nerve to collect, study, and forsake. Thick books read to detriment; tiny, frittery animals—need I say?

Afterward, the woman and I alone, the night gone quickly uninfinite: I kept seizing things—household motes and the like— out of the broad, midbody bosh of her hair.

But if I say I felt something for her, would that make it sound as if I felt things in her stead, bypassing her completely?

Because that might too be true.

■　　■　　■

When you're a renter, a tenant, an apartment-house impermanent, you make do without cellarways, attics, crawl spaces: there's little volume your life can fill.

So you take it outside to the open air—into thin air, you've already corrected yourself.

The eye doctor started calling my husband a "glaucoma suspect." There were drops and a dropper on the nightstand, pamphlets of attenuated portent.

I got better at tugging away the context from around every least thing. Something as unchaotical, I mean, as the compact she had suddenly stopped caring for. It no longer made the daily dainty descent into her purse.

I got alone with it, pried the clamshell casing open.

Spoofed much too much of its powder onto my nose, my cheeks.

Waited.

Waited even longer.

No alarms to report then and there, of course, but I must have, ever after, felt eaten away a little more around the clock.

My weeks with this bare woman dipped deficiently toward winter. She either worried herself back into my attentions, or a day got minced into minutes we just wished away. Her love for me, in short, was a lopsided compliment, longer in the rebuke than in the glorifying.

(The freshest snow on the streets already grooved and slutted by traffic.)

Another night of roundabout apologizing, and she reached for a shoulder bag, not one of her regular daytime totes. She tipped it all out, fingered everything preservingly where it fell.

The whole business was already looking a little too votive to me.

First the smoot, the flaked razures and other collects, she had abstracted from the gutter between blades of an overemployed disposable shaver. (It had taken, she said, the edge of an index card to reclaim this richesse.)

Then, in a mouth-rinse bottle, a few fluidal ounces of sea-blue slosh from a compress that had been used whenever there were immaculate agonies behind a knee.

And a smutched inch or so of adhesive tape from a homemade bandage, onto which pores had confided their oily fluences. All stickage had long gone out of the thing. (She draped it inexactly across her wrist.)

It had all been her sister's, she said, if a sister is who it had been.

I am always in doubt of whoever can't die right away.

She was gone some nights, too. Things happen when you are younger and have it in you to pinpoint your satisfactions.

I would take the bus to look in on my husband. In my absence, life had scarcely scratched at the man. He never bothered going through my pockets or sought secrets in my miscellaneals. His point of view was exactly that—a speck, something too tiny to even flick away. We were in the bathroom; he was razoring the daily durations of hair from his cheeks, his chin. I was sitting shiftily along the brim of the tub. There was the hankering hang of his thing. I let it fool itself out to me.

Days were not so much finished as effaced. You caught sight of new, unroomy hours looming through the old. Then months more: months of fudging forward unfamished. Then a Sunday night, a worldly evening, finally.

We got off the bus, the woman and I, at the first town we came to. It was a paltry locality with a planetarium, a post office, a plaza. The plaza had a restaurant. We went in, ordered, raked through each other's romaine, thinned out the conversation, set off for the restroom together. Somebody had taped to the mirror a reminder that hands should be washed for thirty seconds—the exact length, the sign went on to say, of a chorus of "Happy Birthday." We thus sang as we soaped the other's dickering fingers, but when we came within syllables of the end of the third line, where you have to put in the name of the "dear" celebratee, we broke things off.

It was the same driver for the trip back—not a nice man.

This being my history, I snapped out of my marriage, pieced myself back into the population, prodded and faulted, saw red, then wed anew in wee ways.

This husband and I soon set a waning example of even our own business.

I later fell in with a girl who kept a cat on her head to stay warm.

I was mostly of a mood to pollute, and she was frank in her dreams, which she logged, but a liar in all other opportunities.

Then years had their say.

HEARTSCALD

HOME

When I got back from the mall, everything in my room had been rotated almost a whole eighth of an inch to the right.

I am taping it all back into place.

FEMALE VOICE ON PHONE: "NO MORE CONTACT"

I can't speak for myself, but a job does things to a person, deducts a person pretty brutally from life.

Desks are terrible places, no matter how many wheels a chair might have.

You can't do much about how drawers fill up.

WHAT TO DO WITH THE OHIO RIVER

Drain it, obviously.

Hire me to walk its length and gloat.

PLACE-NAMES

I once thought Ave Maria was one.

Neighbors

He slips a note under my door, says he has forgotten how to talk, so is there something that can be done?

I meet him in the lobby. I bring my instruments in a wastebasket.

"It's my first time," I warn.

I go to work on him.

His first words: "I've got something in my eye. A kingdom or something."

Errand

The girl behind the counter rang up my package of paper towels and said, "Will that be all?"

"No," I said. "I want to suck out all of your memories."

The Trouble Between People Usually Gets Its Start

The pastor kept saying, "Thy will be done," and all I could think was, "Thy *what* will be done?"

I Used to Love LPs

I used to love carrying them home from the store, the big, goofy flatness of the things.

I thought the numbers parenthesized after the song titles were letting you in on the time of day the songs had been taped.

I thought the peak time for singers, bands, orchestras was between 2:30 and 3:30.

Like the Lady in the Play,

I have always depended on the strangeness of my kind.

She Was Cardiacally All Over the Place

What they told me is that when the doctors opened him up, they found lots of accordion files, jars full of wheat pennies, a glockenspiel, a couple of storm windows, and told him there was nothing they could do.

Record Player

I used to play my records with the volume turned all the way down.

I would lower my ear to the needle to hear the tiniest, trebliest versions of the songs.

I Am Awfully Fond of the Internet

Trouble is, I hang on its every word. I have old-fashioned, home-style dial-up that entitles me to seven screen names. I've finally curbed my online activity by using the "parental controls," which I exercise by means of intricate settings from my primary screen name. The controls allow me to set restrictions on the nature and duration of the Internet activity conductable under each of the other six names. So for each of them I've permitted myself exactly one hour of activity each day, but it's a different hour each day for each screen name, and unless I log on during that one hour, I'm out of luck. There's no way, of course, that I can remember the allowable hour for each name for every day of the week, and I naturally never bothered to write any of it down. The result is that most of the time I can't get onto the Internet at all, and it would be much too much trouble to go back and undo all the settings. So you might say, "Well, then, do all your business—whatever that might be, and it can't be all that ennobling if you've gone and placed so many obstructions in your path—from your primary screen name." Yes, yes, very good point, but somehow the Internet access from my primary screen name seems clogged, or something.

Work

My humanity would have been misemployed no matter what direction I might have taken in life, but, no question, I have walked away cravenly from blocked-up photocopiers, paper jams of any kind.

A lot of toner has gone into all I have done.

There Were Wider and Wider Slits in a Day

She had a three-legged table.

I always felt bad about that.

I Am Afraid I Am Nothing So Dear

As is generally the case, the father's love for his daughter was sporadic and awful.

The whole day was tossing ahead of him.

His daughter grew up to throw her weight onto different people differently.

I have to go around her to get anywhere.

Girl

She wanted me to believe her best feature was her shadow.

People Kept Opening Wide

I keep seeing the phrase "a women" everywhere I look.

Trouble is, it can't be just a typo anymore.

SECOND WIFE

The human body is far too hot.

It cooks things right out of your heart.

CAESAREAN

I was hired to pack the old kind of computer disks into boxes for shipping, or maybe they weren't even computer disks, because this might have been even longer ago than that.

The supervisor said, "Just make sure you put enough of that newspaper into every box to pad it." He pointed to stacks and stacks of old papers banked against a wall.

Later, he checked in on me. Most of the papers were gone.

He picked up a box, then another, and another.

"Why the hell are these so heavy?"

FIRST WIFE

I don't know which is finally sicker—specifics or engulfing abstractions.

She said she was just looking for someone to ride out some sadness on.

MOTHER AND BANGED-UP SON

Looking back over everything I might have ever said, I see that I have never come down hard enough on any of the rooms I lived inside.

I want there to be science behind it if and when I do.

FATHERLAND

The state I was born in had to be abbreviated as "PA."

Honor My Wish

I tried drinking, but it wasn't extinctive of the parts of me most in need of extinction. Plus, I had a good umbrella, but it got blown inside out, and I couldn't close the thing. I set it down on the sidewalk and watched it blow off into the storm.

I welcome any drowsy and senseless sincerity.

I Could See Where She Was Stuck

A man I knew had had car trouble for years. He got around by bus.

He had just the one daughter, and I knew what she needed to be told.

I could feel the words already forming into solids in my head: *There's no such thing as parents.*

When the time came for her to go off to college, she picked one in the state that was shaped far too much like the human heart.

She arrived at the airport seven hours ahead of her flight.

The automatic doors that led from the long-term parking lot to the terminal wouldn't even open for her. She tried all three sets of them. The sensors, she guessed, failed to detect sufficient bodily or characterial presence.

She should have brought luggage, school supplies, a change of underattire.

Then an untroubled-looking couple turned up.

The doors parted.

She rushed in behind.

Second Wife

We had to move two towns to the left, which was west, westish, in this case.

Girl

I was singing over wee chords fingered on an electric guitar that wasn't plugged in.

It was a song of infatuation that I eventually passed along to the infatuatee. She said the chorus could use a little something more to fill it out.

My voice was as flat as it ever gets.

It sounded practically ventriloquized.

My Life Takes Place Mostly on the Floor

"Get over here!" I shouted into the phone.

The woman came.

She thought I had meant just her.

This Is Not What I Wanted to Say, but So What?

I wish I could inhabit my life instead of just trespassing on it.

I Later Suffered Attraction to Someone a Little Less Like Her

There should be a way for this to go straight into my short-term memory.

There should be buttons to press, entire consoles of buttons.

This should be more like science fiction and less like hate, pure and simple.

PULLS

It has always been my custom to go hungry for people, then make my way practically from door to door. But there was a time I had a wife and a new best friend.

I was just doing the weary thing of being in my forties.

My wife wanted to be known best for her parting shots, the breadth of her good-byes. I could count on her to be back within hours, though, tidily silent in her chair.

And the best friend? He was an uncrusading man, rebuttable in everything. He looked felled, or probably at least fallen.

I began dividing my nights between them.

This wife and I had a rented house, two stories of brutal roomth. The air conditioner required a bucket underneath it. Our meals were the cheapest of meats thinly veiled.

My best friend had some uncovetable rooms above a garage. We took down hours with our talk.

Here's her name—Helene—though she will probably tell you different.

For a while, I tried to get her steered toward women. We settled on a blowhard of sporty despondence, crude to the eye but newly starving for her own sex. I staked the two of them to a meal and threw in good wishes.

She came home ebbing in all essences, looking explored and decreased.

She wanted to know about my best friend. I told her that he and I fell onto each other more in sexual pedantry than out of affection, that our life together did not grow on us or chew away at our hearts. His body was just profuse foolery.

Thirty-eight years of picked-over, furying age she was—brittled hair, a bulwark forehead, a voice that sounded blown through. There were hidey-holes in whatever she said.

I felt indefinite inside of her, out of my element and unstately in my need.

One night he wanted to know what it had been like to go through with the nuptials, the hymeneals. Not much had held up in memory. I let out that the minister had spoken of a "middle ground" between women and men or husband and wife, I forget—someplace irrigated and many-acred, maybe a plain. I had felt unchampioned that day. The minister got me alone at the reception, snapped his fingers, said, "This better not've been just some skit."

There are only two things, really, to ever say to anyone.
Try: "I'm very happy for you."
Or: "This is just not done."

I made no more than the arcanest of passes at others. They probably never even knew they had been addressed or beset. I worked for a sloganless bail-bond concern. The people closest to me in seating were a rough-playing woman and a man about my age, drowning in the hours. The woman drank liquored sodas that brought something flowerful into her voice: words were petally with extra syllables. The man took a restroom break whenever he saw somebody else come out. Maybe he found something engreatening about being in there so soon after anything dirtily human had been done. I pictured him taking deep, treasuring breaths, filling up on us. Home was probably just an air mattress somewhere.

I lived in the lonelihold of my portents and pulls.

Weeks kept fleeting past us.
My wife restocked her mind daily with factual packing from TV and the papers.

I would want a day to quit. Thinking what, though? That the one rising behind it might have a more encouraging bone structure in its hours or at least be calibered better for my regrets?

Then one night she wanted to know how she might recognize my friend on the street.

I spoke of the ordering of creases above his eyes, the general tempo of both his blinks and his nostril-flarings, the pitch and range of his arms, the usual drift of the rib that slid about inside him.

But nothing eased for her or for me.

My parents were still alive, still short on marvelry, still saying "We're all he has."

I had a sister, too, drying out again in the tedium of debt somewhere.

She was an acher, patient but baneful in her morbid sweats.

I thus sing the praises of my kind, but more often I just look for signals in the faces of grocery cashiers who are required to say "hi"—women mostly, overevident in their agony; features miseried, it must be, by hitches in the upbringing of their men.

We tried pets, my wife and I. Bought a dog at cost, then a budget cat.

The dog was unawed by my guidance, my sweet talk.

The cat behaved—out of a love or regard, though, that was iotal, toiling.

If you bought for one, you had to buy for the other. (Mostly novelties to squeeze for a spectral, unmerry squeak.)

I wish I could remember whether they bailed on us or just died, overfed.

Another generation had shot up behind us anyway.

I had heard about these persons—that they were handling things differently.

This was the generation that was discovered to have been "just reading words" and then was taught how to get through a textbook by coloring the sentences so that a page, when the fingers had finished with it, looked beribboned, or zoned into chromatic blocks and runs. The books were handed in to the teacher, who graded mostly on pizzazz.

Nothing went untouted about these kids.

I went out and found one at a shopping center.

She was aimless of face, but things had been staged in her hair—demonstrations of metal and feather in the low altitudes of stickied coralline. What she wore wasn't so much a cover as a kind of kiting, blown about before her as she thugged away at a mood. Whims of string (from a shoe, I think) were ringed around her wrist.

She had just been graduated from the two-year institute outside of town.

I took her out for one of the current coffees.

She asked whether I knew that cold water melted ice cubes faster than hot.

I nodded learnedly.

She mentioned "sleeping in."

I told her I had been well into my central twenties before it dawned on me that to "sleep with" someone didn't simply mean to take a companion for your horizontal hours and thereby get sleep domed over you so much the higher than it would if you went home to bed alone. I had thought that was how you gave greater compass, greater volume, to your dreams.

She sipped, and shook her head, and said sleep roamed all over her—it was tramply; it left reddening trackage on her back.

"Not that you'll ever get to see," she said.

She wanted my address anyway. I gave her the friend's. I did get one letter later, a good-bye. It was, she wrote, a "bill adieu."

I am leaving out the hobbies, the odd jobs, the aplomb I had that just got harder and harder on people.

But I will admit that I did go to the doctor once about the ache in my face. It eventually swelled my cheeks and slit into my sleep.

The doctor called it a "referred" pain. It had arrived, he claimed, from someplace far away.

He shunted me off to a specialist, who said the body always waits until the last minute to explain itself to you.

And my wife? I had borne some of the brunt of her fresh starts, seen what helping hands could do with someone like that.

Even her arm—the flesh of it looked tilled, perfected in every lurid turning away. It could withstand scrutinies far more spiteful than mine.

She fell in with a man full of biblical quips, brash intelligence about the presaging capers of his Lord. I saw her vivified and steep by his side in the business district one day. I was by myself in the house every other night. I liked the reliable isolations. I spent some time in the book she had been through. There had been obvious violence in her sessions with it. The binding was loose. It barely had a clutch on the leafage anymore. The bookmark kept sliding out.

She came back to me with tiny growths in her groin and a new, striving vagueness of eye.

Then I found a huge laundry room in an apartment tower near the house. For a time, I couldn't do enough laundries there. Nobody ever caught on that my basket was practically empty. I would enchant every machine with dollar-store detergent, then get the things gushing and thumping through their cyclicals.

I confined myself to one item per load. This ensured a cautious, tyrannical clean.

Even better, there was a lost-and-found, a big cardboard box torn down a little from the top. I started bringing things to kick in—whatever clamored up toward me from the lowest of my life. The thinking must have been that I was most devoted to people I had not yet met, that I was best at laying out courtesies in advance.

Thus the box filled mostly with helpings from my wardrobe: shirts gathering further shine; slacks that were negligences of hemmed fabric, down whose twinned chutes my legs had once gone their separate ways.

My best friend and I were now living in a roundabout familiarity that, from farther off, might have been taken for an advance in attachment.

We made it to the yard sales and brought back further caprices of the culture. Once it was just a mug whose hectic lettering said, "READ A MAGAZINE TONIGHT!"

But nothing much was flaring in my heart.

One night I told him that our lives differed in unbeautifying ways. I told him our bodies could never really be in league.

I pointed at his hand. It had just left mine and was started on its way elsewards.

His fingers always looked as if they were squabbling among themselves, undecided about what might next be deserving of touch.

My wife was walking a fine line, wearing herself away from me.

Months broadened in their burden.

Then the advent of her scandal: sprigs of intimate hair trapped, specimenized, in the clear sealing tape all over the holiday packages that went out one noon to "influentials." Her defense? Anything hailing from a body had to be worthy of at least flitting reverence on your way to the sink.

But cracks had started forming in her words. Things ever after were fissured in her speech.

Then the girl wanted to see me after all. Told me to meet her in the new wing of the closest mall. There was a swinge of ambition in her step as she saw me drawing near.

She hated all her friends now, she said—preeners mostly, demanding dripling sorrows of every instant in her shadow. And what about me? she wondered. Did people my age have friends?

I mentioned a couple of people who lifted emotions without giving credit yet expected originality in any affections coming from me.

"Tell me your wife's side," she said.

One evening, I caught sight of a man who had assumed himself anew in my slacks, my shirt, my jacket and shoes.

He was startleproof in some sort of painless hurry, apparently.

The look he gave me was not a grateful one, or even salutatious, but I felt at large.

One night the three of us were in our right minds around the same table. There might have been a birthday. I remember that something consolatory had been ciphered into the icing of a store-baked cake.

I grabbed her hand.

Released its fingers—or set them out, rather, in severalizing meander—onto his arm.

I must have thought I was getting something exalted on one or the other.

The fingers, I could see, were stuck.

I got up, feeling scanted and surpassed.

My life now dates from that day.

TIC DOULOUREUX

My brother and I were the last of the sons still living at home. It was my aunt's job—once a month a pay envelope was propped against a step halfway up the staircase—to see to it that I was kept some distance from him. One afternoon she told me to drop what I was doing and walk with her to the room in which he was kept. I trailed her down the hall as far as the doorway, then stopped.

"No monkey business," my aunt said.

The room was dark and windowless. This was still very early in ragweed season, and my brother was the only one of us the pollen had wanted much to do with. Handkerchiefs were balled up on his bare chest and on the floor beside the footage of yellowed foam rubber on which he was taking his slumbers. There had to be so many handkerchiefs, I was tired of being told, because a single one would have been soppy, draggled, useless, in no time.

"Go ahead," my aunt said.

I seized each handkerchief by the corner and shook it out into a lank spookling and then passed it along to my other hand until I had a dank fraternity of at least a dozen or so of the things squirming together.

My aunt started toward the doorway.

"Go," she said. Her eyes, I could see, were watering a trifle.

In my room I dunked the handkerchiefs one by one into the scummed water in the wash pail and, without rinsing or wringing, distributed them across the floor to dry. At some point, I composed myself—stretched myself out atop the handkerchiefs to cool the backs of my legs. I pictured, as always, the gleaming expanse of my brother's chest, smooth as tile. I might have fallen part of the way asleep.

Every room on our floor was a complete dwelling, with something to fall asleep upon, and a wash pail, and another pail for whatever was going to desert our bodies, and something to cover the food we never could finish.

When you are one age, my father was fond of repeating, practically anything is either a bed or a blanket, no matter what it might have started out to be. But I was no longer that age.

I one day entered a room where my aunt had got ahold of a newspaper. She was trying to find a reliable way to keep a taut double-page of it aloft, kite-like, between outstretched arms. She shoved it at me.

"Read this and tell me what you get out of it," she said.

There was an article about the different things people ate and wore in a different part of the world. It was padded with recipes and sewing patterns, anecdotes, excitant quotes. I could see how old and rotten the thing was. I gave my aunt a chunked, inaccurate summary.

"Nothing in there about brothers?" she said. "How brothers should behave themselves around each other?"

She reclaimed the paper, tried to get it up in the air again.

"It names all the places they're allowed at on each other," I said. "It names everything about the places."

"Show me where it says any such thing," she said. "They can't print that in a paper."

I stabbed my finger through the page, jerked it out of her hands. I returned to the tropical stink of my room and counted the number of times my brother at the other end of the house sneezed next in succession—forty and seven.

Downstairs, it was a regular house. My parents were partners in a failing sales venture that confined them to hotels for weeks on end, but when they came back, their voices rose up through the hardwood floors, reminding us to mind our teeth or running over the details of turning points, of showdowns, with finicking clients. We were expected to make our reactions, our acknowledgments that we had heard, sufficiently audible. Sometimes I just pounded on the floor. My brother often followed this example. I could tell when he was using his elbows instead of his fists, because with an elbow you do not get nearly as much thud. The sound is more pointed. A few times I heard the ball of a bare foot. Once I swear I made out what had to have been his skull. There was nothing from his direction for a long while after that, so I drummed enough for the two of us, moving about in the room and out into the hallway, but whom was I fooling?

During my parents' absences we were permitted downstairs no more than twice a day—one at a time, my aunt first—to choose our food and to fetch our water for drinking and dousing. We emptied our pails in the powder room. The toilet had a new seat that was not screwed on properly. It would slide out from beneath you unless you knew the right way to sit. The sink had no stopper, so you had to make sure there was nothing loose on you or on your smock when you bent forward to wash. Only one burner on the stove was even hooked up. There was a chandelier in the shape of a wagon wheel above the kitchen table, and the table had an extension-leaf slid into it. One afternoon I sat at the table with a dish my mother had covered with foil in the refrigerator. It held a fantastication of stringy meat overextended with cake crumbs and edged with vegetabular sliverings that didn't quite sit right. I happened to hear my brother squishing along the floor upstairs in socks that must have still been soaking wet. That day I began to develop an appreciation for how things upstairs sounded to people underneath. From every footfall, every stride, came a creak that rippled outward until it overspread the entire ceiling of the room. The effect was one of resounding activity, of achievements far and wide.

"If it'll get your mind off of it," my aunt said.

She had disposed herself beneath me, her eyes already shut, her hair a leaden bulk, an infrequent twinkle in her fingernails.

I filled her body with some pulse of my trouble. From the window I could make out the low-roofed town, untrafficable in the haze. One of the housetops close by was handsomely slated and slick. I slid my mind onto it for a clammy duration.

This is what days were now like in the morning if I hoped to see my brother come afternoon.

My heyday was the week or so my brother and I were finally boyfriend and girlfriend. We would arrive together for lunch in whichever room my aunt had lit some candles to keep the food heated. Handkerchiefs would swag from the waistband of my brother's pants, to be plucked, besopped, then set free. I watched them sail toward the floor, each with a fresh fortune of phlegm.

"He always claimed his wife hated him for the wrong reasons," my aunt said. (I am afraid I paraphrase.) "Her despisal, he felt, was wide of the mark. The marriage was far from finished, but there was less to make it stick. The bed they shared was amiss. The mattress was too big for the frame, for one thing. There was quite the overhang on his side of it. He got better at shifting his weight onto other people, or tacking somebody onto himself for purposes of symmetry alone. I was much the same way—younger. But did I run? We were too much alike in our bloodbeat. We'd gone out to eat, finally, and he told me what he had told her exactly as he had put it to her: 'You, you, *you*.' Everywhere you look—why didn't I know it then?—people are repeating to other people what they had said to third parties, and the ones caught in the middle are afraid everyone within earshot will think that they, the middle people, are the ones being spoken to with such a tongue. So they keep interrupting. They say things like, 'You actually said that to so-and-so?' Emphasis on the so-and-so. But I hadn't been around long enough to know.

"My heart back then was more of a catch basin than it is now.

"When he was a child, mind you, he slept so soundly, he had to be taught everything all over again in the mornings—how to sit up to the table, what forks were for. His sisters were Brenna, Linette, and Nioma. They jumped for joy over whatever a foul little mouth could reach. He never wanted me to know their names and their interests. 'Disaggregate,' he'd say if he were here. He'd be throwing up his arms all over again.

"He would doff his shoes the instant he entered the house. 'You've no idea what I've been stepping in all day,' he'd say. He'd bid me farewell before shutting the door for his bath. I once found the poor man trying to read his way around a business card some thoughtless cuss had left as a bookmark midway down the page in a library book. I could see the struggle in him. The thing was slotted right into the spine, like a tiny extra page. It stuck out an angle. It was obvious he did not want to have to touch it. From where I stood, I could see the parallelogrammatic shadow it was throwing onto the left-hand page. I reached over and snatched it away. I was always the one to turn on the lamp and make sure the light fell over his left shoulder. I'd say, 'You'll ruin your eyes.' And he'd say, 'The only way to ruin your eyes is to keep looking at people.'

"So don't think I don't know what you two think you have," my aunt said. "Don't pretend you're the first."

I had my foot around my brother's ankle. One of his hands was in mine; the other grasped at an undrabbled handkerchief.

"He knocked you up?" I said.

"It was during one of the later years upstairs," my aunt said. "The doctors told us it was a termless pregnancy, that the child might not ever come out, that it wasn't going anywhere, that you see these sorts of impactions every once in a very great while, that this wasn't the end of the world, there were ways to get around things, arrangements could be made for its tutoring, its recreations, inside of me, and for a while we kept at it, the drills, the columns of words, the recommended rhymes. But we started hearing less and less in return. 'Pipe up!' I would shout. It got harder to tell its baby talk, as muffled as it was, from everything else that might have been going on in my hellhole of a body proper. I think sooner or later it must have just got drowned out. I know I started shedding pounds."

"Do you ever talk to him?" I said.

"Your father?" my aunt said.

■   ■   ■

A couple of nights later, I heard heavy luggage landing on the linoleum below. We were all three of us on the floor. My head was in my brother's lap. I thought I was the only one awake.

"Who got the decorations out?" my father shouted from downstairs. "Who gave anyone permission to hang crepe paper?"

We lay still. I could see my aunt's eyes unclosing themselves.

"What did I miss?" my father shouted. "Something big? Somebody thinks they had a wedding behind my back? That's what this is?"

I heard drawers being opened heatedly.

"What else could have happened?" my father shouted. "Look at this place."

I heard the oven door slam.

"Which one of you?" my father shouted.

I saw my aunt raise an arm from the elbow, then start to bring it down. I kicked out my leg and caught the arm before the fist could reach the wide, booming floor.

YOU'RE WELCOME

Worse, I had been the husband, most recently, of a sweetly unpoised, impersonal woman, and in the months following the divorce (it would not have been worth the bother of an annulment, she had said; annulments were reserved for circumstances even more gloriously unfornicatory than ours), I had been getting sicker and sicker of living in conclusion in the little riverless city to which I had always returned after any kind of body blow or setback to my likelihood. But the divorce somehow didn't feel finished to me, I didn't feel riddled with it, or partitioned any farther from her; and having learned, from some florid passersby, that she was living in lower Europe with an aunt or an uncle with small sprouts of money, or sponging off somebody at least welcomingly kindred, I crossed the ocean to see what else there could be that might extinguish what I felt persisted between the two of us. There had to be a surer way to consummate the end of things already ended.

I was a stare-about on the nightlong flight, pacing the aisles, pushing aside every meal and snack, hogging the lavatory for half-hours at a time, thinking that my thinking was, "You don't want to go over it again, how you go from being a part to being apart," and how true, for marriage had given us the chance to cultivate our mussed lonelinesses shoulder to shoulder, my lunatic of a penis uncoaxable into even the simplest of bedstead sex.

People were plugged up enough as it was.

We—*I*—landed at length in some city not even worth my putting the stony name to it here, because I wouldn't want anyone feeling envious that I, of all tossed-aside American males, had made such a crossing, especially since from the instant I put myself out onto via this and rue that, I paid the place no mind, took in none of the sights, ate only in the hamburger hideouts of tourists afraid of their own shadow. The hotel was a questionable piece of work, nothing like my apartment, that seventh heaven of meds and stinkbugs, where my dreams either sneaked from sore point to sore point or beat me to a pulp.

It was a couple of days until I met up with her in some plaza or another. There was a man with her almost terribly.

"Maybe you should go take in the town for just a bit," she said to him. He dropped back, the way people commonly did around her.

Her bare arms swung boldenly as we walked to some kind of bistro. A utopian diet had limited her to rigorisms of tofu, but I ate a smattering of bacon and toast. I could tell she was stirring words inside of herself, and then she and I talked over each other about what we had coming to us, every tit for tat of it, reparations conceivably computable. Her gut had always told me everything: that there are many kinds of love, but ours had never been one of them. Need I have reminded myself, then, of the times I had moved around on her, drudged from an underarm to the rear of a knee, but always stopped short of anything that would put me across as someone connubially constituted for a woman so beautied to the point where you had to wonder whether she had ever even been beautiful at all? The marriage had been no time to start.

Her face, scarcely tended to with a scamble of blush, had assimilated some heavily haphazard eyeglasses. (The frames, new to me, looked as if hewn from rock.) But she struck me as not uncomely, if a trifle overhauled, her hair supplemented now, her dress an affluence of daylight-blue tugged over breasts looking newly punched up.

My body—dare I drag the thing in here?—had been exacted baggily over an inner nature unrooted-for and undelighting. I couldn't break free from any of this body's leakages or procedures.

But her eyes, as ever, went vagrant when she talked. Her life was better now, she said. People went easier on her. Even the ones who had it in for her had to hand it to her that she was good at what she was doing, even (I gathered) if all she was doing was gadding about coolly in falsehoods extraordinaire.

"What about you?" she said. "What are the love interests? Let's hear of their displeasing miseries one by one."

I said that people tended to get dislocated when I touched them too much. I stretched things too far.

"Nonsense," she said. "You don't put yourself out there at all."

I took out my wallet and showed her a photo of a woman who had long ago taken refuge in the haven of a sweater many sizes too immense. She looked hardly even noticeable in the picture. But in point of fact she was a skin-and-bones difficulty with arrhythmic outages of affection and a butchery of blue-black hair. She had tapped me, variously, pandemoniacally, for kindliness and money, but then started offering us, as a couple, to others. In no time, people, bamboozlers themselves, had gone through us just to get through with us.

"Who left whom," my ex-wife said—as a reminder, though, and not as a question.

Wine she wanted now. The afternoon had issued itself quarter-hour by quarter-hour into buggy evening, a drizzle-drozzle so soon on the windows.

She was claiming to be pregnant in some desultory way or another. She said she had been having a devil of a time with it. She asked me to ask the waiter if he knew of any old hand at abortion. The waiter had that look of contented demolishment you often see over there. He wore a skirty apron and narrowy shoes, slippers almost, and spoke to us as if straight from his private life. He led us to the front of the place and pointed across the way to an arcade of sorts.

We held hands in a pedal-taxi on the little passage over. I felt derisions of warmth in her palm.

The abortioner's office was at the back of a machine shop and was full of swatters, plumb bobs, toilet plungers. This was a staminal man with dinky eyes and fingers that kept niggling at each other as he spoke. On an ironing board behind him: a midget computer, bluey and ablip.

"This is the wife-in-chief?" he said.

A funny way to put it, because I figured we had always been equals in whatever was most petty or fruitless at the moment. But you had to factor in her tendencies to entice and deprive.

"I am in want of an opinion," she said.

"Remove all wraps, trimmings, fixings," he said to her.

"No reason for you to leave," he said to me.

"I never left," I said.

"I meant now," he said.

She unbuttoned, unzipped. I had forgotten, I suppose, the finely hirsute earthliness of her, that vicious uneternal splendency. (The skelter of moles along the small of her back, the salmon-patch birthmark on the nape of her neck, the bubbly something near the groin—that droll, brazen sincerity of her body had always been a sticking point.)

He reached for a whisklike thing, then something along the lines of an awl. Proddled and poked into her a little. Then, after a clinical minute or so, said to her: "Somebody has been pulling your leg. You're not up to anything at all in there."

He pointed unclemently to me.

"Maybe it's him it's inside," he said. "Maybe I should be scraping around in your man there."

"He's not my man," she said.

"How long not?"

"Over a year now. Closer to two," she said. "I'm with somebody else."

"It takes a lot longer in a man, though. It goes unclocked."

Then: "But just look how crammed the guy looks. Look how chockablock that gut."

"We were against having kids," she said.

"This won't be a kid," he said.

And to me: "Desert what you're wearing."

I did as I was told. Stripped—or, rather, felt things tearing, being torn, away from me. If it's hard to say, it's because of my hands, the way each of them had always been contrary to the nature of the other.

"Your heart is jerking," he said.

All I knew was that I was naked, skeptical, ill-spun, beastly, shame-burnt, dashed and thankless, disheveled in every sinew. (I had always preferred my body sight unseen.)

It was a plastic hanger, not one of the wire ones, he finally came at me with. He hooked the thing into my behind and pulled and pulled educatedly until he let out a peep that just as soon structured itself downward an octave or two until it was harrumph after harrumph of chronic expertise.

"You keep yourself awfully stocked," he said.

He exchanged the hanger for a shower-curtain rod.

Ripped into me again.

Fetched out, and set down on the plane of the ironing board, the expectable barrettes, compacts, lipsticks, and atomizers, but also:

- the serpentinous leathern strap of a shoulder bag (clips included);

- pages wrung from a scratch pad with what must have been phone numbers scribbled over until they were gibberished into inconsultable, unconsolatory faces blurrily girly;

- airline-boarding-pass envelopes, stuffed with an overkill of nervily plucked coils of bikini-line hair;

- receipts for shoes of woman-made materials only, for fair-trade coffee beans, the receipts a little smeary, as if having blotted the oils from the tip of a much finer nose;

- a head-shot photo, scissored from a magazine, of some sacked sit-com actress, taken to salons as a prompt for the stylist to age her just so (bangs, featherings, tints);

- a ropy noose of a necklace in full, but just smashments of chokers, lockets, bangly teakwood—

"That's it?" the man said. He stepped back, the better to hurl the curtain rod at me. "That's the most trouble you've gone to?"

He called me a man of pronenesses instead of convictions, screamed things even more coring, threatened my life, walked me out to the tram to see me off, etc.

I forget if she was still with me then or not.

This isn't all of it, obviously, just some notes I must have taken not much later, overstepping. I had never been the type of man that women reassessed. I do know that in days to come I heard that she and the man had gotten themselves thrown out of her aunt and uncle's, or whomever's, and were living in a bed-and-breakfast in the same ruin-heaped city, and I liked to think that they were going to have to feel it in their bones just as I had always felt it in hers—that lingering business, I figured, about fitting new people and their irritable parts to the old feelings, the feelings that only made you feel as if you were going to have to first get permission, though, to chalk any of it entirely up to her.

Life—mine, I mean—might better be left unattended.

I'd otherwise want everything elegized the instant it happens.

SIX STORIES

SIMPLE

This is the simplest story. Why am I always the one to tell it?

When I was nine, an older kid said, "Hold out your hand." Then tossed a crumpled candy-bar wrapper into my obediently cupped palm.

Walked away, laughing.

I decided to let the wrapper stay put.

Out of spite, or what?

I grew up, rented a room, worked, rode escalators, figured out where and where not to insert myself.

People kept looking at the wrapper in my hand and saying, "Here, let me take care of that for you," or "Are you looking for something?"

I kept waiting for somebody to say something in a language that wasn't shot.

CONCENTRATION

There was eventually a little something wrong with the son, too, though nothing as bad as with the daughter. The parents ordered corrective shoes and sat up one night, writing and recopying and then laminating a note to be passed among all of his teachers.

The teachers read the note and placed the son at a special desk, where they quizzed him about kings and invertebrates. He answered bodily, and correctly.

He came home having been taught how to answer the telephone in a telephone voice.

"Speaking," he had been taught to say.

His one big break was getting told he needed eyeglasses—an encumbering portable fenestration that made props of his nose and ears. It was not so much that the world was now filled in more tidily (things were less destitute of outline, less likely to drown within themselves before they arrived in the thick of his eye) as that he felt he had acquired a wicket about himself, a little cage up front through which business could get quickly and fittingly done.

I Was Surer of Things

Try it this way: there was a woman who betrayed me with a man who had opened a factory in which it was suggested that the workers make things out of glass. The man did not believe in pushing people. He never once looked over anyone's shoulder.

The man had no luck in hiring the woman's children.

They lived off their mother and grew demandingly lovely on two slipcovered sofas pushed together end to end.

Coarse, dandelionish tufts of fabric sewn at intervals into the slipcovers left pink imprints on their cheeks, their foreheads.

I later liked to watch them walking ably away from me but not yet toward each other.

I will not give you any of the gore.

Employment

I'm looking for work in this room, naturally. I'm desiring lots of work in here. I'm very serious about my desire.

I go up to the guy. "Is there work?" I ask.

"I would imagine," he says. He shows me to the desk. It's the same old desk, my desk.

I pull out the chair and sit down.

I open one of the drawers. I find my underwear and socks exactly where I keep them. I open another and find my health-and-beauty aids.

The guy says, "You get dental, eyeglass, life insurance, major medical, death and dismembership, two weeks' paid vacation, seven paid holidays, fifteen paid sick days, personal days TBA. Employee pilfering is the retail sector's filthiest of secrets. Lift with your whole body, not with individual limbs. Don't just be a people person—be a person's person. Come in through the employees' entrance and breathe out through your mouth. This concludes the orientation."

I reach for a pen.

He slaps my hand hard.

"Just do what you'd be doing anyway," he says. "Only now it's going to be work."

SPEAK UP

She wants to know what he saw in her, so I reach right in for it, pluck it out, and hand it to her. It's a grammatical occurrence of something big, something way out of scale.

This is a conversation we're having, an incident. She is hemming his trousers, the six pairs he left behind. I have been encouraging her to wear them herself—one pair per day of the week, time off on Wednesday, middle of the week, in case she runs out of anecdotal material.

In short, I tell her, Hate him.

But she wants to know what if he calls, what if he comes back, what if they're both shopping for tablet paper in the same micromart.

Skip it, I tell her.

To be fair, what goes where? In terms of my life, where should this be taking up places?

The only way this keeps going is if you speak up.

Tell me something.

Tell me every other thing.

How's every other thing?

THIS STORY

This story has two parts.

The first is about his last love—how he got circumstanced in it, and all the antiperspirants and behaving and abbreviations it later came to entail. This part is long—much too long for me to include or even synopsize here—and it darts out at this or that. Please do not hold it against me if I pretend that this part of the story was misplaced or, better, put aside to boil.

The second part of the story is short and familiar. It parallels your own life, so it is that much the easier to remember. It lends itself handily to discussion in groups small and still smaller. I will recite it in its entirety:

Son, you cunt!

LOO

S hall we face something else?
     I had a sister once.

The center square of the little city where she had grown up still had a couple of "comfort stations." That was what they called those belowground public lavatories whose stairwelled entrances, sided and canopied with frosted glass, looked like gateways to some sunken Victorian exposition. She could not remember whether she simply wasn't allowed down there or just preferred holding it in.

This sister was the self-silencing type. She was done up in a body bereft of freckles or shine.

She never found a way to get her hair rioting upward in the flaring fashion of her time.

Loo (for that was the name she used) was already at that stage in her headway toward demise where it was best to tell people what they wanted to hear. What they mostly wanted to hear was that nobody else, no matter her station in life, ever really knew how much it was that she should've by now already gone ahead and packed.

Her sleep in those days was generous to a fault. But she would wake up and feel herself felled by the clarities and definitudes of the new day. Then to work, in the afternoons, in a windowless basement office in an overchilled building on the outskirts of town. There would sometimes be too rational a cast to her mind, and sometimes she nodded off, but this was a dream-free species of sleep, and she felt unwelcome in it. There was nothing to be made of it, either. It left no residue.

She was a remainder of her parents, not a reminder of them.

Her private life was not so much private as simply unwitnessed.

The shops in those days did in fact sell something called a "body pillow," but she had not brought the first of them home yet.

■　　■　　■

Her second job was an older person's job.

She was afraid there was nothing she didn't find entirely mysterious, nothing that didn't make her feel as if she had never once belonged in her life. But the one or two people to whom she had been closest had always been the most difficult to fathom or even unveil. Even their faces seemed to destabilize themselves into new forms of unrecognizability under the hardly forceful pressure of her gaze. She would no longer know who the person was that was morphing disorganizingly before her eyes while the two of them were eating or pretending not to be hungry or whatever they did that kept them together undefended. She would have no steadying sense of what the person truly looked like from one instant to the next. And if the externals were themselves so mutable, there could be no end to speculation about what exactly might be going on inside any human body purposely neighboring her own. There was no reliable way of finding out.

She had the disadvantage of looking like a lot of other people. She was often accosted by strangers who took it for granted that she was somebody they knew. They insisted on resuming conversations broken off long ago and threw fits when she could not supply the precise lines of flattery or remorse they had been waiting to hear.

She had been living for some time in dun-colored small-town apartments with the blinds drawn at all hours. She had never learned the names of the streets. She had only a punctured knowledge of geography. She supposed that it helped her to be far from the center of anything, unincited.

But coach herself forward she did. A heavy-haired girl of terrorizing ordinary beauty cornered her at some upstairs cabaret. Teems of feeling fizzed between the two of them for a minute.

In the catty months to come, there were belongings to buy, and a past already kaput and ready to rebulk, rebuke.

Twenty-two, twenty-three—she was running out of realms.

■　　■　　■

Or was it just that she had permitted such an overfellowship with herself, suffered from such an oppressive overintimacy with her body, that on those rare occasions when she stumbled upon a glimpse of the bigger picture of herself, the microscopic view and the larger perspective did not fit together at all?

There were jolts and didders to her nervous system.

But did she shoplift?

With fingers so thin they looked like snippets from somebody else's?

She was not blessed with a voice in the head that furnished a running interpretation of human incident. Lives around her motioned brokenly this way and that. But not even her own body would honor her. There were flubs in her private locations, and her hands did not mix all that well with each other.

There was in fact less and less talk, and when she did speak, it was as if the words were issuing not from her mouth but from some rent in the murk of her being. This did not sound all that much like ordinary utterancy. It came crashing out of the vocabulary she kept crashing herself against.

Such was the life of hers into which others now and again must have pitched some woe.

Our mother?

Two parties are said to be present at every birth.

Neither ever survives in one way or the other.

While she was growing up, some packages of potato chips used to carry, on their backsides, a defensive notation along the lines of "This package is sold by weight, not by volume. Contents may have settled during shipment."

She thus learned to throw herself at the first perfectly rotten mood to come along in anyone looking more likely to last.

And our father?

As a girl, she must have known it was a coin collection, at least of sorts. But those nickels and silver dollars of his had not been pressed into any of the gloomy folders from some hobby shop.

My sister needed the chocolate teenies, the sourballs, the licoriced dojiggers.

She was big on upshots and bitter ends, and why should she have to see herself at all? Let that be somebody else's affliction. She had learned long ago how to prepare herself for a day without recourse to a mirror.

She did not yet like to drive, she suffered motion sickness on trains, planes were far too aerial for her taste, and on buses she would always get stuck next to the perspirational, the heartsore. The founding fathers, she thought, could have done a better job of laying out the republic so that everything would be within a stone's throw.

Encouragement came for her to audit an Oral Communications class at the township college. The professor said things like "Other things being equal" and backed drably away from her after class. He looked cramped and made sport of in his own life and forums. There was a turnout of papules, ingrown hairs, whiteheads, on his face. Her final grade would have been a Courier-font C.

Of the flight home for the first of the funerals, she remembered little except that the twosome sitting to her left kept rousing her from her narcosis (she had chewn some stupefacients) so they could use the restroom. They always left and returned as a couple.

She hoped she hadn't been talking in her sleep. A big fear was that in her sleep she would "open up" and give untidy, exploded views of her psyche.

Later still: an autumn with a winterly girl (lavish of eyeliner and with that knack for the pathetical). Didn't she owe it to herself to see life flatten desirably in the very design of a day?

■ ■ ■

Then where—Kansas, Arkansas? The paychecks were direct-deposited, so you do tend to forget.

She felt cozy in the time zone, but her days out there were as livelong as all get-out.

In those parts, the supermarket bakeries baked bagels without even a hole.

There was the ruck and malarkey of a diary for a while. She dressed page after page in a sneaky, tossing backhand.

Then she bought a car, a black one, and drove it.

She let the thing fill up with more and more of her trash.

In next to no time, the doors on the driver's side had been keyed intricately, all-overishly, though *keyed* is not quite the word. There must have been ice picks and chisels involved in the job as well.

PARTIAL LIST OF PEOPLE TO BLEACH

S he was either next to me on a plane and turning a page of her magazine every time I turned one of mine, or else she had come forward from way back to be a handful anew, because people repeat on you or otherwise go unplundered. I will think of her as Aisler for any priggish intentions I might still manage here.

Aisler had spousy eyes, and arms exemplary in their plunges, and she brought her bare knees together until they were buttocky and practical. I hemmed and hawed inside of her for some weeks after, but never got the hang of her requirements. A woman that swaggering of heart will not bask in deferred venereal folderol.

Anyway, she had a kid, and the kid's questions kept tripping me up—e.g., if you let people walk all over you, do you become a *place?*

Seven, seven and a half, and there were tiny whelms of hair already all over the guy.

I was flushy, heavy-faced, bluntly forty.

The morning they moved out (this was winter; flurries quibbled at the window), I made a sinking study of the lease. I had never given much thought to its terms before, the deductional verve of "lessor," "lessee." I was worded into the thing just once as an accountable, but the woman's name was right and left, gothicked in fountain-pen flaunts.

In short, I left the apartment the way I had found it— evacuated, fakedly intact, incapacitated for any glorying course of residential circumstance.

This was in the demising district's lone block of limestone heights.

I had lived there wreckingly in pairs, and in notional associations of greater than two. I had painted many a rosy picture. My eyes, it had usually been claimed, were bigger than my asshole.

So I stored some things, some becalming ensembles, in my car of the decade, a four-door sobriety. Set out for a pay phone, called some people to ask after people even farther off. But after a while it was just their biles vying with mine.

Night was a portal to the morning, maybe, but morning was no gateway.

At the office campus: a couple of new hires on my level, a woman and a man. The man was in his meridian twenties, not a quick one to color. It was all I could do to show him the quickest way to disable a paper clip so it could no longer get a purchase on the pages, how to refuse food from people who came in one day with new teeth shingled over the old.

There were spatter-dash cookies all week the week he started.

We had, this new one and I, some jaunty pleasance in the john. We got to the bottom of our camaraderie pronto. He was seclusively beautiful, a crude breather through it all, and I was easy to glut, even easier to usher out.

The other new one, the woman, was one of those life-leading types newly mired. Her hair looked created just for the day.

A daughter of hers came in one morning, came over to my desk, uncautioned. She was jeweled meanly and sloping well out of her twenties, and said, "I do sense a life boarded up inside you."

She let a hand deaden decently on my knee.

I made an appointment to meet her at the close of the week outside some vocational library beyond the county.

The day came (and so soon!) with a new droop to the sky. I drove out to the place, parked, welcomed a wait. She showed, though with a readied but refraining woman of her own. Just a girl with blacked-up hair, attractively uncertain in a man's raincoat, a fraternal-looking thing.

I went off with the second.

Her apartment, a duplex—lawn chairs everywhere inside, an unheightened futon local to the dining room, track lamps watted lowly. It was a vague body she had, the breasts just glib, simple growths. The hair mossy on her wrists—lichen, it looked like—took a weak but exact tack down her back, too. I was grateful for the broadway of bone that ran the wan length of it.

The usual skewing of selves, and then a brother upstairs if I felt I needed a look.

I did later make it up the steps. Found him adrowse undrunkenly in the tub. (The water hued, perfumed, kept bubblish with pumps. Wind chimes strung from the showerhead and set chinkling by an electric fan.)

Above the waterline: the snuggery of his underarms, an unhardihood to the shoulder blades—the healing neck, the face sharp-featured and finagledly beardless.

He talked; said he hoped to be seen as a behaving presence thereafter. Said he wanted to look travelled and dressy from a distance. Saw himself as an original in strickenness, long uncopied.

I took a seat on the toilet.

Did I agree, in maybe theory, that there were the taken, and the takers, and, between them, the kinds catastrophizing quietly?

A hand came suffering upward from the suds.

Tell the truth, he said: didn't I now feel *teamed?*

I sat some more, then felt fickle, went back downstairs to sit a while longer with the sister. But the arms I put around people always met up again with each other.

It was fitting to call our sessions at our desks "shifts," because shift I did—I mean, I fended, scraped along, moved from one point to a point just beyond. There was a lunchroom where I referred crackers backhandedly into my mouth, and a lobby with a guard who stood with hirsute goodwill behind a counter, and a restroom off the lobby. Above the urinals: a "PLEASE FLUSH" sign, with a clip-art elephant and "Don't Forget!" scripted down its trunk. But I wanted my piss pooling, maturing, in the trough with everybody else's.

The day widened as you tired of it.

This still was Thursday. Then Friday finally underfoot. Then a three-day weekend, a second-string holiday thought necessary to observe.

I knew enough to go home. The route was more formal now, with toll-takers trained to thank. Then an oncoming car not far from the turnoff, and I slipped up—got the windshield wipers going by mistake.

I was afraid the swipes might be taken for communication or, worse yet, a wave.

Then a pyloned bridge, the spotless boulevards, thinning streets of close-set addresses.

My folks! They had each overshot their marriage but otherwise went about ungulfed by life. They welcomed me back to their shams. Nothing was amiss or cosmic in my old, dormered room upstairs. A promising first gush of sleep, and then I awoke to the usual voices pluming upward through the baseboards.

I had not gotten a whole lot out of my heritage except a hoarseness like his, a poked heart on the order of her own.

They were savvier in their lamentations now.

Forty I was, and then fortier, fluking through my annual reviews, carrying my deskside trash home at the end of a day rather than running any risks of its being examined.

Just an inkling of skyline to this city. Nobody had thought to get lyrical about it yet. I was living on the brink of downtown but not, so to speak, alone.

There was an injuring party in his tindery fifties, and another, only lately unbunched from a family, querying out of some hole.

Then one who may have gone on to ape something wonderful.

And yet another, much younger: wronged early on, then doctored, restarted, struck by blows again. She had eyes of a deep, speaking green, but it was a green that spoke differently in a day's time.

I could roll off the names, the work numbers, of them all.

I could let a little thing or two ruin every other thing.

Things true of me should be even truer of you.

Sometimes people are too close to call.

Divorcer

DIVORCER

How far back should a man like me have to go?

She needed to buy a bag, a duffel, to collect the things of hers that were still in the other man's apartment. So we went to the odd-lots shop on the corner, a surplus store, army-and-navy. The bags were all of one size, one color (an obvious, becalming blue), one price: ten bucks. How much stuff had she left at his place? "Gosh, gallons, I guess," she said. She imagined that all of it could be squeezed or rolled up and that it would be nice to see the things that way, condensed like a summary of another concluded part of her life, to which there had been so many parts, unlike my life, which had hardly massed itself at all.

This was just an errand, she kept insisting. Everything between them was *between* them now, she said. What didn't I get?

And it wasn't as if she had been living there, she said, though that was where her mail kept going, the packets and chubby parcels that were always being forwarded to her from tearjerker towns farther south.

I had never seen this man. I never knew what might have been firing through him to her or what was yet to come out of the facts about him. The two of them had never gotten around to taking pictures.

We stood in the checkout line, one finger of mine curled around one of hers. Then all of hers ganging up suddenly on my upper arm.

"This is the easiest thing I've ever done," she said.

I had always been hearing this exact same thing from people, always on the kind of day that gets troubled down to its veriest grains. I'd heard it from lady dentists with purplish scoldings of tattoo on their shoulders, from men even older than I, reachers who roped themselves off from whatever they were reaching for.

She told me to wait outside the store while she went to the man's place. It was only blocks and blocks away. The etiquette of the matter would take maybe ten minutes max.

The afternoon welcomed me into its swelters. An hour went by, then cleared the way for another. I had found a bench near the store and stood in quiet beside it. Others came and sat: unfinished-looking men, a pair of proudly ungabby girls I took for lovers done for now with their love, a woman graphically sad in ambitious pinpoints of jewelry. Then a man so moodless, I could see all the different grades and genres of zilch behind his eyes. The city flattered these people who in the country would have been flattened fast for all to see all the same.

She found me at last and sat me down on the bench and said, "He cried and cried."

Then: "I cooked for him."

Then: "I made him something fussy for dessert. I wanted it to be a good-bye."

She made an effort to describe something merrily chocolate that had trouble retaining its shape or else had to be cut with care into squares. Her eyes looked fatigued, glassine.

Then: "I made it clear it wasn't old times."

The duffel bag was empty. She explained that her things weren't all in one place in his apartment. It wasn't as simple as all that. Things of hers had hit it off with his in dresser drawers, paternal suitcases, two snug closets, a laundry hamper, knottily hanging baskets. And some of his things, his finery, looked a lot like hers, it turned out. It was going to take sorting, and the sorting could take hours.

"Then maybe do it?" I said. "He's having a nap," she said.

But she went back, returned not with the duffel but with a bagful of the breviated, revelational dresses she usually wore, and some love-life loungewear now all bunched and abstracted.

"Look at the nice book he gave me."

It was a large, lap-spanning book full of photographs of the city shot testimonially and without sentiment from the air. "Shouldn't I feel sleepier after something like this?" she said.

●　　■　　■

They had her teaching some already outlined social science in the older hall of the neighborhood college. Vicinity University, they kept calling it. Her every syllabus came stapled to excess. She cried anytime it came out that she hadn't done any of the reading either. The book was the kind whose pages could not be tamed to lie flat. The thing kept shutting itself.

Five classes three days a week, and these were quelled girls with queering glowers, older young women unpetted and inexpert in dress, sideburned boys who were uglifiers of their one good feature, a once clean and eloquent arm now petty with tattooery. Called on, they spoke through the cotton of T-shirts yanked up by the neck holes all the way to the eyes. Test days, any essay answers they wrote foamed out of the plumpest of pens.

The multiple-choice answer sheets later went poppingly through an automated grader, and the results came out meaned and medianed in another of the nether percentiles.

Maybe somewhere else she would have been a big fish in a small pond, but here there was something of only the guppy about her in the way her mouth suckily took its coffee.

The remorseful e-mails: "Please …"

Touching herself under the desk, the hair down there mushed moist by her indulgent, unwandering thumb …

You can't generalize about divorce, and you can't get too specific about it, either. The subject either clouds itself up or loves the attention too much. I do know that the marriage was an approximation of somebody else's, someone who had had a theory about the importance of coming in out of the swarm, nothing more than that, but we had put emotional grime of our own into the thing and had expected something a lot gutsier.

The first night ran each of us back to people who had milked us for feeling before. She was no swallower, but I soon had my body conversing with hers in some nervy way. There was some chatter from us as we each transited the other in passing. We fudged something intimate that produced a notable scum of us both.

We peered cravenly into the words *wife* and *husband*, then went after them until they were anagrammable on the backs of envelopes bearing bills:

Wife = We *if* [emphasis mine].

Husband = Bad, shun.

She called her parents right there from the mattress. One was a stepparent, the other thoroughgoing in parentage, a bequeather of that hatred of hers that measured itself before coming out, so that what you got was just squeezings from it, squisses you could almost take for tenderness. I don't know what she might have been told over the phone, only that she went on to fill in the outline of the parent's life with days that got sucked into weeks and then months that disgorged her into a future that moved her from bathroom to bathroom. But it turned out to be just the same life in a different generation, looking gone.

And her stepparent? Her stepparent had starved her for her own good. Her stepparent had clipped coupons and for all but the last day of the month scrimped and saved, but on that final day always made a big production out of paying full price.

The town knew its place. It gave you unnatural human nature in a nutshell, unscared. This was a town in a county several counties over from the nearest city of consideration, a cement-block settlement in the colorless outdoors that itself stood no chance against the capital, where avenues were built up to the third or fourth story and you expected a net shittiness to an ended day.

It was in a dullish four-door with a brat of a rattling dashboard that I sometimes drove to, from, and through these places, then back to my wife and other things she was a baby about.

My life took some getting around to.

True, she did human-kindness kinds of things to people sickly in just the general sense, and was civil to any skunk or ransacking raccoon that broke into the kitchen and crashed through crockery before bowing out.

Dinner, at her hands, was capellini doloroso, with pours of diet cola.

The doctor ran some scans, cushioned the soft diagnosis even further with offers of a prescription soothant, a puny scored tablet, bluish and hexahedral, something to fool with her other appetites and maybe make more of the time go by.

Her handwriting was either all hooks or florets when she finally wrote a check.

Marriage had not worked out to be a doubling of each other's life, though there were duplicate juicers and sources of music. She reviewed her body from time to time, then substituted things in her wardrobe accordingly—a cocktail dress replaced, say, by a robe already pilling.

She was the first of us to be usually looking torn.

Three pairs of pants, seven sweaters, two pullovers, and a sports jacket double-vented in the back remained home to any odors and flakes, all other psoriasic consequentiae.

The city was only faintly more than a town, though a couple of corkscrew apartment towers had gone up to sharpen the skyline.

She would always start off a new notebook on the fifth or seventh page. The hope was that what came to her later would be good enough for the front.

And she had those parts of her I could never bring myself to call her "sex," because sex was what got done with them anywhere else by anyone other than me.

I was always driving her to the airport, only she sometimes came back by taxi, sadly talkative, gobs of new thought in her head.

Our landlord was a bloat of a man who always wore three or four T-shirts sacked over himself at one go. You could tell he wasn't keen on having people living out their awkwardness on his property. He wasn't technically the landlord (he was the landlord's father), but we were to address him as such because the landlord himself was, of all things, a daughter, an only child, slow of breath, uncitified, still shy a milestone or two on her way out of youth but already reigning over him through her mother, who sometimes slept uncoaxed by his side but otherwise left her dulled, left-handed body alone.

The lease was a work in progress. It kept the landlord up into the puckering hours of the night. He wrote on tablet paper in a huff, then wrote over everything already written. It was no more than humped penmanship, though.

He would draw a finger through the significance of stubble on his cheek, postpone his sips of the tonic water, then go back to considering.

No bare feet on the floor, hands off the walls, inspections at a moment's notice—more and more would come to him.

There was confusion about whether by "guests" he meant us or our visitors. Our visitors arrived one at a time with backpacks hung from one shoulder, in make-believe that someone's arm was slung over them warmingly.

Then the dress code for the building started calling for a kind of half-sleeved pullover with flaglike stripes that proved hard to find. Even the landlord wasn't sure where we could get our hands on one locally. "Try yard sales," he kept saying. "Be early birds."

He started charging extra to park, and twenty dollars more if we wanted to come and go by the back door (for that was the checkpoint now), and an hourly fee for each window opened to the western, fresher side of town.

The batteries in the smoke-detector saucers had to be replaced by his hands alone, thirty dollars per treatment, with a mystical tool nobody else was to see. It was a great many tools in one, though far too many at once. He said he was doing us a favor by using it this secretly.

Then we returned home one evening to find the parking lot, resurfaced only days earlier, overspread now with a good two inches' worth of unraked gravel.

Inside: throw rug after throw rug thrown in agitant multiplications over drop cloths dropped just so on the hardwood floors.

Furniture—ours, all of it—piled either neutrally or conclusively against one wall.

Littler things of our life now in wide-open boxes set out.

The spare keys he was selling us on were not exact copies.

"They're originals," he insisted. "You'll find nothing else like them in this world. They're yours alone to have."

These keys did not turn the lock.

My job that fall involved writing eight-page booklets whose titles always began: *What You Need to Know About Your* _____.

The blank could be filled with: prostate, adjustable-rate mortgage, butternut tree, loved one's mildest of autisms.

The interviewer had warned me against ever using the noun *spouse* ("It sounds spitty"); I was to favor, in its place, *other half, opposite half, second half*, or, preferably, just plain, fair-enough *half*.

A footbridge was the only way to get to the building with the lunchroom. There were always people crossing the bridge from the other direction, people needful of greeting. All I knew to say was "Weather we're having," which most of them heard as "What're we having?" So I always knew the day's menu before I got there.

The narrative had, for a time, gone out of my body. Those few weeks I was neither growing nor growing old.

I was slow-speeched, and gone aside in things.

Breakfast was maybe lukewarm bacon to jog my bowels maybe later.

Once, in the men's room at work—and this was a morning I was talkative, sociable, for a change—what I thought I heard from the stall next to mine was: "Lead me alone."

I've been wanting to have said some things about marriage that would get something done to it; I'm not sure what, exactly, but the idea was that it would be something you could make a point of listening to and then miss the gross amount of it regardless, then feel both a little relieved and a whole lot more apparitional, and move on right away to something else, a wee-hours stroll around a schoolyard, maybe, or a bolder than usual meal. I've been meaning to get these things said in steadying words I started saving up earlier for some other circumstance I had been expecting to have to survive (I'd assumed that my sister—a candid shambles of a blond, four years my superior, and my only sibling, though *sibling* is so mewling a word, so petty-sounding and resentful—would give up the ghost in some awfully silly, sexually freakened way or another), but then the wedding came along and pulled these words toward it instead, tugged them into vowlike paragraphs. They became little wrecking articles of wedlock:

First, that the human body had been dreamed up to defeat any plans you had for it.

Second, that I had all along been pressing myself into people or giving them the go-ahead to press themselves into me, same difference, the object being to pass quickly enough through some other body, soaking up some of its inner drip and squish, then come out the other side reasonably different.

Third: but you never got that far.

Fourth: all you could ever do with people was back out of them.

Fifth: so explain, then, all that talk of "going all the way."

So, true, we might not have ever been all that close, but we stirred, went to stores, and from a man with a thinnish quip of a mustache we bought sling chairs and odd-fangled candleholders and some lamps, display lamps at an ad-hoc discount, for some lorn-looking tripod tables at home. We ducked behind wordy menus in restaurants where, unbelieved, I ordered visionary desserts to be whipped up on the spot—spired, candified compositions that half an hour later were delivered to the table as hardly more than ordinary graham crackers stacked around breakages of penny-pincher baker's chocolate.

We stood in the metal-detector lines of courthouses just to visit whichever restrooms were most out of the way. (It was in one of those stalls that I once found a carpenter's pencil with a comforting fleece of dust and lint.)

We showed our faces at the viewing of a convenience-store clerk murdered one night in the store. It was some bloodshed we had read about in a paid notice in the paper. The viewee was putty-faced and dressy, her auburn hair banked upward. My wife gave the sleeve a procedural squeeze, and there was somebody there who stepped forward to shake hands and say, "Maybe it's just me?" This was said in a covering kind of voice. It belonged to an empty-eyed man on a verge of some sort. He was the boyfriend, we later learned, melodially enough, from the girlfriend, who put more and more punctilio into being the one person left of her ilk.

My family: I'd had that sister, and she'd had those kids, those three, who had been taught to win people over by saying, "You can tell me."

They were in a state that on the map looked orderly and trimly cornered.

My nephew had been put in a school so small, field hockey was only for the tinier girls, but a petition got him a uniform that almost fit and an obscure but honorable place on the squad. The coach had a version of the "There is no *I* in *team*" speech, and my nephew knew enough to say, "But there's an *m* and an *e* in it, and that would be *me*." Off the field, he walked with a delayed default stride that made him seem farther and farther behind in lonely tryouts for any life ahead. My nieces were lunarly vacant of face, and as such were unsweetened and unspeaking. They lived in the loonery they listened to on discs a boy kept burning for them on a laptop that was actually right there on his lap, bare and abroil. The songs were not from real records, just false-hearted bedroom renditions sung-spoken by sexual hopefuls online.

My sister: she had boiled herself down to boasts that she could hold it in and hold it in until she no longer had to go at all.

Let me at least get her husband out in the open. There was a human side to his eye contact, but something nastier kept tipping out of his characteristics.

They enjoyed advice, those two.

I remember their powder room's lout of a mirror.

Whatever it was between us that wasn't of a sort that should have warranted marriage: I hit back how?

I soaped my forearms hourly to disown any accruing smell of myself.

My penis might have had reach, maybe, but it never increased itself for her.

Then new tenants moved into the apartment to the left of the apartment where there lived a man of a nature exactly like mine. The newcomers were a couple with all of youth still in their hair. Smuttishly inked necks and arms on the two of them. A third, a girl, sometimes came and went. All three of them parked their locked bikes in the hallway. Then, days later, a plastic crate full of oddments of automotive hardware, jumper cables and the like, came to preside out there as well. Next: a stepstool, a dishpan full of caked dishes, a clothes-drying tree abloom with underfrippery and swimsuits.

Things kept teeming out of their apartment and into the hall. It soon got harder for him to carry in any groceries or take out the trash without bumping into something cubically impertinent out there.

One day it was the kind of hair dryer that ideally has you sitting underneath it, domed. (He found a way around it, though.)

Another day: a painting, cruddily acrylic, of cartons of picture books, saucepans, other potluck apartmentware.

The welcome mat in front of their door put a new confusion in him.

He brought it up with his one friend, a telephoner from horizons away.

"You're probably being invited," the friend said. "I'd try the door."

Then, next day: an entire, dried-up toilet, looking neither discarded nor set aside, but revealed, *featured*.

But did he take a seat on it? (He did not.)

Within the week: a magazine rack full of whisks; strips and squares snipped from possibly some needlepoint; a TV stand on which stood part of a pillar and a sandbag, sievy.

He one day did give their doorknob an experimental turn.

Dialed it a trifle.

There were three of them in there on the sofa—the man, the woman, and, between them, a girl only a little younger than the woman.

It was the man who spoke to him. There was rubbed commotion in his coloring, but he was just a sleepy young man in shorts. His legs had a shaven luster.

"Shouldn't the phrase 'home away from home' be of some upset to you?" the young man said. "Because your *home* home, your apartment, that lovebird of an apartment of yours next door, isn't, to this way of thinking, your home, either? Might I inquire about your birthplace, if that isn't too sickened a way to put it?"

The man named the town. Its name even had *town* suffering in suffix-wise fashion at the end of it. You could not pronounce the thing without its sounding like a gravelly place of unsought population, of traffic hard to come by. You pictured the address numerals of the houses having been painted over by accident again and again, and people not giving their backyard gardens a chance. Pets were all over the place, but treated more like keepsakes than like beings waiting to be fed.

The woman and the girl were kissing unnoisily, their faces getting more and more imbued. The girl was flat of eye. Her hair was blunt and blond, except for purplish overshootings here and there. The woman had marks, notations, on her arm—probably just reminders? The man, the visitor, could make out only one of them: *Be a better beautician.*

"I'll entertain another question," the man said, as if to be of this world.

No response.

"Go ahead, one more," the man said. "Pry."

Then it was suddenly one of those times when the departing minute mates with the oncoming one and you get a tiny bit more out of the moment alone.

He left a little after.

My wife: she was the active one in the marriage, mixing other men into it.

Time had dropped unkindly on her, but her teeth looked lighted from inside.

No, truth to tell, she had a smattering of beauty, a looksiness that would do.

Looking at any of it made you want to make a list of things in your own life that usually went unhated but now came coiling out for denouncement.

My list always begins too late. May it start as never before.

Even if it's just another cock-and-bull chronicle of girlfriends, boyfriends, in troubled outcomes or bleeding insignificantly on some couch.

There were ways she had of letting things lend themselves to loss.

Neither of us had been the better-looking.

Neither of us ever spoke except in dialogue that sounded miked and lonelier than just talk.

My one piece of luck was that I lived only blocks from a narrow little supermarket where on Thursday nights I could count on a mother and a father to be shopping for lunch things with a couple of gray-templed grown children. These were a son and a lab-coated daughter—both, I figured, somewhere in their forties, although the son wore more than one kind of class ring and seemed younger around the mouth. I would look from the parents to the children and have that sense of something or other having been handed terribly and immediately and unreturnably down. Two carts, almost empty, were somehow always hitched fast together, and the four of them conferred over everything, and in conferring got uglier and uglier over what had to be bought. I tried my best to stay close by and to hang on every word, because things usually went from the brazen to the brutal, and things got said about bedsheets that had never known any cleanliness or peace, about private appliances that took more and more juice, about body parts that still had no trouble finding each other through some splittage in the wall between bedrooms through which brother and sister had once passed only candies and erasers; and things would get thrown, left to lie on the floor in the aisles, cellophaned single-serve meats and cookies rococo in their curvations, and I, in life of my own, was usually buying only store-brand things, and the brands were brands like Banner Day and Soirée and House Proud, and the actual items, mine, I mean, often as not, were no more than commonplace clothespins, not the clippy kind but the ones that looked headed and legged but armless just the same, and, of course, the paper plates I used as memo pads, because no matter what I wrote on them, it was always right away wreathed, commemorated, and the final of its kind.

But to move on with my life would have meant what—just dragging the present entire of it five, ten miles to another stop?

And the different ways I was hated by different people! There was the one I'd surprised, sinkside, shampooing his eyebrows—eyebrows whose bristles he kept snipped suchwise that they shot out at you as vulgar perpendiculars.

Like the later me, he had a thing for nurses who had lost their touch.

Too, I'd thought of marriage as a gateway to other people. My wife had had lots of friends, cutthroat beauts she lied to tiredly.

The days of paper-signing came and went for us in different hellhole time zones.

I'm sorry, but they had a different way of talking about subtraction back when I was in school. It wasn't "Take this away from that"; it was never a matter of *minus*. It was "Find the difference of." E.g., "Find the difference of 54 and 41." So go ahead. Find the difference of her and me.

⬛   ⬛   ⬛

She moved to the consuming city, though it barely nibbled at her. The easy part, for me, was tearing up the photographs, because the camera had never cared for her; she looked veiny and lined and coarse-wrought at forty, she lived under a head of downed hair gone even droppier still, her arms lacked sweep and moisture, her knees didn't glisten, a bracelet or two wouldn't have killed her, but then again I had never gone in for the straightforwardly beautiful, I had wanted only whichever beauty came out garbled and fugitive, though when friends—the friends I then had (all of them since lost to ratty marriages of their own)—inquired why I had ended up with someone so unnatural, my answer was only: "But it was her call."

We had loved each other, yes, if only over and around other people, and we had married each other, even if only in a neighborly sort of way. But divorcing was something only one of us could do to the other.

It was her hands, finally, that were inseparable.

I could never get them to let go of each other and seek any hold on me.

Two doors to my right, his hair took effort to behold in its unshortened format. For an older man, there were all sorts of glamour he hadn't cut down on, even in his stocking feet. The socks were silky nuisances of maroon and chartreuse.

This was in an apartment angled similarly to mine, with just one room of worth, and in it a dolt of an old radio. It was a boxy table job on which he lured in the signal of a yonderous station. It carried the same programs as the local one but brought word of prim businesses kept in small families far from his walleted dollar. There were car repairers who would never have the chance to put a stop to the naughtiness of his maiden sedan, exterminators who would never make it to the inner circle of his bedroom's bedbugs, the peppy roaches in chest after chest of his drawers.

He felt that dulling in his heart that sometimes happened when he thought of lackeys other than himself.

He was a minority somehow even in his own lonesome householding.

The radio station was in a city whose name it was tricky to keep spelled aright in his mind.

He ordered a map of this other city. It came on a day that was otherwise no haven for him. He somehow got the unfolded whole of it tacked to the ceiling above his bed. He bought a pair of toy binoculars with the aim of reading the names of the streets. He got lazy, though. The binoculars sank back into their case. Before long, he had the map confused with a map of summer skies at night. The lines of the streets became lines that bundled stars into plausible constellations. Then the constellations were going to have to be called something. He couldn't remember any of the big shots from the myths, so he named the constellations after himself:

Teddy the Tenant, who now washed himself as often, as roundly, as possible, half expecting new things out of his body. (His body just a bin of bile and unused muscle.)

Teddy the Tenant, who looked through everything in the room to the undermatter rotting within it.

Teddy the Tenant, whose preference was for things to come to him quietly wrapped and padded in the mail.

The one thing to do when I finally paid him a visit was to disrobe like any other crybaby soon to be divorced, then crawl into his bed.

I never once gained on myself with him, either.

She is still the same person, no doubt, only with a different person. That baleful preposition *with*: I keep tripping over it on my way to larger thoughts. I've tried writing to her—letters and e-mails, greeting cards, note cards and postcards, all covered with the same trudge of words; but then I remember she is with somebody, somebody uneerily right there beside her, although in the wan case of her and me, she had always been just merely near—in the next room, the spare room, say, talking down-voicedly on the phone to a person maybe in her family or once close to the family and now known only to her, or maybe to the person she now was with, forming a fate for herself, replotting her past, finding ways to untighten me from the stories she would ever after tell of her unrosy and hairsplitting late thirties.

So am I saying only that my life no longer featured even me?

The thing about my sleep was that it had no influence on the day to come, and it set nothing right in the day behind.

I could see by the paperwork that it was on the second of June, a Tuesday, that the divorce had gone through. ("Gone through" = impaled.) I never found out the exact time of day. You don't always get anything but the date on a birth certificate, either, I later was to find. But my receipt from some mart down the highway tells me the hour, the minute, the second, when my wrinkly cash was tendered for the women's deodorant, the women's razors, the women's soaps and foams and creams and bleaches, all of which I was going to put to suitable substitutive use on myself.

Another way of putting this keeps putting me, I'm afraid, at one of those tax-preparation places, a franchise. This was toward the end. I was only just now getting around to having my taxes done. I told the man at the desk, "Married, filing separately." I handed over a brown accordion file aslop with papers, envelopes, receipts. The hands on this man, this preparer, were thuggish and unpreened. I could smell his lunch on him, down to the condiments. He had on a loose shirt of daft, demanding plaid.

He accelerated through my data. "You're fifty-four?" he said.

I nodded iffily.

"We'll need the lady's Soc Sec numero," he said.

"That I don't have," I said.

"But you can get it," he said.

"No."

"I'll get it, no nuisance there at all." Then: "But will you look at you?" Then: "What sort of a woman do we even have to sit here talking about?"

I may be at my best when things aren't getting anywhere, but I knew where this was going. Everything always went this way. So I described her at some dire, tidying length. I tried—let's be fair—to put a kind of cursory drift into the description, especially when it came to her eyes, which gave you a fast sour splash of regard, and her eyewear, the asymmetrical frames that she thought corrected something about her face, the way it dragged its features to the right.

But the man eventually cut me off. "You make it sound like her arms are teetering," he said. "It sounds like she's seesawing or something."

Then: "Do you always talk like you've got a shade drawn down over your voice?"

Then: "Believe you me, you're going to come out of this far more the innocent one."

Then: "Mind if I ask you something under the table?"

"Off the record, you mean?"

"Beneath the desk," he said.

There was, to be sure, just enough room down there for the very two of us. There was just enough light. I had always been partial to the closest of quarters, whichever kind of proximity leaves the person you're with looking suddenly *pieced*, unseeable as a heinous human whole.

His slacks were a button-fly laughingstock of acorn-colored corduroy.

I'd seen unbuttoning with far more gusto in it than his.

"No need for you to touch it," the man was saying. "But can you at least admit how much you've gladdened it? It's not been glad like this all day. It's a gladiolus. So, Mister Man, what would be a very nice last straw?"

She was my wife of five months going on five years ago.

Things hadn't lasted even long enough for people I hadn't seen all that while to have started looking a little like other people.

I wouldn't know how to go about looking for any of them now.

THE DRIVING DRESS

B efore I could fit into the few clothes my second ex-wife had left behind (a couple of filmy summer dresses and a responsible, unrevealing running ensemble), I had to drop a good bit of weight, twenty pounds or thereabouts, even though I was already on the slim side for a man of my unvague fifty years and bone-aching frame. I knocked off the weight by eating the sorts of things she had eaten and in much the same niggled portions, as best I could remember, and all of this food was innovatively unmeated and noodled over, not agreeable to me at all. I ate it at room temperature on the kitchen floor, more often than not spooning it out of the marbleized glass bowl of a ceiling lamp I had never returned to its rightful place above me after substituting a meeker-watted bulb. (My apartment had no tables, no chairs, just a stranded-looking, sheetless cot and, beyond it, stack after stack of the folded towels—dish towels, tea towels, hand towels—this ex-wife had bought for the undampened life she had imagined for us.) The food never became intelligible to my taste, and I soon enough was always going hungry, always feeling dwindled and funny in the head. People at work, mostly foes, inquired whether everything was all right, and I always said yes, in a swooning way, thinking that they had to be thinking of some bigger picture in which I barely figured, or else were asking only so that I would ask something as payback. The fact is that I have never played all that large a part in my life, but I know a lot about what goes on ever so tepidly in other people's circumstances, so I was always ready with one question or another, even if it was only "And your name would be?"

Divorce, I kept forgetting, is not the opposite of marriage; it's the opposite of wedding. What comes after divorce isn't more and more of the divorce. What came after, in my case, was simply volumed time, time in solid form, big blocks of it to be pushed aside if I ever felt up to it, though more often than not I arranged the blocks about me until I had built something that should have been some sort of stronghold but in fact was just another apartment within the apartment in which I was already staying away from mirrors, shaving by approximation, bathing in overbubbled water that kept my body out of sight.

We had been married on a Tuesday, but it didn't work out that our anniversary would have always landed on a Tuesday. (Calendars would not do us that one favor.) This was in a rinsing rain of early July, and the only music came from a music box the minister had brought out from his glove compartment. It played one of those melodies that referred you right away to other melodies beyond itself, so there wasn't much you could do if you refused to play a guessing game. The minister tried to draw us out a little, and seemed tickled that this wife-to-be was the baby of the family. "The one you're from or the one you're beginning?" he said. His lifetime must have been a lifetime of radiances written off, and he carried his holy trappings in a tackle box. To this day, I maintain that the ceremony hit hard but was a lot lonelier than it needed to be. The marriage was a clean enough one in the sense of no missed periods or abortions. Neither of us crammed much of anything at all into the other darling. We had ants in the place we were renting, and the directions to the ant killer we bought said not to kill them outright but instead let them go on feeling as if they were getting away with something. Then, a week or so later, we were to set out on the floor a couple of little plastic disks whose refreshments within would be carried back to the kingdom and shared holocaustically. But we had moved our things out before the end of ant season anyway. We were in a rush to be shown something of ourselves against other backdrops and ledgeways in uncushioning city settings.

We lasted through just two places after that—first the walk-up, and then the one where we're in a picture holding on to some believing, sandy-haired person who delivered birthday balloons to us by mistake, though I have never figured out who would have been around who would have had a camera.

■　　■　　■

Loved or wanted, probably not, but I'd been chosen, I don't doubt, or at the very least I had felt targeted somehow. The whole thing—flirtation behind others' backs, courtship, engagement, marriage, separation, curtailment, divorce—had lasted a little less than a year.

We had wasted no time on accuracy of feeling or any bettering ebulliences in bed.

The wedding presents I sent back delayedly and by the cheapest of mail. The givers had been mostly favorites of my ex-wife's, a cautioned circle of self-bewildering men and an armful's worth of women who didn't believe in spending any time on themselves.

A friendship ring there was, and lots of those stringy, braidy, beadwork friendship bracelets so very burdening that year, and rubber stamps that spelled out her first name in cavorting characters, and sweaters with her name or her initials embroidered many times over, and silvery cylinders abrim with monogrammed handkerchiefs (those twiny, outlasting triplet initials of hers once more, never adding up to a word no matter how you kept disarranging them), and a good half-dozen or so handwrought books of calligraphied poems (with stapled index cards for covers) dedicated to her all but fatally. The poems were mostly list poems, and they listed, again and again, the overlong fingers, the hair that mired itself unfinely on the forearms, the face that reported little of the moods rocking within.

With each gift sent back, I wrote a different note on differently deckled notepaper but always to the effect that there were people bluntly evident to themselves in even their queerest of dreams, and there were people like us, who had to keep feeling ourselves out, looking for hints in all we had done, even when all we had done was discover that others had liked having us around only because our presence deepened their sense of having a place all to themselves.

So I kept to the diet, let my body ebb vengefully, and the day came that I could insinuate myself at last into the dresses my ex-wife had thrown on for meals, for company, for evenings of witticism and the pushing musics she backlogged on cassette. I stuck to the sleeveless thing, the one she had called her "driving dress," because she had once worn it while we took a long, trashy cruise through some woodlands beyond the cooling human ensuings of the county. But there wasn't much I could do in it but sit around on the floor of the apartment, though I eventually formed a habit of calling people—relations, affiliates, usually just an aunt on my mother's side who had lived all of her grown life with a possessive neighborhood lady whose notion of herself as an innocent had gone too long ungardened. This aunt would ask how I was holding up, and I always got around to lying. I lied with the scaly understanding that by lying, I was just doing what my ex-wife would have done, because, to her, the truth had only always been something waiting to be ousted from the facts and then shown the door so that the facts could reassemble themselves more creationally around something else. The facts in this case were only that I had become a man who one day came forward and fled himself.

FATHERING

My son went on to live himself out of life and livelihood in a state not all that different from our own but looking practically empty on the maps. Now it was my daughter's turn at the fore.

My daughter was in the grade where you have to prove that the school can't go on without you. It was going to be a rocky year, because I had a rocky enough job and had already put that son through school, had done as much as I could for the kid, walked him gravely from one teacher's station to the next, left him finally to fend for himself and find his footing somewhere other than under my roof.

I had to begin bringing in men to tend to my wife now that I was spending more and more time on my daughter's homework—the projects, creations, offensives, and enterprises demanded of her at school. It was only natural that my wife would feel scanted, so I went to the bother of introducing her to men I knew, men at bottom baseless but harmoniously groomed and suited. Something in her would sometimes catch on to something of one of them, maybe just a blowout of body language or a steep-rising opinion about bedstead etiquette, but mostly I could see she had hardly been lured at all. My mind was understandably on other matters.

My wife and I, once in the bed, sometimes talked without much thought during those nights when she wasn't out with one of the men I had put her aside with.

"She ignores me now," my wife would say.

"She's a schoolgirl," I would counter.

"Her brother didn't carry on with me the way she does with you."

There had been something crushed and unclear all along about that son, true. He had never once come to me about anything. I assumed he'd always gone to his mother about any of the delicate details. I'd always pictured something, or at least a penumbra of something, spreading itself out between them, or over them. A mother is always better at seeing to it that things get wiped away.

If I say I would eventually go to sleep, I mean I dragged myself high and low to a place where the sleep had to have been preparing itself for me.

I could bank on this sleep, once found, to get any culminated day sugarcoated completely.

My daughter was slow-spirited and emotionally meandering, and she spoke in a streaky way, and she had unsavory hair, mostly bunny-brown but with a plunge of it dyed black, and plumpish arms that looked as if there were no blood inside, and breasts that at this point were limited, unloaded.

The teacher had her wearing those shorts that had a panel of fabric stitched to the front so that it looked as if she were wearing a skirt. The sweaters she could choose herself, and what she chose were ones with neck holes that appeared gouged out.

The only time I went in for a conference, masking tape was stuck in braceletlike formations on both of the teacher's arms.

"Do you push her nearly enough?" the teacher said.

Some married people report pain or inflammation, and others will tell you that a well-adjusted partner feels no need to touch the other. To me, though, marriage had always seemed more like one of those medical procedures that, once performed, could never be undone. I might be thinking of the one where a bow gets tied holidaywise around a tube.

My daughter sometimes took a pair of sewing scissors petitely but hostilely to her hair. She liked to fill her stomach with the most blood-gushing of meats. She had vocabulary trouble, too.

But with my son, in the year when he had been the one on the front burner, it was mostly that they sent him home one afternoon with a couple of illustrations of a cautioned-looking man of inexpansive middle age, abandoned in the easy chair of a living room, a telephone table at his left. The illustrations were identical except for six things, my son had been warned. Could he find all six? They wouldn't push him any further along in his learning until he had made a list of them all.

Simple: in the second picture, the telephone no longer had an old, rotary-style dial, one of the man's shoes was untied, the man was no longer wearing what appeared to be a college ring, his sweater no longer had a peacock-blue stripe running bisectionally across the front, and the phrase *first-aid kit*, stenciled onto the lid of a little carrying case resting on the man's lap, no longer held the uniting hyphen.

But that came to only five things.

Everything else about the two pictures looked exactly the same. The son and I stared into them hard. We stared into them steep-down and from oddball angles and cunning disadvantages of perspective. We refreshed our vision with shocks of cold water, traded places on the sofa, looked with just one eye, then the other, then through a cardboard cylinder. We laid tracing paper over the pictures and traced resortfully. We took them to a place to have them enlarged, and, when that did not satisfy, we took them back and had them reduced.

This went on sundown after sundown.

The kid went to school every day saying, "The man in the one on the right is a twin of the one on the left?" or "A great many hours have passed?" or "The left one is heavier of heart?" or "There is a tainting difference in the weight of the paper?" or "A different mood has come over him?"

"None of those," one or the other of the teachers or aides would say.

The kid kept getting sent home again with the pictures.

I did my part, though. I went in and howled in my tamed way at the teachers, the aides, the principal, the head of the school board. I composed letters in my head and committed one or two of my phantom tirades to paper.

These bashful tantrums got me nowhere.

I decided to cheat, found a specialist in the phone book, called. He made it sound as if his office were right around the corner, but it took me the better part of an afternoon to find the place. I brought him the pictures. He took them off my hands and said, "Never mind these. Don't this boy of yours have a mother?"

So I veered home, looked up my wife, shoved the pictures at her, said, "Okay, so show me the biggest difference between these two."

She wasted no time. "In the one on the left, it looks like the phone is just about to ring. But why should it always be up to me to be the one calling?"

My wife: she had a way of telling me something by evening out the truth in it, leveling everything until the only way I could take it was as the sleek lie it had become.

I built her up for the men as a woman of unslumping intelligence, of goodwill that had real punch.

So okay, okay: there is a clean feeling you're said to feel when you're sure you've been thrown over, but I could never feel sure, so I never felt clean.

I could picture my wife with a man who had climbed out of a differently heaping generation, I could picture the two of them alike in height and mirth, but I couldn't picture either of them saying anything other than "Now we know what?"

I borrowed some of my daughter's paper and one of her ornamented pens, and tried:

Now we know not to trust the kind of dark that promises to have veins of something even darker in it.

Now we know that when people ask if you're married, it can be hard to tell whether to take the question as a pleasantry or as an affront, whether to come out with something snotty or imploring.

Now we know that something stringy in me must have unstrung itself even more.

Then one day the girl came home to report that all the teacher had said was: "Don't come in here having read the paper. Write your own newspaper, or don't bother coming back."

My daughter's paper, when she was done with it, was three pages long. It was the width of a woman's shoe box. It was handwritten on paper-bag paper with one of those pens that gave everything you wrote a silvery shadow. There was only one article, and it ran on and on in swirl after coerced swirl. In the news was one roommate (male) having done another (also male) out of his life, claiming that he (the first male) was the mate of the room and not of the other person. The weapon was a curtain rod that had been filed sharp and wielded first sodomizingly, then knifewise. The article had been written in inverted-pyramid style and correctly trailed off into cuttable statements about the males' rearings, qualifications, and side interests.

The girl delivered the paper to the teacher and brought home the note the teacher wrote. It read: "I'll need to see a scale model of the room."

The mock-up, done in balsa wood and modeling clay, took the two of us a good week and a half. It was based not on the daughter's room, which wasn't quite the otherworldly setup you might right away expect, but on the one the son had grown up in: that was all his roughhouse-scarred furniture in there, and his elegiac lineup of wine bottles, and his clipboards, his heavyhearted keepsake pornography.

Two days later, the model was returned to the girl with the prompt: "Then tell me about males. Tell me all about at least one local male."

Her brother was no longer local, and she had already related whatever it was that exact words would have said about me.

I said to my daughter, "There isn't a boy or two around here with an interest in you?"

"Not with anything for me to tell anybody about."

So I told her about the man I had paired my wife off with a few nights previous: a man of such-and-such upheaved and tellable height and poundage, his wishes for an uphill, farfetched future, his bathroom traditions, his first wife's foofaraw of clips and holders in her hair, his second wife's losses of sisters, and now his heart all hectic in this onfall of immaterial affection for my wife.

I described the man in the act of looking at my wife—at the advancing legs and arms, the arthritic slant to the upmost segment of each of the little fingers, the large-pored composition of her face, each of the eyes looking like the nucleus of a terror entirely separate. I could respect the man's erection even if I could not supplement it right that very instant with a like one of my own.

My daughter wrote some of this down, trapped it in the defensive prettyisms of her handwriting, turned the paper in to the teacher, who wrote back: "Bring in this wife/mother/person soonest."

I have no idea whether my wife, thus summoned, ever showed up, or whether it was only a telephone conference she and the teacher enjoyed, but the girl came home from school that day and made a sound with her mouth that shook me all around in myself. It was a sound that had a little bit of everything in it—you wanted to pick out the parts that were just exhilarants and keep them separate from the parts that were accusation far and wide, then see what else you might have in there that was going for you or against— but all of it came at you in an exhaustive cry, and she kept making this sound again and plentily again. I rushed to make sure all the windows were shut, and I turned up the radio and the television to drown her out as best I could, and I tried to mimic the cry to maybe neutralize it, and in so doing came closer and closer, and when I had all but approached it, she took a swing at me, insisted the cry was her oral property alone.

Days later, the girl returned from school with a squeeze-box-style folder holding watermarked forms for me to sign. The school was going to keep her on, the papers assured. They wanted her for all the time in the world, for as long as possibly life.

It came to all of two inches, my signature, one final fathering bother.

TO WHOM MIGHT I HAVE CONCERNED?

I

To cut things short: she was mortally thirty and was drawn now to the uncomely, the miscurved, the dodged-looking and otherwise unpreferred, so my body must have naturally been a find—breasts barely risen, putty-colored legs scrimping on sinew, knees that looked a little loose, teeth provocative and unimproved.

If I talked, my voice sounded suctioned out.

She wanted to know about my family, so I said nice, encyclopedic things about those dry-boned people shuddering on a back porch far from my pounding opinion.

And my love life? I mentioned a slow-hearted man who had gotten to me first, and the teakwood toy guitar he could form some fundamental chords on, and though the songs themselves were hazy enough in their straying melodies, the words to the songs evaluated me, I felt, unfairly.

"And after him?" she said.

No answer comes back to me even now.

But I moved in with her, pushed my filing cabinet full of stoneware and unrevelatory sweaters up the stairwell. An ailment had left her prim-lipped and prickly, and there was everything the matter with her perfect-looking feet. Her diet was a diet of meatless whimsicalities hard to prepare and even harder to digest.

Her heart was an unharboring thing.

II

Mornings, we bordered each other in bed, her mouth sometimes engaging mine in ways I could take for a kiss.

The living room held only that slattern of a sofa, those two portly chairs, that inane table doubling as a desk (the vase atop it stuffed with mystic yanks of hair).

Nothing rose above five stories in the town, and the month would not budge: this was an August on end.

I wasn't good with life, and it came out that she had had so many of us, women exactly of my type, that an old friend of hers long ago stopped trying to keep our names straight, and took to calling us all Gretel, or simply G, or M, I'm afraid, for the occasional, dazed, break-apart male.

There was nobody fearing for me in particular.

III

She took the money that came to her and motivated it to become even more money. Checks arrived in flimsy forwarded cinder-gray mail.

She did her sit-ups only in a full, slopping tub, and then only if I was there to watch lewdly and applaud.

She would burst out of the apartment, having screamed, "Forget it!"

People, she said—people tiring and self-affectionate to this day—had already predicted why or how soon she would leave me. They said I was "rural," "kelp."

She hated stores, but we sometimes eventually had to shop for food. I would guide the cart along the faltering floor of the town's only carpeted, pricey market. After just one aisle (starches boxed and enveloped), she would shout, "But I am not a person with time for this!" I would maroon our cartful, follow her out to the parking lot, and, driving us home, listen to her count aloud the people she suddenly missed, even landlords, even a druggist who plucked the hairs of his knuckles but had always had good, almost funereally summational things to say about her, based solely on what had been jittered out on a prescription pad—the three grades of domineering medicatives, vividly capsuled, for whatever might take apart any portion of any loveliness of hers in daylight.

The night I had to replace the battery in the clock above the kitchen sink, I left the clock set out like a plate on the table.

The impulse was to find a lid that would forever cover it.

IV

Hair expressed itself tinily on her arms in smartening coils of walnut-brown, and she went about in backless dresses, even slept in them when she wasn't sleeping alongside me, and I was limited, dissipative, slow of mind even for someone of my unreadied generation.

Where I worked, there was noise from the office next to mine. Just one voice, sexless but not unfeminine in its murmury daylong ongoing. It was a voice that soon was scooping out more and more of the pith from my concentration until my skull felt hollowed and everything next door sounded that much more pronounced.

This person was talking either to himself or herself—let me hazard it was a man—or else monologically on a phone. I couldn't put an end to any of my work. It sat on my desk, foldered away but saturated with mathematical offenses and ungracious intelligence. A progress report, two pages max, was already three days past due.

V

She had the world fingered. She knew its every nook and seam.

She had been told that her laughter sounded exactly like *har har*, though I never once heard it that way, and in principle she was not one to laugh, except for that havocking eruption that one night followed my having answered her question *What exactly's an elk?* by saying I imagined it along the lines of a dog, only not quite as blithe.

And the fund of hair between her legs: that tousle alone was filling enough for me, and I liked the way one or two of the coilings would come loose and complicate my swallowing for a dreary while, because I believed in always having a little something to choke on, as needed.

But I could not have even once ever pleased her, and she never once pretended to have wanted to be pleased.

VI

In her defense: her stepfather, from the day she turned twelve, had forced her to bum toiletries off other people—relatives, classmates' comforting aunts, neighbors nicknamed and shaken.

She brought home diluted shampoos, mouthwashes funneled into picnic-day condiment bottles.

The razors handed down to her were ladies'and men's both.

Hair of all shades still concerned itself between the blades.

The deodorants those days came canned. They shot out a froth under your arms.

It was a student teacher who introduced her to dress shields and other confidential protectives.

Any drugs she took were just street tinctures of harder stuff, and the highs hardly revised her. There was a friend for a while, a sparkle-haired girl promiscuous in her sympathies. Their love was the kind of unmuted love, rummagingly physical, you get only from friends about to ditch you.

But mine? My parents and brothers should not have to figure into any of this except as snitches.

What had shaped me was the discovery, at thirteen, that I could send my arm around my back and then make out, at my side, the fingers of a hand doing its damndest to reach me.

VII

She insisted I lie by her side in tedious untouched undress while she read things in which the thinking always plunged, and she would now and again look up jollyingly from her book to say I was "cute," and liked to pronounce my full name in a senseless blabby swagger, with the expectation that I would follow by reciting hers, that richly hyphenous thing, every division of it sounding, with each doting repeating, less like the name of a person, a baby-faced bedmate, younger by years, her youth holding up, than like the name of some buckling mass of land, another unbeckoning territory, clearly inclement. So, true, not every night was brutal, I wasn't always fighting with her, she wasn't always threatening to leave.

She was sometimes chatty—sassily, intelligibly so—in the unruly oblivions of sleep, her night-breaths otherwise tiny but sounding inquiring.

My own sleep? Dreamless, unramifying.

I get behind myself the most when I'm trying to make me out to be only plain-hearted and bewared.

VIII

What she made night after night for dinner was dingily stripped and pasty, affiliated with unkempt vegetables, pea-colored teas.

Later she was working even later at a call center.

I usually got lost on my side of an argument (thoughts pooled in my head until any new ones got drowned), and I had, it's true, grown up believing that "No news is good news" meant that tidings of any kind were always necessarily bad, and before long she was within her rights to be holding me accountable for things I did or did not see fit to have done in her dreams.

IX

She was immured in her charisma, in short, and spoke to me only as if through fissures in it. Sometimes all she said was that my soap was the one thing stinking things up.

There should have been all the time in the world for me to put any of my orienting criticisms of myself into ballpoint permanence in a hideaway notebook somewhere, but I could no longer stomach the sight of my handwriting. My printing that had once had such backbone in it came out all brittle now, and comical, and my cursive kept veering off in weakening wavelets.

The car was always parked out front, and she had cozied it with pillows, bolsters, a coverlet; you felt indoors and unbeheld in there, despite the windows all around and the courteous snoopery of neutral passersby. The backseat library was packed mostly with reference works, all hers: guides to warning signs and surgeries, emergency manuals, and that mighty lapful of a dictionary in which you could look up *couple* and find, beyond the cautiousness of the preliminary definitions, unsolacing confirmation that the word had for ages also meant "not necessarily two but a quantity constituting more than one and as many as a few."

X

Yet I sometimes would not speak to her for days, and we slept in separate rooms now, and I was soon accepting the daily chewable sugared vitamin from her fingers without having to touch her at all. She left for weeks at a time, by bus, rented car, my car (a compact often egged), or by train, by airplane. She liked cities and the obstacles they offered, and the problems only a city could ferociously solve—the way you could style your loneliness into some blunt human trouble that instantly had appeal.

I imagined some glaring girl draped already around her. I could see the girl down to the hue of her lipstick (a rude orchid) and taste her breath (something alcoholically appled in it).

If I cheated, at first it was only with a girl as well, a sad-headed and suggestive young woman, an only child, with the only child's burden of having to be many-sided and rounded enough to stand in for anyone else who could not be bothered to have been born. She would sometimes stand in her own light, sometimes commandeer light from elsewhere and direct it all over herself until she looked bleached out, wraithy. If I say that we had sex, all I mean is that we possessed it one at a time while the other of us had to make do without.

XI

It's not that I was mannish. It's just that I wasn't all that much a woman in my contours and phenomena.

My college had had an upstart highway cutting right across it. The splashy sound that everybody suddenly turning pages made, and all the buildings called "halls" to remind you to hurry up and hurry through: I always got thrown from the books, could not stay put in somebody else's line of thinking. All the profs ever wrote on my papers was "As you like" or "Then go right ahead."

I saw myself even then as merely dirtying and undefended.

After college: an unenduring, stopgap marriage (he was overhumanized, always prompt in returning any reasonable farewell crackle of affection), then employment, and co-workers, mostly women my own life-poisoning age, mostly Kristens or Kirstens or Kirsties: the shouts of violet in their eyeshadow, their moony maneuverings between men.

My apartments were always efficiencies, for the pointed and abridged living they required, toilet and stove each practically within arm's reach, though I conducted much of my body's insurgent business in the most public of places.

XII

But I hardly held it against her for hating the town, this runt of a place, whose principal streets were not numbered but, instead, optimistically honored obvious trees.

And the neighboring neighborhood, where she wanted to make friends and so did: should I not be doing a better job of skipping over the tamed eyes and closing mouths of these undiscourageable people who put up with our surprising company and wiped us into their lives?

The names of the wives sounded like wearied imperatives: *Melissa!*

XIII

Then she left to visit her family for a week that turned into a month. (Punishment I more than deserved.) Her voice over the phone persisted more thinly, claimed less of a radius, but the considerations were always the same: her stepfather was still a parasite, and her brother's every other wife was either calling off another pregnancy or recruiting one or the other of us for some petty romantic triumvirate.

Updates, as well, about her sisters, the unharnessed two of them, the one's heart galloping toward the other's in the attic they still shared in their late, paddocked twenties.

My telephone manner was dicey. It lacked the novelty coughs and tricks of neutrality it somehow has now.

But I told her everything—that I stormed around the apartment in dresses of hers that now smelled only of me; that everything I ate out of our unearthen blue crocks tasted spookingly of things I thought I had eaten days ago; that my body might have meant well, but my life felt merely impacted on it instead of getting dashed off from within.

She read off likely times of departure and arrival. What sort of mistake would she prefer I make next?

XIV

My title at work, to be technical about it, was mitigation specialist. I was the person hired by the defense team to find mitigating predicaments in the history of the defendant, then fashion a wreathening exculpatory context for whichever evil had been brought to bloom. This was done mostly through interviews with the defendant himself (for it was almost always a man, on the youngish side), his family (had any of these clear-cut and constructive figures survived), the extended family, the neighbors, the preteens in their lookouts on the neighbors' porches and patios, the former teachers and olden coaches, the foremen who were historians of grievance, the general practitioner who believed in cortisone above all else and also practiced exciting bedside dentistry in a pinch, the hobbyist who had introduced the defendant to midget hobby knives and ominous pastime chemistry—only it was an assistant I sent out to towns in the troughs between other towns to do the footwork, the spadework, the eye-watering eye-to-eyes. My responsibility was to make enough time for a stocking-feet read-through of the rundowns, the records and transcripts, the Internet-search histories and suchnot, with a nose for anything extenuating. I would learn about hernias that were nobody's business, warning signs mistaken for winning ways, insouciant executions of bedroom reptiles, a school project about the phases of the moons in a jilting girlfriend's fingernails, sullying marital acquaintanceships from still later on, sometimes a sheet of paper that came into dignity as a diary of sorts, on which had been written the bittered convictions of whoever most deserved to be the last two persons on earth.

Today, for instance, a transcription of a chat with a cousin of the accused, a girl in her scantling twenties with little to add, her photograph in the folder bringing her to light as a reluctant mustering of skin and bone in a lax plaid sack of a dress, a face unfavoring itself, my attention angling almost at once to the hackwork of the hair, the little there was left of it, a pittance of dead-leaf brown.

In the transcript, she classified herself as an inferior by choice, talked in a heavenly way about sleeping on cold kitchen linoleum, preferring to be walked over, even stepped on, eating only house-brand foods, applesauces and syruped unnutritive fruits, and then only when they were on sale and, whenever possible, poured atop the guckage already there in the dog's unrinsed dish.

She had taken "brush with death" to mean "apply death smoothly and gently to your life." Every word, according to her, was the alias of some other, which was why any two people came to remember everything so differently. Her body had told her to guide the active ache in her skull down to idle joints and ligaments.

Her name, her number, were handsomely provided. I dialed. "I've told you too little already," she was saying, as if speaking through mouthfuls of waxy collateral speech. I went out to see her right away.

Only she didn't look anything like her picture. She was a haze of late girlhood in a sundress several sizes off. She did not even think to bid me welcome.

All she did was drop to her knees and take one gracious little sip from her own dribble on the floor while I stood by.

This was just a Tuesday that everybody else must have been passing through on their way to later little things in life.

I felt split between myself and receding divisions of my nature, all those traits that had come down to me from parents, parents of parents, ancestral nonentities.

This sometimes happens to people all too awful. You go boring right through yourself. You're your own predator ever after.

XV

Things transmitted by sex: disease, yes, there had, of course, been any number of those roseate sicknesses of one or another cunt visited once too often, and we looked upon them as not punishing enough, but I should be listing the other things of hers that came into me, too, the qualities and uproars and such of this primary woman of mine, my egger-on, the one I always found reason to return to, but I keep, *kept*, myself coming up short whenever I counted us together, and time was piling itself onto my face in ways that didn't necessarily age me but made me look too ornate to be thought any longer young.

Then the clear choices of joint checking, her signature more and more often adjoining mine on unaccepted documents, on greeting cards that left the greeted ones feeling doubly accosted, assaulted; an autumn, in short, already exhausted and coarsening into the septic muck of December, all that sloppage of the holidays and people, nobody cousins and worse, saying, "But it must be lonesome just the same."

And all true of the new year: I put on some pounds, took them off, took off with a noticer who at first noticed only my feet, my besooted toes, the toenails a dribbly livid pink. He was a standing ruin of a man, hirsute, and unpliant where it mattered in the rues in his head. He said I was everything that had been dreamed out of him. We lived in his bargain apartment and fit into each other under the covers, my lips slicked with his drippings, but I was confused and shaming, I didn't return things to their places, I ate in an unforgivable bustle of crumbs at his desk, I wasted perfectly good paper on sketches in the hasty lines of which he claimed to summon the ghostly contours of her jaunting arms as I had described them once with my fingers fast inside me, busily, morbidly twiddling.

Must I remember this man this liberally this late?

He sucked unlit cigarettes and suffered in weighty misfit shoes that were inherited.

His diagnosis was some sort of social syndrome popularly mischaracterized as a glory or a treat. It made him do everything the same way every time.

Mornings, he didn't so much get dressed as duffel himself into an ample bagginess from which his arms, those lugs, had to butt out for their trouble with knobs, burners, thermostats. Then a birthday of his that, until my own came around, left him technically an extra year older than I.

There would be pasta slackening in a pot in day after day that buzzed off in minutes of emphasized decay.

So, in brief, we were not so much a couple as a twofold loneliness, though he could be convivial in his hollers from the toilet, and his guilt conversed with mine in ways that covered old ground rousingly.

But it galled me, all of it—the spaces in his intelligence where the education had run off from him, the picked-at complexion, the little yellowed district of his slanting lower teeth, the eyes that released themselves laboringly on my legs the time I finally bared them with a week's immoderation of hair.

It was thus I went back to where she, the woman, my encourager, lived *unliked* in a brilliance of cooperating finances, of things given neatened definition in rooms now cleaned weekly by cleaning women twice her unsympathetic age.

I went back, and I pleaded every sort of poverty, though mostly what I lacked was anything going for me in the life behind.

XVI

I must have gone on figuring that before things between us could get sharpened to an end, there had to be a middle, if for no earthly reason other than to make the beginning look so much farther off and uncritical now.

She was always out of bed before me, and her breakfast candy was those little knobs of bittermost chocolate, tiny tetrahedrons of pressed licorice. The coffee had to have both ice cubes and a heating element in it.

And it was always the last time she was going to be doing things, because tomorrow, finally, she was going to take any old magazine article and wring an outline from it, then take the outline and situate facts of her own onto it, anything, her tantrums, her cookings, the nutmeg smell of her arms, her junior-year concussion, discarded formats of her lonesomeness, even the side interests of dogs she had since outgrown, then send the thing off to the same magazine, in hopes that when, months later, the article came out, it would be seen right through, read down to the original, to matters that had nothing to do with her. She counted on people far off to at last have taken that much of an active part in her going to pieces for me, or whomever she might have been seeing me as, because, truth be told, I was quite the indelicate myself, and I ran around on my past.

XVII

The building where I worked got itself pronounced sick in a sudden, silencing memo: it told of molds and ignoble moistures on just about everything; poisons in the paints and in the carpeting, the controversial furniture; toxins in the insulation, blowing out of the vents. My co-workers were demanding redress or else got the idea to wear gloves reaching almost the elbow, protective magnetic necklaces, prophylactic indoor watch caps tugged down to the eyebrows.

Some of us began showing up in aprons, snowsuits.

Others tucked chancy minerals and whatnot up their nostrils.

A co-worker came at me representatively, befriended me, took me out to lunch to tell me about things that had creased her life for the worse, confiscations thanks to her landlord, allergies that could not be tracked back to a source. Showers of sorrow kept showering through her. Her face seemed hoisted toward me straight from these griefs. She had a grove of terribly bone-brown hair, and eyes a little incivil.

The lines I could not help seeing drawn from the spree of moles on her cheek to those on the shaft of a forearm were suddenly strings I should have plucked for what must have been the pipsqueak, duping music of her.

Truer still: she was beating the dead horse of her middlemost twenties.

She wanted my phone number, but only in Roman-numeralled perplexity, if possible.

I gave it to her in slow, begriming pennings on the butterfat of her inner leg. (Her dress was a whim of sink-washed gossamer.)

Then dessert: a shared block of chocolateless cake with decorative obstructions she spooned into some zippery sanctum of her purse.

She must have known I expected speedy proof that she was my type—at once befooled and wounding—because she said, "This has been dainty."

She mentioned some errand to run before returning to work, so I walked alone along the vacant avenue and considered myself even further. What had I been formed for? To whom might I have concerned? I wasn't foremost even in my body, where my parents spoke themselves up out of my disposition. They had me hard-faced in their honor, these two. They had guided me to junior versions of their infirmities—the scalp all scaly, flakings under even my eyebrows, crises requiring a toilet not quite every hour.

I was their oiliness far and wide.

And my brother, the oldest of them: why think of just him? This one always dressed up even for bed, but there were hexes all over him, jinxes in his essence. The doctors had talked and talked of what was drowsing in his vitals, in no rush to rot him just yet.

He was the very figure of anything better off beyond. And I? As ever, the merest pinprick of a sister.

I was now in the part of town that was part run-down park, part graveyard. Then, the marble-arched totality of a museum, dyingly devoted to the paperwork and dropcloths of municipal history, then the three blocks of conditional business district, mostly misnomered delis. Then, returned to the office, in the corridor, the one answering our need for a midway, I ran into my supervisor's assistant. He told me I was awaited in Meeting Room B.

I took one of my bogus deep breaths, went in.

There were interns in there, the newest shock of them. They were mostly girls, mostly immodest in their make, the indicia of their diets evident in triumphant complexions and the force of their focus as I carried on about double-sided photocopying and the only sure unmenial way to staple.

Two or three of these were imperial things precise in the bicep. Another was still in shower shoes. They all had names that sounded mostly rhetorical, or else they had been named after paints. This was a silken generation, with their own way to spell. (I was later to learn I was "biast.")

The one boy among them regarded me in a splurge of reverence, raised a hand to ask whether I was a Mrs. or a Ms.

I said, "*Mrs.*, pronounced *misses*, to be construed as the conjugation meaning *suffers the absence of.*"

Afterward, back in my office, I tried to bring myself off, tried to picture the cake-sharing girl from lunchtide. I itemized her as, first, the smirched and doodled-over Band-Aid on the chubby left thumb, then the to-and-fro of that restless fine-gauge bracelet, then the backs of the elbows I treated as equals instead of going right away for the dirtier and rougher of the pair.

And those moles again, both singly and as a schemed, strewn set.

The honorable and unmodified breasts.

The legs, the vital difference between them being a scar dimming a little of the shine of the left knee.

She was a full tree of features in one instant, just a stick figure in the next—such is the story, I guess, of how quickly you're rid of people just when you most need them in distinct figment form to accord with what your fingers best get bent for.

So, all right: my deskscape, my desk-set pen aiming at me rocketwise from its holder, the coercions of folders in front of me, packed paragraphic matter about people packed with unquiets—I called my woman at home.

No answer.

Which was not the opposite of her having answered, naturally, because she could have been there, giving answer in some hiding way, or privy to funny feelings about somebody else she had hoped might still be good for a call.

But the ringing, at my end, in my earpiece, had a for-all-time ridginess to its trill.

It sounded more and more corrugated.

And the only food in my drawer? Something blundered from a recipe calling mostly for things other than what I'd had. But now I ate it as if it were a particular alien bread.

Six o'clock seemed distant, chimerical.

It was sometime after five, I guess, that I rode the bus home, alone with my loneliest thoughts, the woman from work, this new, rawest friend of mine, already proportioning herself into whatever sectors of my heart were still discretionary about anything worthy of regret.

But within a week she quit, or was told to quit, or had been told she had quit—I forget the specifics, or even any general drifts in however time got itself torn from the year.

XVIII

Then, come summer, the returned-to woman and I moved the better of our things into a sublet in a city. This was the city that had been built to be subordinate to the steeper one across the river, and we rode trains daily to this other, monumented place. We displayed ourselves in restaurants, in concourses, scrutinized each other through zany sunglasses fitted over our regular pairs, spoke of no shared future beyond whichever narrowing evening now neared.

I was always five years ahead of her in time that went by in torrents.

The city: it was understood that you came here for things to get amplified inside you that anywhere else would have gone forever unheeded, unheard, but they were minor things finally, talents you just got touchier about.

There was some hush-hush work she had to do on index cards in a library, and she would dismiss me at the base of an escalator, where I was to meet her hours and hours and hours later. Her greeting was always "But I accomplished nothing!" She abominated me in public angers but suffered my touchings and wanton severities later in the walk-up.

We were neither of us givers, and our affections came garbed in impatience, annoyance, spite. The heat wave lasted little longer than another seizing week.

XIX

Dragging our feet across the grandest of the bridges, exercising our temperaments at the riskiest of intersections, the sky usually misleading us about whatever might come next. Then, one night, a sudden, ambitious rain shoved us under an overhang. A vendor wheeled toward us with his carted disarray of tall, gallant umbrellas, sold her an entertainingly plaid one. The downpour let up, she junked the thing, and then the real storm: the raindrops pluttering on her hardly sleeved arm didn't smell cleansing at all. We rushed uncanopied to the subway.

The thing about the sublet was that the walls had been markered up with slogans, digs and indignities difficult to fathom, more difficult to ignore. They determined the course and pitch of conversation, put militancy into our smallest stabilizing talk.

E.g.: "Just be yourself; nobody else wants to"—though I cannot recall whether that was something already troubled out onto one of the walls or something she put to me much later in impatience in the first of the heavyweight papers I had to get notarized, legal-enveloped, then sent certified and stupendous.

XX

For it was in the city that we had the rite, if that is the word for it, finally performed. This was in that pound cake of a borough building downtown. She had an eye infection, and I was missing a button, though not one pertinent to any bosomal propriety. Just the two of us in dresses, sleevelessly synonymous smoke-blue numbers, and then the presiding, flat-spoken functionary in her robes, and an ardent Latina girl recruited as witness from the hallway's waiting queue.

But it felt more like a conference than a ceremony. It took all of two minutes.

No rings, no bouquets.

The picture of the witness was one of the ones that came out as duds, and the drugstore developer flubbed the rest of them with a vertical line ghosting through the center, true, but rarely dividing the two of us bodefully in any of the shots captured afterward by strangers we had compelled on sidewalks, in the laked park, at the restaurant with the poster-sized, isolating menus.

We were not much for fucking, but the things we saw done to each other in that union: you can stomach only so much of the humanly finally possible.

XXI

We walked around and around the outsides of museums, and her money brushed against mine in frumpled batches we handed over to servers and salesclerks, and she tried on whichever dresses I selected in hole-in-the-wall boutiques—strappy, indefinite dresses that brought out her shoulder blades in full and volunteered a gleaming preponderance of each eloquent leg.

In the taxi to the train station, she made certain the driver knew I was a slob, a shirker, a cheapskate, a sponge, hurtful and unreliable, and why was it again we were leaving this bold and defeating city so soon? Why didn't we end it right there?

XXII

Or the two of us again in our domestic spectacle, a day already profaning itself into furthermore of yesterday: over and over, all I had done was say, "There, I've said it," though it would leave me feeling only exposed, not unmasked.

XXIII

Either that or she talked and she talked, and I watched her vocabulary go by in its pretty balloonery of self-reproof.

This was winter now regardless. Her arms were pushy even in the sleeves of the devouring sweaters she wore to and from the airport. She had impractical but professional reasons for all these departures and forlorn returns.

There were informant squirts of truth in the lies I now told too.

XXIV

The violet finery of veins in her forearm, a full day's fetch of stubble in her underarm, the moistening curve of her voice around the words of outpouring discouragement it took to turn herself even further away: it was one unexalting night or another toward the end of that second year, and we were having it out in the bathroom again, and she had me mostly right ("failures of empathy," "vengeful withdrawals"), and my conscience must have had other polyps on it, tumoral guilts and disgraces, because we were together only grittier after that, and then came newer pivots and revolts in her loyalty to me, pairings I might have even put her up to myself.

If people say the marriage was a passing thing, what they mean is that it shot right past us. We couldn't keep up.

XXV

Or the dulled lucidity of her eyes, and her hair now a clamor of outright brown-black, newly clipped: she would return to our table at the restaurant after taking forever in the restroom and say, "I think there might be somebody crying in there."

The days nagged at me about days not yet come or else kicked me into nothing exquisite, because I must have loved it when criticisms of me came so gingerly detailed, as hers now did. There is something arousing when you figure you're about to be dumped—the benefaction of all that trauma right around the corner to keep your nights and days accursed and replete.

XXVI

I found myself among other annihilated people and places in the eyesore poetry she wrote.

Not so with Amelda—I'll name her—whom I knew only in her stinkard of an apartment, and then only as a bag of bones, a sunken personality. There was a balderdash of blond in her hair, and it was hair retrenched to extremes. Her health looked obscure on her.

I liked to follow her heart in its disenamoring way toward other things in the room after the fancier setback of some coitus meant just for me.

There were wads of time during weeks we looked out of sealed windows at the cold, burdening girth of the world.

Around the house she dressed only in towels or, just that once, an impromptu slit pillowcase.

Our life ran away with us in ways that withered only her.

XXVII

To be sure, my wife left me those three times as practice, as exercise, and once in a demure, evermore sort of way that didn't stick, and there was the time we went our separate ways but in intimate parallel, shoulder to shoulder and still under the same roof, and the time she put her things in storage by picking up each thing in the room where it lay and then setting it down again in the very same place, but with the understanding that it was merely stashed away there now, in holding for some later date, and then the times we lived together as friends who were practically sisters who might as well have been husband and wife, and then finally the one time she breathed verifiable permanence into the separation: there was vermouth on her breath, and a fellow in a blazer holding the bottle. They collected the least of her things and were gone just like that, though she later left him for someone she referred to only by her profession: this was "the metallurgist," though I suspected a person of a different, entirely unlaboratorial pursuit, maybe lecture-hall sociophysics, likely the only local female in the field.

XXVIII

Or the phone would ring and ring, and there was the question of whether the peal of it sounded any more yearning than before. But I would not pick up.

Or, days later, she was calling again from an airport, only minutes until boarding:

"Am I to have come back?"

XXIX

The things the removed beloved did not take with her—rucked packets of chocolate tomfoolery; skirt hangers; a carton of drab, wheaten cereal; the blockiest of paperbacks; a camera case packed with hair clips, barrettes; an empty garment bag of thick, clouded plastic; a snatch of gift wrap bearing telephone numerals over which her handwriting had panicked in obscuring ribbons and roils: all these I arranged in obtuse relevance on her side of the mattress, and, at night, I rolled over onto them without demolishing enough.

I must have breathed on it all.

I took over the lease.

I go on signing her name to things the same pruning way she would have no doubt done so herself.

MIDDLETON

For one reason or another, my wife, a baby-talking, all but uninterpreted woman only a couple of years older than I, died in one of those commuter-plane crashes that reporters were never sure what to do about. It happened on a day when the third of three famous people in a row had finally died, in this case some moody entertainer, and no one aboard the plane could have been anything other than worn out and morbid to begin with, and anyway my wife was not even a commuter: she had been flying across state to visit a stepsister, somebody more sturdy, who had taken sick after some apparently recreational uncertainty about a newly glued upper tooth.

The call came while I was on my own again in the men's room at work. I remember a weekend of customized, ethnic condolences, soaked bouquets dropped off on the doorstep, then two nights of viewings that showed her off as a contented, slugabed beauty of a pierced and bony sort. The burial was put off to a Tuesday, a morning rounded with cloudages and gleams in a single packed but unclarifying hour. The minister, I thought, might have struck too possessive a note, and there was a banquet afterward in a rented hall where the stepsister, newly recovered and unruly, told me there were whole sides to my wife I had been blind to.

"I knew the core," I said.

But by now I've forgotten whatever she said in return— something, I don't doubt, about the core being the least fruited part, or the part least rotten, but the part you were going to be throwing out regardless.

My wife's brother had been there, too, with that hair that looked knitted on, and dirigible aunts of hers, and the gushing but refusing arms on them, and the cousins in teasing sleeves, and fuller-witted meekling uncles, some nieces and trivial, bejeweled nephews sinking even further into excusable youth.

"You're how old again?" one of them, legs milky in low-reaching shorts, said to me in the men's room. He was angular over a sink.

"Fifty-fifty," I said.

Death didn't have any of the detergent effect I had been led to expect. Things that had looked violently dirtied before looked even dirtier now, and there was a marital malodor to our place, but make no mistake: we had been lovers, my wife and I, meaning mostly that we had coated things and people with love, had used our love to cover things up, to see to it that layer after layer got put over everything. Not even once had we ever had to resort to any of the tender belittlements of sex. There had in fact been talk of divorce, but we talked about it the way other people talked about getting a pool or maybe just a pool table, even just the miniature kind that rests atop a regular table, even a card table. But the pool table would not have been for me, I always had to make clear. (I preferred brochures of things over the things brochured.) It wouldn't have been for my wife, either. (My wife had gone in for porcelain figurettes of comfortable-looking tomboys and certain of those hypoallergenic dogs that had to be addressed just so.)

So it was a clumsy way to go about living it up.

I had been making myself scarce by dozing away the morning she drove herself to the airport. The last thing I could remember from the night before was treating her to a foot-rub that must have felt practically abstract through the thick woolen socks she could not be brought around to taking off.

The Saturday after the funeral, some sort of small-business carnival was still going on at the county's exhibition hall. I drove out to have a look at urgeful suburban humanhood, stood in line at the ticket shanty. Ink from a stamp pad was splotted redly onto the back of my fisted hand. "Keep coming back all weekend," the woman with the stamp pad said.

Inside, I made my way from booth to booth and looked for anyone who might have looked anything like my dead wife.

My wife, thank goodness, had been merely a type, her body just another of many greatening recurrences of a fixed repertoire of feature, limb, bone. (It had forever pained her to keep coming face to face with so many depleting forgeries of herself.)

So: loads of persons, mortals, existents, whatever you will, in undooming circulation under exposed beams, and in no time I found her, my wife, an unrelieved reinvigoration of her, in an accurate young man in perspiry repose behind a bug-bomb booth.

His hair an aloof dark uplift, but shortened to an incoherency around the ears.

One earring looking more like a button, the other like a cuff link.

The nose in overfleshed revolt against the rest of the flat, coping face: an even complexion requiring no adjustive tints or enlivenments, unbalancing brown eyes suddenly ablink, a suddenly opening mouth.

"I've known you?" the mouth must have been said to say, the voice coming out of the lukewarmth of a life obviously already padded with involvement, fulfillment, fatiguing praise. I had to break some ice, the same ice, over and over (e.g.: "Sick yourself?"; "Life pointing you away from yourself?"; "Father still living at home?"; "Must it always look as if everything in creation has been positioned just to see whether you can keep your fingers off it?"), then brought him out to the house, fed him funeral fruit humbled into wedges and cubes, welcomed him into her wardrobe—first a shirtwaist that he drowned in just a little around the knees, then the cocktail thing in which he popped seam after seam. Things just got muddier in my heart, and then he must have found his way to me in some life of ours from there on out, every hour of it getting razored into ever keener minutes that could barely cut anything away.

I HAVE TO FEEL HALVED

I

We had to sit for an annual review at work, but the catch was that
there were sliding criteria, standards unstable from one assessment
period to the next, so I would usually be told that my voice on the
phone sounded like a voice still slushy with sleep, or that there were
things my co-workers felt they couldn't exude with me around, or
that I extended my hand to clients as if awarding it to them; and I
would get referred to a large-pored lady down a lonely hallway or
to an intake person at a societal-arts building across the boulevard,
once to just an eye doctor who spooked the examination room
with floatings of milky light and blew onto my eyelids, then tried
to atone.

II

Other things weren't firming, either. Word was that as a man you
were expected to make the jump to women, but I was lunking
through late middle age, my even spongier fifties, and living with a
man younger by decades. Whatever I felt for him must have been
way out of balance or all too little much the same.

It went unrecouped.

My heart kept bullying me into letting people like him pull
anything.

III

I had found him in an onlookers' bar on a short street that squinted
off an avenue. This was in the extremity district. He was got up

in some rayon trashery with three-quarter sleeves, a girl's slippery belt, fingernails flashened. I was a workingman after work after all. I menaced myself with examinations of his manner, his spruce, sweatproof practice of himself.

I sent out a hand, let my fingers pile themselves onto his.

Neither beer nor mints on his breath. (Maybe traces of merest salading.)

He pointed dimly to some further indefinite figure on the dance floor.

"Let me go finish a good-bye."

IV

Some nights my young man spoke up in his sleep—mostly solemnities, sometimes mostly spitten slang.

He slept in the bed and I slept in the chair next to the bed, or he slept on the floor and I slept endways along the foot of the bed (this thus left most of the bed available and bereft), or each of us slept on the floor at either side of the bed, or he slept in the chair and I did without sleep with throes in my stomach, gratings in my skull.

The bed had started out as just a mattress and a frame on casters, but it had then become a formal summit of sorts, unwelcoming heights of some kind, as a bed sometimes must whenever two persons are guessed to be close.

The bedclothes were of a faded, jumpy purple plaid. They looked unlikely to envelop.

And the chair—the chair was in fact only one of those valet chairs, the kind with a trouser hanger bolted to the highest of the back slats. The seat was a lid you could lift. I began storing things in the hopper underneath:

Some quarter-length socks of his, long unlaundered, looking now like pouches, meaningly unfilled.

Rimpled empty packets of those concise, hard-cased chocolates he had esteemed for a week.

A swidge of his hair, lifted once from trimmings in the sink.

Mornings, he would go off to work in curio retail I knew not exactly where.

V

A hashy complexion, hair pluffy and unmastered, a blush in bare arms barely offered—some days there was no bouquet to be made of him.

Other days I felt sexually concerned.

VI

An accelerating metabolism meant he needed starches within arm's reach—pillowy regional bagels, pretzels candied in their contortions.

The next month: a diet of practically milkless milk, slabbed or crumble-pattied substitutes for everything else.

The coffee he demanded was coffee that had to be ounced out expensively by hand into bags that cost extra.

These were luxuriations funded by a mother who mothered him skeptically and kept narrowing her love until it was a thing that gored.

VII

I never got the truth out of him, only things peeled off from the truth, things the truth had shed.

Then one night a woman, young, was asking for him at the door. She was scrawny and obscure in some sleeveless construct. Matte-black hair hung from her head like curtains stiffened.

The face? Homely, abrupt. The nose? Respecified with cosmetics.

There was fight, though, in the eyes.

I did not have to ask who she was, only what she thought she was doing.

"I am asking for him back."

VIII

Another night, another visitor at the door: a regretful man almost my age but more hit-or-miss in his panic: hands so swooping and opposed to each other, he seemed to be crossing himself out as he spoke: "He won't be needing the rest of his clothes?"

IX

This was a lean apartment that threw itself out notionally over one side of a garage, though the garage was not mine to use. The place—there were three divisions of it which you had to go ahead and count as rooms—was lengthwise unrealistic, but I lived with him within reason.

One day got chocked into the next: there was a blockiness to time, like a month's evident rectangulation on a calendar tacked fast to a wall.

His mother and stepfather made the trip aggressively from a metropolis of stone lawns and unhumid heat. They looked me over for signs that a life by my side would not mean years lopped off his future.

These were unpleased people in airplane attire. They could see nothing azurean in me.

X

Besides, his teeth always clicked at the instant he fell asleep. He rioted quickly inward, and the next morning would wake up sore, bitten, bruised, infuriated. There was always an ache broiling behind a knee or a dream to be repudiated straightaway.

He must have valued me as somebody valuing him, for anything on his body accorded itself with something on mine, we matched in every fashion, but I had carnal recourse to him only rarely, and, even then, I never could go through with it, because it would have been only for minutes. I would have been only filler.

XI

A job like his—I knew the trouble it could take to get one hour jointed to another until you had an afternoon finishedly articulated.

After work, he travelled among other vague-waisted young men of temperament in taverns and tinderbox cabarets. He was allowed a happy hour and one hour of costlier socializing thereafter.

I am sure he danced and in the gaps between dances compelled a hand of his onto a neighbory shoulder and rested in restrooms after initiatives. I am sure he did whimsical things to make tears teem when he brought up how nippy it was at home, and how the laminated note taped to the thermostat counseled him to keep his prettily vagrant, bashable hands off.

He would come back to me with things written in sentiment on his wrist—e-mail whereabouts, mostly, or telephone integers already blearing.

XII

He hated it when it was the first of the month, and he hated it worse when it was a month that was no more.

The mail seldom brought him to satisfaction.

He could count to ten in different rampant tongues.

He kept his shaving ephemera, his quiver of tweezers, in a little trolley on the skirted table alongside the sink.

The frontiers of this sink held toners and tinters vesseled pricily, effervescers by the jugful, cologne in a bullet-shaped bottle that I feared, had I brought the thing to my nostrils, would stink bitterly and forgivably of his ass, because his ass could hold its own among the presented openings of this world.

XIII

I had grown up in an outlying county of unfarmed farmland, shantied ridgeways.

Childhood was precisely the word, because I rose through those first years as if cowled, blindered.

How could "the country" be both the sticks we were living in and the state-laden, encompassing nation?

Then middle school, high school, a back-facing junior college—none of it came to magnitude in me, either.

I thus drove myself to this guttery midget city for the gropery possible wherever people went drastic in numbers.

XIV

He took along everything he owned even if storming out only for the weekend, or maybe he entrusted it all to a rental crypt somewhere, and I would turn the place upside down and prospect even the trash until I found something fortunate of his touch. Once it was a box of photo corners, those tiny, gummed triangles you licked to position snapshots squarely and evidentiarily onto the pages of an album, in this case a "presentation" album he had presented to his mother, double page after double page of us in poses of germane separation, never the two of us in the same picture, not even a long-ranging shadow to intimate that the other one of us was of degenerate consequence just outside the frame.

My signature mood was a maneuvering tenderness that bears forgetting.

XV

He was not the first, this one, and the second still wrote to me all the time, in pressuredly typed letters and notes, printouts and packed follow-ups, paragraphs crammed over the sentiment panels of greeting cards, but the words seemed caged in what he wrote, not free to mean much of anything, and I did not show these to my partner, my match, my counterpart, who anyway was not a reader or even much of a listener to things read out loud, though he was a talker, unless by talking we mean the way I talk, which is not the way I am hoping to have finally spoken here.

XVI

And the first one?

The way his name broke itself out of the alphabet and could barely be held to its spelling: it queered the mouth that pronounced it.

He was laid up the while I knew him, but his symptoms lacked a guiding disease.

XVII

Middle of the week, a pissiness at work again, and a suspicion that my features were not entirely concerted in their paining expression of same.

Then an unenjoyed, prettified doughnut creaming ever so little.

Then my young man called to give me some guff about a shirt.

(It is said, isn't it, that you "make" love because it's otherwise not really there?)

The afternoon afterward got pursed with a worry first about an incisor (its glint was gone; it was no longer situated so stalwartly in the gums), then one about my car: the engine of late was letting out a cryptic gibberish before it turned over. The papers I was supposed to be approving had the tread of someone's flatting intelligence on every clause. The matter of it had been trampled something terrible.

I tend to take notes when my reading fails me, and then I pleat each page of notes. I fold it all up, make tears until I've got practically a tulip. Then I go next door to the vending-machine nook for whatever is most orangely galore.

XVIII

He bought strainers, graters, spoon rests, corers, and filled shelf-papered drawers with still more, but we ate out at his daily insistence, though he scarcely ate—and the unforked entrées, things fruit-fringed and unpleasant of scale, got themselves committed to take-out catchalls by waitresses severe in the wrist.

He had had a chandeliered childhood, I have made delay to mention, and had grown up trading spectral affections with grandaunts, letting great-uncles pant and prevail.

XIX

He had left a roommate for me, or so he claimed, and their room, once he was gone from it, had rebounded by calling insects and rodents out of its walls—long-sequestered, veteran roaches, mostly, that now gave a syncopation to countertops and floorboards.

The roommate took to wearing overshirt over overshirt, and came down with a raucous, blistery sickness that brought him closer to the door to some other ill.

It was a door extant only in fits. Its existences were equivocal.

The door to the room, though, had photos, Polaroids, push-pinned to its backside. A house-calling doctor, a stockpot of a man with a satchel, told him to take them down or he would have to do it himself.

In these photos my young man was even younger and more abusive in his every sign of life: the steep features of the stoutened face, the fluke mole on the right cheek, a stricture already in the eyes, veins awriggle on the backs of the hands, the snippy hair on the knuckles—

But the roommate pulled through. There were days, weeks, of feeling plugged up with recovery. Then came elongating gurgulations in his sleep, unmotivated stiffenings of his dick all the standstill day.

He was soon directing himself retributively at girls. He gave them the most disorganizing of attentions.

People knew this man later only for the cologne he had whipped up. It was a cologne that didn't hit you all at once. A citric breeziness at first, then an implication of other, less placeable fruits, and then it would strike a scolding afternote, then just as suddenly leave off, and you would be smelling matter-of-factly of only yourself, only more publicly now, and uncoverable.

XX

But whether it was my lonesomeness hosting his or the other way around, I felt his momentary devotions, or I felt belted to him and no more.

He was twenty-two years my junior, my miniature. My life to come had come to be a wee thing.

And my hearing was practically shot. It was sometimes only the vowels that reached me.

They came out of his mouth like pastels.

XXI

Even so, he did not know enough about many things, but he veneered his ignorance with guidances from TV. (Hold your breath ten times during a tornado. Never feed your fish if you're feeling cross.) I was a radio hound, attentive to head-case polemics on the talk stations, though I never called in, and I was plenished with grammarless dire data from the daily paper, but it was in a leaflet reaching me physically through the mails that I first learned of a utopian procedure called "prostate milking of the semen"— fingerings of the gland, conducted rectally and by partner, that promised release without release. You felt nothing from your surge.

It was thus we expressed any bodily regard for each other those dashing months that dashed year.

XXII

As a rule, I kept a couple of friends, one of each, a filmy-eyed woman and a fellow who vacuumed law offices overnight. I had known them when they were the demolitionary darlings of their crowd, but they were tamed, absolving people now.

The man was the more departing of the pair, always putting words to your wave of farewell.

The woman still had that voice that kept boiling right out at you.

Her hair had gone gruff.

XXIII

Or he spent a lot of time exulting in the tub. His soaps were kept sleeved between soaks. I wanted to be clean in his manner, but water was never to be my element. I used a dry shampoo and a chunk deodorant and powdered myself many times over before I drove to work and sat up straight to the desk to get my lower body relievingly removed from the rest of me.

I had to feel halved.

The desk had come with a floor protector beneath it and a desk dictionary, not the household or college kind. The front matter boasted that the light thrown on the words defined therein was a light appropriate solely to the immediacies and sight lines of today's office backdrop. But when you poked your way to the definitions themselves, you were nowhere closer to things at all. Nothing was getting called what it was. You apparently had to look to your dreams for that, but to dream you first had to fall fast asleep, and I was not sleeping, not even when I was dead to the world.

XXIV

Those blackouts and fast little faints of his—I assured him that they were his verdict on me for only that day alone.

Those pocks and pittings I could explain, too: life had bitten tinily away at him out of a hungering no unmonstrously different from mine.

I gave him mouthfuls of the like; I consoled; I rubbed his feet, which were narrow, tidy-toed, unbunioned, unpungent feet; and I did his laundry one item at a time to give full deterging concern to its petite but worldly dirts; and I seized on every chipped and discolored thing that came up out of his vocabulary when he talked his emptying talk on the phone.

XXV

My family—I was barely gatherable with them for milestone birthdays, anniversaries soothed over with reasons because. Life had always pointed us away from each other. But I sometimes went home just for the day, or maybe just the long and short of a morning.

My mother liked to let a ringing telephone ring itself out in tribute.

It was only things from far off that came out of her bowels, she claimed. She considered herself a conduit.

She preferred a footstool to a chair, and wore one pair of glasses over another to get superior definition.

My father would circle almost anything at the back of a magazine. There was knowledge that jutted out of him oddly or forked itself unwanted into your brain. A cancer meandered in him.

And I had a sister still living at home: eyelids detailed darkly, and breasts alert even under those rolling sweaters, and always an arm coming toward you with a glut of bracelets, and a mouth that slanted actively when there were things yet to ask of you.

In sum: Father, Mother, Sister, Self: the four of us now and then grouping ourselves genially around some cousin's graduating niece, or contributing signatures to a gala kind of get-well card.

The extended family was exactly that—a bloodline carried too far.

XXVI

"Thinks the checkout girl at Foodfair won't know what crap he's buying if he turns everything upside down."

"Eats supper off newspapers on the floor."

"Puts that stuff into his voice to make him sound sadder."

He wrote such sooty truths about me in an otherwise hapless diary, but the penmanship of the pampered—such cusps, such struggly descenders!—was always hell on the eyes.

XXVII

He was smoking opinionatedly now, subsisting on seltzers and bars of absolute chocolate.

The bones he kept picking with me were skeletal of something bigger I should have been beginning to picture.

Then we were both reading the same book, but on different shifts. This was a leveling thing, a true story of a man's ruin, boosted from the hospital's lending library of no-joke literature of self-rescue. He read for just kernels, main points, alone, but carried the book into the bathroom with him. Brought it to our breakfast corner. Had it slammed open before him in bed while drawing things out from between his teeth or disporting a razor a final time for the night. The book accepted his shavings and flakes. They settled frankly into the narration. He kept at it until the book was autobiographically crudded, a sampler of his cells and immoderate bodywide mire.

XXVIII

It's not that I didn't weigh on him, but I was hauled around in his mind without any of the buffering my life and my living of it required.

Then it was heavy-skied autumn already. I had him cheating on me with my blessing.

I sent him off to whatever was eddying in other high-foreheaded men—scholarly lavatorians, killjoy attendants of fitting rooms suddenly popular.

There was one who divided the world into "have-nots and half-wits," and another whose money had pieces of other money paper-clipped to it, and their ilk was always more likable than mine, because I am of the kind that picks the wrong week to have finally had it with people.

My young man, though: I watched him pull from his tongue a hair displaying itself as a perfect, plucky ampersand.

XXIX

Living, you see a lot of yourself, and what I saw was a man of straightforward hair, teeth reclusive in the tottery smile, one hand trysting with the other underneath any table or desk.

I wore ventilative shoes and took my foods at room temperature and wanted more out of people.

To hear me tell it, I had been one person, then condensed into somebody else, somebody more idiotical of our times.

XXX

Or you would have seen him, often as not, sitting alone on the low retaining wall outside a tourist center or at the foot of some moot monument or other. You would have fallen all over yourself for having been just the one to notice so utmost a loneliness in so baseless and unvisited a city. You would soon be flattering yourself that nowhere in his life was there so much as a co-worker who knew him to say hello to. Then a cloud or two would beg off overhead, or a blown leaf would blow right at you, because there was maybe a lake breeze from the brute lake that was farther off beyond the palings and bulkheads and embankments and the like. You would look his way again. He would not have moved so much as an atom. But you would see your mistake. For you would now be in the grip of the conviction that people, one person in rivalry with one or more repining others, were just that very instant waiting for him in other fractions of the city, having waited for hours, likely as not, and hating him for it, and hating themselves now, and ready to sever ties once and for all, if ties were what these stringily strung things, already shredded, must be suffered as terminology here.

You would have been right at least about me.

The others, had I gathered accurately, were the part owners of a concession-equipment-rental service, and then some molely someone with a mustache that looked mostly munched away.

XXXI

Or I pictured myself three, four months ahead, being advised to "move on." But you could enter into people only so far and then had to come out the same way. There was never a way clear through. You were always back to where you started.

XXXII

He kept packing his things until they were parcelly and hard to make out under the twined rucklings of butcher paper.

Then they formed a lamentable plenty on the backseat of my sedan, driven finally through pinchy sunlight to the post office, where the clerk said, "These will be going how?"

It was a reluctant city, this home of mine—a center of population but otherwise not at all solid to the local eye. No sooner did you leave the memorials downtown than the streets went uncertain.

Then the highway to the airport, four unlively lanes, and the airport, a torn-up one. Parked, went through the entrance sheds, let the moving walkway separate us between others. Then the terminal. He wanted the popular coffee. We read the program of departures. We kissed quickly and shrinkingly, in the manner of foreigners.

He left me leaving him.

WOMANESQUE

The woman who was later to become my wife had gone off to a state school in a faraway state and parted from it baccalaureately but no better in the head. She afterward moved to the dormlike district of the modestly rising city downriver. Streets sheered through it to avenues out of the blue, and the skies usually kept fooling you about the season. She went in for an overlapping look: cloud-gray cotton predominations above loose, seclusive skirts coming down as far as her socks. She pushed into employment as a medical transcriber, built up her personality with girlfriends, boyfriends, mothery older women who wanted younger women with arms as thin as kindling. She streaked her fingernails a meteorological bluish-black, learned to read things into the shreddings in the lining of her coat. She nerved herself sore into people. Her loves would take just days to wane.

She gave herself over to weeks with an overgrown man whose hair lacked government. He had read chapters of the classics and could put names to faces and then take the names back in ways that left the faces looking unclaimed.

Life, he preferred to boast, came direct to him and not, as to her, through curtains, screens, thickenings. Under heavy medication, this man moved her around from room to room during nights of candlelit quiet. She could hold a mood, even the most moonish of them all, for days upon days, and she would report to him in dismal minimums of French he never got the gist of. It was good to feel herself red in the face.

He, this fellow, had a remote life and a daily one, and it was only in the latter that he was the notary who had to make himself visible for anyone bearing bunched stapled papers to be stamped or given the prissy commonwealth seal. He was all for helping these unjoking folks to shimmy out of human affairs, though he thought of himself more as an omitter.

Small wonder, then, that her body kept telling her the only story it knew—the one about all roads leading to only one or another other road.

She shoved her heart at a batch of different, uncourting people after that. In time, she found herself invited to move in with a woman whom nobody else had ever seemed to have any bearings on before. This woman was mostly houseridden, and unclothed, and there was not much blowback from her youth. Her failings weren't even personal. But what was there to talk about, then, except the meals, which they kept simple—sauces and syrups dippered over rices taken too far?

She, my wife to come, kept a notebook this time:

"Think of this as a one-month residency, a retreat."

"Depression keeps you young."

"Friends don't let friends stay friends."

"Be wishful of what you care for."

"Women taste mostly alike down there, but with men you get variety in their alkalines."

The luggage this time practically filled itself. The city wasn't getting any younger. The dailies kept saying social-scientific things about droops in the population.

Thus those racking weeks thereafter with a man worth a bundle. His feelings for her came out without foundation. Then, after him, the fuller-fraught half of a skeptically respectful couple, about whom more never.

The watchmaker, or the man who repaired watches, or maybe resold stolen ones, was a man of jammed mind, coughs coming out of him like chuckles. He informed her that she was living out of her life, out of just tiny pockets and corners of it, and not in it, or through it. "We should see about fixing that," he said.

His apartment had a tall person's bathroom, but he was a shorter guy with an aloof Labradoodle who (he warned) had it in for everyone, though the dog (the thing was called Signe) was soon enough weirdly adhered to her on the ticklish, tufty couch.

"A good sign," he said, and then went on and on about how he had stepped aside from his past, how more and more people looked created instead of born, how the days kept puffing themselves out instead of coming only to an end, how the body had only so many quarts of water in it in which the soul might as well just go and get itself drowned once and for all.

His pants were suddenly neither here nor there. He was loiny, and pustuled, with an utterness of hair, ginger squibbles of it all over, and his thing was atilt and capering toward her.

She gave out some sniffly forerunners of a sob.

"Good call," he said.

The story she later told was that it had not been a rape exactly, and by then, two or three months had already gone by anyway. The doctor at the abortion center remembered her but said he had never seen anything like this. "Let's try something different," the doctor said. "Eat a lot of sugar two days before. Let's make this one the sweetest one yet."

The doctor referred to it as "the individuum."

She went home and ate marzipan and oddly chunked chocolate and twistings of licorice tugged this way and that and was back a couple of days later in some poly-cotton wigwam of a dress.

She chose "twilight sedation."

The thing came out looking stymied but composed.

"No more meats after this," the doctor told her in the recovery bay.

"Okay."

"Same goes for fish."

"So it shall be."

"Shoes of synthetic materials only."

"Long as somebody makes Mary Janes that way."

"And nothing from the plant kingdom."

"Ever?"

"You weren't born yesterday."

"You want me to starve."

"There'll be others."

■   ■   ■

Then a marriage, annulled in a couple of months, to somebody running a Laundromat with a storybook name. The whole thing had been a lot like dating, but just in one place, that drapey apartment of his in which body-part periodicals were still everywhere strewn.

Let me get the air cleared of him for all times' sake. He was a faultsomely soaped man who knew a lot about the danglier things in life. The car he more and more had to drive had something possibly berserk or voodoo in the upholstery. He was spermy and hurtful. A vagueness hulked inside of him. The way he talked, every word stubbed out the one before, so his statements came to you lonelier and lonelier.

If anything, it was nice of time to come out by the quarter-hour only. A minute by itself would have been murder.

The two of them were soon enough living in abutting privacies I was later to cut across.

This man, though, turned out to be just a drablet of his parents. They were all I could get him to talk to me about, though, to be precise about it, they had not come forward to be his parents until he was some near-adult still doggedly up for adoption. He never once thought to bring up his wife, though this was how she came to me, this was how I came into it: she was just about to leave town to see about a plant, the merest and stringiest of vines, which was said to have died, and would I still be close by when she got back?

We went in for the recommended counseling some months before the ceremony. The counselor had a chatterbox stomach and a voice, alto, hospitable to singsong scripture and sexual hogwash alike. Squares of toilet paper had been piled trimly in a corner of his desk. Almost everything he said was prefaced with "Just out of curiosity …" or "One wonders … " We didn't figure out until later that he was the head minister.

He asked the two of us to sit in different rooms and work on pages from a workbook photocopied in obvious haste. We could make out, in the margins, ghastful traces of the hollow-boned fingers of whoever had stood so drainingly over the machine. The pages called upon each of us to make lists of things that the other person, the "partner," sometimes made us feel "rooked out of." We had to come up with six "site-specific pillow-talk topics." Some items were just fill-in-the-blank:

"The way I grew up, it's a wonder I don't still _____."

"I should be better by now at _____."

"Love him/her or hate him/her, you have to _____ him/her."

Then he motioned us back in and made us read our answers out loud to the other.

E.g.: Me: The way I grew up, it's a wonder I don't still picture chicken wire around people. I should be better by now at bodily life. Love her or hate her, you have to love her.

His advice was not to send out any "Save the Date" cards. He said, "People'll take it to mean, 'Save that day from having to be the day we get married.' Just wait and send out regular invites."

Then he had one of us sit in the outer room while he gave an incontinent talk to the other. To me he said nothing that hadn't occurred to me before—viz., "Why must those innermore parts of a woman come out sounding so much like brand names, trademarks? Doesn't *clitoris* smack of something patented, something over-the-counter? Did you know that *gal* is actually short for *gallon*? Are you game for the monthly gush of herself? Are you really going to just sit there and tell me she doesn't look to you like the type who goes for whoever approaches? Hasn't it never not been said that the only thing that will ever even begin to understand a penis is another penis?"

Later, after her turn, I asked her what he had told her.

"He had a lot on his mind," she said.

Then the wedding day itself. I wasn't allowed to hold her hand in public after that because some man who might still love her could be living just about anywhere now.

For a few months the marriage went through the roof. Welterweight wooden chairs, throw pillows, things entirely called throws—the happy home was an L-shaped apartment with four rooms doomed with molds. We really did carry on as a couple, as husband and ice-chewing wife. We were colleagues in momentums of undressing. We slept at diagonals to each other, and in that rubbishry of a bed spoke in shaking, swallowy ways about nothing more than a pinhole we had noticed in the floor. Through it (because the thing kept getting us up), we could not really see all that much of the room underneath, just a funnelly enough peep for it to sink in that our privacy wasn't having any of us.

Her arms were hardly rovers of me ever. They bolted out of canopying sleeves toward things she formed into other things that weren't quite fully dolls.

How soon things went so minute between us!

I of course loved her, though love always gets revised right out of what people feel, and different things get fished out of the feelings, different words get put to everything that's been fished out.

Add to that the telltale drollery of empty streets glimpsed basely at four a.m., again at six; then sleep shallow enough to prepare me for spells on the sofa; teeth-marks on my arm that looked to be only from my own idle teeth.

Every other month gave us a long weekend. A Monday usually got bundled with it. I would walk off the first hour or so of a late-starting day in the petty stores of our district. "Did you find everything all right?" the clerks would ask as I made to leave. But there were two ways you could take that. One was: "Did you find whatever you came for?" The other was: "Did things really look okay to you in here? They still don't to me."

She thought of me, at most, as an outpost of herself.

We were further foolings of the human form.

We ate wastingly in restaurants at shared, incensing expense. She rarely finished a first forkful. The food, she later claimed, was "just bait."

It was always a bother to her that *adulterate* couldn't mean something a little more upbeat, maybe "to have come at long last into adulthood."

We had gone to dictionaries more than once over this.

Also *nasturtium*—not "an enclosed, considerably sized, usually domed structure in which were kept all manner of nasty things."

Granted, I was a rumpus-assed man all but fifty. My life kept coming clodly back to my body. I had to wear a T-shirt over my T-shirt to keep from soaking the blousy things I wore beneath jackets, but people saw through me straight through to themselves.

I could have done without myself, too.

My wife, as I now had to think of her, this woman I'd picked over all others to handle me in the dark: I could never route my passions to her in any contenting way.

She would make cut after cut through the almond-brown incessancy of her hair until the edits left it looking even longer in the droop.

And what was I if not someone not unwomanesque myself? Had I not been seen often enough sealing an envelope kissingwise, then twinkling my fingers over the flap until everything dried?

Not to keep harping, but in my case, it's just that I was born, grew some, started differing, didn't stop.

I remember my mother as a woman who took the world hard and knew enough to say "Get ready for bed" instead of "Go to sleep," because one does not go to sleep, you had to beg sleep to come to you and not be afraid to be a whore for it.

She herself took "bird naps."

Life had horsed around with her enough.

But how much could you do about yourself on only a twenty-minute drive home?

My parents, their house, my sister still living there in her penny-counting and choleric twenties: she had skrinkled her hair, stressed it quillwise and sky-reachingly into trickily purpled setups. She did her body's bidding and was said to be believably diagnosed.

Mother and Father lived abrawl in heart and bowel.

And I'd had everything backwards when I was young—that it wouldn't matter where you went to school, that your teeth were the last thing people would ever see.

"You're just as good as anyone else," my father would tell me. "But how good are *they?*"

This wife wore flats and liked to walk through the public parts of hospitals, the free parts of expos. She would point to a huddle of almond-topped creations in a bakery case and demand, "These ones!" She liked chewing out waitresses, shopclerks, customer-service dignitaries, but they had to be the slimmest of things, love-eaten women in their lipstickish upper thirties.

She kept her body shushed in bathrooms even when supper came bawling out of her behind.

Her last words before bed: This will have been my life, my weekend, my period, etc.

Person, I guess, would have just about been the word for her.

As for her parents, remind me again: who was it who came to visit whom in whose condition?

She was moneyed on her mother's aunt's side, and her father's hair looked filched off anyone else's head. His diet had since been limited to bagfuls of salad greenery and health-store potions impersonally poured. The man could stand to lose his talent for fouling the family nostalgia.

Of her brothers, the youngest and the oldest were, respectively, dead and venomous. I give the middle one credit. He went back to school and took good notes on his bad arm.

We naturally went to movies, shrines, boat shows, anyplace open, but must I go into any of that?

Her hair sometimes winged out a little. She kept a folder entitled "Indignities to the Person."

Waking, you sometimes find something already stated in the day, and it's all you can do to keep yourself from repeating it, letting it compact itself into a chant, even when it's only: *Thanks for the response. I don't buy it.*

■   ■   ■

Work did not magnify me much, either. They had me picking through inventories. But I always felt called back to my desk, the metalline discomforts of it, its surplus widths and oily veneers, its mostly emptied but dividered drawers on one side that rackled whenever I pulled one out.

I was of two voices when it came to answering the phone. One would say, "It's just me." The other would say, "He just now stepped out."

People, co-workers, would stop to talk to me, but only long enough to reconfirm that reverse directories were making things doubly worse.

I reported to a manager who wore sports coats with pockets in extra places.

Lunch was usually a cube of brute cheese and cookies fallen apart before I got to them.

Afternoons, after work, I was jealous, too, of the locals who rode the local buses home, people so sure of their destination that they didn't mind all the halts and delaying roundabouts of the route.

We had a phone, true, a static-stricken landline, but no answering apparatus to collect incoming mutter and coo. The phone was unjacked half the time anyway. To get through to us, you had to come over and practically knock your knuckles off. Most people eventually got cussy, left notes. These were mostly rushed and spelled in all galoot capitals, mostly saying, "I FEEL SORRY FOR YOU."

Other than that, it was wrong of us to count on doctors to always be finding something funny running through her blood.

You get tired of always wondering anew why life has to take the place of youth.

It had always been up to my mother to shout, "Occupy yourself!" But I was already in there as far as I could be made to go. I was all but incarcerated in the unglazy allhood of me.

■   ■   ■

It hardly helped that her breasts were dumbed by a bra too bewildersome for me to undo. And that lasting drought between her legs, those little affluences of hair on her in the least fitting of places: hair that looked one moment forthright and untouched-up, then pranky or curated the next.

She was a photographer herself and had mostly concealed her mooted, junior career of it. (Close-up after close-up of what looked like curds in bathwater.)

And things you wouldn't know to look at her, thrivings I can't go into here, because things are looking bad for the facts.

I could see how she was starting to release me into a category of people she had already weeded out.

Her hand on anybody but me looked better put.

I remember a pallid young woman making emotional fortunes for herself in just a crocus-colored hand towel of a dress. An even younger one was always either being sure to be pulled from rivers or putting out just-lit cigarettes between her legs.

In bed, remember, this lady just read and read. (Softcover biographies unbenevolent.)

She had always called me only by the lone, unlevel syllable of my first name, except she flexed the vowel of it, bent the thing so far back from its given tonal hold that the name seemed to be summoning somebody other than who I was.

But hers, her name, even the first one of them, had a curvature to it in her toddling lilac longhand on the signature lines she later signed on the attorney's overstepping paperwork.

It was a name that sounded spiny when you pronounced it.

I wish I could say it now without an old silkiness setting into it out of spite.

She liked being seen off, put on trains, left almost for good at airport ticket counters, her luggage bowling along behind. She liked to be given back what she gave. Once it was a scarf, a straying thing of slate-gray that looked no better on her; another time a bracelet of masculine diameter, gambled over her wrist. The thing was certain to slidder free before she even boarded.

Loss—I liked at least how the word started off laggardly enough, before sickening itself into all that sibilance.

Any worthy sorrow came with a catch: you had to have asked for it.

As for the e-mails that came from her later, I would have wanted my reply, the only one there would be, to have been written in miniature on the back of just a slip of paper, a supermarket receipt most likely, in the dark of a weekday midnight, and I would have wanted to be afraid I was writing over something already written, something, at bottom, about my wanting to take more of an interest in people, at least in their shoes, the different ways the heels got worn down as the wearers kept tipping their bodies toward the world in tilts and leanings we never could have made out.

Last I checked, there I still stood, loveless and hateless either way.

These days, I launder anything before I say it. I make sure there's something still sudsing between the words. My remarks thus boast a certain rinsed impurity. But back then the dirt came out all over my speech.

We had once rented a hatchback and driven to a violent natural wonder, fought attractively against the falloffs. There was later some flooded scenery for us to back up through, too.

Something else is that, for months, her one satisfaction had been fattening up trash bag after trash bag with recyclables, mostly the stubborn plastic jugs my uncaloried colas came in. She was saving everything for a crosstown recycler. One day, her thinking went, we would haul all of it over there, sling it triumphantly into the bins. It was part of the new hate she had for me for hating all of the gutsy nature on our planet.

So I waited until she vanished for a weekend. She was always flying back to that wearing-away city of the overfulfilled, then returning days later with new grievances caked over every panel and slant of her temperament.

All I did was lug the bags one by one out to the Dumpster.

I treated them like any reasonable, regular trash.

She came back and ended everything.

Assisted Living

ASSISTED LIVING

Whether she came on to me or just came at me testily, without much sleep to her name, should make no bit of difference to anybody now. I tried to be a father to her, and she wanted to try being a daughter—that was to be the understanding, effective whenever.

Twenty-three, twenty-four, she was already sinking in a life of mild peril, of shortages sought out. She had run away from one of the middle counties to that blocked-in, secondary city, the one summoning itself clumsily upwards downstate. I was down there temporarily from the tertiary one.

She was staying in what had once been a magnificence of a building—eleven limestone stories—with three roommates, though each had a room, and she knew people of all walks and wrongful pockets of life.

She wanted to report to me. That was my importance to her. I forget her earliest accounts, but a later one was about her youngest sister's knack for looking at people a little older and thinking only "hostel … house … hospital … hospice."

I never got the roster of siblings right, but they were mostly sisters dropped off at peewee colleges that each had a pond and a climbing wall with trampolines underneath. They were all majoring in medical billing. They all adored her and told her to stop fooling herself away on straw men, older men, ones who knew their place only if you walked them to a map and pointed out just how stringy and facetious their part of the world really looked in a cartographer's dullard colors.

Another report: her mother these days was reachable only through regular, slowpoke mail—fatted envelopes that came back unopened but bearing signs of purposefully rough handling, cross-room tosses.

She had larger, veinier hands, her TMJ was creakier than mine, her hair had been pruned to incoherence. (It looked sketched onto the skull, then scumbled.) She had me beat with her pirated culture and that unjust élan of the validly but modestly depressed. She wore sweeping sleeves reaching all the way to thumbnails gnawed raw. She claimed she was paid to sit with stay-at-home couples while they sent their kids out for papers, coffee, out-of-town tobacco. Her other job was at a custard shop.

There wasn't enough testing of affections on each other. At most, one afternoon, I wound a couple of sidewalk-vendor necklaces around her wrists, which were thicker in the bone than mine, though who was I to be limbed so cleanly at fifty?

She had been portioned to a little over six feet. Life had harshened on her dearly. She asked about my former wives, and why, in my describings, I'd let what they ate look like the vegetal grime it was. The second of them, I said, was just one of those overcared-for types, a belonger last seen caught awkwardly in a crosswalk.

But this one, this grown but unboosted girl, had different, sounder hurts.

Everything, I repeat, was on the level. It was so level we could set things out on it, the whole of whatever it was, with its jumpiness and discomposures, without anything of hers ever having to touch anything of mine.

We faced each other in a bed just the one time, at my hotel. She woke me in a tremble and said, "I know what's going to happen, but I don't know just what."

I soon enough had to go back to my city, where I feared for my livelihood. She was against doing anything over the phone and could write only on a severe sort of gray stationery that was harder and harder to find at a good price.

I fell into the old, retaliatory life. I saw a lot of a nervy man some years my junior at work. Everything to him had to have a sexual result. I called things off with him after a few weeks of giving myself the third degree. It was as good a time as any to just cross yourself out. I wandered one day into one of those warehouse shopping clubs. I wasn't a member, but a man in a smock waved me through. I walked and walked until I came to an aisle where my eye was caught by a box with the taunt "24 COUNT." It was all I could do to stop myself from breaking the thing open and counting them out one by one, whatever they fuckingly foolishly were—pouched chippings from something crackly, I gathered.

Nine, ten months later, I bumped into her at a bus terminal. Or maybe it was at a car service. She was wearing old-looking clothes that were new to me. She had a handbag—a first. She was applying to veterinary schools, she said. (We shook hands over it.) I said that at my age, you start to realize you might have loved only once, if that. This came out sounding topical and impatient.

She said, "It's been years."

YOU ARE LOGGED IN AS MARIE

I was not so much the quiet kind as the kind quieted. Had a daughter in cram school, plus a son not much older, though life had mostly fizzed off the kid.

People like that—prematurely worn, still ungrown—start a day with a cleared heart. (Pocketed intoxicants, unrolled tobacco from a night table, futile fruit-flavored incidentals.) Distinct on the streets in approximations of undress, yes, but by midafternoon they're bashed up again, back home, underlining every preachy word they read.

These two didn't live with me.

These two were from a bygone wife, an ex only if we let *ex* equal *extinct*. The recent wife, the deserter, was the truer to life of the two, an ex if *ex,* just this once, is allowably abbreviative of *expeller,* or *excluder,* or *exiler*—take your pick.

This marriage had had a running time of one year, three months, sixteen days, forty-two minutes.

Her name still had its run of the growlier lower vowels.

My ex-wife: she was to have been the woman by my side, though I had other sides, and she must have had other people, dumbfoundingly young things in cloches or berets, none of them cut out for life in its longer forms.

She delivered herself into a day with pills she crunched with unmilked cereal.

She pestered the alphabet in craggly poems of groped-for woe. I quote from "Bedclothes":

> at any given
>   moment there are
>   only half as many marriages
>   as there are
>   people
>   who are married.

It's not just a rumor that old men stink, and I was just about sixty, but the dollar-shops obligingly stocked confectionery fragrances, bottled lollipop pitched at preteens. PINK WHIM one was called, and PINK DREAM, PINING PINK. I bought a lot of the stuff, doused myself liberatively (forearms, chest, shoulders) before setting out for a day's errancy and dare.

But how much can you do for a sister practically fifty, except visit her five, six times a year, the two of us shivering around her kitchen table, though she ate off the TV tray by her bed?

This was in a newer town that had gone up hollow, then slowly filled in with discounters, a clinic, a competing clinic.

Her body displeased her, so she barged away from it toward sometimes even mine. That led to sweatful, recondite disquiet.

Then the day I had to deliver news of Mother.

Said this sister: "What's she so dead about?"

I don't want to be going over this again, but it keeps going over me: how there were months when the days would not stand themselves up into weeks, how there were way too many moments when we cost ourselves our lives, how there were people who were the billionth of their kind and yet had days when their place in their home and their place on earth were just one and the same.

She had put a premium on starting almost every other sentence with "I will have you know."

She had a body bullied by insomnia, but another body, sometimes showing through the depilatories, the cold cream, was sometimes offered for a leak or two from my own.

She dispensed a drastic but heterodox affection to grabbed and frugally loved pets.

We were the seediest of our set, no question, invited to after-dinner groupings just because of her, because of her shoulder tattoos, each of the three a rebus. I was unpopular, unmodified, underportrayed, never meriting a full first impression.

Something else about the ex: she was forever speaking of things as *last* (adjective) when I, stupid-surely, tended to think *last* (verb).

I either jumped out of myself in my sleep or intruded on myself in dreams, woke up, let faucet water run all over me, then let a new day brain me with its frights.

Life wrinkled out at me on the streets. I'd follow somebody for blocks, a woman, say, looking jolly and maybe unmanning, but this was a city whose avenues ran out pretty quick.

Longtimers looked skeptically at the skyline. You'd close your eyes and hope that the thing would hold up.

Sentiment kept turning against the world, people in the world, the things the people wore and looked up in books. She hadn't gone to the bother of puttering with me much anymore. A well-deserved partner always needs reasons to say, "It's not what you think."

Okay, okay: the podium is what you stood *on,* the lectern is what you stood *at,* the class is what you stood *up*. Because I cancelled a lot, last-minute, phoned-in, fancily sick of a sudden.

Hadn't I always tried to keep my life respectfully unspecified for parents, employers, sister, wife?

They called them restrooms, but I never got any peace, any respite, in there. Pisses of a man my age were just dawdly drizzle.

They pushed me over into Human Resources, every incoming résumé looking more and more like a ghost story to me.

Every quarter-hour a fresh stanza of minutes to be oblivionized a.s.a.p.

Let me talk of it as another time in my life when I must have been described as a man who walked a lot, was often seen jogging, trotting all over town, covering lots of ground day in, day out, though not looking any fitter, and when asked what kept him on the go, said, "I know where I'm not wanted."

■　　■　　■

People and their things that kept changing places on the face of the earth; remorsing moods that halted midstream and became just present-day hate; the thriving story of her family and their quick-quitted keennesses (her sister sucked the sweets out of even poorer people, boys went for her brother, etc.). Then more and more poetry driven out of her, naturally, and mostly with me as the concern.

For a while, I tried keeping up with the news. Everything, the newswomen said, was "worse than thought," which I took to mean "worse than thinking," because thinking had become even worse than feeling when I thought about how I felt about her.

On my laptop, I'd read, "You are logged in as Marie."

Then: "You have not provided sufficient information to reset your Account Security Question."

Then: "Please select a new Account Security Question from the menu, or compose one of your own."

I typed: *You'd let her go sloping off after someone after someone?*

"Please type the answer for your self-designed Account Security Question."

I typed: *To count for something, life kept shoving herself apart.*

"Your answer exceeds the allowable maximum character count. Please try again."

Oh, and having had that youth, having had that husband, she complained of being hemmed in by phenomena. She was the glummer of the two of us, more out of sorts with herself and the harangue of our heartbeats. We were a pair of the unpairing. Her e-mails always started: All,

"Your answer exceeds the allowable maximum character count. Please try again."

Believe you me us.

"Confirm we're not of like mind," people were usually saying to me now. "That would put things square."

I spent enough nights in the movie house, making faces without being faced. You try your best to outrange yourself.

Then a breastless special case, fresh from a wedlock of sorts with a woman herself worn out by greeting cards and household balladry. This one moved in with her data, her trappings—even ramekins, if you can believe that. I could see life storming around in her to no purpose, a person among other reviled people going about their puniness in apartmentry. You learn to infer a "for now" at the end of anything anybody like that might one day delay getting said. You wait your turn with everyone else to get yourself collected again in whatever was still held to be human.

I tipped this way and that to get out of the country and found work teaching Oral Business English, as the course was called, in some bulging empire or another in the Far East. I knew nothing about business (I was in fact "unbanked" myself) and sounded slushed and indelicate when I spoke. Most of the students were Americans with lots more youth still due them. They could afford to kill an afternoon listening to me talk about "opportunity cost" and money orders before going off to their dorms to convolute on futons.

Now and then one of them would of course have had enough of me. She would display herself malignantly in the doorway to my office. (It was a cornering nook I shared with a younger man on the faculty, an authority on prepaid cards. He had facefuls of glutted expressiveness.)

"You don't motivate us," the girl would say. "You don't make us want to go out and start something. We feel we're being hosed. We pay your salary."

"I'm on stipend," I said this time.

"Oh, God," she said. "Please forgive? Please be well?"

We looked each other over. She wore her share of placeholder jewelry. She had a frivolity of moles on one arm. Her body, granted, had done wrong by her, but there was a kind of beauty thrashing itself out in her eyes. The dress, rumply and sleeveless, was of a rescuing water-blue.

I could feel her turning me fore and aft in her mind-set.

"See you tomorrow?" she said, and left.

I shut the door. My cock felt boggled for once.

Said my officemate: "So far so good."

But I hadn't been over there for more than a couple of months when word arrived that they were flying my ex over at heroic expense for an hour's worth of jargonic charm about her new specialty—Minionship, or something like that. Allow me to forget the particulars, but it had to do with keeping your opinions to yourself, not speaking even when spoken to, letting others take credit for your work, preferring being discouraged. She had probably pilfered the whole of it, this spiffy new subdiscipline, from me.

"You don't have to come to the dinner, if there even is one," she wrote in an e-mail.

So I sailed back home and fell in with some flat-talking people intent on seeing things in each other just to feel hampered by what they had seen.

Then it's settled, I thought. I'll let my life live *me.*

I will say this for myself: there was only the one of me—unflaring of mind, overthankful, entertainable with the least dregs of affection, dry-handed, living spinsterlike in a problemdom of bedless street-level rentals, privy to people when at long last they were least themselves, fittingly famished, anal to a fault, never lacking for a loss.

This later one came to me not quite figured out. She looked hurriedly lovely enough at first.

She was a day-shift aide at a nursing home and would return to me with dental floss of all colors threaded thoughtfully through her hair. A resident had done it, she'd say. She would not want to wash it out just yet.

"Things don't always have to be miracles," she'd say.

Like most of some kind, she had lived and loved spottily, with lonesome turns of mind and an unsporting heart.

I took my messes and eases with her, but she turned out to be a lot like the others, each with her pharmaceuts, her vasovagals.

Sign-offs for e-mails shifted downward from "Best" to "Take care" to "Best to take care."

Weeks would warp themselves away from the year.

To an inquirer, I described the apartment as three sickrooms, kitchen, and bath.

My father? Funny I should have thought of him through all these ills. His saying was: "There'll be other days." And this was the afternoon of just another of them, the weather plentiful, a jilted watch of hers tight on my wrist, unticking, and still that unstoppable call and response between the heart and the crotch.

Other than that, it's understood that in life looted of thrill, you're to buy doubles of everything. Even a carton of detergent deserves to be with its own kind.

Things I had been mouthing to myself throughout the marriage:

Things don't always turn out, or turn even a little to the side.

To wit: wherever there are two people, people even anything like us, one is forever the casualty of the other.

Press further into yourself, as far as you can make yourself go.

When asked whether it's chronic or acute, say, "Residential."

Cultivate your disgraces.

My ex-spouse: her past was so frozen now in anecdote, it couldn't be accessed other than through quips.

Girlihood, as she'd called it? Her parents had thrown things at her to eat.

What she said did not deliver you directly to a personality. It ran you around her.

I'd been her doorstop, her kickstand—something, I mean, kickedly and meanly hers.

Spousality (her word). There were pacts and pledges, covenants, a contract for me alone to sign: things spelled out for me to do and not do. I could not, for instance, hide from her for more than five hours at a stretch, and there were only a couple of places I could hide, and she had the only keys to both, because one was the room where she slept and the other was the room where she made those gouaches people still begged to buy.

Hatred, in short, but not in so many words?

Thanks, though, for asking.

The story, later on, as it got itself passed from one chummily divorced couple to another, was that we'd been turned away by jeweler after jeweler the grievous week we went shopping for the rings. We showed the clerks our rubber-banded hundreds, but they said, "We doubt this very much" or "If you're buying for somebody else, we don't do that, because you may have noticed in your travels that fingers differ in circumference from one person to the next."

A manager at one place, a woman, came out from behind the counter and said, "Let's see you even kiss this lady."

What I could do was drop to my knees and grind my face against her midriff. I'd been doing that for months, and it was no different there in the glare and glamour of the sales floor.

"What about you?" they said to her, my intended. "What is it you do? Keel over?"

"We'd like to keep this between us," she said. It sounded little.

"Maybe you should take your make-believe outside," the manager said.

But a browser, a faltery woman braceleted the entire route from elbow to wrist, trailed us out to the sidewalk and whispered that there was a man with a cart at the farmers' market on weekends who could maybe do something suitable for us, but could we be happy with white gold?

"White gold doesn't even look like gold," my copemate said.

"But at least it won't look white. Nothing white is supposed to look like anything." The woman's voice started curving off into what could have easily gone philosophical.

We got the rings, all right. Later, in some fullness of time or another, it was a matter of deciding where and how to dispose of mine. I've still got the thing, though, the way I've still got this sense that sometimes there's just news, and then sometimes there's news to me.

THIS IS NOT A BILL

I was either a bad reflection on my parents or their one true likeness. But my own kids? You promise them anything their little hearts desire, but how little their hearts always are, and how unethereal the desire.

The son wanted nothing so much as for everything to have been ever so long ago.

The kid was having none of himself.

He tried hiding behind his similarities to me—the oftenness of my earaches, the prickled miseries in every joint.

Ideally, this should be all about him, his personalisms and all the topics his second thoughts could hold. But I can't get him magnified any larger. This is as big as his marvels will ever get. Men kept saying, "Put it there," and he was supposed to know they were hankering for no more than a handshake?

As for the daughter: she was a dampered little dispatch already orderly in her dolors.

Things she learned in school she rubbed out in her sleep, because, come morning, she thought feldspar was a plant, larkspur a bird.

Others were soon bunching about her, the mood of a morning always slow to premiere.

Sad about what now?

She snapped out of her youth with a riffraff of hair on her arms and a filing cabinet that was mostly for show.

What she took away from college was something heard in a lecture about snakes or maybe starfish, that the things could grow to refreshedly full size from just a slice of their original selves, so why couldn't that be true of people—that from the odd hair or scab you could get, if not the undivided human being, at least the excellence of an entire arm around you?

She never let on whom it was she had slapping about in her heart.

Then again, not discussed nearly enough is the bodily risk of sleeping with someone—the danger, I mean, of getting crushed by some dozing amoroso rolling over, though the prospect of bruises must have been what got her wooed into bed in the first place.

So, true: she was somewhere there in the physical hooey that went with being human. The love itself she could laugh off.

She went through with the wedding, and when they had kids, the kids were girls, the two of them: athletic and unhauntable, I would have bet.

It was a town in which things later came down to a car that should have lasted her until well into her thirties but was recalled first for this, then for that—transmission, starter, part after part repudiating its duty until loaners felt better than home to her now.

Then mail that was mostly window envelope after window envelope bearing doctor-office statements claiming, "THIS IS NOT A BILL."

I have not mentioned her mother, if only because one part of her would have referred you to another part, something more secluded, then along to where you were alone with maybe just the back of her knee, then farther along until you were off her body completely and at the feet of someone or another who had let himself in and was even more wanting.

I go into a day saying, "I won't let myself know."

NOTHING CLARION CAME OF HER, EITHER

As these things go, a woman I'll call my wife and a woman I'll call myself were not yet finished burning the bridges between us or even sharpening the sorrow down to something enough like a stick that a third party could at last take into her fingers and snap practically straight down the middle.

Let me at least drag the third party into words, because all we ever did, the three of us—in pairs of her and her, of her and me, never the three of us chordal together—was leave messes of wordedness in the air for any others to have to poke their way through.

And how we two wreaked devotion on her!

When you stir a marriage like that, the things that keep rising to the top aren't, mind you, the choicest stuff.

And I know, I know, people don't look like what they look like, thank goodness, but here is how she looked at least to me that day of name-calling over complimentary toast in the lobby of the motel: she had built such a fortress out of her unbelovedness that it was tricky to have beheld her for those months as just a plain underneath being with holes some earrings could have filled lyrically enough.

The moods amassing in her eyes (greenish eyes adrowse, though evidently truthful), relevant moles on the left arm, hair begloomed and aptly directed sideward (then later mostly hatcheted away), knees arranged buxomly, accentual acne on expanses of her back, all of these parts carnalized only in retrospect: she was a brightly miserable and unperspirant physical therapist out of keeping with herself.

She was nothing if not downright neither of ours, finally.

Plus, she was a submundane twenty-eight to our fifty (woman), fifty-six (self).

She lived with a gullible dog, a water-purifying system she could never get to work, and a sister, a slow starter whose sleep had no authority. She painted discouraging waiting-room erotica. Her saying was "Someday somebody'll look back on us."

But this third party: she was the type that, when you touched her, stuck to herself.

Me, I stickled over very little. One day it was a breadstick mossy with mold. I made it three-quarters of the way through. The core was a coaxing green.

How I swallowed!

So enough of her.

Let's picture her pelted with age!

In a marriage, the deathly custom goes, you have to choose sides—yours or your spouse's. My side had all the wobbliness on it, the debt forgivenness, the gastrointestinal meds that came with printouts saying: "IF YOU MISS A DOSE ..."

Her side had backbone in the penmanship, dollars dulling in CDs. Everything had finishes on it. Her parents came over to pamper our furniture, spoiling it rotten with pillows that foamily remembered how they'd taken every jab of my elbows.

People usually couldn't place me, but certain cushions always could.

I would have anywise settled for any old chain of events, other than morning revoking the night before, the night before revoking the day, and the day no horn of plenty, either.

Besides, someone had gone ahead and set up a business school in what had last been a buffet. My job involved elating the girls and the furiously timid, discolored-looking young men enrolled in Developmental Bookkeeping, Secretarial Philosophy, Receptionist Science. There was a body of truths for me to fatten and blotch. The PowerPoints I'd pinched online.

The kids dirtied their worksheets and turned them in. I sometimes checked them in the restroom, the one place I could be alone. They texted in there, took their heartfelt, peremptory poops, were otherwise likely quiet, though now and then there were snipings between stalls:

"But blood is thicker than water."

"But not as thick as cum."

The second voice I'd recognized and put the face to: some Kaelyn, a girl of garbled symptoms, of life accrued foolishly, and a saying: *What wasn't there to shave?*

I'd had her twice, two semesters of menial betterment.

But I checked the papers. Literally. Scraped check marks, with weighted pencil, at the top of each.

Took me minutes.

On my way out, I had to step around a cornucopian vomitus on the floor.

And going home wasn't always a hoot. There weren't always brutal acuities to sock away in some datebook.

It was an open marriage that leaked from both ends.

And another development: one of our parents died. Must it even make a difference whose? We'd left everything up to the impresario at the funeral house. He was somewhat of a man dressed with epaulets. He gave us the stock solacing face. He recommended forgoing the obits, the notices, the online guest books.

"This of all things, you don't want it to be topical," he later that night claimed in an e-mail. "You don't want a thing like this to date."

He had us over to meet the cremator—a brother of his. He spoke in yokelisms. Then the other brother took over.

"Anything else you ladies might want going up in that smoke while we're at it? We had a lady in here last week with lots of sewing machines she couldn't find homes for."

I looked my wife in the mouth, at that teetery front tooth of hers.

"There's all that underlinen and the push-mower in the storage cage," said said wife.

I went along with everything—the payment plan, the vouchers, the grandeur of the carton that would do for a coffin. I've never minded signing things.

Out of character? Yes, if it's taken just this once to mean no longer having any of it.

Anyway, who was I to be myself?

People were tedious with me or said, "This is neither the time nor the place."

As for work, school: I let myself in one weekend to make my mark on some papers and, after an hour or so, treated myself to a prissy piss, merely a trinkle, barely disturbing the water already there. But when I flushed, the bowl overflowed, and this wasn't the expectable worth of a tankful of stopped-up toilet. This was outpourings galore.

A mischance in a pipe?

I followed the water out of the restroom. It was already way ahead of me, darkening the carpet darker and darker.

I called Security.

"That building's closed, ma'am," said some man. "It's Sunday. Nobody's there."

"I am."

"You're who?"

I gave my name—which, granted, doesn't really sound all that much like a person's name but more like a corollary to what a person's name might be, something running parallel to the humanly admissible. The name sounded faked, or at most only exploratory.

"Who's this?"

I repeated. He wouldn't hear of me.

"Let me look that up in the directory."

I had to tell him that the *p*s stayed silent, that a thud had to go on the second syllable, that the hyphen was for the moment permanent.

"Someone'll be around," he said.

That had been a saying of my mother's. The other had been: *I get it all the time.* She was another woman untuned to the human constitution.

In sum: an e-mail went out on Monday in overtaxed passive voice: *Water has been found,* etc. No classes for a week while the place dried up.

Then things took a turn for the same. We tried staying true to our sexual excruciations, but I was envious of the stretch of her friendships, the way she drew some people out and took cover in others. She could pass the time of day by literally overtaking it, skipping ahead to the unstinking parts.

No matter the fronts I put up, the gateways I drew open to myself, there was always the same talk behind my back: "What difference would end times even mean to a person like that?"

We had been to bed, in sum, and we'd come back from it unblended.

She worked as an adjunct to a couple of certified nursing aides at an assisted-living sorority out beyond the industrial park. She helped people helping people to help themselves coggle their way down hallways to the Remembrance Room or the Activity Kitchen. She enjoyed the remove the work afforded her but felt the minutes flaking off every hour, then the hour peeling itself away from the day. There were double shifts and overtime, undergarments under other undergarments, requests to tie shoes "the modern way." The caregiven were never to be addressed directly. She was to remain an unseen hand. It should have been compensation that, coming home, she would feel exposed, overrevealed. But it was fine by me that she never once disrobed completely.

Around the house we wore wrappers around ourselves, drawstrings drawn taut.

Love was something squally and pickled among us.

Notice I didn't say *between.*

It never once got that specific.

Then a magazine came out with another list of the eight things every woman could not do without. I had one of them: a raincoat you could turn inside out to get another raincoat almost exactly like it. But shouldn't they have counted that as two?

I say this as someone who, growing up, had to abandon her growth. Life had made it known that it didn't want me in it as anything other than a girl who scared the daylights out of herself when trusted with so much as a pair of kiddie scissors.

You phase yourself out little by little, spread your presence thinner over the immediate things of this runaway world, dim yourself by degrees. All life aspires toward the sureness of erasure, you say? At least yours does, fucking lumpen underpunished self of mine.

My body broached its symptoms wastefully. It was resourceful in decay.

A therapist wanted to know whether I had ever "been" with men.

My answer: on double-decked budget buses, on escalators, in ticket-counter lines when I was there not to buy but just to be moving ahead of others in a publicly observable way.

The therapist's report: "Has no unity of self."

What else? The water-towered town, the city—whatever this place was called that was at such a loss for topography? People either stayed skinny and off-limits or were filthily losing their looks in showerwater that came out in earth tones.

All roads led to the one road that wasn't going where you wanted to go.

Except now and then people make a show of themselves, make themselves fathomable in something cap-sleeved, and jam the small talk with wherefores vast and mattery. It was thus I lapsed with one of the other instructors, a malcontent whose bitternesses were neatly layered (school/home/husband), a parfait of a woman, really, and life looked so good on her that week we picked clean.

It was just rotten luck that the things I found at the bottom of her temperament, the backfiring spites and such, were a lot like mine.

And then a month or so later, another instructor, this one wanting me to undo the mentoring of still another—all that besetting and misdivulged advice, all those fruits of freaked eureka moments, gone to waste on her.

In over her head, she said. At sixes and sevens.

Except she was a welcome tribulation of flatted hair, brows singed and blackened. A necklace that threaded itself this way and that through a course of piercings. A scrawny norm of a girl cracking her way, I guessed, out of the last of her velvet twenties. But she gained amplitude in the men's suits she wore abbreviated to shorts and a shell from which arms would encounter you in feeble forms of capture.

She said: "If you bring out the worst in people, isn't that a good thing? Wouldn't that be doing everybody a favor? I mean, out with the bad, right?"

She insisted on giving me her passwords to everything, all her accounts. I never tried them out. The most I did—and this was just once, and at her place, with its screens, its dividers—was to put myself in the way of the scathing hustlings of her heart.

Nothing clarion came of her, either.

Days skated by, I let life scribble its pending drolleries on me, but my gut told me nothing, my body was mum, I pressed myself next to my wife in restaurants and hideouts, we were a couplelike pair in stormy civilities, in burlesques of togetherness. At a store that sold a little of everything, all we ever bought was friction tape and mattress pads. But things must have shot out of her in her sleep (how else to explain, come morning, the sudden booty on the floor, once even a snow shovel that had obviously been through a lot?), and then a suspicion at first, then later a hope (that in the set of her feelings for me was a subset of gustier feelings spun off for other people), and then another death, another parent.

This one had wanted a viewing, a "visitation," full-body burial, a tarp for the interment. An arousing wall of brothers, sisters, cousins, family men, and any last, hoarsened aunts. Rounding them up fell to me. The rebuffs I took as gloats.

Convenient that they had a boilerplate thing for the death notice. I filled it out as follows, though I'll skip the names:

At the time of her death, her life had occurred, or was forthcoming, in New City, Old Town, Lower View, Upper Falls, Eastwood West, and Beach Canyon. She had been awarded life from a mother, _____, and a father, _____, and held a marriage license from _____. Twice a candidate for second-trimester abortion, she was the co-founder of two daughters: _____(19__) and _____ (19__). Furniture, trumpery, and dental bric-a-brac of hers were collected in seven rooms and one and a half baths. She was the motor-vehicle operator, most recently, of a 20__ _____ _____.

The morning of the service: weather digressive: a sun-shower, a cloudlet or two, then the sky seemed sealed off from us.

She didn't look as gawky for once. Life had fallen through her completely. She had aplomb there in her bin. Packed and on a pedestal again.

In the guestbook: mostly chicken-scratched *You will be missed*s.

The basement luncheon afterward, the tainting embraces.

"What does the commute do for you, other than maybe keep you at bay?"

Good question!

But must I ask it myself?

Classes were half-hours of heaving the right facts up out of the right chapters.

I was overdefinite of face, I'm afraid, and my body looked flung together from muckered, wished-away parts of others. (The brittle of my wristbones, the shoulder blades out of true.)

And others in that tournament of love interests I'd called my forties? Must we look back even just this once?

Lucerne, of the slowpoke pulse: I'd return to find her not so much asleep as nursing some oblivion within.

Aiden: fated-looking, skimming her feelings off what others had felt first, her opinions thinning themselves into whimsy.

Elara: lacking other facets, yes, but that spill of bracelets down her arm when she raised it to put another stop to her tolerance.

Emme: boisterously despondent. Infections, abscesses, things bubbling up where there oughtn't be bubbles.

The last you heard of some of them was that speed was believed to have been a factor.

All of them lively, lovely, and tiring: the motifs in their complexions, the drift of their arms, the hallowing of their absence.

Then the one who tiptoed roughshod over and around me.

But, true, not everybody gets to live in the state's fifth-largest city. Not everybody gets to be met with familial fanfare at the bus station. Not everybody gets to peak too late. Come to think of it, the landlord had a new stove brought over and parked it obstructantly in the middle of the kitchen. The thing was black and wouldn't budge for us. It wasn't even hooked up. (Hoses, wires, and whichnot, left on the sideboard.)

Something for us to walk around together, something to set us apart, something to come between us?

All three could have worked.

Make no mistake: we didn't "break up," my wife and I. It was just that we all of some sudden both moved out, separately, on almost the same day, and went off in different directions. But one afternoon I dropped by the assisted-living in hopes of seeing her no matter what. I had to sign the guest log like any other. Residents puddled by in wheely contraptions. They faced me with faces of febrile unconcern.

And then there she was, plain as day, that day anyway.

It was one of those days when it finally just comes to you—when to end a conversation, I mean, and when to renew an ordeal.

Stories Lost and Late

MY BLOODBATHS

I t was not a full life, but I liked to watch anything falling out of it.

Evenings, I would visit used-car lots—there were enough of them fringing the town—and give the salesman the impression that I was on the verge of a purchase. He would ask what was holding me back, and I would explain my need to know something influential about the previous owner. The salesman would excuse himself—by this time we would have been seated around a folding table—and return in minutes with a slip of paper to which some facts had been fastened. The most I ever found out was the profession (spousal-desertion advocate), sex (female), approximate age (last-minute forties), and circumstance (moving up in the world). Too young for me, but there were never enough facts to do the trick. Wherever I went, I took buses or walked. I had no local friends left.

I spent plenty of time in the larger discount stores where there was always the chance that previous owners of the cars I'd inquired about might be browsing under the same roof. I would buy something—maybe soap. Maybe there would be a "buy one, get one free" special. Back at my apartment, on the floor, I would disburden the cakes of soap of their wrappers and clack the cakes against each other. I would clap them together until they almost stuck, until I had almost one big cake. I was interested in getting the soap to do at least this much for me. This is not merely an example. I want to make it so it is not even partially an example. The last thing I want to do is give the impression that I chose this from a big list of things I could have done instead. The hardest part is knowing how I know how.

The library has exactly one book that touches on the one thing that matters to me, but only for exactly half a page, then gives up. I sign the book out time after time. I keep renewing the thing. Nobody at the circulation desk ever asks, "Still not finished?" or "Never thought of photocopying?" or "Too cheap to spring for your own?" Once, I get some blood on the page, because I've been flossing sloppily with the book open on my lap. I'm in bed. The day is shot. There's just one splotch of blood, maybe no more than a droplet, that landed on the page, and it's so faint that it could easily be taken for an imperfection in the paper, which is newsprinty and cheap. But I take the book back. I never check it out again.

I don't seem to pay my bills very often anymore. I'm good about slitting the envelopes open. But the bills usually feel already paid, or else they seem off-base. When I get a delinquent notice, I write a check for an amount much greater than the amount due. Yesterday I received a notice from the Greater Eastern Township Sewage Authority. I owed $12.60, so I made out a check for $162.00. I evidently sent the phone company a very large sum during the summer, and every month since, I've been receiving a statement that says: "PLEASE DO NOT REMIT PAYMENT."

There's a girl who sometimes cleans up after me. She's an adrenally depleted, vanishingly physiqued company-keeper in the same woolen jumper from week to week. I've found that when you're in the company of a mimic, you need to give the person something to mimic, but with this one I'm always at a loss. I don't have anything gesturally of use to her. Still, I watch her walk all the way across the room toward me just to sell herself short. She tells me her troubles. Her moods come out in cavalcades of a kind. She's got streaks of marigold in her hair. I suppose I encourage her. She starts calling me just about every other night. But how much sadder can a person like that get in the time it takes me to put down the phone, go to the bathroom, and then come back to the phone? She says that during her period she always wears a jockstrap. Words, endearments, are suddenly slushing out of her. I wonder whom they're for.

■　　■　　■

Some years ago, I had a best acquaintance who every night called, long distance, right before he went to bed, which was always a little after midnight. The conversations were always short and hushed; his wife was always already asleep, he would practically be half asleep himself, and he would apologize for calling so late and promise that the next night he'd call earlier. But the next night the phone would ring at the usual time. The calls always followed the same pattern. I would have something in mind to tell him, I would start telling it, and then I would stop. If I heard him say, "Go on," I would continue. If there was no sound on his end, though, I would know that he had already dozed off, and I would lay the receiver down and go back to obtuse needs of my own.

This best acquaintance of mine was five years older than I and had a bustling marriage and three unpunishable daughters and a duty-free business all to himself, but he wanted to end every one of his days with my voice. We had agreed many times over, once even in writing, that there was nothing very wrong with what we were doing, and that the little bit there might be wrong with it was no longer worth a worry. Even now, I believe that everything people said in those days had a surplus of truth in it, though the best acquaintance is now divorced, bankrupt, and full of unhalting hatreds of me.

I often worry about throwing myself into different areas of experience, but I was in the significant city for once. The woman was flirtatious, indifferently aggressive. She persuaded me to have a drink. Then, just as suddenly, she was distracted and withdrawn. She asked for my number and vanished into a taxi. I spent the night in a hotel, where I dreamed about a different but almost equal city that an acquaintance of mine was just now trying to make her home. I felt like a busybody to be dreaming about her new city, because she was unusually proprietary about it, even though she claimed to hate everything about the place.

I receive a letter from a friend who writes that I have not spoken to him "in 29.33 years." That sounds about right. He had been my best friend from sixth grade until he got married. I did not attend the wedding and never had anything to do with him again. In the letter, I learn that the marriage lasted a little less than a year. There's a thrill in the prospect of being in touch with him again, as well as the certainty that disappointments will be revived and refined. He's something of an arithmetician, and from his letter I learn that when he's got time on his hands, he hides himself in the uniform of a Revolutionary War soldier, visits schools, and pretends to be confused by life in this immediate, unpleasant century. I have never felt any need to dress up. I am often told I have an awl-like stare.

My only marriage had been to a woman a third of whose head was always kept hidden underneath one hat or another. At this point, I wouldn't know how to make the agony of it any more evident. The marks we left on each other were, often as not, indistinguishable from blisters. The divorce had been expedited by a woman she insisted was her lone labial lover always. I never saw her again and vice versa. I think we both introduced major changes in our looks to make sure.

About a month and a half ago, I awoke with the abrupt conviction that I had become a bad person. The evidence was there.

Then just last Sunday. S, a weakling former lover of mine, was in town and took me out for a late breakfast at County Dairy. The place was crowded with persons feeling themselves out after church. S and I sat down in a booth, ordered juice, then moved to a just vacated, more secluded booth. A busboy cleared away plates and coffee mugs, and S examined an inspirational medallion that, along with a few nickels and eight, nine pennies, had been left as a tip by our forebears. A waitress appeared and said, "Would you two mind moving back to the other booth? A gentleman is irate." Instead, we settled into a third booth and watched a short-coated man guide a woman whose smile was untidy. They settled into the booth we had just left. The man gave me a hydrochloric look. Then his look turned sporty.

Then this morning. Bits of adhesive tape still stuck to my arms as reminders, I'd imagine.

Bulk purchases are bulked against the walls.

I keep imagining a body securely and afflictively onto the feet of the woman walking back and forth in the apartment above mine. I want to build a case for her as being, in fact, the peep-voiced person who has just now called the radio show I've been listening to and dedicated a song to her father, saying, "Thank you for making my life a better place."

When I was in a drastic year of high school, my stepmother bought sex guides written for tyros and hid them all over the house. What I got out of them made it seem almost like a game: first you find a female, then you find the hole in her, then you fill the hole.

In one of the books, a whole chapter listed beseechments to memorize for times of sudden need: "This way it doesn't have to be completely only platonic," etc.

I think of O and how her life pulled itself together, all but strangling her in the process.

I know it's no good to spend too much time in a phone book. One should do one's business (run down the name, mouth out the number, shut the book, make the call) and then be done with it, put the thing away, advance to the next errand or disadvantage. But the new edition was delivered today, and I loitered within it, and I am the worse for the hour or so I gave myself over to a viewing of the names. For isn't every entry an admission that somebody is still at least partially up for grabs, waiting or willing to hear a little more? Much later in the day, I indelicately looked up the woman's name and found it, reinstated after an absence of three or four years. There was a new address after it, a lane somewhere, with a gardenish name I did not allow myself to remember, and a scrambly new number.

Another thing I regret is having to keep finding new places for a miscut, slightly rhomboid paperback called *1,001 Names for*

Your Baby. I have to stash it somewhere else every day after I'm done with the thing. Some of the names land so heavily on the mind that they seem to have acquired the weight of full-blown babies. I am thinking specifically of names like Finola and Reeve and Naomi, though those are never the ones. It could take a half-hour or more to go through the book and find the right ones every time I lose them. My memory is mostly shot, but I've never once starred or check-marked anything in the margins. That would be asking for it.

All along, in fact, I'd been just a harrowed fellow whose life was not worth a row of pins. Like everybody else, I was watching coverage of the event as it unfolded. My heart sank when I learned that the trouble had been the work of a religious cult and not a band of people upset with the local retail.

But you've got to watch your step in the past.

On my mother's side: an aunt who lived in a trailer court and grew grass in tiny clay pots "just for nice." She tended her portable lawns with manicure scissors and a squirt gun.

All of that clock time to dispose of, all those dimes piling up in sauceboats.

And my father: always the rudiments of a mustache on his face, never the thing fully grown.

I became a person to ask for directions. I pointed people toward streets and purlieus, cream-colored metropolitan ruins.

At thrift stores I bought whatever I knew would be too tight.

The way to get close to people was to wear out the things they once had worn.

For a while, one gets away with being a mystery, and then one finds oneself merely a receding mystery, which is not much better than never having been mysterious in the first place.

On the parking lot of a restaurant, an old friend in town for a holiday opens the trunk of his car to give me a look at three large shopping bags. In them are the hats his triplet sisters had long ago lived their thin-featured, abashing lives beneath. He had acquired the collection in roundabout fashion and now set about arranging the toques, the bonnets, the pillboxes, the tams, in three identical fleets.

He says, "Go ahead. Pick one, if you want. My treat."

I can't bring myself to upset the symmetry.

He drives us to the only bar left that caters to the older crowd. It's in the antique ward of Old Town. Worse, it's karaoke night. The only available seats are along the lip of the performing area, and the undroll fellow working the machine scolds me twice for not applauding. My friend does not once applaud but goes unscolded. He stares into the men. I take sips from an unscrubbed-looking glass of orange juice in which I taste the afterflavor of residuary alcohols.

Afterward, in his car, I quiz him on the number of barstools, the pattern of the wood paneling, the patterning on the floor. He misses all the questions, and I miss all the ones he puts to me (number of video-game machines, highest number of lighted cigarettes at any one time during our visit).

He drives us to an ice-cream parlor. He flirts with the waiter. The flirtations go unminded.

It's still early, though. I ask him to drop me off at a discount mart. I tell him I can walk home from there. Inside the store, I notice a high narrow rectangular window, three feet or so beneath the ceiling (it had been cut out of a wall), from which a woman is intently surveying the sales floor. Her head moves from side to side, slowly, mechanically. I've never stolen a thing in my life, but I keep waiting to be nabbed. I keep killing time by touching everything I can get my hands on.

Hairs, or much worse (bits of bone, even hardware), keep cropping up in the food I get served. They're still not enough to deter.

I let myself get tugged out into a day, then clouted by it. V calls back, says he's finally found the sleep he lost. Says it's being sold in tiny plastic capsules in a vending machine just inside the doors of a home-improvement store. Kids are buying it, cracking open the capsules, trying to bounce it, then trying to chew it, finally giving up, shying it across the parking lot at the shopping carts. Says he stooped to pick up a dollop of it, balled it between thumb and forefinger, took a whiff. Says it gave him a groiny feeling.

But stop just this once and think about your mother having lugged your fetus around inside of her.

Your first consideration is: So how's your fetus doing now, lady?

The cleaning girl is back, cleverly haired and with nebular new tattoos on one arm, though these could be just bruises. She can't talk. She reaches for a pen, and I watch her handwriting take its course on a sheet of memo-pad paper. She hands it to me. "WISDOM TEETH OUT!," it says. She rattles her orange-bottled meds.

I've sometimes wondered about any unharshened inner riches of hers and whether there are any walks of life left for her to walk out on. But she's got a kid, a spirited bedwetter and junior bon vivant, aged two and a quarter. She needs the work. It was from her I learned that *double bed* and *twin bed* weren't different names for the same thing.

My body had never been laid out for marriage.

"Maybe do something about that five-o'clock shadow you've got on the backs of your hands?" my wife had said.

"Maybe suck on some toothpaste first?"

This was to have been a new year. Yet N still stodges himself with chocolates. R, who still works, calls to tell me that she's heard she is about to be "iced for excellent cause." The faxes F keeps sending me in typewriterly typeface arrive with a band of crazen, random letters and symbols at the top: check marks, smiley faces, playing-card hearts and spades, triangles, octagons—with enough mathematical symbols mixed in to give the long sequence the look of an overweighted equation.

■   ■   ■

The story was that a man wore denim skirts that he'd had stitched all the way up the middle so that people on the street who thought they were seeing a man in a skirt and who were about to announce this fact loudly and derisively to a companion or a stranger would venture a second, confirmatory look, conclude disappointedly that he was just some poor stick-legged guy in floppy shorts, then chastise themselves for not minding their own business and for so easily thinking the worst of people. But it was only a story. W had pointed me to it when he called to complain that there was nothing else left to masturbate about. He said he was otherwise down to weakening facts about bodies he'd once sat next to or behind in auditoriums.

Some he has to pay by the hour to listen to it all. Others will put up with it only if it's in a nutshell: As a kid ill-suited to youth, loadedly older already, he'd felt unfated, unblendable even with his friends, those passionately unopinionated attractables who roamed closer and closer to home. By fifty, he'd put a brave face on lover after lover he'd coaxed to throw him over. Then he met the woman of abler caliber and of skittery affection who, I'm guessing, is with some other, better monster now.

In another fit, I'm no older than nine. My mother and I are seated deep in the bus on opposite sides of the aisle. We're on our way to another movie she's chosen to disenchant us both. I feel menial affection coming from her in hurries. It's from her I'll later learn that the trick is to figure out how best to butt out of yourself.

The girl who cleans has from week to week introduced little adjustments in the positions and *attitude* of the things in each room. One night, I return to find the handset of the telephone upside down in its cradle. The ear- and mouth-cups perk upward, like alert ears waiting for me to have some say.

Overheard or overhearing, I let my body give me pause.

The only teacher I'd ever learned much of anything from had one day told the class: "There's only the nineteen of you, and you're none of you any different from one another, so there's no point in even spelling out your names. Save your ink."

She wanted to save us from later having to go through the stages. The scheme of things wouldn't necessarily even have to have any people in it, she claimed, except for maybe "underneighbors" and "overneighbors," and those could be counted on to fight anything out among themselves.

"Don't just befriend your body!" she'd shout. "Long for it! Pine! Woo yourself through and through!"

That was toward the end of an early year of high school, when I had it too good.

The sole visit to my apartment in all those years was from a man almost my age who sweated bare-backed on my sofa and revealed every blottiness possible of himself.

He'd once been another of the dullheads unduly held dear.

But here he was: kicked-off shoes of boaty disposition, slouch socks gone through at the heels, and he was smoking irritably now, poking critically at my pyramids of reference books, because reference books were all I had any use for even then, because there was nothing that did not need to be looked up and confirmed again and again and again, whether it be a symptom or some spoilsport statistic.

Then of course he wanted to talk about his kids. A son still cutting himself just to flaunt his blood. A house-hunting home-wrecker of a daughter suiting herself just fine. They'd gotten their punchy intelligence from their mother, not from him. Neither of them could ever see far enough outside of themselves to take a shine to anyone else.

Besides, he'd disbanded the whole family months ago, he said. Put them out. Had since had his pick of younger men, none of them with an enemy in the world excepting of course now him.

"But once again, as before, as always, I come to you."

I'd always been barely averagely desirous of people in need of a sexual victory, but for this man smelling so thinly of his liniments, of menthol, I felt nothing even whimsically indecent. There was a disposable razor I'd been hoping to prolong the life of, though, and daredevil doldrums I could count on coming. So I told him about those. I rarely got around to setting just the right traps for myself.

Most of the time it was usually too late in the day for there not to be some truth in what people kept saying about me, especially when it was only: "It goes to show."

What I got out of this expression, what I finally thought it meant, was that in order for it to make itself known, in order for you to know it, it has to leave—it has to get itself away from you.

I get up and feel recompacted after a nap.

At the ice-cream place, the snuffling girl behind the counter scruples my vanilla into a clear-plastic dish.

Besides, I no longer drink milk. I gave it up. By this stage, my bones are the way they are. Milk would be nothing more than the sound of itself getting poured.

This could be said by any of my few woman friends with a grown son, but only one of them has said it: "When I go out for a walk with him, it's like I'm on a date."

I peeked through the blinds at the fire trucks. Extending from one of them to the door of the lobby was an inflated portable tunnel, huge enough for somebody to walk through. Something was being either blown into the building or blown out.

Later, a long but promisingly final phone conversation with S. It was interrupted by a series of abrupt and vehement hang-ups, all from his end, and then he would immediately, apologetically, call back. It was a conversation so difficult for me to get the drift of, so nonlinear and spiraling, that I resorted to writing things down, trying to outline. I didn't know what to say, because I didn't know what was being said, other than that he does not yet have the money to pay me back, work hasn't been working out, he's just gotten out of a relationship with an eighteen-year-old, he's overknown in the bars, he's been taking free, abbreviated IQ tests on the World Wide Web, his car is being repossessed, and his doctor claims that anything can go bad in a day. He didn't sound stoned this time, but his daily life and his character have always been a bad match, and I don't like being kept boiling about in his brain this way.

A day toward the end of one of those short-weighted, thirty-day months, and not much doing on the face of the earth except people looking strapped for facts, trying to get away with saying only "I'll tell you what."

Granted that marriage doesn't grow on trees, but there was foul play in her tenderness for people, and her self-criticisms should have come in for suspicion, too.

H: I would see his truck just about everywhere but where it was parked.

Earlier, I'd wanted to learn how to like this city and where I lived in it.

The reasons were, I guess, zerofold.

The maintenance lady was standing in the lobby with the caretaker and some tenants—a mother and her runt of a juvenilely adult son, some watered-looking young men, the woman with the scalding eyes and unattached personality. I typically walk right past them to the stairs.

"Up there," the maintenance lady said. "In the chandelier."

It took me awhile to see it, because I'd never known the first thing about birds, and even when I saw the thing, none of it seemed like an event, something to have happened, in my life.

"You see it?" the maintenance lady said.

Something had to get said, so I came up with "Well, I hope it gets out."

I walked one flight up. My apartment was right next to a little balcony overlooking the lobby. I was going through my keys—I carried three identical sets—and could hear the talking below.

"He stood there and looked at it," I heard the caretaker say.

"That much he did," said the maintenance lady.

Somebody made an ailing sound.

Opposite the door to my apartment was a door covered with aluminum foil and, on top of that, decorations left over from Easter—rabbits, crosses, eggs. On a sheet of construction paper, the tenant, a stocky young woman who always wore a smock, had crayoned the words "Tina's home."

I had been wondering for days whether that was an announcement (invitation?) that she was receiving visitors or a proprietary declaration that this was where Tina—somebody's Tina—had ended up.

Finally heard back from W. Always a hint of bribery, though, in his ingratiations.

L calls, and I say it's a shame about the furnace and the unreachable, barnbound repairman. So I *do* have friends. I've got their answering-machine messages saved from the age of the cassette.

All of a sudden people are saying all of *the* sudden, as if there's only one.

Poor Q, though. He liked to think without any patterning to the thought, and kept his arms at crooked removes from his body when he hid himself to sleep. He was always saying things colorfully to women waxening further in their anemia. But he'd been loved aside once too often and found he could no longer apply himself to life. Nobody had left him with enough adhesive, either.

The obit was a tell-all.

Some constructive criticisms in the book of condolences, though.

After the service, I run into a store to buy more memo pads. They come six to a package, fifty sheets apiece. I've been setting money aside for this for hours. The scowlful lady behind the counter says, "You've got any plans for all that paper?" But instead of trying my best to be overhumane or shower her with kindness, I get her pegged right back: to make the years go by, she grew up, felt unfostered, got married, bothered other people until they got married too, had kids, stuck her neck out for the kids, and all that just to get whose goat exactly?

I'd had enough of a brother myself. He was younger by nature if not by years, and I give him credit for stretching his shortcomings out to last the unrunkled length of his life.

Plus I'm expecting a check for ninety-eight cents in response to a complaint letter I mailed to a supermarket only just yesterday.

As for C, his every remark would start with "As of yet" or "As of tomorrow," but the rest of it was always only about his childhood and a house set so far back from the street that, technically, it belonged to the alley. The alley had a street name, but nobody could remember what it was. Mail would arrive with "REAR ALLEY" in elaborate postmasterly script, though it wasn't even really a house—just rooms atop garages, a treeless lot out front. But so much can go wrong with a toy that is made to look too much like what it was supposed to be only pretending to be. In this case, a snow shovel he brained the neighbor boy with, and that just because he loved to hold hands with the numb.

Always these leakages in my voice, little runny foresounds before I actually speak, though I'll speak only to have said that we were always taught that it's best to always have something on yourself. We were taught to keep that one black mark in reserve. "It'll come in handy," they said. I never had just one, though. Plus, I had always expected that everything going forward would be handled as a matter without any facts.

My apartment is next to a laundry room with one washer, one dryer. The dryer is well-behaved, but the washer has a disorderly twenty-two-minute cycle during which it tries to rock itself loose from its hoses. The tenants on my floor have enormous backlogs of laundry to do. There are embankments of it in the corridors—stamped-down piles of sweat-sodden, mildewy underwear and sundresses and towels and uniforms that reach from the doors of their apartments to the machines. The machines are kept running at all hours of the night. Through it all, though, I never once lose track of the neighbor upstairs. I think she always knows just how hard, how firm, her footsteps need to be, which is one measure, I suppose, of devotion.

Here still, and still hunched over human affairs, I turn on the news, but "at least three people killed" sounds too much like a brag.

With B, it was never the beauty itself—that was never enough (through some moonshaft in her mind, though, she thought her body was ruined by strawberry legs and an unexpunged birthmark)—but her custodianship of that beauty that drew me near, and near her is where I first saw Y, who was killing time by her side at the little station, then kissed her good-bye, and, in so doing, revealed the full razzmatazz of his face, with all that makeup, all that styling of the eyes.

I followed this tressy, twitterboned thing into the train.

He pratted himself into a seat next to a man in a suit. I stooped into a seat next to a dish-faced girl, mid-twenties, I guessed, her head swagged forward in feigned sleep. I watched rheum trickle out of a nose-ringed nostril. She unsealed an eye just far enough to admit one of mine.

Y got off at the next stop. He could've walked those few blocks!

I am tired of explaining that, yes, it was officially called a subway around there, but after only four underground stops, the thing got hiked up to street level and juddered off as just a trolley.

I got off at a suburban junction, boarded a bus, called B as soon as I got home, inquired. Things too easily get unfeelably emotional with me.

"You could've at least said hello, you know," B said. "Anyway, his policy is no fats, femmes, feebs, or fogeys."

B has long since been thin-bloodedly married, has long been gone through by man after bandage-bearing man outside the marriage.

She no doubt still keeps at least one of her clocks set fifteen minutes fast to give her life that extra push.

But had I been good enough to my parents, or had I wanted to shame them out of their lives?

G is in town, though, and invites me to lunch. He's an oniony, abbreviated man. (His face is blooded as usual from the dry razorings he still favors.) For the past half-hour, he's been trying to shake loose an apothegm from his throat. "What a piece of shit is man," he says, finally, then keeps repeating. It sounds thieved from some inadequate classic.

We part, but by evening he's on the phone, en route. "I saw a reproduction of *The Last Supper* day before yesterday, and all I could think of was a Friars Club roast. What do you call those things—those little paddles with a ball on a string that kids thwack around with? I want to patent one—only instead of a ball, there's a little head of Christ, and instead of the paddle, it's a cross. *Talk.*"

I'm doing another two balmy loads.

Things being what they are, growing up past a certain point was politely called *attaining* or *reaching majority,* but there was still only the one of you, outnumbered just as much as before, though in my case I learned to revere strangers, and I returned from the dirty work of college such a differencedly wretchful, wrongable, fucken thing, sleeved and inseamed and bereted suchwise that no skin showed except fingertips, neck, and closed-eyed, shut-mouthed face.

Nobody in my life has ever succeeded in turning me against anyone else. But why is it, then, when I'm trying to type "farther," that I almost always type "father"?

When I'm around certain people, the tides of my saliva get thrown out of whack. I end up repeating things I would otherwise never consider saying even once.

Case in point: that tree outside my window keeps making an awful lot of noise.

But it helps that the clothes I've been buying, even the pongee cover-ups and step-ins and such, are somehow called "separates."

On the other hand, I could take a fumy, retributive walk around the block, or I could tell people how I felt. I got used to the people saying: "This puts me in a spot."

My life, so help me, was a simple, uncurving line inching itself out ruleredly into early middle age, and then old age came over me in a *poof.* I didn't have much to say or do about it at all.

Somebody keeps leaving things outside my door. Primers, foundations, toners, blushes. The blushes I have trouble with.

For a while, I start wearing women's pants and shirts that look exactly like men's pants and shirts, except for how the shirts need to be buttoned. I'm rarely around people anyway, and, besides, nobody has brothers or sisters anymore. Everybody's nice about saying *sibling* instead, to make sure the kids get cleansed of gender. The one time I'm asked about my own childhood, they're intent on finding a kink in my every straight answer. But my mother, mind you, had a saying: "By the time I get through with you, there'll be nothing left but a grease spot."

She had no earthly or supernatural use for me.

From supermarkets, though, I've been hauling home some boxes, three or four a week. I've never been without reason to set store by clean, crisp cardboard.

I upend one of the boxes, push it in front of the little utility TV. I turn the brightness knob almost all the way to the left. I want the screen blank of anything but these fluttering patches of white.

Then one night, on the spur of a moment, I stopped what I was doing, which was making my way from the bathroom to the kitchen. I'd intended to eat something, the first thing I came to. But I stopped. I stood as stockstill as I could. This was not easy. I could hear the woman living above me come to a stop, too—a stumbly, unprepared-for halt. I imagined the people above her, and the people beneath me—this was a high-rise, after all, a five-story apartment block—coming to a stop as well. For a moment, we must have all been lined up perfectly vertically, in standstill formation, each of us with nothing much in life to go back to doing.

But I went and found that box of bacon-flavored crackers I knew I had around here somewhere—dog food, practically—and waited for weightier snow to come.

Feeling more dutiful, I return to the nursing home. The disease has left him partially discolored. The room is a deodorized strongbox sealed with measled wallpaper. A tiny shaded window admits mealy light. I admire the curatorial positioning of the water tumbler. He has to be levered and pulleyed out of his sleep. Now and then there's some leftover movement in a leg.

Loud as I can, I pretend to be his mother and wait for him to finish his life.

On my way out, a woman in the hallway hands me a religious tract in which Bible excerpts are grouped under lively headings. One of the headings is "Seven Things God Hates." These aren't the seven deadly sins, though. These are more like peeves.

Today the library was practically empty. I let the books—all of them unread, none ever even opened—tumble into the narrow slot at the return desk. I was already on my way out when I heard the cry. "But, ma'am, these aren't even from our holdings."

P calls after seeing his youngest daughter off to college, a depreciating university that looked cheap even in the leaflets. I'd taught once enough at one of those. The first day of the term, the class was half women, half men, but something crossed the men's minds by the end of the week (I could see alarms going off behind the eyes), and by week two, I was left with only the girls, and by the third week, half of the girls were gone, too. I eventually got a call from the dean. "With whomever you might still have—I'm assuming you've still got at least two or three, yes?—just go forward with it as Independent Study." Years, many semesters, later, I ran into one of the women. We were in line at a pharmacy. Her beauty must have been timed to bloom in just that very twinkling, because there was a precision to her features now, and her dress divulged her arms entire. She explained that she'd graduated and found a job at a factory where she operated a machine called a palletizer. "I have a favor to ask. Can I store some stuff at your place?" she said. "It'll just be until I move out." The next night, she brought over a coffee machine, a broom, some cleaning buckets, a set of the very plainest dishes. I'd still have them, too, if I hadn't grown so attached to the things, and all they spelled out about the wideness that could suddenly seem given to the world, that it was either ditch them or resume spying on her, but not just out of the blue this time.

My hair is long, black, or prone to black. I've asked for it to be dyed the same suspect shade.

My voice is squeaky and off by about an octave.

At the bookstore yesterday, too many cruising women doing suicide groundwork.

As time permits, I'll take what gets dished out.

The sky today is pushed low over the town. It pringles my skin. I've been out for walks, looking between the people. There are far too many opposite sexes. I spend far too much time.

In the dream, I return from a late-night walk to find that the building I live in is gone and that the houses on either end of it have expanded and spaced themselves out to conceal the disappearance. I report this to a policeman.

No hands but my own, though, to slap me back into the form I feel I've lost.

For a good week or so, P has been calling me late every afternoon, another of the difficult times. "New Year's Eve a year ago, horribly o'clock, I'm in my car, parked outside a supermarket already dark, listening to piano on the radio, I'm thinking of nothing much in particular, looking at nothing, my eyes are drifting on their own, all of a sudden I realize I'm staring straight into the face of a man in an adjacent car, he's motioning with his hands, I roll down my window, I turn down the radio, and the man says, 'Is there a problem?,' and I say, 'Can you believe it's really taken me this many years to realize that *LA* rarely means Louisiana?' He came over and sat. Turns out I knew him from a rest stop outside of the capital." I hear the sound of cake being chewed smackingly.

"To be honest," she would start, just to keep up the difference between the sexes.

But in this room I'm eighteen and my father is washing the big plastic box fan I've been relying on of late. He devotes the better part of a day to it. He's using old dishrags, cotton swabs, a couple of paint-by-number paint-set paintbrushes. He's getting the gunk off the grilles, the blades. Now and then he carries everything out to the porch and hoses it down, carries it all back in. He's finally drying it down now with an old towel. He finishes, and says, "What do you think, inspector?" Later, though, I'm alone in my bedroom. I plug in the fan, dial the "low" setting. A firefly flies right through the grille. Tiny slashes of shredded phosphorescence sail across the room.

My life's story all over again: There are three of us. I see her keep trying to read my face as I keep trying to read his.

As for J, we'd gone to college together, except he was rarely there. He spent most of his time drinking at a better college down the road. He would play the lottery if the jackpot was attractive, then make a point of never checking if he'd won. "Let them come to me," he'd say. He said that after graduation he was going to send me some postcards—the skylines of cities whose names he all along must have been making up. Plankton, I believe, was one of them. I have always been waiting for my mail, or going through other tenants', hoping for any word of him. He looked out for me.

I keep coming back to my wife, though only in thought, in cerebrations baser and baser, and never once in deed.

Failure has its drawbacks, too, but I met her before she'd been perfected, back when she still had spare time. We'd been thrown together by a sensitive scorn for others. We were like-looking enough, and most likely looked ungreetable, though the eyebrows on her were shaped a little more like the *f*-holes of a violin. We always took turns being the older one. Days we didn't feel up to feeling much else, we regarded each other with the simpatico prurient misgiving I always took for something potentially even starker.

She was dead-set on a future. She envisioned herself forgottenly famous one day, and unmurdered, listening to a plastic surgeon prizing the lines on her face one by one, saying, "I'd leave them, if I were you."

The humbling gloom can get to be too much of a good thing.

We fought over which one of us had ended the fights.

She was mum on the subject of whomever I was a replacement for. (Turns out it was a girl who gagged even when guiding gossamer-gauge floss between incisors.)

We each inventoried the other's childish ways to be given up in remorse taken to the public.

She looked for sinister detail before she flushed.

She was thirsty all the time. We had to stretch the water coming in those provocative bottles with homelier flows from the tap.

The marriage mattress kept having to be flipped, or spun, and there were turnovers of every animus, too.

We weeded through our pasts. (Her popularity in college had been rescinded early on. There had been sides of my life never to be guessed at from only a timid frontal view.)

Not that we didn't have a good half-day here and there, but any silver linings were the kind you could just zip right out of whatever was keeping us cloaked from outlying life.

She more and more often found it politic to misreport our marital conditions. But why bother making it seem as if we were awaiting outreach to reach us?

When she got done with a day, it was just another disarray of time displayed just to taunt. You'd have been dragged straight from morning to midnight without the buffer of cloud-drowned afternoon or evening's slow souring.

Night vision wasn't among her fortes, either.

Things she'd do for you left you done for.

The sense in which I too was an ingrate was not even a sixth sense. You didn't need a soul to know it.

I'd gone to all the trouble of letting another night die down. Awake too early, I watch—through a swatch of faded denim tacked over the upper part of a window (my air conditioner is shoved through the lower part of the frame)—the outline of the window-washer's arm going about its monthly swipes. Later, I'm waiting to buy a soft pretzel in a nut shop on that street whose name I always get wrong. There's a little boy ahead of me in line. His forearms are chained together with toy handcuffs. The woman behind the counter puts the boy's change in its own little bag.

Sleeping on the floor, putting up with the new tenants downstairs. The first few nights, I mistook their snores for pillow talk.

Morning, I come upon a sheet of paper still smarting from the words she'd ordered onto it.

In divorce, I must have parted from myself, too.

One night I did it—walked next door to the laundry room and disconnected the inlet hose, the drain hose. Pulled all the plugs. By morning, everything had been restored to working order.

My personal history has too many long, unrecorded stretches, as it should. Today, in the city, a panhandler was saying, "I need exactly seventy-seven cents," but he wasn't saying it to me. And he was saying it not as a plea but as if it were dispassionately autobiographical, a summation of everything finally now stable in his sphere. He was saying it to some guy in his mid-twenties looking unrested, thought-worn, full of untended-to trouble. I wanted the guy to say, "I could get by on less." This was near an animal shelter I like walking through. Lately the dogs have been looking shifty and bigoted.

Another discovery: certain of the washers the plumber had left behind could be worn in a pinch as wedding rings.

One day I pull myself together and take a taxi to a medical pavilion for a flu shot. It's administered by a nurse in a hallway where a couple of other nurses and a receptionist are standing around in fragrant adult complication. I ask for a shingles shot, too. In the lobby, on my way out, I see my regular doctor, a former teacher (music, junior high). He's an unhale-looking fellow manipulating the soft-drink machine. He seems to recognize me and says a couple of worthy things. The first is: "Let me set the needle back." The second has something to do with life rarely being much more than a diversion of the hands from the body.

Vengeful nostalgia for my forties, I guess? I had not kept up with my life but now and then walked in on myself almost butchily with W. Her body was poxed with dotty tattoos.

Eight, nine months later, she expected me to come over and pay my first respects to the baby.

I didn't have another hour to knock out of a night already caving in. Some women are better left to their husbands and their husbands' nice tries.

And the other, the earlier P, with those raggle-taggle eyebrows tinted an untitillating turquoise: she got around to her life too late to get much out of it, though I could feel her heart chugging away under that tunic that afternoon in a befriendedness preferably foregone.

■   ■   ■

Correction: walking out of an early movie, even a decent one, you do *not* find the light any more generous than before, and it most certainly does *not* confer upon the city any such thing as a definitive version of itself. Don't talk to me of sudden smiles returned to you in a shopwindow, or of fishing out of memory the word you've been searching for all week. It's definitely *not* "rill," cocksucker.

But I get lulls like this. I also get breaks between the lulls.

Another of those hurtfully sunny Sundays when nothing stayed hidden or recessed. People were messily intact. I hardly knew what to do with myself. I walked into a fast-food place that was gentrified on the outside but inside was close-packed filth. The woman who took my order and arrayed the items onto the tray had a big stiff bandage on her forefinger. It was clownish swaddling and no doubt richly unsanitary. I carried my tray to a table and discovered that the soda was not the one I'd ordered. I got up, but before I even turned around, I heard a voice shout, "It's all wrong. Bring it all back."

Some nights, though, it's my mother talking straight through into my sleep.

"Did I ever hit you?"

"No."

"Should I have?"

"No."

"Then what did I do?"

She'd given me her stringy hair, her oily nose, her crumbled teeth, true, but those are the kinds of things you bring up only with the dead.

A new day pitted with minutes. I'm just another affrighted individual acting alone. What's left to be said about other friendships about to end?

D: no matter what we were about to do, he was all for calling it a night before we did it. K: she was interested only in keeping herself covered with some lotion or another. I await any acceptable radiations of her intelligence. M: reliably disappointing, again and again letting his life get the better of him, always on the phone, always calling a lot of people. Add to that the fact that the person on the other end of the line usually wanted to know what that jingly sound was, and he did not want to have to keep explaining, for the rest of his days, that it was the prong of his undone belt tinkling against the buckle.

T: a grouty little sulking thing who could sometimes be worth some while.

By the time I got to the home, life was clearing itself out of her.

"She's doing the work," the nurse said.

She already looked a little deceased to me, but this was no time to be splitting hairs.

By morning they had her colored up.

They spoke to me now of "the decedent." Decedents have to make do without pronouns.

A last fax from a "personal individual" I once dumped: "Life serves us right. It started with just a drop, really, that I'd left on a pair of cheap, overdecorated jeans I was trying on at Kmart. Nothing noticeable, practically an accident. The fitting room was no larger than a ladies'-room stall, so I was right to think of swirling waters, of toilets. Then I drove to an old, free-standing Sears and tried on a divided skirt and released a little bit more, a lukewarm trickle this time. It was roomier in there, and I caught my eye in the mirror. There was a darkening on the fabric, a definite showing. I got dressed and carried the skirt back to the racks. In Value City, it was a sheath dress in greenish-blue, and I had to remove my briefs because they were sopped through by now—I threw them in my handbag. On my way to the car, I dropped them into a trash basket. I am almost always having to go. I drove to the newer mall, the one with the elevator with glass walls. I drank a medium Diet Sprite. At Macy's I trained my stream onto the seamwork of a woolen skirt at my feet. At J. C. Penney I drenched the seat of some trousers. There was another department store, a local one, not part of a chain, with a whole suite of fitting rooms, a bench in every one. I tried on a jumpsuit, then went out barefoot for a look in the three-way, dripping sparingly as I stepped. In the side-wings of the mirror, my hair looked sticky and thin—like streamers, almost. I could barely see anything on the crotch of the trousers part. I passed a rack of travellers' aids on my way out of the store and bought a sleep mask, one of those elasticky things, like blacked-out goggles. At the food court, I drank a diet lemonade. I drove to a shopping plaza. At T. J. Maxx there was a limit to how many items you could take in at a time, and I did not even bother with that many—just a linsey-woolsey skirt, some poplin drawstring pants, a simple hyacinth-violet cotton dress. The skirt I doused along the hem without even trying the thing on. The pants I left alone at first. The dress I wriggled into, then got down into a crouch and soaked a shadow the size of my hand onto the underside of it. I left the dress in a heap on the floor. I reached for the pants, then let them drop. I put my foot down on the crotch of the pants and bent over them and dispensed the piss so that it guttered down my inner leg in a rivulet that eventually reached the fly-front of the pants, but barely leaving a mark. I wiped myself on a sleeve of the dress and got back into my clothes. I left everything else on the floor. I bought a feather pillow—thirty ninety-nine—because of what it said on the bag, the name of the brand: Sure-Sleeper Plus. I drove home but left the pillow, the sleep mask, in the car. Still no sign of him. I drove to a neighboring city and in a little mall there took a thorough evac on a metallic, sleeveless thing—a cocktail dress in red, size eight—"

I walk downtown to enjoy the steadfast companionship of the few taller buildings. I return without much integration inside. My inner life has a different chemical structure to it now. Lots of partitions have gone up within. Emotions are confined to tiny allotted areas.

Y calls and tells me he tore off the shrink-wrapping of some monthly or another of women's fashion, then prowled its advertisements in a spirit of goatishness and carousal. I tell him that any religion without a god (or angel, or saint) of mail is incomplete. There should be shrines where one might pray or make sacrifices in advance of the day's delivery. The old, temple-like post offices at least had the requisite grandeur, the marmoreal hush. Y has gone quiet at the other end.

The cleaning girl keeps my place tidy, but that doesn't mean I haven't kept a lot of the wrenching stuff around. I almost never look at any of it, and I would probably have a hard time locating any one particular item, but it's all close by and as of yet unredressed.

The mailman has been coming later and later these days. I have to watch for his truck, which means opening the blinds—something I oppose.

I am a son, a stepson, now sixty-one. This birthday hour is already shattering into its minutes.

Didn't I just read somewhere that if, after a certain point, you no longer worry about growing old alone, it's only because you've already finished doing exactly that?

I'll wait for what's left of the day to work any correcting havoc on me.

I have to come to some sort of decision, or at least figure out what I might really need to decide.

U calls to talk cars, because he still believes I'm still looking for one. He says, "Mine is due soon for demise. It has one hundred and ninety thousand miles on it, and not even half of them can I call my own. They still belong to the original owner. I want to see that they get returned."

Z used to be an expert on how very thin young women with boyish hair got distributed evenly throughout the lobbies of apartment buildings, the concourses of airports, the TV lounges of supposedly private gentlemen's clubs. There was always one per site, holding an unlighted cigarette, a clothbound book open on her lap, the sleeves of her oversized shirt rolled up past the elbow. He interviewed them individually and in groups to find out how they decided who sat where and what was in those books. They kept their voices low but were helpful to a degree. They showed him how they rolled up their sleeves. He bought them better cigarettes. They reciprocated by chipping in to buy him a big shirt like the ones they wore. They walked him to his car. Afterward, citing death threats, he became an expert on something else.

There's just too much time between morning and midmorning. Then that ogre of an hour before you can peaceably sneak a nap.

A man of my generation flies a quarter-day's driving distance to tell me, between slow swallows, that when he was in his late twenties, he twisted his mother's thumb during one argument and, during another, tore the bifocals off her face and snapped them apart at the bridge. She took it all in stride, he says.

He tells me he used to visit his parents all throughout his thirties, his forties, for weeks, sometimes months, at a time. Once, during a visit, he poured what was left of the box of puffed rice onto the kitchen carpet, then reached for the half-gallon carton of milk he had just opened and poured the milk on top of the cereal on the floor. He stepped backwards, watched his mother watch him search for the sugar bowl. He found it on the counter, threw it, lid and all, onto the mess he'd already made. He heard his mother scream "Joe! Joe!" His father's name was Elmer, but because Elmer's boss at the plumbing outfit was also named Elmer, Elmer had become Joe first at work and then later at home. This had been going on long before my visitor was even born, before he was given the name Joseph, for the abasing formality of it.

I listen, but I don't know what to tell him. That to be taken advantage of is, after all, a life? That most people don't want to be thought about all that often, even after they're dead? That I am ruthful and in a bad light myself?

He leaves.

Later, I can't sleep. People are talking in another apartment. The talk is not splitting itself apart into words.

A little more than two years after my mother died, I finally find her birth certificate. It's from 1929. Everything on it is typed, except this, written in stately, proclamational backhand: "Born alive."

GROUNDS

T hen she found something out about me but wouldn't tell me what it was. All she said was "Why would anyone say such a thing about you? What's your side of the story?" I told her that it was probably not a story with sides to it. The sides were what would have held it in if there had been a way to keep it from getting out.

THE ONLY CITY ALL BLUE ALL NIGHT

The person ready to draw my blood says name any name at all. So I come out with something barely of the alphabet.

"Fair enough," he says, and takes the form from my hand.

What I tell him before the question comes up is that I have a wife. Because, after nine years, what do you call a person you picked to stand in for everybody else?

In my case, it was a person with a wife of his own, in a hometown somewhere close by. Why would I otherwise be bothering so much about blood?

I'm supposed to come back in a week to ten days.

To make the time go by faster, I watch the weather take on volume. The snow I shovel in the alley gets heaped into the wheelbarrow, and then the wheelbarrow gets wheeled through the garage and out into the front yard or even as far as the sidewalks, should I say so.

The only lights allowed on after dark are pilot lights. Ours is the only city all blue all night.

The other remaining thing is that a person at work, the worker to my left, is under the impression that the shit I take from others and the shit I take from myself are somehow one and the same. As time permits, this worker always looks uprooted, pale, coaxed. His emotions aren't always easy to spot. Sometimes we take our eyes off each other, but only to get a better idea of where else we might be. The building is possessed of two washrooms on every level. Just this once, I wash my face the way clothes get washed. I get plenty of agitation into it. A certain amount of my life has to be faked to satisfy my craving for absolute honesty in everything I do.

PLEDGED

The name of the town depended on whichever direction you were coming from. We were approaching from the east, so it was called West Southfork. Before we knew it, we were in somebody's backyard. We felt cheap. There must have already been piles and piles of people exactly like us, every one of them stopping just short of saying: "I haven't the heart."

And yes: the grass felt less and less steady underfoot.

And, yes, the dirt beneath the grass felt awfully mushed.

And, yes, the planeting underneath the dirt felt even mushier.

We got down on our knees and dug at it with our long-fingernailed fingers. The bangles on our arms were soon caked with mud. Some of the flimsier chainy-type bracelets got torn right off. We watched them get sucked off into the sludge.

We weren't dressed for it. Anything with sleeves, anything longer, would have been better.

We kept digging, not even looking at each other anymore.

And under all that planeting, wouldn't you eventually expect to come upon plates, some tectonic whatnot or suchlike, or at least trusses, sheets of rock, something to keep holding everything up? Wasn't that what we'd been taught? All we found was stuffing that looked a lot like graph paper—quadrille, I believe it had been called at school.

We reached in and pulled some of it out.

The world went a little limp.

The planet slumped a bit there for a sec.

That wasn't our intent, even if we'd each been a little sick of the other of late.

"Just stuff the stuff back in," I said, and that's what the two of us did.

The surface soon felt firm enough for us to walk atop it again, so we found our way back to a road, followed the road, kept our eyes forward, then came to a nice restaurant, went in, ordered likely meals. The server seemed awfully interested in us. "How are we doing here, really?" the server kept asking as we started on our food.

"Fine," we kept saying. "Really."

"Can I bring you anything else? Can I top off those bevs for you?"

Then: "You're sure you two're all right?"

We didn't say anything, and she left.

"She must have meant our dresses," I said. We didn't usually go around smutched and so bodily mucked over. We were twenty-two and twenty-two and two-fifths, respectively and for dear life.

Her knee knocked against mine.

"Let's do something later," she said.

"After our baths," I said.

"After our *bath*," she said.

Then a man in a car coat came over and stationed himself at the edge of the booth. He pressed his palms onto the tabletop to get himself propped. He watched us eat. He had eyes that were a tad red and had some bedlam in them. His mouth looked stirred up.

I don't ordinarily eat for show, but this time I tried. I'd ordered the sauerkraut over a missy cut of pork and some potatoes modestly mashed. I ate with an exaggerated bashfulness and chewed as abstrusely as I could. My girlfriend did some sort of abracadabra with her salad, never actually touching it but getting it to look dabbled away at until the bowl was practically bared. I'd bring my tumbler of ice water to my lips but never take a sip. My girlfriend brought a fork down into my pork.

The man's arms were now shaking pretty bad. I'm not in the habit of giving people any pity, but I would have said something if he hadn't beat me to it.

"Don't keep picking at it," the man said. "Stop your picking at it like that. You're not going to keep on with that, are you? The way you've been going at it? You don't have to go on picking away at it. If you're not going to finish it off, leave everything be. Don't be doing it just to see what you can get away with. Is that why you're doing it? Just to be doing it? Just for the sake of it? You think people don't see? All I'm saying is don't be picking at it all the time, all right? Leave well enough alone is all I'm saying. You ever stop to think that somebody else might still come along and want it? Leave something for somebody else. Don't go back to it. For crying out loud, just let it all alone."

The waitress came over and shoved a menu at him.

She said, "Look, mister, either talk about the food or get out."

NOW AND LATER

The uncle showed me a tablet page of arithmetic his niece had done for him once. He tried to get me to see the grandeur in it. This was some three-digit addition. "Look at the way she carried that five," he said.

I looked at the five. It looked dippery to me all right.

I think I said something to the effect that math isn't necessarily autobiographical.

"You're saying she didn't know what she was doing?" he said.

He was an altogether different run of being who pinned his hopes liquoredly to what the world had come to, but I knew enough about her parents. They'd gone out of their way to fall prey to their fates. What else were people for?

Much later in life, the niece enjoyed an entire floor to herself. There was a private entrance and steps that led down into the yard. Afternoons, I started going up. She was kneeling under the rafters with the bug lamps. I could see the places where the therapy had been done and the places that might have been missed or skipped over by design.

She sat with her arms loaved out in front of her, crossed at the wrists. There was her hair, poodley and brown, daring you to pour things onto it. Others had left tracks of their trouble on her. She often lost the very thing she was supposed to have been wearing all along. There was the book whose pages were bundled together smudgily with rubber bands. There was the thing she'd gone to the dentist to have hung inside her mouth. All anything ever called for was an easy signature, and hers had those swirls. On our way out, there was the fret of the engine when I tried to start her car.

Something would always come up, and I could always talk my way across it.

A lot depended on which part of her face you were looking at, anyway, and how you divided it, whether it was by halves or by thirds. By then, the day would have come out. Her eyes would hold everything in.

I had to drive her to the mall doctor just that one time. He had a clever way of pacing the diagnosis—throwing enough foreshadowing around until you were confident you'd caught the drift, then dropping something major on you out of the blue, then backing off, reconsidering, batting his hands. In the end, he recommended something over the counter, some yolky sort of balm or another. At the drugstore, they actually had some candy called Now and Later. It came in little wrapped squares.

COSIGNOR

I f it takes all kinds, there were three of them still in town, four if you counted the only one least likely to count here, because this one couldn't sleep with anyone unless it was just actual sleeping, and that is all I probably wanted: sleep in its flattest, least faltering form.

I banked myself at her side.

I was thirty-four, thirty-five, and in need of somebody to keep an eye on my life.

She made a daily search of the unclaimed-money sites on her phone. She squared up her hair somehow. She got it looking chunked. Her arms were so thin, my wristwatch could wind itself around both of her wrists together. Her clothes—the shifts, the sack dresses—looked leaden on her. She was provocative on the topic of makeup. "You know why they call it foundation?" she once said, her fingers tickling her cheek. "Because there's nothing underneath."

She insisted that she could not eat in front of allies, so whenever she got hungry, she excused herself and walked the extinguishable blocks to a lunch parlor. The town had a main drag touched up with planters. The place looked as if it had been founded on a dare. There was a boarded-up campus and some doctors' offices. I doubt there was a doctor around whom she hadn't talked to on short notice. But her life wasn't anything to judge her by. She never once mentioned a childhood, or customs, or work, or matters made worse, or places forsaken, or people laid away.

Life seemed to rise through her without outlet. We had moments, though, of familiarity of a sort. I sometimes handled her arms in a way she didn't think forward of me at all. She spoke now and again of "thyroid storms" and put on a pair of half-glasses to unwrap paper-shelled specifics that she claimed helped her only if she quintupled the dose.

Once a week, she squirmed into a cocktail dress and set off for a room where, I assumed, she hoped to pursue novelty in her solitude. She would shut the door, and eventually, maybe an hour or so later, call somebody or other. All I could make out, from the room with the bed, was one word being lugged past another, then another. What I mean is that every word seemed to bypass the one before it.

What it sounded like was a density being undone.

To all appearances, there were months more like this. I worked from home. Boxes arrived. They were sent back not much heavier.

Then one day she rushed at me and said, "I'm going to need some things. I'm going to need some things co-signed."

I don't know what I said.

"You were married to a business traveller," she said.

I might have nodded, or it might have been just the shaking as usual.

"What kind of person were they otherwise?"

Who was I to know?

"Territorial, I'll bet," she said. "I lived with a lady who smelled like hotels. She never had people over. She had the bright idea of wanting to nurse me back to health. I told her my health was out of this world. She was not one to believe. She said this would be the time to let any sickness blossom. She said she wanted to get to the bottom of my hardship. She said my every organ was misguided. She said I was a candidate for a bigger bed and for backbreaking adoration. She said she saw snatches of herself in me. I was with her for a little over a year. We took in the escalatorial vistas of the stores. 'My heart,' she'd say, 'is the gaudiest organ I've got.' But she was a tiddly little bitch, believe me. There was a puniness about her that made me question things she'd remembered about herself, like having once upset the water table just by growing out her breasts. She said she sensed every sort of pestering aspiration in me. She put me on a program. The slogan was 'togethermost in foreverhood.' She had me walking on the balls of my feet and hugging the walls for balance. I didn't like the way I could feel myself being taken so far through her thoughts. She claimed she owned some properties, multi-unit rental investments that could one day be half mine, but it turned out that the walls dividing the apartments from each other had to be knocked out and the apartments themselves somehow got lost in the process. She took me out to dinner one evening. We took a bouncing bus to the restaurant. She put her hand over my puttering heart. She ordered bleak blocks of meat for us both. The waiter refreshed our dessert by gunning further deservings of fudge atop the basilica of chocolate cake she'd insisted we share. Other days she tried to pay for our coffees with wan currency not of this country. It got so I could almost feel the veins serpenting through my arms. Then one morning she announced that from now on she'd be dividing her time between me and some lazily busied woman to whom she was determined to give the full run of her insides. I said, 'You never mentioned this person before.' Leave it to her to reply with cheery, diversional sounds from her mouth—just clicks and smackings. I decided it was finally time to write the note of good-bye. I put xo before I signed off. Then came the second thoughts. I drew hatchmarks and added some more xs and os, a grid, so it looked like I had just been playing tic-tac-toe at the bottom of it all. I walked to wherever there were buses and watched them arrive and watched them drive off."

I took all of this in without much use for it in mind. I knew that the days compounded differently in other people than they did in me.

Still, for another week or so, I looked after her, meaning I followed the line of her squint, mostly to a window and a tree, a noisy sweetgum thing I'd long wished gone. My house was set back sensefully from the road, and I'd never asked for trouble.

Then she came back from town late one day looking babied, with fresh generations of color in her hair, penitential edits in the complexion. Days later, she returned with hair the sicklied orange of chemical fires. Another day, she came home, late, in somebody's bathrobe (it was of a coarse orchid terry cloth). She now reeked of other people. She started going through my food. I'd catch her snacking by flashlight. I'd find her eating pie meats out of a grease-thinned paper bag. She claimed she ate one bad thing the better to throw up an earlier eaten thing that was even worse.

"I just wish I could've held off a little longer," she said. "If Texas weren't so big, I'd probably be in Canada by now."

"What would you be doing in Canada?"

"Whatever takes tact."

Packing wasn't an ordeal. The things she now wore could barely fill a shoebox loose of lid.

I hadn't realized the trains still ran so soundly around here.

She took my hand comfortably on the platform. She was in the carbon-black dress with severed sleeves. It was a dress that bunched up with every intimate turning of her arm.

Then, just as promptly, she was off.

Let's jump ahead to the public opinion of my initial forties. Rather, let's jump right over it. (Everything back then tore too easily anyway, even when you were given those few more minutes.) Much later, still aforty but measlier now, I met the lady who would sell you houseplants only if you first showed her around the house. She took one look at the horizon through the living-room window, then at the sliced rendition of it through the blinds in the kitchen. She said, "If I come back with some plants, do you promise to be at their beck and call?"

She brought the things over.

These were worthies.

They still hold court.

COUSIN-IN-LAW

P eople were forever claiming to be surprised to learn that he worked at an end table. They had been picturing a workbench, a counter, a coffee table at the least. But the things he did were not necessarily all that big, and after a certain point an end table stops being an end table. It becomes just another table proper, something easily centerable anywhere. Then one day he suddenly felt a doubt being cast over everything he was doing at the table. He looked in the direction the doubt was coming from. There was a woman standing there drinking water tinted pinkly. She claimed she could tell what people were going to say before they were even born. She said it pained her that streets did not go on forever. She was tired, too, of having to see everything with sky behind it. She said he would come to see she was exactly like him, definitely his equal, only younger and his duped opposite in everything. You have probably been through much the same sort of thing with no true nature waiting to make itself known. That being said, there was a sickly curvature to the two of them together, though she never once wreaked anything on him that resulted in goo or a goodness.

WALKING DISTANCE

I t was just something a woman, a girl, was doing mussily to something just barely born. It's tricky to get words around any of it, even when I'm feeling little by little obitual again, because there were at least two different shades of blood involved.

She shredded some cardboard and construction paper into strips, tossed them into the water, too. I watched them curl up and noodle. She believed in getting a tub filled all the way.

This is how she will have answered me every time since: "I yourself. You myself. They ourselves."

AM I KEEPING YOU?

T hey gave my mother seven months. After that, the ground was just one more thing over her head.

It's a wonder I can remember my father for anything other than running off with a woman who did not so much come into the picture as black everything else out. But I was young, eleven, twelve, with plenty of time for time, and I didn't mind that everything had been left up to my aunts. They were all on my mother's side, these overwiped women of long silences and ruckled smileage, and they one by one took me in to take me apart.

The first aunt had a monitoring eye and fed me from flatware too wide for my mouth. There was a lot of fabric under her roof, cottons and linens—balloon cloth, clokay, huckaback, georgette, express stripe, whipcord. But I never once saw a sewing machine or even so much as a needle and thread. She told me to get out of the house and bounce a ball. "You meet people that way," she said. I did meet a girl, older, with a batch of acne and darkened, doused-looking eyes and dimmed hair that one minute was stilled with clips and pins and the next minute seemed to be sinking back into her skull. She grabbed my ball, tossed the thing into a tree, then exempted herself from her dress, an airy rayonesquerie of a thing, balled it up, took me all around her body to where it was open and raw, and that's where I saw the thing that stuck out, a thing that could not have just come out of nowhere. She warned me that her heart had long been laid to rest in somebody else, a sister, and this was a sister whose breasts were precise little integers and whose fingers, dunked into mackinaw pockets, were tipped with nails snipped to the quick but painted, whole-coloredly, the daylight-blue of however much was left of a day on which you had to decide whether to get broken up that very instant in whichever way you saw fit or else honor the cracks you'd already been finding within it—so what exactly was I proposing to offer? Her knees gleamed futilely. A hand of hers was already escorting one of mine along her cheek, her throat, then lower and lower down. Then her hand hardened boldly onto the bones of my own. I must have decided not to stick around to see how the rest of any strings might yet get pulled.

The next aunt lived with an eliminated middleman. He had once sold storm windows. I might as well still picture him as a man forever driving at what he should have long ago walked away from. The few things he had done had always lacked a certain doneness. There was always something missing from the finish. This aunt let the days flake away and of course had her reasons. "Don't keep looking to me for everything," she'd say. "Look out a window." And, sure enough, in any such light, it helped to know whether it was blood or just chocolate you were suddenly spitting out.

This aunt could never see herself outshining a child, but there she was with two daughters, neither one a marrier. They were, the both of them, overgrown, unconformed to each other, activatedly morbid, denied even a stylish and successful loneliness. They came from either end of the same generation and had dodged their lives as best they could. The sticking point was that each had her own room in that deep, wide-winding house. The first one kept repeating *If something were to happen to me* as if it were the most hopeful thing in this world a person could get said. I had to cup my ears to hear her. She was the tiptoeing sort. She was pretty-spoken but had pageants of pain in her face. Her dress was one of those filmier things that looked as if it had just breezed over her from nowhere mappable in this hemisphere. She had a shoulder bag packed with backward-read paperbacks pampered with wax-papered covers. There were two electric fans in her room, three speeds each, and she knew which settings in which combination would muffle whatever it was she was up to, if only turning pages.

She got me alone in the bathroom one night when I really had to go. "We're not to flush," she said. "Pee in the sink. That's how the others do it. It's called consideration." I did as I was told, and she said that the joke was on the older kids in some really close family, a giddily tight-knit one, because what could they do but get even closer and then grow up and have to marry outside of it anyway? It was just one of many thoughts of hers that turned thoughtless in my mocking turnings of them. But it turned out we were both afraid of the exact same two things: rats and travel.

I think she actually did think our hearts would one day come brawling toward each other in a full and tiring life. And I did reach for her ropingly that once. I must have kissed her, I guess, and I must have grubbed around in my mind for somebody more puppety to think about. I must have settled for a small-mouthed tablemate from school, a kid whose blunted brainage had put him on the map. (The kid was always in the news. His inner world was said to be full of outspread spaces. Things would slide out of his hands because they didn't want to stay there. When he opened his mouth, parts of speech dropped out.)

Her kisses, though, came back measuringly. What they were measuring was anyone's guess. She would go to her grave sexually unscathed.

As for her sister, she was grown up or at least was finished with becoming something. She worked at a courtesy counter and picked all day long at something incipiently sicklied on her arm. She had a dank voice, and a youthless drift to her eyes, and there was hardly any swank to her hair, which was long but not of its time. She survived from one interim to the next in those strappy open shoes that offered brute displays of her every haggard toe. The kinds of baths she took left her looking even blearier. She lived in fear of the hot-water heater—that it could blow at any moment. So she kept her things, anything of import, propped atop plastic crates. "But you live upstairs," I assured her. "Hot water rises," she said. I never expected to see her arms swinging that martially. I wondered when the chair in the sitting room had become *her* chair. She sat in it because it faced away from the window. The window gave out on the garage, but the car was kept out front. In a vase was a splurge of plucked and skinkled thistles, and in her brassiere she climbed over hulky furniture to a stepladder that led her to where she hoarded words for some forthcoming bedpost ballad of the obvious. I got to know her fingerwise and by mouth but never nailed her motive.

If my history is correct, this was a house in which one room led directly into another and then another without the relief, the solace, of halls, hallways. I should not have to spell it out that for the longest time—months, no doubt—I had been wanted on the phone. I would set aside whatever I was up to (by now I had picked up a skill or two) and make my way to the room where the receiver awaited me. The phone was on a part of the floor I never knew my way well enough around. A tangle of cords pulled me down into what I want to think of as a swimmer's stance, the crawl of somebody athletic in water.

I was expected to talk. I answered in a voice that sounded as if it were sealing itself off from within.

It was another aunt calling. "Drop whatever it is you're doing," she said.

I kept my grip on that dumbellish old phone. The talking was all up to her.

"If you're even doing anything, right? Because what would a son of my sister's ever have to do? I assume you've been hearing it night and day about your mother? And your father—you're in on it? Or you're just bashful? You've been fazed? You're nobody's sunshine now?"

It was thus I was handed off to this next aunt. She never brought up my parents again, but on a shelf was a photograph of them at a frankfurter shack on a play-park boardwalk. I looked at the two of them flaunting life and limb in sun-lotioned leisure. I was expected to live and learn just like that? The photograph was in a side room with curtains that curtained off only certain parts of things, watershed bric-a-brac never to be touched. My aunt motioned me to a seat on the sofa. Was she pulling my leg when she said she had wanted children because she assumed they would come with answers, or because she wanted somebody to look after her when she was dead? I did not ask about any of them. I did not even know how many of them there might have been, or how long ago they had filed out of the family. She was in her fifties now, she said, and the pills did not go down right. It was always the longest day of the year, she said. No matter how fiercely she felt the hours grouped and grouping around her, she liked to talk about the people who ailed her, but she had a squelchy way of telling people off. I must have yawned, or done something too fussingly with my hands, for she got up and showed me to what would have to do for my room. The only other beings in the house were low to the ground and stole in at night to draw off the little they could of my warmth. I gather that I no longer scorched.

I never got towed off any further than needed in my sleep.

A leg of hers, crepe-papery, twined around one of mine, other fleshes of hers cresting against my side—I'd awaken in the aunt's widespread bed to her airbursts, her intakes, and I would pore over her to the point of despoilery.

Then one day a son of hers who was said to have left no trace was suddenly, distantly, back. (Hadn't someone once told me that the homely always return home?) This son had the upstairs and left an awful lot up to the eye of the beholder. The life asurge in him must have surged only obscurely. I had to get used to him, though. Things happened, in fact, inside of a week. He liked to come out from behind a night's showing of beard to get blunt again about our places and duties on the bed.

"We're not roommates," he insisted. "We live in the same room. Let's observe the difference."

We shared the towel, though, damp as it always was, and all those stickied salads he threw together.

Those safety goggles of his never came off as he ate.

The drinks he slurked out of a measuring cup were at bottom mostly cludded sugar.

He was forlorn because there was nothing to look forward to in pornography anymore. In the snaggily handwritten notes he wrote to me at night, he added bonus letters to the spelling of almost every other word.

He led me in what he said would be half an hour of exercise— the stretches and lifts, the slaps and shrivels. A couple of unorganized birthmarks on the left side of his neck gave it that dirtied look. The hair on his legs was as unflourishing as a girl's.

He inquired about my hiding-places, any milestones put off, welcomes worn out, my rights and dislikes, anything I had yet to take a slam at.

I remember whole mouthfuls of what I told him. It came out uncomely spoken, and lacking in exact words.

But by then, his mother had caught an interesting cold, one that could advance in any number of directions, so would any of us care to venture a guess as to what would be first to redden?

The eyes, I figured? Those scringing, scummed-up, spottled, stinkpot eyes?

Then one morning I felt all motory, as if things were about to get going. I involved a whole arm of his in the one thing I didn't care to keep doing to myself. There must have been more and more of a bodily situation of this sort over the weeks, because, you are sure to remember, girls were cutting corners and going directly to other girls anyway. Because, to repeat, any woman with a man is only a woman with a man. Everybody knows this, but they forget to build their lives around it.

Even worse: no carpeting beneath us, just a tacked-down green baize, and then, to get out, there was one of those doors destitute of knob or handle: you had to plump yourself against it to get the thing open.

That city, if you could call it that, was just soiled scenery against which people kept letting the moment pass. I walked unfollowed to the bus shelter and waited. I let the first bus go by, then a second. I turned them all down. It was an afternoon of wasteful wavings-away. Then an aunt showed up showily in a taxi. For once, there was too much sun. She had her hand planed out visorwise or as a salute.

This fourth aunt was the youngest. Don't look here for a list of her failings, her college troubles, her wrongs and belongings. Don't look to me for any settled description of the rougher stuff in her diets and dealings. I can't really order her all the way back into the order of things. She liked to drop friends and pose problems in public. Nobody had ever taught her how to feel left out. She liked to loiter where the action was, even when her luck was running late. But having a kid, she said, had felt like getting fucked from the inside out. She'd inflicted the whole battery of motherly emotion onto the kid, and halfway through toddlerhood, the path the kid's legs took and the path the kid's arms took didn't always overlap even notionally. The kid had trouble keeping weight on her, problems with holding a shape. The kid grew up to have an indoor disposition and learned that, when there were people around, it was enough just to show them to their coats, then get them going. Would I ever meet this girl?, I wondered, but my aunt made fun of me for even asking. She said she wanted me to leave her as I'd found her—a woman I'd otherwise one day be in a position to insert some rocks inside. The lineup of her fingers on my arm that afternoon left what felt like a permanent burn.

But the day came when I was old enough to live on my own, old enough to wonder what I should want of myself, just how far I could count on myself, and then I discovered women close to my age and then the women's unabsorbed men and then the women again with the men no longer much to care about. I tended to avoid people who were larger than life, but one of them had rigged things so that the only life any larger than hers was her own. You never could tell how close to sit or how farther out she might spiral.

It was a midland city we were in, a city beset by seagulls.

The city was built just far enough up to ensure a tight squeeze among the people fleeing.

Outgoing buses had all been painted to look like trolley cars.

Stamps that year featured the faces of resentful-looking inventors, and there were new bounces to any life sidelined from its better nature.

Written up in the municipal literature was a restaurant where the dining parties were led into little closets to sit. You were welcome to eat as long and as alone as you liked. You could let the meal mudge itself around inside of you. You could come close to your life yet not be taken in. It was expected that you would think back on people who had trailed away from you in average time or to whom you had never quite come right out and said, "Don't do this to me." The line always stretched around the block.

Everywhere you looked, people had been portioned into apartments in which there was always some creakage from above, and somebody always allowed you to stay long enough to hear her say, "Do you have any idea what that fucking person is doing up there? That fucking person is about to put on a pair of pants."

It's a touchy subject, I know, but the thing about living in cities is that somebody was already doing something exactly as you would have done it, so you were excused.

Plus, you could thin out your things with walks to corner trash baskets. You could make one offering to each. One after another of the houseplants you'd slain. Lumps of soap dulled of any sandalwood. Old school papers, with that immemorial finish to those widths of arithmetic.

Eventually you'd have to work, of course, but there was certain to be a woman at work whose bosom looked lugged in obvious, gutsy suffering. In fact, she'd spoken to you exactly once. "The thing is this," she'd begun.

I worked, you see, for some weather service. I was a receptionist first, then a secretary. Clerkly, low-salaried, overrriden in everything, I wore workwear sewn roomily and was admirably undistracted.

I deposited the for-deposit-only checks in person at a bank with a marble-pillared front. The teller there was a man around my age who wrote things on the back of each receipt—pleasantries, predictions. I would turn them over as I gained the street: "Have a good evening. You will come to discover that selfhood is not a victimless crime."

I lived on my own that year and loved the cubing efficiency of my room. I would sit hot-stomached in a dark that felt adhesive. I would let the nights get plastered to me. I'd crawl to the fridge and say, "Let's see, let me just see." In my sleep, if it came, I was good at pulling things out by their roots.

Work and apartment—I had just those two stations in life, wearing out the one through the other and improving on neither. But the streets between them were busy with people getting zeals out of their systems. People rovingly lonesome with brains apatter and nobody to stamp anything out. The woman who gave me that packetful of smidges of hair scritched from her legs, her underarms. The blinkful lady who claimed that the actual set of her features misrepresented her beyond all libel. That girl with the stormish eyes and strayaway incisors, who grilled me gently about birth-order lore, then deepened my vocabulary with "banishee," "platonic parent." Should I have felt nothing but a deadweight sympathy anyway?

All I know is that late one afternoon I felt pulled into a museum, a low-vaulted hall of art, and the things dearest to me in there were the pedestals, the prop-ups, the bases. The actual statuarial crap, the sculptures and suchnot, was a little too humany for me in the mood I couldn't see myself losing soon. Afterward, though, I sat thoughtfully in a stall in the restroom off the lobby and listened to the pips and petite ruptions of my neighbor. Then he was suddenly, mouthily, vocal through the partition, though he rapped on it a few times first. "I'm only here for the day," the neighbor said. "Can you beat that? Have you ever been here for only one day? Or are you here every day? Round the clock? Watchman? That must be it. I can sense things about you, guardianly things, just from the way you hold your quiet. Can you tell me something? What is it you can tell me of everything? Can you help me lose even a little of my life?"

I waited until he lost faith and, not having troubled himself to flush, emerged. Then I heard the quiss of the faucet, the roaring of the hand-dryer, the ungracious progress of feet toward the door.[1]

---

[1] The man had left a note, though, on the sink—a sheet of paper folded in half, and with many a puncture where the pencil had poked through: "Those so inclined to have ever gazed hopefully into the waters with a mind to undertaking a taxonomy of discharge, whether or not the specimens have been left to stand for only minutes, or, less happily, been allowed for a good hour or more to drift or disperse or spoil or mature (and let us assume, of course, that the produce has not been obscured by a gauzy haze of tissue)—those souls, I wager, would count themselves among the first to admit to an unsatisfying recourse to the classificatory terminologies of other sciences, whether it be the dreamy nomenclature of cloud figurations or the crisper formulations of the geomorphologist;

In sum: you grow up, you grow a little too much in one year, you pass for a toothpick in another, you look to your fingers only to see what they are just now letting go of—I can give you only an estimate of what I must have felt for any of the people mobilizing themselves so hurtedly. There was always something I'd know before I knew it. Even, I mean, if all there was to know was that from any window in the world the world itself always looked too awfully sure of itself?

So mustn't we thus come, at last, to my one, unbettered wife?

I was forty-four; she had barely been dipped coldly out of her twenties when we met, though this was her third marriage. Word was she'd been thrown from the first. Nobody could have been sold on the second. One day, she claimed, it just felt adjourned. The husband's love gave out, or something. She walked away from the house, made it as far as the corner, and there I was, on a side street, looking a tree up and down. It was a cloud-laden morning, and I felt unculminated.

It may be well to explain that in what became our house, several avenues over, I covered the doorknobs and other household projections with taped paper warnings out of fear that, astoop for this or that dropped earstopper, I'd crack a tooth or put out an eye. I had to know what to watch out for.

And she, this dangerously natured woman of unshimmering wealth, didn't believe in utensils, or openers. If something had to come in a can, you were probably not meant to have it.

---

and to compound the disappointment, once in a great while there appears a comprehensive evacuation, a single but multiphase release, that embraces a full range of phenomena—first, a barely discernible basal formation of firm, introductory issue settled deep in the throat of the bowl (countable units, say, appearing as constellatory pellets or, less often, as broken sausageal curlings); and, second, above and around this foundation, a stewy diarrheal guck, or slatter; and finally, centered at the top, and the first to meet the eye, a thick, compacted puddlelike and perfectly circular floating mass (the 'mudpie,' as children sometimes are apt to put it)—and such a one, vented to confound and defeat even the most determined of catalogists among us, you will here have found."

May I have more of a say about this union? My wife and I were the wrong people, yes, but the same general type. A love of a kind might be said to have been caused to happen, but any new day was just a mongrel of everything a day before. Must I go into the pinprick nicks of time in which we lived? We wrote to each other on noteboards. "Later," one of us would venture. Or: "Until very soon." But in actual moments of domestic civility, she would budge the evening forward toward dinnertime, bathtime, bedtime. When you made everything just a *time,* please understand, duration was less of a niggling, streaming thing, and more of a bearable stagger. I answered her phone in a voice smokily close to her own, held hour-filling incensed chitchats that way with her parents and brother. Any sex I had with her was less and less collaborative, rarely frontal or topical, barely even in person. Besides, she had backup loves, a specified fruitsomeness to her breath, a maiden name no one dared undo. In no time, there were entire gutted schools of thought about us in widening, spurning circles of friends washing their hands first of her, then of me, and what's there to keep me from saying, even this late, that I would rather there have been facts of life different from the ones there actually were? But I knew her in the absolute.

So: per my ex-wife per the woman she next favored (though nothing in the world seemed to have much of anything left of her impress) per the girl next in line for her (this one, as well, had never been one to dwell all that easily in twos and threes) per some later soundsick intimate of my own (his kisses were spitty and pushy and must have gone right through me to whomever he was after) per a narrow-hearted party in whose lopsided eyes there was neither hokum nor hoopla (but who soon preferred muddling herself away on some other party) per the lately unpeeped-at person now collectedly typing these words:

Life gets old.

It stunts your growth.

This was by now in the day and age of my early sixties.

I was a gala wreckage of decades, I guess.

I had a hash of thinning hair. I always ate out for the lesser chance of choking alone.

At work, the emphasis had long since shifted to forecasts for tri-state areas, then later for city-states. There was money in what I did, yes, but then, all of a sudden, people no longer wanted it done, or I no longer could do it. Either way, the money went all wrong.

And there were no longer any people in my life to speak of, though one day the daughter of the youngest aunt showed up with the news that all of the aunts were dead. Their final sayings had all been taken down, if I was interested.

She wanted ice water in a pitcher. She liked the bouncy-ball sound the old refrigerator made when I let the door close.

She'd had a couple of kids too late, she said, and they weren't the sturdy little stalks of childhood she'd been led to expect but just scoops of flesh, mucks of skin and vein, and she'd left them with her husband and left him for an unsunned sliver of a woman who liked to be around people when they were whispering about the unending finishing-off of a friendship, liking it even better when it was up to her to see to it that another of them got steered beyond the brink.

Oh, but these were brazenly globuled tears to behold!

So could I put her up?

Her name now was a strange choice of words, her hair was a mown brown, and she insisted her arms smelled differently—the left one like cinnamon, the right one like burnt cloves.

She needed to get some things off her chest, she said. One I remember: Never keep anything on the passenger seat of your car. Not even a flashlight or a map. People will know how often nobody else ever sits beside you in there.

And another: Never expect more of a greeting than *You again.*

She was soon speaking of the few people she'd been you-know-who to.

I let her talk, because anything you could put into words could be taken right back out, and who was I not to concede that people like her (this included me) knew our place—it's just that we were determined never to set foot there? This explained all the extra, oppositive steps that had to be figured into everything.

Plus she wanted to know whether our doctors even knew we were alive.

She stayed a few days, she needed to sleep with rainwear creasing beneath her pillow just in case, and when she slept, even the plainest of the day's emotions were left strewn on her face. She found a job where sickly wheels of tomato had to be lowered onto the bigger wheels of the meat. Then, one morning, there was the newly razored gooseflesh of her legs, and things must have gotten a little too one-on-one. I recited the thing about how I had all the time in her world but who knows how much left in mine. She was quick to agree grievously to how easy it was to fit everything so snugly into a duffel. Then the bare arm trending toward me, looking exercised but unendeavoring. Then just the minutes until the cab finally came.

From a dredger of dusting powder she left behind, I applied some of the baby-pink to my cheek. How soon until it could turn to soot to suit me?

She went back to her husband, I later learned. They had a place built out in Parkwood, Woodside, Sidegate—one of those.

People will go ahead and tell you that the rest of it all happened punctually—the mandatory "phased retirement," as they now called it in Human Resources. Half the hours, half the pay, but full health.

That was the year, mind you, when keys were cut with too long a stem. They kept breaking off in the locks. It was forever hell to get yourself back inside. Worse, the world had sorted itself out into the people you once might have been and the people you never now would be. The only other person left who still had a key to my place was somebody recent at work, a level-chested, emotionally unassembled woman with deep-set, practically impacted eyes. Teeth stacked anew, paprika-colored hair that looked capped on. Not one mole on the narrow barrel of her throat. She was tight-mouthed but spoke several long-quieted languages, sometimes in homemade words of her own. From the oyster-white ovality of her face, she told of days that stalked her all their length. She chased after sleep and looked to her dreams for entertainment, but the dreams sputtered away before she could play enough of a part in how things turned out. Her sleep was rarely to her liking. She bought the popular book that advised thinking of the bed as the vehicle, not the destination. "Treat the bed with care," the book said in the woofery voice that came out of me whenever I now read aloud. "Have it inspected. Dress it sensibly." We had a stopgap set of bedclothes made out of old ponchos and peignoirs. But still she struggled. For a while, I kept my life cater-corner to hers. In concerted secrecy, we observed disturbances of wedlock through oriel windows. We unnamed a neighbor's dog. Mornings, we would back off from ourselves in verdictive light that the blinds shredded onto the floor.

Then one day there was a gargly, submarine quality to her voice. The words came out funny. She talked paltrily of "travelling pains."

The earliest the specialist could see her was in five days, but she stopped thinking "days" and instead "sets of hours," which could be as long or as short as she wished them to be, so she made five hours equal a set, which pushed the appointment a full twenty-four sets of hours safely away.

But every day covered her with new colorations.

The doctor called it a rot caught too late.

On my account, she made sure her final steps in retreat were loud and countable.

I let an hour or two pass for things to sink in before I set out to search for her on the fundamental avenue, in the arterial complicacy of the central streets, along the slants and crookings of residential lanes.

I could see everything through the weather but her.

I came back, jumbled through her stuff. Spilled sortings of skirt buttons, jiggly piles of underapparel, a pillow yet to be dandled—I wasn't a handyman. I had no handyman solutions to any of it.

The signature of her lips left on a glass—such are things best left unwashed.

In her purse: the spring and silvery push-button and further internals of what was once a ballpoint pen; dimmed dimes; an outfolded candy-bar wrapper on whose glossy inner surface were handwritten figures that had been taken up in rash multiplication with an eyebrow pencil (projected earnings, payouts?).

I fell asleep on the doll-mobbed bed until the new day's sky was already incurring its surety of blue.

The first few days streamed out of the week and into a memory of minutes here and there of not yet being unpaired. Then a sign that had always said "INDOOR POOL" got itself painted over.

A counselor ventured that the mistake might have been in picturing the matrimonious state as a territory, a body of land, then treating it *geographically*—having both parties agree on how farther off each of us should have looked to each other when seen even further from afar.

"We weren't married," I told him.

I was referred to another counselor, who counseled me that people don't change, but the ways you look for them do.

"You'll hear eventually," he said.

Meaning, I took it, that in years to come, the worst that could've been asked of me if I did not answer the door right away was "Do you have anyone else in there with you?"

Further, you can fend off your body for only so long. You sooner or later have to have your look at it, even if just in the long view. There needn't be a scrutiny. Besides, it was like me to have always taken my baths in the dark. One night in the tub, though, I felt something of myself, caught a touch of something more than what had once been abided there.

The thing was the size of a golf ball when I went in for the first ultrasound. The woman in the clowny scrubs was young, mid-twenties, at most. Everything about her seemed untapered, untucked. But why the decanters, the candlestands, the candles burned almost all the way down? This was a clinic, a lab at a medical park.

She wielded the wand with a distaste I must have craved. Her voice now and then released a meager dirge. I was in there for twenty, twenty-five minutes.

A doctor called the next day with results. He sounded elderly, pronounced the diagnosis (*hydrocele:* an inwash and pooling of something liquidy into the tissue or whatnot protecting a testicle, if I heard him right), and said they had found quite a bit of debris in there, too.

I naturally did nothing for months. Why worry about a little water or whatever this fluid amounted to down in that pouch when I now had my whole life behind me to drain?

The thing was as big as a tennis ball when I went in for a second test.

The technician this time was older, maybe fifty, with that detailed allure of someone having long welcomed a life of edifying carnal blight. She was bold of hand. The procedure felt more like a massage—lots of brushy sweeps of the upper leg with one hand, the other hand guiding the wand. I could sense her talent relaxing itself. She made me feel endorsed.

"Touched less as a kid than later?" she asked at some point.

"Not much really either time."

Then, from her: "Might I be critical of you? Look, I've known you—*of* you—for half an hour, hardly."

"Please do."

"Your body is making a scene. But in my line of work, these are a dime a dozen. What are your plans?"

I said nothing.

"It will get bigger," she said. "It'll keep filling up in there. Don't think it won't. I've seen these things get bigger than a grapefruit."

Still nothing from me.

"What use are you getting out of any of it anyway?"

I went back to my place, divided the bedroom into quadrants, fractionary zones (each with a theme, a motif), though a lot of good that would ever do.

This was not a lively disease, no question, and not even a disease at all, and less a condition than a predicament, a flooded scrotal circumstance, but also no question was that I kept getting baggier and baggier down there by the week.

Months more. Called the doctor again. Said the doctor: "Come in, my friend, and I do mean friend. A buddy of mine'll numb you, we'll get out the syphons, it'll be over and done within minutes, you'll walk out of here lighter on your feet. And it's just a co-pay, pal. That sound good, my young man?"

But, knowing me, knowing myself, I went out to find a cutter. Not the kind the kids had become. I mean the other kind. But the only one in town was doing only abortions now. "Tell you what," she said over the phone. "Come on over anyways."

This was in an apartment tower revised into a condo block. Nothing leathern or left-behind-looking in the lobby. I took the elevator up, found her unit, knocked. She opened the door in just a general way. I was in the vague myself.

Inside, beneath a high-arched ceiling, I found her to be clear-faced, upright in tunic and tights, hair provoked into roils of sorrel. (Her ring finger had a surplus ring.)

"Why don't we just see it and go from there?" she said.

She busied herself believably with one of the reins of her necklace.

I disrobed my lower half.

"So we'll just be throwing the babies out with the bathwater?" she said, surveying. "That what you have in mind?"

I was all nods.

She shut her eyes and spoke to me in some stab at a parable about the kind of men who had ever made it this far.

This sounded like a Bible-study lesson. My face must have gone wavy.

"Okay, so let's not be so imaginative then," she said. "Let's not think things too far through. Let's just take simple things simply. This might just be the simplest thing ever."

While she talked, she no longer seemed to be whirling other, unspoken words inside her, and when she went quiet for a little, I figured she wasn't thinking hard at all.

"Something the size of a tennis ball might need nothing more than a tennis racquet taken to it, agreed?" she said. "We won't even have to get medical about anything."

And it just so happened she had a racquet, she said, recently restrung. It was merely a matter of fetching it from a far-off room, farther off than a visitor might first have envisioned. (That vaulted place of hers must have been practically arcaded. There were roundels, too.) While she was gone (a quarter-hour?), I eventually found the chapel where towels were kept and laid some out.

Back, she said, "Okay? You won't be a baby?"

Then started whacking.

A few sovereign bashes, then the things just dropped off.

The blood might have been lush, but there wasn't even all that much of it.

"See, mostly like water anyway," she said. "No mystique. Didn't I tell you?"

Then sutures stitched with a sprung safety pin instead of any needle.

"You'll feel it for a few. No big decisions for a couple days, okay?"

I reached for my underslacks, my slacks, then my wallet in the slacks.

She said my money was no good in that part of her life.

I dressed, rode the elevator down, hailed a taxi.

I called off a week's worth of work. I took a leave to give my groin leisure to spoil and swell. I let it redden debonairly. I skipped the dressings, the ice packs, the tablets to degrade the pain. I sent no infection away.

Within months, with nothing much of its own to do, my dick had dwindled a little, and this too was a boon.

I was pegged ever after as the person who sat way at the back of the last planetarium left in that neck of the woods and stared at whatever stars the operator would get slung up. I liked feeling covered by a fake, finite sky, and I liked how shifty a night sky was supposed to make you feel. I don't think the guy ever even knew he had an audience until I would clear my throat, or crackle a chocolate-bar wrapper, and he would dial the house lights up all the way in retribution. There was a rail built into the back of the row of seats in front of me, and I must have always been gripping the thing pretty possessively when I always said, "Do you take requests?"

This fellow, of course, ignored me.

Outside, afterward, the world would look planetary not at all. Everything looked overpainted. There was a glister over all of it. There were just close-going roads and streets, low-set buildings, people, not many, and there was nothing—not one thing—that said the most or even the least about me. I could not see even any of the people looking my way.

But answer me this: by how many minutes, how many days— or months, years, however you want to reckon it—must you keep insisting that life is too short?

I'm not keeping you, am I?

Am I keeping you?

Is that what it is?

Then what else is it then?

Mother!

What else can the dead be taught?

Acknowledgments

To Gordon Lish I owe everything.

With deepest gratitude to Giancarlo DiTrapano and to the editors and publishers of the books in which most of the stories in this collection first appeared: Gordon Lish (Knopf), Derek White (Calamari Press), Kevin Sampsell (Future Tense Books), Vincent Standley (3ʳᵈ bed), and John Yau (Black Square Editions).

Deepest gratitude also to Lisel Virkler, Thomas Vasko, Brian Evenson, Adam Robinson, Brent Bates, Elle Fallon, Jim Steranko, Lauren Leja, David Winters, Christopher Kennedy, Kramer, Jane Unrue, Paula Lifschey, Shari DeGraw, Jeff Clark, the National Endowment for the Arts, and the Foundation for Contemporary Arts.

Grateful acknowledgment is made to the editors of the journals in which the following previously uncollected stories first appeared, some in significantly different form: "Am I Keeping You?," in *Egress;* "Cosignor," in *Sleepingfish;* and "Now and Later," in *Blood + Aphorisms.*

In memory of my parents, of Diane Stevenson, and of Alfred K. Thomas.